WINE AND GODS

CAUGHT BETWEEN WORLDS

CANDICE BUNDY

LUSIOS PUBLISHING

My life changed in ways I never could have imagined from a simple hike in the woods. The rocky cliff where I almost met my end became the birthplace of my new destiny.

After my dangerous trek through the Colorado mountains, my fortunes transformed overnight. Dionysos, the golden-skinned god of wine and madness, brought me back from the edge of death and granted me powers beyond comprehension, igniting my desire to bring change to the bleak, poverty-stricken and daemon-riddled city I called home.

When I first met him, I had no idea that the man I'd danced with around the fire was my enemy, Governor Blaine York. His iron grip on the city left little room for progress, but my determination to win him over was unwavering. I knew I'd destroy him if I had to.

As I struggled to control my wild and chaotic powers, Blaine's calm and collected nature offered me a steady anchor. But as we worked together, I couldn't deny the growing sexual tension between us. I knew he was wrestling with his own desires - for power, and for me. And I couldn't help but feel a thrill at the thought of being the one to bring him to his knees.

Our attraction was undeniable, but I couldn't help but wonder if Blaine's affections were genuine, or if he was simply using me for his own gain. As we fought side by side to uplift the city, the line between love and enmity blurred. I knew I was playing a dangerous game, but I couldn't resist the pull toward the very man I once considered my enemy.

In a world where gods, demi-gods, daemons, and mortals collide in a power struggle, I wrestled with forbidden attraction and conflicting loyalties. An old threat lurked in the shadows, threatening our fragile alliance. I had to navigate a world where powerful forces threatened to tear apart my newfound family and the soul of my city.

Dive into Erin's exhilarating journey in this paranormal romance sequel, where gods, demi-gods, daemons, and mortals collide in a struggle for power, love, and the soul of a city. Immerse yourself in a tale of passion, madness, and revolution that will leave you breathless.

CONTENTS

CHAPTER 1

ORIAS

Orias jolted awake, a throbbing ache in his head signaling the silent siren ringing loudly within his skull. He surveyed the room, his mind's eye filling in the details and giving the darkness substance. The shadows flickered and crept across the walls like a living creature. Pressure built inside his mind like a dam threatening to break.

"Visions, visions, always teasing me with useless glimpses of the future," he muttered, recalling the time he foresaw the perfect cookie ingredients for one of Kobol's recipes and the ending of an inconsequential drake brawl at Blood from Stone.

Orias threw off his covers and strode to the mirror wall, slamming his fist against it. He despised the visions. What would they show him today? Something necessary or something frivolous? A piece to a larger puzzle, meshing into a pattern he already tracked? He'd spent hundreds of years in the study of a seer, and he felt no more accomplished than Miss Cleo, a two-bit psychic hotline charlatan. Sometimes, he hit the mark so hard and true the moment felt epic, like a shock wave rolling through space and time. The inconsistency of his particular skill set continued to rankle his hide.

"Why couldn't I have been a skilled warrior like Kobol, or a master of energy like Azimuth? I'd even trade this curse to be a scent-hunter like Nadir."

He faced his mirror wall, the lightless room devoid of motion and sound except for the beating of his heart.

And the shadows. The endless, ever-present shadows which whispered to him incessantly.

The sensation of a gravity drop kicked in, like a free fall into the deepest trenches of Sheol. The borders between the real and unreal faded away, and a kaleidoscope of color filled his sight, radiating out in circular patterns around him.

First came an image of a grapevine, laden with ripe fruit that began twisting and transforming before his eyes. Thorns erupted along its length as the vines warped into the shape of a massive serpent, scales glinting in the dim light. Fangs bared, the snake lunged toward him, mouth gaping wide enough to swallow him whole. Orias recoiled in horror.

Next appeared a blade, its handle ornately decorated with silver filigree. The metal glowed, turning a brilliant crimson as flames engulfed the sword and searing heat washed over Orias. He watched in dismay as the inferno consumed the blade, leaving only ashes floating down around him.

As the ashes settled, the images shifted and coalesced into a moonlit glade surrounded by ancient oak trees, their gnarled branches reaching toward the night. An arch of stars materialized before him under the night sky, twinkling and radiant, yet he could see nothing on the other side. Only darkness. The stillness of the forest was disturbed by flashes of color flitting in and out of view. Orias sensed an enchanting presence, beckoning him forward. A profound sense of foreboding gripped Orias as swirls of brilliant light poured through the doorway with graceful and unearthly movements, dancing through the glade as if freed after a long slumber.

He knew of only one thing this could mean, but it was impossible. Fae. The fae were harbingers of chaos, creators of illusions and madness. They were relics of an ancient world that no longer existed in the mortal realm. To see them again could only mean a great upheaval was coming, an unraveling of the order of things. Orias trembled, unnerved by the implications of the vision.

Then came a vision of captivating golden eyes, blinking at him. Orias didn't recognize the eyes, and there was no accompanying face, yet he felt assured one day he would look into those same eyes.

The images sustained, and he noted their permanency for more than the usual quick succession of flickers of potential. The arch remained for minutes, glittering under a quiet night sky.

This was no doorway into another world, but a new future.

This doorway was an ending.

The images faded and Orias pulled on a robe, chilled from the visions. He had no precise sense of the time span involved, but knew this vision was true. At least, as true as they came for him. This was no flicker or potential future.

This was coming. Or perhaps it was already here? And the golden eyes. Who did they represent?

As the room fell silent, a mysterious sound reached Orias' ears, making him wonder if the events of the vision were already beginning to unfold. Only time would tell.

CHAPTER 2

ERIN

Erin hit the trail hard, her backpack shifting in time to her pounding footfalls. The crisp morning air tasted like a refreshing drink, washing away the stale, choking pollution she'd been breathing behind the city walls. Only here, in the official outland territory, in what used to be known as the Colorado Trail in Pike National Forest, did Erin feel fully alive. Fully free.

She crested a hill and ground to a stop, not wishing to spook the herd of whitetail deer she'd stumbled upon. Erin crouched down and grabbed her phone, capturing a few quick shots before the lead buck caught her scent and urged his does away from the interloper. Erin stowed her camera and took a drink from her water bottle, allowing the herd to move on before she continued on her way. Deer could be aggressive when cornered, so she gave them a wide berth.

She'd learned all this, about the trails, the deer, and the mountains, from old paper books in the library. Books in the archival section no one ever visited anymore.

This area of wilderness was officially off limits. Unsafe. Unsanctioned. Uncontrolled.

Which was total crap. Just because Western S-Mart Division couldn't make a theme park out of nature meant you weren't allowed to go there. If corporates didn't have a way to profit, you weren't allowed to explore. Erin had to lie and say she was traveling to Blackhawk, where gambling continued to flourish, just to get past the city walls and onto the mountain roads. Of course, she was warned. *Don't go off the set routes, ma'am. They aren't maintained and there are criminals and unsafe sorts out there.*

Yeah, because a little danger and excitement might actually make life worth living.

Erin hated the cities. Hated everything about them. If she could rip them to pieces with her bare hands, she'd do it. She ran a hand through her short and now very sweaty hair, pulling it back from her face. If she didn't work this anger out of her system, she'd end up telling Maria exactly where she could shove those proposals on Monday.

Erin slid the water bottle into her backpack and took off at a run, her shoes screeching against the rocky trail as they fought for traction, a sound that grated on her ears and nerves. It couldn't be helped. No one sold trail or hiking shoes anymore. Everyone in the city jogged on carefully manicured running paths around perfectly groomed parks. After paying a usage fee, of course.

The lodgepole pines stood like majestic sentinels, their branches whispering secrets to the wind as the sun painted dappled patterns on the forest floor. The fragrant scent of pine needles, sap, and spring wildflowers wafted through the air. Her anger at the cities threatened to explode from every pore. She wanted to scream in frustration. Instead, she ran faster, more recklessly.

Anything to burn the frustrations out of her blood. Up here, Erin could let her wildness run free, and there were no security patrols to tell her to slow down.

Her breath sawed in and out. Sweat ran down her back, soaking her t-shirt.

On Friday, Maria, her boss, had scowled and asked her to rebind proposals to change the font color header on page forty-three from cerulean to sea green. All two hundred of them. The job paid just enough for her to afford a studio apartment in Class D housing, just a step up from the de facto slums.

Erin's arms pumped, her thighs burned, her eyes watered.

Sometimes Erin was convinced she was simply born in the wrong fucking century. Hell, perhaps the wrong planet. Not that she knew the right time or place she'd fit in, but this certainly wasn't it.

The trail dipped down and around a formation of boulders three times as tall as Erin, and she rounded them with ease, using her momentum to propel her up the slope on the other side.

She was going so fast, Erin had to throw a foot out in front of herself when she saw the brown bear lumbering down the hill. The sound of her feet skidding to a stop was painfully loud in her ears. Erin immediately crouched, making herself small and non-threatening. The bear wasn't even looking in her direction.

Erin had read up on wildlife in the Rocky Mountains,

but she'd never seen a bear before. According to the text-books, they were extinct. Beasts of history and lore. This one was now less than four hundred feet from her. It was smaller than she'd thought it would be, perhaps about five feet long and just over three feet high, but by the shimmer of its fur with every lumbering step, Erin could tell its bulky form was packed with muscle.

It was beautiful and Erin cherished the moment, even while she anxiously waited for the animal to continue on its merry little way. Just then, the wind picked up and the bear's snout sniffed the breeze and its gaze swept unerringly toward Erin. She'd seen a dog's hackles rise before, but watching the bear react to her was another thing entirely. It dropped and swayed its head from side to side, a low rumble issuing from somewhere deep within the bear's belly.

Erin scanned the area, and behind her, next to the boulders, the ground rose steeply and crested a ridge. She couldn't see what lay beyond, but it was uphill, and she knew from reading up on bears they moved slower uphill. Erin was a fast runner. Was she fast enough?

It might give her a minor advantage if she had to run for it. Erin heard the bear make a huffing noise and focused back on the beast. Its snout was raised, and it let out a loud growl. Erin held her ground and kept low, refusing to look at it directly, attempting to appear cowed. She certainly felt intimidated. Couldn't the bear tell it had won the pissing match?

The bear charged, and Erin sprung into action, racing up the hill. She heard thundering footsteps pounding behind her as the bear crashed through the underbrush, hot on her tracks. Its roars spurred her on, forcing more adrenaline through her veins as she dodged rocks and leaped over fallen trees. Soon, she reached the crest of the hill, and to her horror, discovered it wasn't simply another hill.

It was a cliff, with a drop of easily over a hundred feet, down into a ravine below. The sight gave her immediate vertigo.

Panicked, Erin spared a glance behind her at the enraged bear, which was now only about a hundred paces away, and then down into the ravine. Without thinking, she got down on her belly and shimmied down the rock face, desperately seeking footholds and gratefully, against the odds, finding them.

She had no experience rock climbing, but looking up at the bear only fifty feet away, it now looked like the time to learn.

Erin's moves were quick and, in hindsight, extremely lucky. She got a few feet down the cliff wall before the bear arrived. She was far enough away that she had escaped the creature's reach, if not its powerful roar. The bear, clearly the more intelligent of the duo, chose not to climb the cliff. Instead, it snarled and snapped at the crest of the hill for a while before trudging away. Erin did not know how far it had gone.

With her luck today, definitely not far enough. Going back up would be the shorter and, it was likely, an easier route, but she did not know if the bear remained nearby. Thus, not entirely safer.

Going down would be hard, but Erin was strong.

Erin steeled herself and started down the wall, taking her time now. This differed from any other exercise she'd done before; it required strength in her fingertips and forearms that she hadn't trained for. Her arms quivered with each new grip and foothold.

She made the mistake of looking down. She'd only made it less than halfway down, and the bottom was littered with sharp rocks and bushes. With her luck, the bushes sported inch-long thorns.

Erin pushed onward, determination her ever-present partner. Unfortunately, her stamina continued to fade, and there was nowhere on this nearly sheer pockmarked surface to rest. Every movement was a struggle, plus her fingers were raw from gripping the coarse and sun-warmed rock.

Erin fought back tears as she found the next hold, the sharp angles of the rock cutting into her hand as she squatted into position, but she needed the hold, and there wasn't another option. Erin found a more comfortable one for her left hand and then began seeking footholds blindly. Her feet found two different spaces, widely spaced, but they were there. Erin let out a long breath, and let her weight settle onto the new footholds.

When both feet gave way at once, Erin's body stretched out against the rock, her hands slipping in their grips as her feet flailed for footing and found none. The rock bit into her right hand painfully, and Erin looked up to see blood dripping down the rock. Her bruised fingers slipped from the hold on the left, and then the flash of pain in her right hand was simply too great, and Erin let go reflexively when she felt the joints in her fingers begin to tear.

The free fall lasted only a heartbeat before Erin hit and scraped against the rock wall, banging her forehead painfully against the stone. It tossed her backward and her downward glide continued unimpeded until Erin hit bottom with a sickening crunch as she crumpled to the ground, landing mostly on her back. She tried to stay awake, her vision blurring and darkening at the edges. She fought the encroaching darkness, terrified of what might happen if she succumbed to it. As her consciousness slipped away, she held onto one final thought: she had to survive this, bear and all, to prove that she was truly alive and free.

CHAPTER 3

ERIN

The pounding in her head roused Erin, followed by the awareness of throbbing pain all over her body, with a screaming, shooting pain flaring from both her left ankle and her right hand.

If only this was just a nightmare. If only she could wake up from it now. The city guards were probably right; the wilderness can be a treacherous place for a lone woman like her. Yet here she was, lying in agony, with no one else but herself to blame.

Erin didn't want to open her eyes. Heat seared her flesh. Her throat was parched. Her twisted back screamed for attention, and for a moment, Erin remembered the bear, her scrambling descent down the cliff, and then her complete loss of control.

Erin struggled to open her eyes, and when she did, the light was blinding, and for many moments, she couldn't make sense of her surroundings. Images were fuzzy one moment and clear the next. Perhaps she had a concussion?

One thing was sure: no one knew where she was right now. If Erin wanted to survive, she needed to pull herself together and drag her own ass out of this screw-up. She had no other option.

Erin groaned. She would not be a poster child for the dangers of the wilds. Hells no.

Looking down at her body, her limbs were all askew. Or was that just her fuzzy brain? She was surrounded by granite rocks, and hadn't landed in the bushes after all, which was likely a lucky move. From the ground, they appeared more like spindly branches than soft leafy bits, and imagining one of those branches impaling her wasn't at all reassuring.

The smell of pine needles filled her nostrils as she tried to move her arms, and only the left responded, flopping around like a dead fish. "Fantastic. One working arm and one working leg. Halfway to being a functioning human," she muttered. At least it didn't hurt to move it. However, the more Erin moved her arm, the more natural the movements became, until, finally, a semblance of natural movement returned. Erin reached up and grasped the backpack strap, which was still in place and most likely why her back felt horridly distended, and slid the strap over her shoulder. Her right arm was trapped beneath her body, and she'd lost most of the feeling in it.

Free of the harness, Erin tested out her left leg. Pain shot up her leg, and she looked down, focused, and saw her left ankle was twisted, swollen, and bruised beyond reasonable use. "Well, at least it's not bleeding," she said out loud, trying to find a silver lining in her situation.

After a few attempts, her right leg proved functional, but

painful to use. Erin slid it along the ground and curled it close to her body, and then used her left arm to leverage herself off the ground behind her and away from the backpack, unfortunately putting her face into the dirt. Erin's right shoulder screamed in protest as the joint came back together, and she had to ignore the twist to her left leg that begged to be left alone. She quickly used her left arm and the strength in her right leg to lever her body into a sitting position, freeing her right arm from under the backpack.

When her right hand erupted in pain, Erin doubted the wisdom of her chosen course of action. The arm was still difficult to control, so she grabbed it with her left and laid it across her lap. Blood trickled from cuts on the central three knuckles, which had been kept in check until now by her own gravity. Woozy and nauseated from the motion, Erin knew she had to act and stay focused.

Using her good hand, she reached for her backpack and dragged it closer. The metal canteen hadn't been damaged in the fall, and Erin grabbed it first. Using her teeth and her left hand, she unzipped the bag and located the smashed remains of the first aid kit. Its plastic case had helped cushion her fall, and splinters of sharp white littered the inside of her bag, spearing and ruining the lunch she'd brought to eat.

Sifting through the remains of the box, Erin found several alcohol swab packets, gauze pressure packets, and some fabric tape. Nothing else looked useful or intact. Using a similar one-handed and teeth technique, Erin ripped a strip of fabric from the bottom of her once white t-shirt to use as a bandage. After another look at her damaged hand, she ripped another one to serve as a washcloth. It would have to do.

Erin popped the top on the water bottle and gingerly rinsed off her fingers, mostly just trying to get the dirt off, swearing loudly when the pain got too intense to tolerate. The cool water felt soothing on her injured hand, but it also made her shiver slightly. She'd heard about needing to keep wounds sterile to prevent infection, and guessed the only way she would keep an infection out of these cuts would be an expensive shot from a hospital that would put her back a month's salary. Maybe two. Great. So much for scraping together a deposit to get out of the slums.

Next, she wet one strip of the shirt and wiped her hand down. Besides the abrasions, the rest of her hand was okay, which was good news. Erin tore open the alcohol packets and wiped around the edges of the gashes. She let out a scream. The pain was so intense. The blood kept coming, so cleansing the wound didn't seem to do much good. Finally, Erin held her fingers, so the gashes were mostly closed, pressed the clean packed gauze against the wounds, and then wrapped the other strip of the t-shirt around her fingers to hold them in place. The tape held decently, and after a few minutes, it appeared the bleeding was at least slowed.

Erin took a few sips of water and began pulling everything out of her backpack. Erin sorted all the trash and ruined items into the backpack's front pocket. There was a sweater covered in squashed banana she wasn't likely to use. She threw the remains of the fruit onto the ground some distance away, unwilling to eat it herself. She found some ibuprofen from the first aid kit and took four, hoping they'd help with the pain, and put the rest in the side pocket of the pack for easy access.

Assessing her right arm, besides the damage to her fingers

and her sore shoulder, it was mostly bruises. Unfortunately, her shoulder was so sore it had almost no rotation. Erin sighed. At least her left arm was fully functional.

Now she turned her focus on to her legs. In her odd forward lean, her right leg was bent while her left was fully straightened in front of her. Feeling down the length of the right leg and moving all the joints, Erin concluded it was good to go, just unhappy and bruised like the rest of her. The left leg scared her. Her thigh was fine, however, a bit bruised. Erin bent her leg at the knee and pulled her foot closer, aware of the extreme swelling and discoloration around her ankle. Her exposed skin screamed at every moment of contact with the ground.

Erin debated for a few moments, and then gingerly removed her shoe. As soon as it was off, the relief was instantaneous. The pain didn't go away, not by any means, but it no longer felt like it had a vise on her foot. She stowed the shoe in her backpack and peeled back the sock for a look. Black and blue bruising met her gaze, and she quickly put the sock back in place. Was it a sprain? A break? Nothing was poking out through the skin, and there was no bleeding, so that meant she had more time to treat it, right?

Erin knew there was no way she'd be walking on her left leg out of here. Therefore, she needed some sort of crutch. She looked at the briar patch, which had many long, dead branches. Erin wrested her backpack painfully onto her shoulders and then scooted herself over to a promising-looking bush. She found a thick and long branch and uprooted it rather easily, although the bark was rough on her hand.

Maneuvering herself onto her knees, Erin got up onto her

right foot and then hobble up into a standing position with the makeshift crutch. It wasn't ideal, but she was low on options.

Erin got her bearings and figured if she followed the cliff wall in the direction she'd come from, then eventually she'd find a way back to the main trail, and thus, back to her car. She'd run over two miles down the trail before the incident with the bear. Now the sun was almost directly overhead. "At this rate, I'd be lucky to make it back in time for my funeral," she muttered to herself.

She sighed again and checked her bandage, relieved the wound wasn't bleeding through. Erin hopped and blundered away from the base of the cliff and over to a slightly wooded area which was shaded and had less rubble underfoot. After just a short while, the briar branch showed signs of sagging, so Erin looked around and came upon a pine branch and switched it out. She had to be careful not to drag her left foot, which was a growing strain on her thigh.

As Erin navigated the woods, the sound of her own labored breathing mixed with the rustle of leaves underfoot and the distant chirping of birds. Eventually, she came to an area where the cliff receded, and Erin could make it up and over the terrain and back toward the trail. It was only mid-afternoon, but Erin still did not know how far she'd come.

Exhausted and sore, she laid down in the shade of a pair of lodgepole pines. A quick nap was just what she needed. Only a short one. The sound of a babbling brook somewhere in the distance caught her ears, but she didn't remember it from her maps. Nonetheless, it lulled her to sleep.

Just as she was about to drift off, a mysterious noise jolted her back to wakefulness. Her heart raced as she tried to identify the sound. Was it just her imagination, or was there someone—or something—out there with her? She strained her ears, hoping it was just a harmless animal, but the uncertainty gnawed at her.

CHAPTER 4

ERIN

Erin awoke to darkness surrounding her in a bed of soft moss that tickled her skin and a fuzzy pelt resting heavily over her limbs. Her ankle ached, but the once-sharp pain had faded into a dull throbbing. Everything about her body existed in a buffered state, thrumming to the steady beat of rhythmic drums and heat suffusing in the air. The brook which had lulled her to sleep no longer invaded her consciousness. Whether it was drowned out by the other noises or too far away to hear it now, Erin didn't know.

Puzzling over the noises roused her groggy mind enough for Erin to find the strength to open her eyes. And when she did, she rubbed her eyes, certain she was hallucinating. The scene before her was so bizarre, so surreal, Erin knew she was lost in a dream. Sure, her ankle hurt badly, no doubt a remnant of her waking mind, but the rest...

Erin lay on a pallet at the edge of a meadow. In the center, a massive bonfire surged toward the sky in time with the drumbeats. She couldn't see the drummers, but trusted they were somewhere past the throng of strangely clad dancers, swaying and pounding their feet to the ground in a circle around the fire. Their feet stomped so wildly, so fiercely, Erin could swear the ground itself shook. Instead of scaring her, it thrilled her to witness such an awesome show of force.

How lucky she was to see this theater of the bizarre, if only in her dreams.

There was no moon in this dreamscape, nor stars. The smoke from the bonfire hung in the air, enshrouding the small enclave. Every sound echoed back into the space, amplifying the grunts, hoots, and hollers of the dancers. If not for knowing it was a dream and seeing with her eyes the trees at the edge of the meadow, reassuring her they were indeed outside, this might be a formidable web to be caught within.

"Who are these people?" Erin muttered to herself as she focused her eyes on the dancers themselves. They were a wonder each unto themselves, barely visible by firelight. Each was costumed to mimic something from the forest. Several of the ladies appeared similar to tree nymphs, assuming Erin remembered her mythology correctly. Their skin was painted with knots and bark like striations, and their hair was strewn with leaves. Each appeared to be a different tree as well. If she was right, those few were pine and spruce, that group aspen, and, on the far side, a few beeches. All trees she'd seen around the state, but now bizarrely humanized. No, they had curves. Sensual hips and buxom chests in contrast to straight-trunked trees.

But not all the women were trees; some were flowers. Columbines. Daisies. Wild roses. Erin lost track. Then there were women who were wild in a way she couldn't catalog. Curiouser and curiouser.

The men were another matter. They were consistently uniform in their lack of humanity: all were satyrs. This she knew from the horns on their heads, cloven hooves on their feet, their shaggy legs and rumps, their prominent and erect phalli, and the lascivious grins they sported in, well, the direction of every female around them and occasionally other satyrs. Some of them didn't appear overly picky about who reciprocated their attention, as long as their interest was returned.

"What kind of bizarre wonderland is this?" Erin wondered aloud, a wry smile playing on her lips as she briefly considered whether she had stumbled into some sort of cult gathering.

Despite the late hour, the heat from the bonfire spread throughout the glen, raising the temperature under Erin's pelts. She shucked them off, already sweating through her t-shirt and shorts. Her shoes had been removed, laid aside next to her backpack. Had she taken them off herself, or had one of these motley crew? Clearly, someone had attended to her while she slept. Or perhaps it was all just a subtext of the dream?

Unencumbered now from the weight of the furs, Erin sat up and breathed in the heady musk of the assembly combined with exotic incenses and oils. The effect was distinctly potently wild. When a priapic satyr set upon a nimble aspen nymph and fell on her between nearby spruce trees, her cries were not those of panic, but instead of heated urging.

Her imagination was definitely running on overtime. Erin couldn't help biting her lower lip to keep herself from laughing. There was no way his extreme lower anatomy would work out with the dainty and willowy nymph. Yet the nymph urged him on all the same.

At that moment, a man laid down next to her, breathing like he'd just run a marathon and availing himself from a bloated wineskin he brought with him. He was tall, barefoot like the rest of the dancers, and clad in an embroidered burgundy tunic covered with exquisitely wrought golden grape leaves. The fabric was so delicate; Erin was sure it was an expensive silk and itched to touch it.

When he finished drinking, he turned to her with a lazy smile, his eyes flashing gold in the firelight. "How are you enjoying the festivities?" He offered her the wine, his casual demeanor at odds with the frenetic energy surrounding them.

Curious where this dream-state was headed, Erin accepted the wine while her eyes appreciated his long, wavy blond hair falling over broad, muscular shoulders. She took a sip of the potent vintage and swore it singed her stomach and then her veins on contact. Erin couldn't help but take another, longer pull from the skin, and this time felt the effects from the molten liquid shoot down to the tips of her fingers and her toes. "What type of wine is this?" She gripped the wineskin against her chest.

He grinned and threw back his head with laughter, and Erin was surprised how the reverberating sound rang across the meadow. Yet the drumming and dancing didn't cease; if anything, they increased in tempo. A moment later, he leaned toward her conspiratorially, not reaching for the wine. Oh no. Instead, he nuzzled up close to Erin, his chin, his lips hovering at the cusp of her shoulder and neck. She felt her pulse race in response to his mere presence.

"Nothing unusual for this sort of gathering," he whispered into her ear.

Erin's entire body hummed with an electric thrill, even her throbbing ankle. Was it from being so close to this stranger? She didn't want to chalk it up to sexual magnetism, but his allure was striking.

"You're sure there's nothing unusual about the wine?"

He leveled her with his gaze and then leaned back, giving her some welcome space. "It's sacramental wine. As my honored guest, I insist you have as much as you'd like."

His full lips appeared wine-stained, yet he spoke with clear, melodious tones. "Who are you?" Erin took another sip of the impeccably superb wine.

"Your gracious host, of course." A smile played around the corners of his eyes and lips.

This was a game to him. Erin was supposed to understand and be clever enough to figure it out. Well, perhaps if she hadn't fallen down a cliff earlier in the day, broken her ankle, and then landed in this wonderfully luscious dream, well then yes, perhaps then she'd be able to figure it out.

She took another sip of the wine. Oddly, she wasn't feeling increasingly drunk. Instead, Erin felt larger than life. Her consciousness expanded outward, slowly noticing, and connecting with, those around her. It felt like an out-of-body experience, except she was still in her body.

"Have you drugged me, fine host?" Focusing on the man, he at once appeared human and yet not. She could tell he was like the others, something more, but what, she couldn't say. He hadn't even touched her or tried to take advantage of her like the satyrs were with the other females.

"As I said, the wine was blessed, nothing more. There is no trickery here."

He was so serious, his face so grave. Erin's laughter bubbled forth, but his expression didn't change. "But this is my dream. This isn't real. No matter how delicious." She took another swig. It would be grand while it lasted.

Storm clouds gathered in her host's visage, and for a moment, Erin felt fear. "This is very real, Erin. You've wandered into my domain repeatedly. You've felt the call. Now, with my vintage on your lips, you feel the pull to greatness, do you not? I see it upon your face. I feel it echo in your blood. It's not simply wine to you, is it?"

There was no contact between them but the breath of air, yet she felt surrounded by him.

Erin dared. This was all a dream, after all. "So what if I do?" She took another long pull from the wineskin and reveled in the feel of it coursing through her veins, permeating her skin. "Yes, I feel it thundering through me. But what does it matter when this is all just a dream?"

Her companion relaxed, smiling and smoothing his tunic. "Well then, I suppose you're right. I would, however, ask for one boon in return for the gift I've given you."

"Just one?" Erin asked, suspicions abounding.

"Yes. One." His mask of innocence let Erin know she was in for trouble. Big time.

"Okay. What is it?"

"A kiss."

"Just a kiss?"

"One kiss. I'm afraid you couldn't handle more of me." He licked his lower lip, and Erin felt an insane urge to lean forward and bite it. What was coming over her? The earthy scent of the wine and the intoxicating sounds of the surrounding crowd clouded her senses. It must be the wine.

"You've got a healthy ego there, mister. I bet I could take a lot more. I'm already feeling like I can take on the world." Erin lifted the wineskin high, feeling the forest floor's cool dirt beneath her feet. This evoked a resounding round of shouts and affirmations from the assembly, and she hooted in return. The drumbeats increased into a frenetic tempo, and the stomping of feet pounded the forest floor.

Her host guffawed an appreciative laugh, enjoying her humor despite her insult. What an odd person, or whatever he was.

"Soon enough, the earth will tremble under your feet. But for now, will you accept my kiss?" His golden eyes mesmerized Erin. She wondered why she wasn't crouching in fear, but she looked into his eyes and urgently wanted what he offered.

When Erin leaned in for the kiss, she realized a hush had fallen over the assembled masses. All eyes were turned on them. Looking upon his wine-darkened lips and the dark promise, Erin waited for someone to challenge her right, to stop her. The knowledge that she'd be willing to fight them for this opportunity of a single kiss shocked her. Her host remained effortlessly reclined back, propped up on one elbow, leisurely taking in her measure, his expression decadently inviting.

Erin's pause led to a surge in the crowd, and she thrust out a palm and practically growled. "No!" They stopped in their tracks, but Erin sensed it was a momentary thing. Their hunger, directed toward their host, was a palpable thing.

She turned back toward him and leaned in, and his power

rolled over her, encompassing Erin with waves of heat and need.

"Last chance to turn back," he whispered, his words barely audible against her lips.

"I have a feeling I'll regret this forever if I don't." Erin pressed her lips to his wine-stained ones.

All the outside sounds stopped, replaced by an intense rushing noise in her ears. The flavor of his lips was exquisite, tasting of the finest vintage, and Erin completely succumbed to the sensation, lost in the moment. Her body inflamed with a heat she could never quench, and he breathed into her mouth the sweetest breath. Each movement he made was crushing, bruising Erin's lips in the most delicious way. And yet, as he continued to breathe into her, the pain became more bearable, and Erin could respond with fervor.

Erin couldn't later say if the kiss lasted a minute or an hour; there was no time in this place. He kept his word and didn't touch her beyond her lips, but her body writhed and burned from the small amount of contact. She'd never reacted this way before. Her body had become a live wire, shocked repeatedly by his wine-soaked touch.

When he finally pulled away, Erin uttered a sigh and didn't even have the shame to blush. "Now it's time to dance."

"My ankle is broken. I can't dance. I'll just sit here and watch."

"No. It's not." He smiled with such confidence that Erin frowned and then stood up, trying her foot. She favored it for a few steps, not daring to place full weight on it. Sure enough, it held her weight just fine.

It's all just a dream.

A shock of disappointment ran through her, and then she brushed it off. "To the dance!"

She flung herself into the crowd. The simple joy of pounding her feet along in time and swaying her body to the drums was a solace to her soul.

Erin couldn't remember ever being more at peace in her life.

Even when a randy satyr got close and laid his hands on her, she spun and lifted him by the neck until his hooves flailed in the air.

Erin took a swig of wine, waiting him out. "Beg me for air with your eyes, scamp!" The nymphs gathered behind her laughed.

He did, appearing most contrite. Well, as contrite as someone can with their eyeballs about to pop out of their skull. Erin waited until he was a deep shade of purple before dropping him to the ground, where he gasped for air.

"Never touch me without my consent. That goes for the lot of you." Erin made her point with her mostly empty wineskin. The nymphs cheered her on. The satyrs nodded in agreement.

Erin's eyes met her host's across the bonfire. He inclined his head and appeared to be holding back laughter. Erin saluted him with the wine and drank deeply, and he smiled, all seriousness again.

Spinning off in her dance around the fire, Erin's feet stomped the ground with such force she swore surrounding branches shivered in response. Singing an unknown verse yet moving with sure feet, Erin took the revelry deep into her soul and expressed it through the undulations of her body.

Just then, one man in the crowd caught her eye. A

distinctly human man, unlike the other satyrs and dryads present. His piercing blue eyes met Erin's across the fire, and a flash sparked across the lightning-shaped tattoos running the length of his muscular arms. The tattoos appeared to glow as if by some otherworldly magic. Captivated, Erin directed her dance toward him. His eyes roamed her form as she approached, appearing as enthralled by her as she was by him. The satyrs surrounding the human backed off on her approach, perhaps scared by her harsh treatment of their brother.

Nudging her way into his personal space, Erin sought to understand the magnetic force that was this man, his aura emanating a grounded and steady presence that somehow pierced through the chaos of the bacchanal. She noted the intensity of his gaze, a testament to his undivided attention.

"What brings a man like you to a bacchanal like this?" Erin husked out, her throat ragged from the incessant singing and chanting that painted the night with wild abandon. Or perhaps it was the wine?

"I could ask you the same thing," he shot back, the deep resonance of his voice vibrating against her skin, sending shivers down her spine that had little to do with the chilly night.

A spontaneous laugh bubbled from her throat. "I just woke up here. But now I wouldn't have it any other way. This night, the creatures I've met, it's all so extraordinary!"

A coy grin pulled at the corners of his mouth, his gaze heating as if he could see straight into her core. "That's how it is in dreams, lovely. This wonderland carnival promises delights of the most exquisite kind."

Electricity sizzled along Erin's skin, the charged air

igniting a burning curiosity within her. Would his lips taste of the same mystery that his gaze promised? Would they carry the same golden warmth as that other man's?

"Exquisite, you say?" she purred, her laughter giving way to an intoxicating smile. Her heart raced as she leaned closer to him, her question suspended in the space between them until he finally swept in to capture it with his lips.

The distance between them evaporated as he leaned in, his lips claiming hers in a searing kiss that was anything but tender. This man was a wildfire. His touch was an all-encompassing blaze that devoured her, leaving behind an insatiable yearning that echoed in her bones. His kiss held the promise of an unexplored adventure, an invitation that she was more than eager to accept. As Erin surrendered to the irresistible pull of his allure, she realized she craved more. She craved everything this mysterious man offered.

Their passionate encounter escalated rapidly, tongues dueling and teeth nipping in an all-consuming dance that stripped away Erin's awareness of her surroundings. His hands, strong and sure, traced paths across her body, each caress amplifying the intoxicating sensation coursing through her. Her heart thundered in her chest, the frenetic rhythm echoing her desperate yearning for *more, closer, deeper*. His ragged breaths and inaudible whispers blended with her own, creating a symphony of desire that rivaled the wild revelry of the bacchanal around them.

Erin was completely lost in him, in the tantalizing mystery of the man before her and the electrifying unknown of what might happen next. The contours of his muscular form under her exploratory touch sent a thrilling shiver down her spine. She reveled in his commanding presence, his powerful arms a solid anchor in the whirlwind of sensations threatening to consume her. His clear arousal ignited a responsive flame within her, and she matched his ardor, spurred on by the intoxicating blend of desire and curiosity.

She realized fleetingly anyone might watch, but the thought barely caused a ripple in her heated reverie. After all, she reasoned with a carefree shrug, this was only a dream, wasn't it? Why not give in to the pleasure, to the exhilarating unpredictability of the moment? In the realm of dreams, there were no judgments, no consequences, only the enthralling dance of desire unfolding between her and the mysterious man.

Just as she was falling deeper under his spell, allowing herself to be swept away by the tempestuous tide of their shared passion, a sudden flurry of activity disrupted their tryst.

With an exuberant burst of giggles and rustling leaves, a grove of nymphs appeared seemingly out of nowhere, pulling Erin away from the mesmerizing man. Their cheery voices chattered away as they led her into a small copse of trees and presented her with a dress fashioned in their likeness. Short, breezy, and woven from a haphazard assortment of leaves—in her case, freshly pruned grape leaves. It seemed a precarious ensemble, but a soft underlayment of mossy substance held it all together. As the nymphs playfully formed a barrier around her, Erin, still dazed from the abrupt interruption, shed her t-shirt, shorts, and undergarments to don this extraordinary gift.

However, when Erin reached for the dress, a few of the flower sprites stepped in with paintbrushes and insisted, without words, to adorn her flesh with elaborate painted-on vines and grape clusters. They had no shame, covering almost every inch of her skin, but they worked quickly, the paint drying as quickly as they applied it, although the process did sting slightly. Erin amused herself in the meantime by finishing her wineskin. It was a sad moment, and she passed off the empty vessel to the lady with a frown.

No sooner was the painting completed than the sprites slipped the skimpy dress over her head, and the troupe was urging her back to the fire. For a time, Erin danced with wild abandon, lost in the moment, amazed at the combined energy she was now a part of. When the drums reached a crescendo, she raised her voice as one with the others, and the very trees shook. It was heady, and Erin loved it.

While the drummers found their cadence again, Erin watched many couples pair off and cavort against trees or in the shadows. And yet, in the glimpses of firelight, nothing was left to Erin's imagination. She knew she could be one of them if she so wanted, yet she craved the frenzied motion of the dance. Erin spied her enigmatic host across the fire and caught his eyes, watching her intently as he lounged amongst his revelers. She noted that although he had a nymph kissing along the flesh of his bare arm; he paid her no heed.

How curious.

Erin broke eye contact and stepped round the circle. When Erin looked back toward where the lightning-marked man had been standing, she observed with some disappointment that he was no longer present at the gathering.

She sighed, and then bellowed out, "I require more wine! And drummers, return to your posts and lead me in your ecstatic dance!"

Trills and good-natured laughs met her decree, but

shortly, another round of deep, rhythmic beats set up and set her feet moving.

A timid satyr with a bruised neck tapped her elbow. "Begging your forgiveness for the touching, Vessel. Here's your wine." He held out the wineskin, bowing low.

Vessel? What was he going on about? No matter. She took the wine from him and scratched between his horns. "No worries, my furry friend. You were within the bounds I set forth. Well, this time. Now go on, for the frenzy is yet young, and I intend to dance until the sun rises!"

He grinned mischievously and then howled into the starless night before turning and dancing off into the throng. Erin smiled and loosened the stopper on the wineskin, and as she raised the bag to her lips, her eyes sought her host instinctively. A second later, Erin found him, well entwined in a pair of willow nymphs, their long arms and legs wound about him in a horizontal dance which should have brought a flush to Erin's cheeks. Instead, she simply smiled, kissed the stopper, and then she saluted her host with the wineskin. His eyes flashed burnt umber, giving a brief nod of acceptance.

Erin watched him return his affections to the nymphs, and she took a long draught of the wine. She rejoined the dancing, and realized there was a tempo, not just to the drums, but also to the vintage. It was a Rioja, hot and fiery, brought to pair with the intensity of the celebration. It would smelt them together through an iron forge of will and passion.

How she knew this, Erin neither knew nor questioned. It was a dream, after all. She had little to no wine knowledge in her waking life.

Erin thought wistfully of her mother, wishing she was still around to experience the carefree joy of the dancers before her. The place she called home in the city was a universe away from this altered space, this theater of revelry.

And yet she'd never felt more at home.

She guzzled the wine, sharing it amongst her newfound friends, blotting out thoughts she could do nothing to change. They danced until the rosy fingers of dawn touched the sky, and then she collapsed in a heap onto her bed of moss beneath the lodgepole pines.

CHAPTER 5

BLAINE

Blaine hadn't felt this wild and carefree in years. His laughter rose and mixed with the smoke hanging heavy in the night air, punctuated by sparks of embers floating up on heat-drafts from the bonfire. He wore only his boxers, yet none of the characters moving around the bonfire took any notice. Half-dressed bodies danced to the rhythmic, unseen drumming, some moving at a slow, sensuous, deliberate pace while others spun wildly, deftly threading their way through the others.

Raucous laughter erupted around him. A rough, leathery wineskin was thrust into his hands, and Blaine took a pull of the tannic and spicy draught, the bite of the wine making his tongue tingle, before passing it along. The aromatic smell of the wine wafted from the wineskin as he studied the faces of those in the small group standing near him, passing it. A furrowed brow and a nervous gulp betrayed his unsettled feelings as he noticed a wild, animalistic look about them all.

In fact, they didn't look altogether human at all. A hirsute man clapped Blaine on the back as they all laughed together; were his legs covered with fur, or was that some sort of costume the man wore? Or perhaps a effective hair growth serum? A feminine face across from him smirked, her painted face and mud-caked hair wild in the flickering light. A slight, androgynous form clad only in a loincloth and swirls of paint leaned against the sprite, whispering something in her ear. The smell of earthy paint and the rustle of the loincloth added to the peculiar atmosphere.

The wineskin again passed to him, and Blaine took another drink before he passed it along. The incongruity of the situation hit him. Where was he? What was this place? And who were these—assuming they were human—people?

A Burner conclave, that must be it! He'd heard how they behaved like animals, dressing in wild, barely there costumes and partying until the dawn.

But how had he gotten here? And what would bring him, the Mayor of Denver, to such an uncivilized place beyond the safety of city walls? Imagine the disapproval of his council members if they knew. A vote of no confidence would be assured, and surely some would contest his leadership.

Just then, an athletic female form spun past, her lithe body a shadow backlit by the firelight. The glow of god-touched sigils illuminated her form, but Blaine couldn't make them out through the movement of the other dancers. Pushing forward into the fray to get a better look, Blaine was swept along with the rhythm of the drums, the swaying of bodies around him, and the building energy of the crowd.

The full-body sensation was electrifying.

Blaine kept catching glimpses of the woman's form as she danced, a wild, fearless, and potent energy encapsulating every movement. As she moved around the circle, the fire-light played off her skin, casting light on the sheen of sweat across her chest. She wore a simple t-shirt and a set of faded shorts, her bare feet and calves covered with dust, a testament to the intensity of her frenzied dancing this evening.

She rounded the fire again, and by mere chance, the woman looked up and their gazes met. His breath momentarily caught in his chest. She made a beeline for him through the crowd. Was it his imagination, or did they part before her like a river around a stone? A wicked grin played across her face as she consumed him with her eyes. Her tongue flicked out to capture a stray drop of wine that was caught on her lower lip.

The woman came to a stop just inches away, her intense focus captivating him. Blaine was consumed by the desire to feel her skin under his touch, to taste the sweat on her throat, to claim her lips. Never had a woman elicited such raw emotions within him.

"What's someone like you doing at a bacchanal like this?" Her voice was a raspy whisper that sent a shiver through him.

"I could ask you the same thing," he countered, his voice deeper than he expected.

Her laughter rang out, carrying the power of her self-assurance with it. "I just woke up here. But now I wouldn't have it any other way. This night, the creatures I've met, it's all so extraordinary!"

Her surprise mirrored his own, and yet she seemed completely at ease amid the surrealistic atmosphere of the gathering.

"That's how it is in dreams, lovely. This wonderland carnival promises delights of the most exquisite kind," he responded, trying to hide the curiosity that was sparked in him.

The sound of her joyful laughter echoed in the room as she drew closer, her gaze sparkling with mischievous delight. "Exquisite, you say?"

The electricity in the air seemed to crackle as she leaned closer, her question a whisper in the space between them. He met her halfway, the intensity of their connection manifesting in a searing kiss. The kiss was a wildfire, burning away the last vestiges of his self-restraint. He wanted her; his need echoed in the depths of his being. This woman was an adventure he hadn't expected, but was ready to explore.

The intensity of their emotions grew quickly, sparks igniting between them as they exchanged passionate kisses and gentle touches. He found himself swept up in the whirling storm of sensations. His hands moved over her body with a fervor that mirrored hers. Her heart pounded against his chest, matching the rhythm of their shared desire. The ragged breaths they shared only heightened the intensity of their encounter, creating a symphony that rivaled the wild party around them.

He was enthralled by her, by the contours of her body under his touch, by the thrilling responses she provoked in him. Her body was a siren's song, enticing him further into the depth of his desire. His arousal was clear, and he could feel the matching heat within her. The thought that someone might watch didn't faze him. After all, wasn't this just a dream?

Just as he allowed himself to be completely consumed by their shared passion, a loud outburst tore them away from their blissful state.

Just then, a grove of nymphs approached and dragged the woman out of his arms and off into the trees. Blaine soon lost sight of her.

He hadn't even caught her name. Not that it mattered, since it was all just a dream.

CHAPTER 6

NADIR

Nadir, also known as Meriwether Storm, daemon summoner extraordinaire, lounged at her favorite street café, watching children play in the autumn leaves in the park across the street. Their carefree laughter rang through the crisp mid-morning air, blending with the bustling sounds of the café and the occasional gust of wind rustling the trees. Her bagel sat untouched on the plate, the scent of toasted sesame seeds teasing her nostrils as she sipped absently at her steaming latte.

She caught a whiff of Azimuth's familiar vanilla and musk scent on the breeze and grinned. He pulled out a chair opposite hers without a word. Nadir took in the guise of his human form, one of the few times she could view the extensive daemon ink he'd had before turning Liminal. His sandy blond hair was the same cut and style—long in front but short in back—as it was in daemon form, his face the same. His marked skin even had a whisper of a tan.

"You almost look normal in that human form, Azimuth.

Almost," Nadir teased, grinning foolishly. "To what do I owe the pleasure? You've been so knee-deep in research I didn't think you could get away."

"I needed a well-earned break. I hadn't seen you all day, and I figured I knew where to find you."

Nadir grinned. "Caught red-handed."

Azimuth raised a brow. "What have you been noodling over at this café? It's a pleasant enough environment, but this is the third time this week you've visited."

Nadir considered her words, knowing she owed her partner Azimuth more than a half answer. He had been bound to Belial, a Prince of Sheol, for far longer than she. Nadir realized Az and her other cabal-mates had grown so accustomed to their sire's often psychotic behavior that they'd also become numb to his abuses. In contrast, every time Belial spoke down to her, ordered her about, or otherwise treated her as an animate tool devoid of emotions or opinions, was a fresh cut to the sliver of a soul she had left. But Azimuth hadn't earned her ire today, so she held back, hoping her mood might take on the sun's sunny disposition by some act of magic.

"I suppose I've been avoiding Belial. I know I swore an oath of loyalty to him and the cabal, but if I'm not around, he can't demand things from me. Besides, I know you can always find me if you need me." Azimuth arched his brow, and Nadir expected to get a lecture, but just then, her phone rang. She pulled it out of the back pocket of her pants, checking the caller ID. "Saved by the bell." Annamie. She shot Azimuth a pointed look before answering.

"Hello, old friend. What's the occasion?"

"Oh good, you're in town. I've been tuning into the security scanner you lent me, and last night they found something suspicious in an empty house in Aurora, specifically in the Mission Trujillo neighborhood. A pile of dead bodies; but get this, there's no smell. They haven't been decomposing, and they appear to be missing organs, too. I tried to call you yesterday, but you didn't answer." Annamie's whispered words were easy enough for Azimuth to overhear across the table. His frown and the shadows filling his eyes matched her mood.

"I wasn't in town. You could have rung me if you wanted."

"You know I don't enjoy using that warded rock. It's covered with daemonic shields!"

"Those are my shields."

"I still don't have to like it."

Sigh. "I understand. What's the address?"

She rattled off the street address, and Nadir committed it to memory. "As always, thank you, Annamie."

"Just take out the trash, Meri. I have friends who live in that neighborhood."

"That's our deal, gal. You call it in, I clean 'em up. Consider it handled." Nadir slid out of her seat and put the phone away in one smooth motion. She left a hefty tip, along with her tab on the table. Azimuth stood by her side, his protective aura cooling her heated response to Annamie's call.

As they walked away from the café, Nadir glanced at Azimuth. "We should try to keep up appearances, you know. Meri is supposed to be single, after all."

Azimuth smirked. "Ah, right? Can't have the locals gossiping about our scandalous love affair?"

"My car is right around the back. Let's walk."

"Do you need to move it?" He asked his query in the same way he had so many others over the months of their shared experimentation. The tone of his voice was curious and composed, seeming to probe what the next step in this strange interaction would be.

"Not for a few hours. By then, we'll be back with rein-forcements." He gave a curt nod and followed her into and through the café, then out into the damp, musty-smelling alleyway out back. The rough texture of the brick walls on either side seemed to close in on them, but Nadir's keen senses told her they were alone.

A covert glance around and a whiff of the air assured Nadir no one watched them, despite the sun blazing high above them. Her nose never lied. "We're clear."

No sooner had the words left her lips than Azimuth was kissing her, his entire body pressing her against the wall of the alley. Nadir was lost in his embrace, and the scent of him filled the air. When he teleported them to their bedroom at the cabal, she knew immediately by smell; plus, the cool brick behind her was replaced by a much cooler temperature.

Her heat swept around them in an isolated whirlwind, his hands sliding up underneath her shirt with practiced ease. Nadir hitched a leg up around his waist, drawing Az's lean form even closer to her own. She dug fingers through his hair, groaning in pleasure.

When he chuckled and picked her up, one hand cradling her backside, and headed for the silken sheets of his bed,

Nadir pushed against his chest with her hands. He paused, the playful question plain in his sapphire eyes.

"Wait, no. Not this time. We need to get the boys and head back to Denver. We have daemons to kill."

"Then why are you still wrapped around me like bindweed? I'm not sure it would be safe to unwind you now, even if I tried."

He slid his hand lower, gliding tantalizingly along the connection between her jeans and his leather pants. She groaned in frustration.

"You're a terrible influence," Nadir accused, nipping his lower lip.

"I try my best, darling," Azimuth replied with a wicked grin, taking a harsh intake of breath. Yet she lowered her leg as the kiss lingered, and then raised up onto her toes and buried her nose in his neck, luxuriating in his unique scent of vanilla and sandalwood.

"If you're determined," he said, running light fingertips down her neck and across her back, "we can deal with business first." She could hear the smile in his voice.

"It's best. The last time we made them wait, Orias became a tad impatient. You never know when he'll notice we've returned."

He pulled away, lacing his fingertips with hers. "You're far too rational for your youth."

"Compared to what? The young Azimuth? Do tell." Nadir's curiosity over his early years, alone and with Belial, had been an ongoing interest to her, but not something Azimuth spoke of often.

"Not now. We have business, remember?" He led her

toward the door. She pouted, offering a duly exaggerated stuck-out lip and puppy-dog eyes. "Fine." He pulled her to him, kissed the pout off her face, and whispered, "Perhaps a bedtime story?" The hungry look in his eyes promised much more than a simple story.

"Deal."

CHAPTER 7

BLAINE

Blaine jolted awake, heart pounding in his chest, his mind foggy with the memory of bonfire smoke in the air and with a thin sheen of sweat across his skin. Images of dancers pounding their feet against the bare earth, dust billowing up around their scantily clad forms, and guttural chants echoing through the tall lodgepole pines played through his thoughts.

The green eyes of a blonde-haired dancer as she stalked toward him, framed by firelight, flashed through his thoughts. But he couldn't make out the details clearly.

"What on earth could this mean?" he wondered aloud. He didn't recognize the location, but knew it was nowhere in his city. Was it a message from Zeus? Or perhaps it was just the late-night takeout food playing tricks on his mind.

There was a light rapping on his bedroom door. "Sir?"

Blaine sat up in bed, swinging his legs around to the floor. "Yes, Jake, come on in." His majordomo must have awoken him from the dream, but Blaine didn't remember the initial knock. "That's strange."

Jake entered the room, his footsteps barely making a sound on the plush carpet, carrying the business phone in his hand.

"Another emergency?" Blaine stood and stretched, shaking off the remnants of the dream.

"Sorry, Sir. It's Maria this time." Jake held out the phone to him, his gaze apologetic.

"One of the many joys of being mayor of this illustrious city," Blaine responded with a hint of sarcasm. He took the phone and added, "Jake, you've been a trusted friend and servant for years. Thank you."

Jake nodded, acknowledging the gratitude. "Can I get you anything?"

Blaine shook his head. "Get some more sleep, if you can. Tomorrow's agenda is long."

Jake bowed and exited the room.

Blaine took a deep breath and brought the phone to his ear. "Maria, to what do I owe this three a.m. call?"

"Thank you for taking my call, Chief." Maria's breath came heavily, as if she'd been running, which Blaine couldn't imagine happening in those heels she loved to wear. "You know I'd never disturb you at this hour without good reason." Exhaustion strained her vocal cords, cracking not just once but twice as she spoke. "As the city's oracle, I have little control over when the gods send me missives for your ear, Sir."

"I understand," Blaine replied, pacing barefoot in his room, luxuriating in the plush carpet under his toes as his skin cooled from the evaporated sweat. "Apollo works on his own schedule. To what do I owe the pleasure of this one?"

"There's a new player in town."

"New god-touched are called into service as fits the gods' needs," Blaine replied by rote. "What's so unusual that this one required disturbing my sleep?"

"First, this vision awoke me from my sleep, which rarely happens. Usually, my visions come during quiet times of reflection. This vision felt like a slap upside the head; like I'd been hit with a shockwave of energy."

Chills ran down Blaine's spine, and he paused at his floor-to-ceiling bedroom window overlooking the city, foolishly hunting amongst the twinkling city lights for anything amiss. Dancing forms from the dream replayed through his thoughts.

"I can see how that would be concerning."

"Exactly. Second, in my vision, this new person took a seat at the city council table with us."

"A new god-touched of that rank wouldn't just appear out of nowhere, Maria. The elevation process takes years. Decades for some. Perhaps the vision meant someone on the council got elevated up a rank?"

"Well, I understand my visions can be muddied, but I'm certain this person is an entirely fresh face."

"Can you provide me with a description of this unknown person?" Blaine asked. "Or their deity?"

"The vision didn't make those details clear, but what I saw was truly terrifying."

Blaine's mind raced as he considered the implications. "I can see how this turn of events would be upsetting to the entire council. I appreciate you bringing the possibility to my attention."

"Respectfully, Sir, I should note this was without doubt the strongest vision I've had all year."

Blaine could tell she wanted to say more, but held off out of respect for his position. He ran a hand through his hair, preemptively feeling echoes of the exhaustion of the coming day. The information Maria brought wasn't actionable, per se. Or was it?

"I meant what I said, Maria. Your contributions are invaluable to your fellow council members and in service to our city."

"Thank you, Mayor," Maria replied.

"Be assured, I will put our security forces on alert for a newly called devotee."

"That's very comforting, thank you, Sir," Maria replied. "By their will."

"By their will," Blaine replied, and then hung up the line.

Giving up on getting any additional sleep for the evening, Blaine began his morning routine with a hot shower. Mobilizing his staff to search for an as-yet faceless and unnamed god-touched, who may or may not even exist, would be an interesting challenge.

As he mentally prepared for the day under the steaming hot water, thoughts of his dream intruded into his thoughts. The scent of the bonfire lingered. The timing made him wonder if his dream could be connected to Maria's vision. Could it be a coincidence, or was there a deeper, more sinister connection? Focusing on what he recalled, Blaine remembered no faces or names from his dream. The energy was one of wildness, empowerment, sensuality, and freedom, which he supposed could be connected to a variety of deities.

Shrugging off the feeling, Blaine refocused his thoughts. He needed to be sharp for the day's agenda ahead, which included annexing lands around the city for future industrial development. He'd do his part to manage the potential concerns posed by Maria's vision and then move on to more productive efforts.

Little did he know, his dream and Maria's vision would soon come crashing together, changing his life forever.

CHAPTER 8

NADIR

*A*z and Nadir entered the main meeting room where Kobol and Orias were lounging on the couches, engrossed in a video game. They were fighting off a horde of aliens with an arsenal of futuristic weapons.

The pair's entrance went unnoticed until Azimuth announced, "We have news." Orias and Kobol stood, abandoning their game. "Nadir's contact, Annamie, has identified a possible daemon lair. Something is leaving human bodies in some form of stasis. We need to move quickly."

Kobol, a stocky, strong-looking man, chided them. "Why didn't you say so sooner, instead of dallying in your room?"

"We weren't dallying," Nadir replied. When Orias arched a brow in her direction, she shrugged. "Much."

"How many bodies?" Kobol asked.

"No idea," she replied. "It sounded like less than a dozen. We also don't know if they're killing one or two at a time or taking them all at once."

"Still, a single location and one group of victims suggest a small group of daemons working together," Kobol concluded.

"Agreed," Azimuth replied, his gaze narrowing on Orias, who had been silent, arms crossed, and face downcast while they had talked. "Anything to share, brother?"

"Nothing of relevance," Orias said, not looking up. He held his stance like a tree in gale-force winds, shadows swirling around his feet.

"Why don't we talk about whatever it is later?" Nadir suggested.

He snorted and shook his head. "Yes, add it to your list of conversations that we won't be having anytime soon."

Nadir grimaced, guessing he meant the conversation she hoped to have with Azimuth later. "I will. Count on it."

"If you're done bantering, let's grab our gear and head out," Kobol said, massaging the back of his neck.

Belial strode in from the library, carrying a wrapped bundle in sparkling silver leather over to the kitchen counter. Nadir recognized the rare animal hide but refrained from asking more. There were things she'd discovered she'd rather not know when it came to Sheol.

"I overheard you talking. You're heading out on a mission again?" Belial's eyes glinted with anticipation as he unrolled the leather.

Nadir nodded. "My friend, Annamie, called in a daemon lair. We were just heading out to investigate." She walked closer to the counter and saw a set of four delicate-looking daggers, as silver as the moon, lined up upon the supple hide.

"New weapons?" Kobol reached out and took one, hefted it, tested for balance, and then shot Belial a doubtful look. "These dainty things won't hurt a flea. Are they related to the tre'jor?"

Belial flashed a row of sharp fangs. "For someone who's

lethal despite his compact package, I'd think you'd know better than to judge a weapon by size alone, Kobol. The tre'jor rips a daemon apart, breaking it down into its molecular essence, and then binds that essence to the wielder of the blade. These are my newest inventions. I call them sancre." He spoke the word reverently, his claws danced lightly along the length of the blade.

Azimuth picked up a blade and inspected it. "How does the sancre differ from the tre'jor?" He cast a brief, wary look at Belial, who was too busy admiring his handiwork to notice.

"The sancre is an entirely new class of weapon. I've been trying to perfect it for years, and I must brag. It's my masterpiece. Instead of binding a daemon's essence to the wielder, the sancre consumes the essence and dissipates it into the universe," Belial explained with pride.

Nadir reached out and picked up a dagger, feeling the cool metal between her fingers. "So, it's a daemon-destroying weapon?"

"Exactly. And it has the added benefit of not binding the daemon's essence to you, which can be unpleasant," Belial admitted.

Orias finally uncrossed his arms and stepped forward, picking up the last dagger. He examined it with a critical eye. "They are deceptively lightweight."

Belial chuckled. "That's the beauty of them. They may be light, but they are remarkably durable. The metal is an alloy I developed specifically for this purpose. The dagger's power lies in the enchantment woven into its core. When it pierces a daemon, the enchantment activates, and the daemon's essence is absorbed and neutralized."

The team members exchanged glances, each holding one

of the sancre daggers. "We'll need to test them," Azimuth stated, his eyes locked on Belial's.

"Of course," Belial agreed, a sly grin spreading across his face. "But not on me. Find a suitable test subject, and you'll see the sancre's power firsthand."

Kobol nodded. "Alright, we'll try them. Let's suit up and head out."

CHAPTER 9

NADIR

*A*rmed with their new sancre daggers, they felt a renewed sense of purpose and determination, eager to test the effectiveness of Belial's invention. The prospect of a weapon capable of destroying daemons without binding their essence to the wielder could change the course of their ongoing battle, offering a powerful new tool in their fight against the darkness.

Kobol headed toward the training room where they kept all the other weapons, Orias hot on his heels. Azimuth grabbed Nadir's free hand and drew her close to his side. Their silence spoke volumes, the tension palpable.

In the training room, the boys quickly equipped their weapons of choice: Kobol with his hammer, Azimuth his two short swords, and Orias his curved, ornately engraved scimitar. They had no need for discretion on this mission.

Nadir approached her black lacquered weapon's dresser against the wall. Her favorite weapons rested on the top shelf, nestled amid scarlet silk. She selected an assortment of daggers, metal arrows, and thin wires, strapping them to various parts of her body. The arrows and wires went into the specially crafted containers attached to her boots.

"How close can we port to the site?" Orias asked.

"I don't know the area very well, but it's not a far drive from where I left my car," Nadir explained.

Kobol laughed. "I've been meaning to ask. When are you going to upgrade your house to match your Hummer?"

"I like my house. Besides, it's established with my alibi."

"You need a bigger house. Who says the powerful 'Meri' can't upgrade? Or at least get a bigger garage." Azimuth ran a hand between her shoulder blades, and she fought to keep her breathing even.

"Let's deal with it later," she replied.

"Everyone ready?" Azimuth asked.

"Hold on to me," Nadir directed. "We're porting into an alley near my car."

They did as directed, huddled together. Nadir chose a shady location overhung by buildings and blocked by dumpsters. Scanning the area visually and by scent, she detected a human nearby.

"Kobol," she subvocalized, "there's a guy. He's just a few feet away. He's..."

He leaned in, mouth to her ear. "On the other side of the dumpster, I know. I don't have your bionic nose, but I can smell a sweaty lout eight feet away. Give me a moment."

He winked into invisibility, and a few moments later, a sickening thump against the brick wall made her stomach turn. Nadir pushed away from Azimuth and stalked out of their hiding spot, not at all happy to see a busboy from the restaurant crumpled into a pile on the ground next to the back door of the restaurant. An again-visible Kobol crouched over the man, checking his pulse.

"I assume that was necessary?"

Kobol spared a glance up at her, nonplussed by her attitude. "He'd just brought out the trash and was coming around the dumpster. You wanted us to remain unseen, so yes, I made a snap decision. It's what we do every day. In case you're curious, he's fine. Go get in the car and drive around the corner. I'll knock on the door and make sure someone tends to him, and then I'll join you."

"Fine." Nadir grabbed her car keys and stalked off toward her car, aware by scent alone Azimuth and Orias followed. When they got within ten feet of the car, the push of a button unlocked the doors and started the engine, and she jumped into the driver's seat.

"You're upset. One of us could drive, if you prefer," Orias said, holding open a back door.

"It's my car. I'm driving. Besides, it's not like you know Colorado."

Azimuth and Orias got in and closed their doors. "We know enough to navigate. What we don't know, you could co-pilot." Orias' voice of reason made perfect sense, but her hands gripped the wheel until it groaned under the pressure as she put the car in gear and drove out of the parking lot.

"My car. I drive." Nadir pulled to a stop along the curb and put the car in park.

"Girl doesn't like to share her toys." Azimuth claimed her knee with his hand.

"Don't distract me, Az. We're here to help humans, not hurt them."

Kobol appeared outside of the curbside car door and got

into the car. "Calm yourself. I gave him a minor concussion and his friends just called medics to check on him. He's already coming around. More importantly, no one noticed us. If you're so concerned, pick a more secure location for the port next time."

Nadir laid her head against the steering wheel and took a deep breath, then shook her head and put the car into gear. "I'll plan ahead better next time. The alley was a poor location for the group of us."

No one replied, which was likely for the best, considering she needed to reset. She left Lo-Do and traveled east, catching the highway and heading toward Aurora. A few turns later, they turned into the suburban neighborhood Annamie had indicated. Checking the exact address, she located the subdivision and drove through the area. It was bisected by a wide greenbelt with a park filled with equipment for kids.

Not where you'd expect to find daemons. But with the depression, no doubt there were plenty of vacant houses ripe for their use.

Nadir parked down the street from the first address, and when she got out of the car, the scent of daemon kin drew her immediately. The others followed.

"What do you smell?" Azimuth asked.

"The residue of three daemons," Nadir replied. "One foul and musty of greed, one heady bay and acacia, smelling of power, and one some sort of flesh eater, smelling putrid." The others shared a glance. All could smell other daemons, but only Nadir knew their powers by scent because of her acquired hunter abilities.

"Good to know," Orias replied. "Lead the way."

She did as requested, not at all concerned about being the first through the door. A few houses down, she located a home that reeked of daemon essence and led them around via an open back gate into a backyard void of other structures. The back door to the house was locked but was made from metal, which Nadir easily bent open with her powers.

Once inside, she sensed no one else was there. There were no bodies; the police must have removed them yesterday. The boys fanned out and looked the place over, but it was empty.

"They aren't here now. But recently." She opened her mouth wide, tasting the air. "I know their names. I can taste them." She rolled her tongue at the foul taste in her mouth.

The guys drew weapons and formed a circle, backs to each other. Azimuth turned to her. "Draw your blades and whisper their names when you're ready. The curiosity will be enough to draw them back."

Nadir nodded in understanding, held her sancre dagger aloft, and whispered the names she tasted in the air.

CHAPTER 10

ERIN

*E*rin awoke, eyes opening to sunlight dappling down through the outstretched arms of the lodgepole pines she remembered falling asleep under last night. Or was it this morning? Birdsong filled the air, their warbling joy untouched by her plight. By the angle of the light, she could tell it was already midmorning.

She stretched a little, languorously, and could still smell the smoke from the bonfire in her clothes and in her hair. Surrounded by her backpack, walking sticks gathered from last night, and her body arranged in roughly the same position she'd fallen asleep in, all appeared in order. The forest creatures hadn't even gone after her meager food supplies.

It was all just a dream.

Her laughter rang out in the night air. What a crazy dream, no doubt spurred on by her injuries and fatigue from the day. Maybe she had hit her head when she had fallen? That was always a possibility. All of yesterday's events were jumbled up like slices of a shattered mirror, reflections in her mind that seemed to form an impossible landscape that she just couldn't piece together.

Had she honestly faced down a bear? Danced with satyrs and nymphs? Slipped her hands across a gold-skinned man? Surely not.

Then why did her lips still feel bruised? Erin brushed the fingers of her left hand across them gently and suppressed a yelp of pain. Blaming dehydration, she moved to prop herself up on her left elbow, preparing for her body to protest every motion.

Meeting no resistance, warning bells clamored through her mind. Erin hadn't desired discomfort, but it had been assured after yesterday's fall, which she was fairly sure had happened. *Hadn't it?*

Erin grabbed a canteen and drank deeply, but it tasted weak. *Off.* She sighed, craving something with more substance. She held the bottle out and sniffed it with her right hand, but it smelled fine. In shock, her eyes took in the entirety of her right arm as she moved it back and forth, placing the canteen on the ground. The fabric she'd bandaged her fingers with the day before was gone, and her movements caused no pain. Although there were a few bruises and small, thin white lines on her fingers and mild stiffness in her shoulder, Erin couldn't rightly call it pain. Not compared to the lancing heat she'd experienced the day before.

She sat forward and gingerly peeled back her left sock, again finding no bruises. Frowning, she slipped it all the way off. Poking and prodding her mostly pink flesh, Erin searched for the damage so fresh in her mind, but, again, only mild discoloration remained. She flexed and stretched her foot, rotated it back and forth, all with no protest from the joint.

Erin replaced her sock and sat back. Had she imagined the fall? No, her shirt was still ripped where she'd made it into an impromptu bandage for her hand. Perhaps she'd instead hit her head in the fall, and her actions reflected some form of temporary insanity?

A smile crept along her face as she deeply breathed in the forest air, the slightest hint of smoke lingering on her clothing. She shook her head and laughed. If she was mad, so be it. She preferred it over beaten, bloody, and broken.

She ran her hands through her hair, finding and then pulling out pine needles and lichen. Lovely. The animals had left her alone, yet she'd dug herself into the mossy bedding in her sleep. Her damp shirt stuck to her back, the effects of sleeping too far into the day mixing with the rising temperatures in the relative solitude of the forest. Erin sat stupefied, dazed at the sudden change of her circumstances.

A pinecone landed on her head, followed by a chittering rant. Erin scrambled to her feet, easily locating the offending chipmunk in the limbs above her head.

"Hey! That was completely uncalled for! Get outta here before I throw one of those right back at cha."

The chipmunk stared at her raptly throughout her speech and then scurried down the tree and off into the woods. Well, at least she'd scared it off. She loved her time in the forest, but those chipmunks with their morning antics and cries for territorial dominance could drive a woman to the brink.

Standing, Erin stretched again, testing out her ability to move, and discovered only minor sore spots. Nothing to hold her back. Grateful for however it happened, she dug her shoes out of her backpack and put them back on her feet. She gathered the rest of her things, leaving the walking sticks behind, and shouldered the backpack. Checking the sun's position and the forest for recognizable landmarks, she settled on a north-western path, which she reasoned should rejoin the main trail and get her back to her car.

Although she walked hesitantly at first, both fearing another encounter with the local wildlife and afraid of pushing her foot too hard, her confidence soon returned. Despite the bear and her subsequent fall from the cliff, the forest remained her refuge. The sighing of the wind through the trees was a solace to her heart. The sunlight filtered through the air, dappling the pine-needle littered earth and warming her back, a hug shining upon her very soul.

The essence of the forest filled her. Completed her.

Erin didn't want to leave. The moment she spied the abandoned trailhead and her dilapidated Dodge sedan, she heard the call of pan pipes echoing through the hills behind her. She spun around, searching for the source of the sound, while her heart beat in time with the haunting melody. No one—or perhaps more accurately, *nothing*—was there.

Something in the forest waited for her. Beckoned for her to return.

Shaking it off, Erin stumbled back to her car, flung her backpack in the passenger seat, and then climbed behind the wheel. Her head ached. Today was Sunday, and in a few hours, she'd be expected to serve drinks at her second job late into the evening, on her feet, before getting a scant few hours of sleep and heading back into her corporate job on Monday. She had responsibilities. Commitments.

It promised to be a very long week.

CHAPTER 11

NADIR

"Wrathkin. Athazagorath. Rakshasa."

The smell of the greed daemon, Athazagorath, hit her first, the sound of his swift footsteps coming a moment before he materialized right in front of her. He was an enormous creature with blackened skin, ragged clothes, and long, thick fingers. Before she had time to react, the daemon was on her, crushing her body back against the others with his substantial bulk. He reeked of greed, desperation, and a hundred other unsavory things. His hands gripped Nadir's throat and forced her head back. She struggled under him, skewering him with one blade after another, but she wasn't able to free herself from his grip even with all of her strength enhanced by daemonic powers.

The sound of steel on steel filled her ears as the others faced Wrathkin and Rakshasa, but Nadir's focus was completely upon the immovable daemon with his hands around her throat. Her lungs burned for air as one of her daggers fell uselessly from her fingers, sinking into the floor at their feet.

Azimuth appeared out of nowhere behind Athazagorath, driving his sword through the daemon's back. Nadir gasped for air as Azimuth withdrew his sword from the daemon, who slumped forward onto the floor between them with a mighty, gurgling exhale.

"Thanks!" she coughed out. "I almost had him."

"Of course you did." Azimuth winked at her, and then pulled her close, spinning them around just in time as Kobol suddenly came flying across the room. He hit a wall with such force it shook the entire structure, and then he fell motionless to the floor. Orias moved quickly past them toward Kobol, enveloping them both within the void of his shadows. Although Nadir had seen him do it countless times, the sense that they'd ceased to exist always nagged at the back of her mind.

Nadir shook off the sensation and shifted her attention, sizing up the other two daemons, Wrathkin and Rakshasa. The former was a large, imposing figure, blue-skinned and gaunt, with a pair of horns curling from his forehead. The latter was a human-like female figure with a slender frame and golden eyes that seemed to burn with a deep, inner fire. Rakshasa might have appeared to be the less dangerous one of the two, but Nadir knew, since the daemon was a flesh-eater, that she likely also had an ability to incapacitate her victims.

"Hey, Rakshasa. Wrathkin. How about we don't choose violence?" she asked. "Tell us where the others are, and we can all part amicably."

It was a lie, and by the dubious flash in the daemon Wrathkin's yellow-lined eyes, he knew it.

Rakshasa seemed to sense the tension in the air and was

starting to move. She took one step back and then another, her eyes flashing between Nadir and Azimuth and Wrathkin. Suddenly, as if she couldn't control herself any longer, she rushed toward the shadows wrapped around the fallen Kobol with a ravenous look on her face.

Nadir reacted without thinking, launching forward before Rakshasa could reach her fallen brother. A host to a flesh-eater daemon herself, Nadir understood the sometimes near-undeniable compulsion to feed, especially when the victim was already incapacitated. With a twist of her body, Nadir drove one of her blades through the daemon's heart, killing her instantly. The sound of the impact reverberated in Nadir's ears as Rakshasa fell to the ground in a lifeless heap. There was a moment of tense silence, followed by a sorrow-filled howl from Wrathkin.

Nadir turned to face Wrathkin, who was now the only daemon left standing. He'd moved closer to her, body shaking with overwhelming grief at the loss of Rakshasa. Nadir could see the torment etched on his face, even as he eyed his companion's blackened blood dripping from her upraised blades.

She didn't fear the remaining daemon, trusting that he was no match for Azimuth and herself. "I'm sorry for your loss," Nadir said, her voice filled with genuine empathy. "But you must understand, you left us no choice. You've been feeding on the humans here, drawing undue attention."

Wrathkin looked up at her, his eyes filled with tears. "She was my mate. My everything. And now she's gone."

Nadir felt a pang of sadness for the daemon, despite the fact he had just tried to kill them. She had seen enough death to know the pain of losing someone you loved. As she met the gaze of Wrathkin, Nadir didn't react as Azimuth raised his sword to the daemon's throat. As the icy steel touched his flesh, hatred bubbled up in Wrathkin's gaze.

"What's the location of your nest?" Azimuth demanded. When Wrathkin didn't answer, he went on. "Give us what we want, now," Azimuth said, his voice low and menacing. "Or suffer the same fate."

Wrathkin stood still for a moment, his gaze shifting between Nadir and Azimuth. Nadir watched him with barely concealed contempt as he thought through his options. She kept her blades at the ready, knowing that she would have to act in an instant if Wrathkin chose wrongly.

But eventually, he decided. "What's stopping you from killing me after I tell you?" the daemon grumbled, a fiery gleam in his eyes.

The shadows in the corner roiled and swept away, revealing Orias and a very cranky looking Kobol. Nadir let out a breath, relieved to see the redhead standing, even if he looked a little pale. Orias moved with catlike grace, walking up to Wrathkin, his face a mask of serene calm.

"Nothing will stop these two. Despite all the raw power you yield, you're going to die tonight. Either by their steel or by my more artistic means."

"I can fight my way through the hordes of hell, shadow-walker. Why should I fear any of you? I'll fight to the death, and whether I live or die, you'll never know where to find the others."

Orias lifted his hand toward the hulking blue giant's arm and then paused. "I can pull the truth from you, or you can give it freely. If I force it, you'll die in agony as I rip your mind to shreds, fiber by fiber. If you simply utter a few easy words, I give my word, your death will be swift."

"There's nothing easy about betraying your family for a painless death," Wrathkin sighed. "You wouldn't even know that I'm giving you the right location."

"I'll know," Azimuth added.

With defeat written on his face, the daemon's shoulders slumped in compliance. Misery twisted his features, but he spoke. "1801 California Street."

Orias and Nadir both looked to Azimuth, who nodded in confirmation that he'd spoken the truth, and then, without further warning, sliced his sword through the formidable daemon's neck. The hulking, blue giant's body crumbled to the ground as his dark red blood seeped into the ground beneath him.

All four watched the daemon bleed out onto the carpet, the air heavy with grim resolution.

"Do you know the address?" Azimuth asked Nadir, his voice low.

She nodded, knowing he'd taken no joy in the act. "It's in a busy district," she said, thinking through the situation to make sure she had all the facts. "The idea of a daemon nest there seems improbable."

Orias replied to her after some consideration. "We'll see what we find." He turned his attention to Kobol next. "Are you recovered?"

Kobol ran a hand through his ginger curls and winced as his fingers hit a sore spot. The skin had broken, and a drop of blood appeared. "My ego's more bruised than my pride," he shrugged. "But they'll both recover after we rout the nest."

"Let's port these bodies back to Sheol first," Azimuth said.

Orias nodded, a frown forming on his face. "We didn't use the new weapons Belial gave us."

Nadir glanced at the daggers in her hands. Daggers that had become almost an extension of her hands during battle. "Damn," she said, "we'll have to remember to use those at the nest."

Orias' frown remained, and Nadir had a feeling he was doing some mental calculating under the surface.

"Anything we should know?" Azimuth asked him.

There was a pause, and then Orias shook his head. "Nothing of import."

Nadir wondered what Orias' visions or intuition might have brought to his attention and how heavy it would weigh on his spirit.

CHAPTER 12

ERIN

The pervasive beat of industrial music rolled through the club, displacing the pounding in Erin's head with a steady rhythm and cadence, which lulled her into a languid mood. The aches in her body had continued to fade throughout the day, and now she felt uncommonly vibrant.

Who knew falling off a cliff could be therapeutic?

"Hey Lola, here's your drinks for table fourteen." The bartender shoved the drinks over, his wary eyes scanning the crowd. He was always waiting for trouble. There often was.

"Thanks, Bear." Erin gave him a quick wink while she loaded her tray.

No one used their given names in the illegal den of iniquity, known simply as Porters. If the security forces ever busted them, Erin planned to hightail it out of there and never look back.

His curiosity over her playful demeanor didn't lead to questions. Instead, he harrumphed and set about fixing the next order.

Erin sashayed in her red high heels, ridiculously short black skirt, and a matching black tank top which did nothing for her willowy yet athletic frame. Yet it fit the dress code, which was what Charlie, the boss, demanded.

Porter's simple rule was to appease Charlie or don't get paid.

Erin dropped the drinks off for a pair of regular customers. By their factory-issued tan jumpsuits, she assumed they worked in one of the local manufacturing centers. For all she knew, they worked in one of the production factories, producing one of many local varieties of signature beer Colorado continued to win awards for. Because of their identical outfits, she'd nicknamed them *the blond* and *his bearded friend.*

"Here you go, a vodka tonic. And a stout for you." She set the drinks down, all the while bending forward to give the men a show as her skirt hiked up. It helped with the tips. Their eyes, however, were on the stage, fixated on Brie, one of the strippers.

Erin wouldn't dance. She had a deal with Charlie and he'd never pushed her. He could be a hardass, but at least he respected her boundaries.

"That'll be thirty for the drinks, guys."

Only then did Erin merit their attention. The blond pulled out his wallet and fished out two twenties and handed them over. "Keep the change, Lola." He smacked her on the rump, and although she cringed inside, Erin forced a smile.

"Thanks. Enjoy the show, guys."

She turned to walk away, pulling a ten out of her apron, making the correct change, and then slid the tip into her bra.

"Hey, Lola!" the bearded friend called out.

She turned back and leaned on the table. "What's up, guys?"

"When'd you get that ink done, girl?" His tongue licked his lips, his raw hunger directed right at her. "It's wicked hot."

"Huh?" These guys hadn't been here long, and she'd only served them two rounds of drinks. What were they going on about?

"The vines across your shoulders. How long did it take to get 'em done?" asked the blond. He wasn't lewd like his friend, but the appreciation in his gaze was obvious.

Erin craned her neck around and glimpsed delicate, dark purple verdigris swirls gracing her shoulder blades under the thin straps of the tank top. What in the world? She couldn't see how far the design extended. It would require a mirror to get a full view of her own back. *She needed to get into the bathroom.*

"What, you get it done after a rough night of partying?" asked the redhead, laughing at his own clever joke.

Erin's thoughts flashed back to her dream, remembering the nymphs painting her skin in the *dream* and how it had stung in places, including her back. She laughed aloud, shaking her head at the ludicrous concept.

But if it had all been a dream, why did her lips still feel bruised? What mark now adorned her back?

Could the golden-skinned man and his revelers have been real?

No.

Impossible.

Which is why she now had a mark on her back, which a shower hadn't washed off? A shiver ran through her body, causing her to wobble a touch on her heels.

The men stared at her, and Erin stared right back.

"Lola!" Charlie's voice bellowed.

Erin almost dropped her tray, but pinned it between her arm and ribs. "Sorry guys, I gotta run." She flashed them a wide, fake smile and spun toward Charlie, who was in the back of the club in the VIP section.

Dragging her scuffed heels to the low-lit area cordoned off by worn, red velvet ropes, which Charlie must have stolen from a shutdown movie theater, Erin tossed her short, flippy hair coquettishly at the stoic bouncers before acknowledging Charlie.

"What cha' need, boss?"

The tall man had short-clipped hair, dark brown eyes, and harsh, angular features that intimidated almost everyone more than the bouncers. But then, as the boss, it was only fitting to be the most imposing figure on the floor. "I've got a client requesting you."

She almost laughed at his hubris. "I don't do *clients*, Charlie."

He barked out a laugh. "Little Lola's got a backbone today?"

"I wait tables here. I'm not one of your other girls." Erin crossed her arms and leaned back into her hip, arching an eyebrow.

"Man says he just wants to talk to you. Do me a favor and have a drink with him?"

Charlie had never asked her to do anything before. He'd always ordered. "He's an important *client* to you?"

"Very."

Erin fluffed her hair in the back, poufing it up a bit. "I'll talk with him, Charlie. But I'm not *entertaining* him."

"Whatever you're comfortable with, Lola. He's the one all the way in the back corner booth."

"Fine." Erin let out a low growl and slid past Charlie and the bouncers, snapping her heels against the concrete floor in a staccato beat in time with the music, her hips swaying provocatively. She dropped the serving tray off at the VIP bar and wended her way back to the corner booth and Charlie's *special* client.

The high-backed, black, circular booths provided insular bubbles of privacy lining the dimly lit chamber. Some tables were empty, some filled with customers enjoying a lap dance or more intimate form of company available to them here in Porter's VIP lounge.

The corner booth held a single occupant who already nursed a longneck. He wore an expensive-looking red suit shirt encompassing his thick torso and had a thick five o'clock shadow dusting his prominent chin. It was in stark contrast to his bald head, which sported a tattoo of a gleaming silver spear she could just spy above his left ear. *How did he get away with that at a corporate job?*

"You already have a drink, I see. I don't suppose you need another?"

He didn't smile back. *Odd.* "I'm fine, thanks. Why don't you get yourself something, and then we can talk for a while?"

"Sure thing, hon. I'll be right back."

Erin sauntered back to the bar, in no hurry to return to her VIP, but figuring she'd show off her long, toned legs. If the man wanted a show, she'd give him a show, because he wasn't getting anything else.

"Hey Lola, what can I do you for?" Mick, the bartender, asked as she leaned on her elbows.

She licked her lips. Only one drink appealed to her. "Wine. What all you got?"

"House red or white," his enthusiasm was as dry as the options.

"Be more specific."

He frowned. "What, you're a connoisseur now?"

She flicked her fingers at him. "Just tell me what types, Mick. I ain't got all day."

"Fine, whatever. The red's a merlot and the white's a chardonnay. I think the rose is a merlot or zinfandel. Crap if I care."

Erin rubbed her temples. Merlot would never do; it would only make her melancholy. The chardonnay was a sunny and upbeat wine but would solidify her connection to her *client*. Not something she was aiming for. The undefined rose was an automatic pass.

"Do you have a Nebbiolo back there?"

Mick rolled his eyes. "I've told you what we have, Lola."

"Can you double check for me, please?"

"You know something I don't know?"

She shrugged her shoulders. Nebbiolo's ability to focus her mind and keep her crafty would be perfect. Erin didn't know how she knew, but the clarity of the answer was rooted in her like a living thing.

"Fine." He disappeared through a door into the storage room behind the bar and returned two minutes later carrying a bottle of Italian Nebbiolo and an astonished look on his face. "You could have just told me the VIP had it brought in."

Except he hadn't. Thoughts of the man with the amber eyes flashed through her mind. How could this be possible? Erin watched in wonder as he popped the cork, handed her two glasses, and then handed both the glasses and the bottle over to her.

She squelched a private smile as she picked up the bottle, held it to her nose, and breathed it in deeply. The aroma was divine.

"Thanks, Mick."

"Next time, just tell me flat out and don't mess with me."

"Sure thing." She hadn't known what she'd done, just like she hadn't known about the mark on her back. She needed answers more than Mick did.

Erin carried the glasses in one hand and the bottle in the other, slinking back over to the table, her lips pursed. She set up the two glasses and Mr. VIP leaned back in the booth, waving her off.

"There's no way I'm drinking anything you pour." It was said neither in accusation nor amusement, just in his earlier flat tone.

"Yet you had me get a drink? Why?" She poured herself a glass, unable to resist the bouquet emanating from the bottle over the stench of sweat and mildew of the club.

"I figured Charlie would expect you to drink along with me. I also wanted to see what you'd do."

Erin finished pouring and had the glass resting against her lips, on the cusp of tasting the wine, when his words hit her. She paused, raising her eyes to meet his narrowed, calculating gaze. Her tongue flicked out, capturing a few drops of the dusky, berry-laden wine.

She craved more to her marrow, but knowing he wanted her to indulge made her fight the impulse. What did he mean, *see what she'd do?*

"Have a seat." He gestured at the space next to him. "I'd tell you to sit across from me, because I can assure you, I'm not planning anything other than talking with you, but it would make Charlie suspicious."

She took a drink then, slowly enjoying the feel of the aged vintage while she sized up her host through half-open lids. The wine burned a welcome path down her stomach, and from there, through her veins, emboldening her actions. Whatever this man was, he knew things. Things she wanted to know, too.

Erin sat down on the bench and slid around, getting nice and cozy with the corporate suit. When her hip and arm rubbed up against his, he initially pulled away before settling back down.

Interesting. When he backed away from her, in that instant, she glimpsed the tattoo on the back of his head. It was a pair of crossed spears done in black and highlighted in silver, gorgeously wrought. A man of war?

"You wanted me here to talk. I'm here. Talk."

He took a deep breath and looked her over while she drank another sip of wine and studied him. Anxiety rolled off him in palpable waves. It wasn't something she'd noticed before, but his inability to sit still, especially with her this close, was downright comical. For all his posh veneer, sleek presentation, and displaced 9-to-5 appropriateness in this parlor of sins, he hadn't come undone until she'd snuggled up next to him.

He shivered under her gaze. "If you touch me, Wild One, have no doubts, I'll bring you up on charges so fast your head will spin." His words threatened, but the fear hung heavy in his eyes.

Peals of laughter rang from Erin's throat. "Pardon, sir. *You* asked me over. *You* invited me to sit. This meeting is entirely at your discretion. What's your name, anyway?"

"Daniel. Yours?"

"Lola." She poured herself another glass, ignoring his insta-frown.

"No, your real name."

She gave him a sideways glance. "You've got to be kidding, right? That's not how we play things here, or at any club. Even you corporate types have to know how it works. I'm not having you report me to the security forces."

He spread out a hand, flat on the table, muscles tensing across his shoulders. "This isn't about the Corporates, not directly at least, and you know it. This is about what we are, besides all of that. I need to know why you are working here, and why you feel it's appropriate to display your adoration to non-initiates."

Erin stared at him blankly. What? The? Sheol? He thought she was a part of some club and had some in, but she had absolutely no idea what he was rambling on about. However, the more tense he got, she knew one thing for certain.

Erin wanted to punch him. She'd never been the violent type, but his obscure lecturing inflamed her temper. Sure, he was a corporate shirt, but nobody threatened 'Lola'.

That might have been the two glasses of wine talking, she considered, before dismissing the fleeting concern.

"I work here, Daniel, to make money. Some of us aren't as lucky as you corporates. As for the other, I have no idea what you're rattling on about." She finished the second glass of wine, which had slid down even smoother than the first. Of course, she poured herself another. He wasn't drinking any, and it would be a shame to waste the bottle.

He leaned into her, the hard edge of his steely musk an assault on her senses, and gripped her wrist firmly, so hard it bit into her skin. "You have great favor. It's obvious by the extent of your markings. Surely you can secure better employ than this seedy dive," he whispered into her ear.

Erin's lip curled into a snarl. He was no better than the satyr who'd tested her limits at the forest's bonfire. How dare this man handle her without permission? The music pounded through her veins, her heart surging with the fire of the vine.

"A smart man would remove his hand about now." She set her glass down on the table and leaned into him, but this time he didn't give. "What markings are you referring to?"

Say it. She needed him to tell her what they meant.

Stoically, he held his ground. "A wise girl wouldn't flaunt our markings," his eyes lingered over her nearly bare shoulders for a moment, "to non-initiates. You know what'll happen if I report you?"

"What, someone's panties will get in a bunch? Those are some stunning blades tattooed on the back of your head. Won't you get in trouble for showing off those too, *Daniel*?"

He laughed and then looked her up and down like he

couldn't quite figure out if she was joking or not. "Of course you can see these. You're a devotee. But you're showing yours off to everyone. I know for certain because those men asked about your prominent display. I heard it over the music all the way across the club. What do you have to say for yourself, wildling?"

Erin's tolerance for this discussion of shadow and innuendo had come to an end. "I said, *Daniel*, take your fucking hand off of me. Now. Or I'll remove it for you."

"I'm not the type to back down, sweetheart." His grin transformed into a grimace, his grip twisting her wrist, pain spiraling up her arm. "You need to hide your markings now, or I'll report you. Heck, I'm going to report you anyway, but how I pitch the report? Well, that's entirely up to you."

His glancing leer toward her slight cleavage left Erin dropping her mouth open in shock. "I'm afraid we're not destined to get along." Despite the pain in her wrist, she used it and her shoulder to press him against the back wall of the booth, leveraging off her left leg. Surprised, he released his grip, and once again tried to slither out of her presence, but she had him pinned. "I gave you fair warning, didn't I?" Erin's lips brushed from the corner of his lips up his cheek to his ear. Anyone watching might have confused the moment for a sexual overture.

They'd have been mistaken.

"I should warn you, little lady, I'm a renowned fighter. It's rare that anyone bests my skills."

His bluster was at odds with the way he continued to try to squirm out from under her. Erin straddled him in the booth, preventing his escape. "You manhandled me. Such behavior isn't allowed." Why Erin couldn't back off this nonnegotiable point, she didn't know. He'd crossed a line and she wouldn't, couldn't, back down.

"Fine." Disgust rolled off his features, wrinkling his nose, curling his lips in an unattractive snarl. "But not here, have some decorum! Pick a time, a place, and I'll meet your terms. I'm honorable when challenged."

She barked a laugh right into his ear. "You already picked it. You should know better when dealing with, what did you call me? A wild one? A wildling?" she spat at him.

Grabbing his shirt by the lapels, she stood in the booth and dragged him out, despite his roar of protest and attempts to dig in his heels. Although he far outweighed her. Standing up, Erin could tell he had the hefty but lithe build of a wrestler. She'd been able to pull him out without too much trouble. Perhaps because of the slick surface of the vinyl seat?

His face had darkened with rage by the time she tossed him to the floor, but he had her by the shirt, and took her down with him, where they fell to a heap.

Erin had never been much of a scrapper, and in seconds, Daniel had rolled them over and pinned her arms to the dirty, sticky floor. "Your ways aren't fit for the city, *Lola*. You should run back to the hills where behaving like a madwoman will be tolerated."

His words lanced through her, and Erin knew in that moment she wasn't insane. She hadn't imagined what had happened. She couldn't explain it, but it had been more than a dream.

The bonfire. The satyrs. The nymphs. The man with the amber eyes. The bruising kiss. *The Vessel.*

Somehow, all of it had been real.

Which meant she'd changed. Daniel knew what it meant

better than she. Erin didn't understand the depths, yet she felt the power of the wine coursing through her veins and understood it as truth.

With a sigh, she released her doubts, her questions, and gave herself over to the profound sensations beating in her chest, spreading through her entire body. At once, Erin experienced the same energetic high as she had danced around the bonfire. Her body hummed with power, and by the flicker of fear furrowing the brow of the man above her, he sensed it as well.

"Didn't I warn you about handling me improperly?" Erin pouted, and then drew up her legs and used her leverage with one knee to fling him off her sideways. He rolled to the side, but maintained his grip on her wrists. Erin used the momentum to bunch up and narrow the angle of her wrists, forcing him to continue the roll onto his back and then punched him under the collarbones, at which point he finally released his grip.

For a tough guy, he laid there stunned and breathless. Erin pushed her advantage, kneeling onto his gut and landing a series of all-too-satisfying punches across his jaw, chest, defending arms, even shoulders. In a matter of moments, his eyes were rolling back in his head, and yet her anger only was stoked further.

Thick fingers laced around her arms, and Erin broke out of her destructive trance. Hauled up and off Daniel, Bono the bouncer held her back to his front, her feet dangling in the air, but Erin didn't fight him. She had no beef with the man who'd intervened and saved her from more than one patron who'd crossed the line. Charlie stepped in and helped Daniel to his feet, while Bono set her back down on hers, although he didn't release his grip. Not that she blamed him. Her knuckles still itched to swing toward her opponent.

Daniel recovered remarkably well, and spoke to an irate Charlie in hushed tones, his arm wound around him, and their backs turned away from Erin and Bono.

"What's wrong, Lola?" Bono whispered into her ear above the din of the music.

She dug the toe of her shoe into the painted vinyl of the floor. "He's an asshole."

Bono grumbled out a laugh. "He's a VIP, honey. Comes with the territory. I admire your fire, but this was not a viper you should have tangled with."

"But I won."

He snorted. "You *never* win with them."

Erin sighed, frustrated over having the trouncing cut short. "I will. Perhaps not today, but he'll get what's due."

Charlie and Daniel turned, icy glares matching the hardened posture of their bodies. When Charlie spoke to her, all semblance of any prior camaraderie they'd shared was nonexistent.

"Needless to say, you're fired. Bono will walk you out. If you even step inside this club again, I will get the security forces to arrest you for prostitution. Is that understood?"

Cold fury flared through Erin over his baseless claims, but she knew he could make it happen. The smug look on Daniel's face behind him, although bruised and beaten, left little doubt. How long would it take her to find another job like this? Would Charlie spread the word to other clubs that she'd be trouble and prevent them from hiring her? Erin bit her lip. The consequences weighed on her slumped shoulders.

"Fine."

"Take her outta here." Charlie walked off in a huff.

Daniel remained, and as Bono turned with her, spoke up. "Just a moment. I have a parting thought for the chit."

Bono hesitated, no doubt worried Erin would take another swing at Daniel. She remained limp in his arms and nodded a go-ahead to Bono.

The self-satisfied smirk on Daniel's face fell short, considering the impressive black eye he sported. He leaned in, arms crossed, and she noticed his torn collar from the fight. "I'm reporting you to Blaine, real name or not. You can be sure he'll find you. If you're smart, you'll flee before he catches up to you. You're clearly not tame enough for our city."

"If he's anything like you, big boy, I'd be quaking in my barely there skirt. But with a name like *Blaine*, I doubt he's even a real man. Pansy's more like it."

"Lola," Bono growled behind her, but she remained limp in his grip. Erin didn't intend to start another fight, but she'd be damned if she'd back down from Daniel's verbal threats.

Daniel held a single, lecturing finger up to her nose, and Erin barely suppressed a laugh. "I'll let him know you said so. He won't be amused." He swept past them both, almost knocking Bono over when their shoulders connected with brute force. Erin laughed, not bothering to hold it in any longer.

Bono ignored her, hauling her body through the club, shoving aside anyone along their way, earning a few squeals. Erin couldn't stop laughing, despite the circumstances.

When he pushed her through the dilapidated club door and into the alley, which served as the club's entrance, her mood sobered. He set her down gently, and she was impressed with him for his kindness.

"Thanks. You could have just booted me out here on my ass. It's what Charlie wanted, I'm sure."

The big guy rubbed the back of his neck and stared at the ground. "Sometimes the boss doesn't know how hard it is for the girls. I watch. I listen. I'm sure that VIP had it coming. Besides, watching you beat the crap outta him," Bono sneaked her a grin, "gal, I never knew you had it in you."

Erin licked her lips, the taste of the Nebbiolo still fresh upon her flesh. Somehow, the wine had changed her. *Or had it?* Had it been the tipping point to push her over an invisible line in the sand? Or had she been there already, deep inside herself?

"Sometimes I even surprise myself. Take care of yourself, Bono." Erin turned to go, her heels scraping on the asphalt of the unlit, dank alley.

Erin's stomach lurched at Bono's question, the sincerity in his voice piercing her fabricated bravado. It took all her willpower not to turn and collapse into his powerful arms, to cling to the comfort and safety he represented.

She couldn't stop the derisive laugh which slipped out. "Don't worry about me. There's always work for desperate girls who are willing to work in shit holes. I'll find something new before the week is up," she replied with a conviction she didn't feel.

His sigh echoed against the narrow walls, but Erin refused to look back. She heard the door close behind her as she made her way out of the alley. She'd stashed her bicycle around the corner. The metal chains and locks had held it secure against the dilapidated concrete building pylon she'd relied upon time after time.

Freeing the bike with the key she kept secure in a pocket sewn into her panties, Erin rode home, pushing the pedals with the toes of shoes better made for dancing. Yet she'd gotten used to it.

It never ceased to amaze her, the things one could become accustomed to out of necessity.

As she rode through the deserted streets in the wee hours, she crooned to herself. The lyrics creeping unbidden into her mind, half-formed, but the tune carried through her mind, a drumbeat grounding out the distress of the past few hours.

CHAPTER 13

NADIR

Nadir tread on light feet, leading the cabal up the concrete staircase with the downtown high-rise office tower at 1801 California. The stark, whitewashed walls held little contrast against the industrial bright lights overhead. Reaching the next stairwell, she passed a sign painted in red on a black door. The number fourteen marked the floor.

Thanks to her daemonic strength, she wasn't even breathing hard. Not that she enjoyed climbing endless flights of stairs. So far, the most interesting part of the mission had been doing her mojo on the lock in the basement parking garage.

It never hurts to have a metal manipulator on the team.

"Are we there yet?" Kobol whispered. Nadir glanced back at him, watching for any sign of lingering issues from the blow he'd taken to the head earlier, when her nose finally caught a whiff of their prey.

The corner of her lip curled up a notch. Annamie's intel

had proved correct, yet again. She hadn't wanted to believe her friend's claim that an entire daemon nest had taken up residence downtown in a busy office space, but it appeared they'd gotten pretty damned bold.

Or desperate. Daemons knew something hunted them, but not what. They'd upped their game.

Nadir looked at the sancre in her grip. They weren't the only ones.

"We're getting close. Another floor, perhaps two. Remember, there are humans here too on the other floors. We'll have to be quiet," she whispered.

"That's not usually how these things go down." Azimuth's lips thinned. An icy aura emanated from all around him, long blades held in both his hands. Nadir couldn't help drinking in his spicy vanilla-laced scent as her eyes feasted on his tall, muscular form wrapped in a long-sleeved, cashmere black sweater and black leather pants. No doubt that lovely sweater she'd bought him would get ruined today, but it was completely worth it.

She rolled her shoulders, an all too familiar heat wafting around her body. "We need to *try*, boys. Discretion and all that, remember? C'mon."

"We can't enforce their behavior, Nadir," Orias replied, striding past her up the stairs. She caught up, soon matching him step by step.

"Are you picking up anything?" She searched his impassive features, yet his focus appeared completely on today's hunt.

"My powers serve no one's whims. They come when they will."

"I just asked because you had another vision this morning. At least I thought you did?"

Orias glanced her way, shadows haunting his features. "If it had pertained to our activities, I'd have shared."

Nadir flushed and looked away. What had gotten into him today? "I didn't doubt you would have."

As they reached the 17th floor, a powerful smell pricked their noses. By her estimation, there were at least twelve daemons inside, but no guard was stationed at the door. The few surveillance cameras in the stairwell had been painted or vandalized. No doubt the building maintenance had a hard time keeping up with their efforts, and who would have expected a daemon nest like this in the middle of downtown?

Orias held out his hand, blocking Nadir. "The door is warded. Allow me."

She'd been too caught up thinking about Orias's abilities and doing a daemonic headcount of their enemies to notice the wards. Looking closer, she caught traces of them in the crevices between the door and the frame. Nothing too complicated, as they weren't intended to hide the door, but the energy read was beyond uninteresting.

If it hadn't been for Nadir's heightened sense of smell, she'd never have picked up traces of daemons from the door itself. It read as innocuous. Boring.

Had the daemons expected others of their kind to come looking for them? Why not hide their scent, too?

"Can any of you smell them from out here?" Nadir whispered. The other three shook their heads. *Right.* They didn't know any hunters could sniff them out.

"There's a problem," Orias said softly, his hands mid-gesture, focus absolute. "I can sense another ward tied to this one on the other side. As soon as I deconstruct this one, the other will trigger. It's encapsulated, and I can't access it to work."

"You're saying we need to blow the door and go in, weapons hot?" Kobol replied. A single swing of his hammer swished through the air with a momentum destined to crush bone. The eager look on his face made Nadir wonder what he'd done before being recruited into this cabal. Sport fighter? Athlete? Whatever it was, he appeared born to bruise.

"That's an accurate assessment, yes." Orias's face was grim. He didn't bother to say that going in blind wasn't ideal. He didn't have to.

Nadir tried to remember back to 'ideal'. It was another lifetime, literally. She shook off the funk before it dragged her down into the past.

"We'll go with the disorientation tag and bag," Azimuth said, eyes crystalline blue in focus. "Nadir, throw the bolt on the door. Kobol, you'll be first in, wrapped in invisibility while you do your thing. Orias will be next. Cast your shadows about and attack them while they don't know what's real and what's not. Nadir and I will take the rear, and she'll bar the door, preventing any exits."

"Won't they just port to escape?" Orias asked.

Nadir shook her head, hanging her free hand on her hip, causing the various metal weapons on her belt to clink. "This is a large nest. They're here for a reason. I'm betting they'll stay to protect whatever it is they're hiding."

"Can we get to it now, before they hear us?" Kobol sighed.

Azimuth looked at Nadir, and she gave a quick nod.

Manipulating the handle and lock on the door took less than a second. She arched a brow at Kobol, and he winked out of sight. Damn, how she'd like that power.

Nadir took a deep breath, watching as Orias spun shadows around him in a circle, casting outwards for visions, yet with no intent this time, and when the hallway was filled with his black shroud, she swung the door open.

No audible alarm sounded, not to human ears, but there was a sense of prickly wrongness which slid over her skin and a tremor which shook her to her core.

She scented Kobol as he flew past her and felt Orias move by a moment later. Azimuth's light brush of an arm against hers grounded her and set her feet into motion. In a handful of steps, they were through the darkness and into a dimly lit room. Nadir closed the door behind them, bolting the door and fusing the metal into place around the frame. Only someone with her gifts, or someone able to blast through the door, could get out that way.

"I'll look for other exits to block." Nadir palmed two thin, sharpened daggers in her free hand. She still held the sancre in her right hand. "You do what you do best."

"We could hunt together." The light crease of a frown graced Azimuth's brow.

"I'm not likely to die *again*. Now go, before I stab you myself." Nadir picked a direction and crept off, leaving him to his own devices. He seemed to need a kick start lately, else he tended to hover over her. How could she prove to him she'd be fine hunting alongside the rest of them, if he never let her go on her own? Belial had faith in her, and in this one instance, she agreed with Mr. Big Blue.

She heard Az's faint protective growl behind her, yet

continued onward. Her feet stepped through wisps of conjured shadows which swirled in eddies at her passing. Nadir refused to allow her gaze to drift over them lest she become mesmerized. The air in the dark space was thick with scent, making it difficult to pinpoint any singular daemon. Instead, Nadir focused on getting her bearings and gleaning what she could from the foul stench of the nest.

The packed space held row upon row of office cubicles, all in a dingy state of disrepair. She skirted the outside, looking for the elevator. The inconvenient height of the cubicle walls once sported colors in coordinating beige, eggshell, and coffee tones and stood a few inches above her eyes, preventing any reasonable line of sight into the middle of the room. Nadir heard the sounds of her cabal-mates in that general direction as they smashed heads and invoked screams. They would no doubt keep the inhabitants well occupied until she caught up.

Nadir rounded a dark corner and located the elevator doors, as well as a pair of youngling daemons hiding out under what used to be a receptionist's desk across from the elevator. She focused first on the elevator while monitoring the pups, who couldn't have been more than a few years old. They were over waist-height on her, but daemons developed quickly despite their immortal lifespan. She mentally fused the doors' metal seams together in mere moments, and then she shifted her complete focus to the wee daemons. Hiding her weaponed hands behind her back, she sauntered closer to the desk and kneeled down beside it. She didn't scent any other daemons nearby, just these two.

They appeared to be of the same brood, purple-skinned

with tufts of black hair covering cream-colored horns, running in ridges down their spines. They had lovely, round lavender eyes. Had they even had their first kills? How could she tell if they'd dined on human souls?

Bile rose in her throat. She had no way of knowing. Belial's orders stood. Kill all you find. Oath bound, she risked death at his hands if she didn't follow through.

"Come here, little ones. Let's go find everyone else, okay?"

For whatever reason, they ran to her and threw their spindly little arms, all eight of them, around her. A heavy weight rolled around in the pit of her stomach as she reflexively hugged them back with weapon-laden hands. At that moment, a male daemon crawled down the hall, limping from a deep gash in his leg. From his purple coloring and wide eyes, she guessed he was the youngling's parent.

When he noticed the blades in Nadir's grip, he faltered, his eyes begging for mercy. "Mercy, please. Whatever your purpose, spare them." She let two of her needle-daggers fly, wrapping them around his wrists and then mentally forcing the metal ends together where she twisted them in place. Portable handcuffs were never easier.

The younglings tensed under her grip, turning and attempting to flee to their father, but Nadir held firm. She didn't run an orphanage for daemon children whose parents had been put on her master's hit list. She pinned the one on her left to her side and sunk the sancre into the one on the right, hating herself as she watched the horror in their father's eyes.

A sancre destroyed daemons differently than the tre'jor.

Where the tre'jor caused the daemon's essence to become tied to the wielder of the weapon, the sancre simply destroyed the creature, powdering it into a fine dust.

Thus, as Nadir watched the child issue a wordless scream, the father fought against his makeshift cuffs and wailed, and then the child burst into bits, covering her with a fine layer of silt. The youngling's sibling screamed, uselessly struggling in her powerful grip.

Nadir moved to sink the sancre into the second youngling, but before the blade made contact, the child's flesh rippled and contorted.

The father lifted his head. "I beg of you, not both..."

As one, both father and youngling erupted into dust. Nadir rose to her feet, shaking the layers of powder, which had once been a family, off her face, hair, and clothing. Yeah, they'd been a daemon family, but a family all the same. Before today, she'd never killed younglings before. Another dubious first she'd done in Belial's name.

Nadir regarded the brilliant reflection of light off the sancre's edge. What sorcery had Big Blue forged and enmeshed with the wrought metal?

The scream snapped her out of her trance. She charged straight into the chaos, not stopping to think about what could be in her way. Fangs and claws tore at her clothing, searing heat scorched her skin, and daggers were thrown from all sides. To ensure she was protected, she sheathed the sancre securely against her thigh.

A large, dark hulk of daemonic muscle who lumbered into her path didn't even have a chance when he leaped out in front of her, eyes blazing. In passing, her gleaner warned that his tusks held deadly venom, and she used her lust to confuse him, then punched him hard enough to knock him on his ass. Using her razor-sharp claws to rend through his rhino-like hide of his thigh. Nadir pounced and tore open his leg with her fangs, indulging an internal daemon she'd kept on a short leash for too long. She continued to allow her lust aspect to flow over him. Poor bastard didn't know whether to cuddle her or fight her off. Before long, he could do neither.

Wiping her face onto her sleeve, she stood up from the empty husk, which had once been a threat. Nadir could consume ten more if she let herself, but for now, she relished the raw power coursing through her veins. It had been too long since she'd fed. The austerity plan Azimuth and the others adhered to was for the birds.

Heading deeper into the nest, the cubicles here were torn apart and thrown aside. Her cabal-mates stood over the final three who were clinging to life. Kobol bent down to run through one with his sancre, emotionless in the cleanup process.

Why shouldn't he be? How many times had they done this? Nadir sighed.

"Find any humans?" Azimuth asked.

She shook her head. "No luck on that front. Did any of you notice any of the daemons disintegrate without being hit by one of us?" She scraped her claws together, noticing the slight lisp of her speech from the fangs. There was a time she'd be disgusted by looking so daemonic. Now? She didn't care.

Kobol killed the next brood with equal efficiency. Nadir pressed the back of her hand over her forehead, and it came away bloody. She knew immediately by the scent that it wasn't her own blood. *Oh bother, when did that happen?*

Azimuth, who'd been sifting through the rabble, likely looking for clues on whatever the daemons were doing, holed up downtown, turned to her, eyes narrowing. His aura spiked ghostly white in the darkness. "That your blood?"

Nadir shook her head. "Nope."

He nodded, his aura dimming. "I lost track of a female. I'm not sure who killed her, but it wasn't me."

"The timid one hiding out in the corner?" Orias asked. "Cream-colored skin, horn-back ridges?"

"The very one," Azimuth replied.

"It wasn't me," Orias replied. They looked at Kobol.

He held up his arms and shook his head. "She must still be here."

Nadir scented the air but knew what she'd find. When she'd first entered the space, it'd been hard to track all the daemonic signatures. There must have been at least twenty present. Now it was down to the four of them and one last wounded daemon, lying limp against a crushed cubicle wall.

"No, she's destroyed."

"I don't get it. Who killed her?" Kobol asked, bending over and sinking his sancre into the last of the wounded daemons with perfunctory efficiency.

"I did," Nadir spat out through her fangs. When she didn't explain further, the others turned to Azimuth, knowing his truth sense would confirm or deny my claim. He nodded with bewildered confirmation. "Are we done here?"

"What aren't you telling us?" Azimuth asked. An electric spark of his power laced down his sword, lighting up the room.

"I'm not the one withholding information, as per usual. Let's go." Nadir waited for the others to clean off and secure their weapons and gather around so they could all port back to the burrow at the same time. Leaving a cabal-mate alone at a location, even a cleared one, was never an option.

Her thoughts lingered on the sancre, hating Belial all the more. They hadn't been given the full story, but she'd get to the truth, one way or another.

CHAPTER 14

BLAINE

Blaine sat stoically on a low altar of carved oak, polished through the regular contact of his limbs over the grain from these past many years of service. His inner calm was rocked by the portents stirring his private shrine. Although Zeus hadn't made one of his rare personal appearances today, the god might as well have for the wealth of messages scrawled out around the spacious room.

This secret alcove was in the penthouse suite of York Tower, as in *the* Sebastian Blaine York Tower, and known only to the other Zeus devotees, or god-touched, as the uninitiated sometimes called them. Dim light provided by candles lit the cella, casting harsh shadows against the plain, gray-painted walls. At the center stood a larger-than-life Zeus statue trimmed with gold accents within the crown atop his head, the trim of his himation, even in the texture of his oak staff.

From Blaine's vantage point, the statue appeared to glower. An unusual turn of events. Normally, the mood in this room reflected the god's approval of his performance.

Today something had been found lacking, and yet Blaine was certain nothing he'd done had fallen under the god's scrutiny.

Blaine cast his gaze about, checking to make sure nothing in the naos appeared disturbed. The trophies on the plinth hadn't been touched. The fresh offering of barley and wheat sat mixed in a bowl at the feet of the iconic statue. A bronze bowl filled with rainwater laid alongside. Between the two, a brazier with copal burned. He'd anointed and cleansed himself with the rainwater before entering the shrine, and even now wore only a pair of dark gray silk pants.

Everything should be in order, but here, in this place, he sensed the presence of the god powerfully.

Zeus's displeasure gave color to an otherwise gray world.

Blaine had constructed this space years ago to curry favor with Zeus. The rectangular cella had doorways on the far end and was flanked by two aisles. Thirty-four Doric-style columns made of limestone in the old Etruscan style ringed the entire space. From the outer aisles, murals of the twelve labors of Heracles graced the walls in true fresco fashion, reminding the devotees of the heroism of the son of Zeus. If you'd devoted yourself to Zeus, this reminder tacitly implied the level of dedication expected: Absolute.

Blaine watched and waited. The disapproval drove him almost as much as his love of solving puzzles.

Patterns formed in the air, thunderheads of incense smoke invoking images of emotional turmoil. Smoke shifted, forming patterns of grass over the gray, baked, pentilic tile marble floor. No, not simply grass, but wet grass. Grass alone meant a blessing. Wet? Perhaps tainted, skewed, or just not how you'd expect it to arrive. The portent's clarity left something to be desired.

Then, up against a wall, the smoke formed a gate shape. It stood closed for many minutes before swinging open. Did it mean a new beginning or a new possibility of some sort coming up?

Blaine raised a brow, but he didn't otherwise move, unwilling to disturb the ether of the room. He was content to wait until the energy played itself out. Emotional turmoil, a new beginning, and a potential blessing—or was that a curse—all played out in Zeus's message tonight. No wonder the mood within the cella had turned dour.

Blaine's phone vibrated in his pants pocket, and he had to stop himself from cursing aloud. He had it set to emergency contact only, therefore avoiding any superfluous contact while in devotion. Yet he wouldn't, *couldn't*, leave until Zeus had finished with him.

He waited, alert for additional signs, for another forty minutes while the ether cleared, but none appeared. Yet he didn't regret waiting. Whether Zeus was simply testing him, or on some subconscious level communing with him, it didn't matter. Once the presence of devotion had passed, Blaine arose, strode forward to the statue and placed his hand over Zeus' on the oak staff.

He had no way of knowing if the portents applied to his legal clients, the other devotee members of the city council, or general issues relating to Denver as a whole. Regardless, he'd figure it out.

Blaine strode out of the cella, through the nave, and to the outer door. He activated the palm-coded lock with his hand, and the black metal door clicked open. He moved through to the dimly lit hallway beyond and closed the door behind him, which locked automatically. Gliding down the carpeted hall on silent feet, the sound of voices raised in anger came through the door at the far end.

Adrenaline spiking, he hurried his pace and slipped through the hidden door, entering his plush living room, ready for a fight.

Daniel, a devotee of Ares, had Blaine's majordomo, Jake, by the collar, lifting him up onto the tips of his toes. Jake gripped Daniel's forearms, trying to pry them off, but he had nowhere near the fighting skills as the devotee of war. That hadn't been why Blaine had hired him.

"This information can't wait! You alerted the Chief nearly an hour ago! What's keeping him?"

Daniel's single-minded focus on Jake prevented him from noticing Blaine's swift, quiet footfalls on the plush carpet behind them. Blaine placed his left hand above Daniel's right elbow, and with his right, he grasped Daniel's right thumb from the tip to the base of the digit. Confusion swept over Daniel's face as Blaine simultaneously bent Daniel's thumb inward upon itself while also sliding the pad of his left thumb between thick muscles until it hit a nerve. The swift intake of breath and fading color to the man's cheeks let Blaine know he had the man's full attention.

"I observe devotion regularly at this hour. Daniel, kindly unhand Jake before I kill your grandfather." Blaine applied extra pressure to his thumb, and Daniel squealed like a stuck pig. Daniel, sweat forming on his brow, released Jake, who staggered back a few feet, catching himself against the back of the couch. Normally quite reserved, his majordomo appeared to have his feathers ruffled and no amount of running his hands through his mussed hair or straightening his skewed shirt would fix the problem. Then Blaine noticed the bruise on Jake's right hand and had to restrain himself from lashing out. "Jake, is the bruise on your hand the only one?"

Jake's gaze flitted up to Blaine's. He turned his face so Blaine could see the scuff mark coloring his right jaw. "Just these two. Man wouldn't see reason."

"You understand, Daniel, you owe my faction a penance for this slight. I expect all sworn Hellenes to behave with a higher standard of decorum than *this*," Blaine spat out the last word.

"I'll pay whatever you determine is reasonable, Chief." Daniel's voice came out strained through thin lips.

Blaine gave a quick nod to Jake. "Why don't you get cleaned up and ice that jaw? Take the rest of the evening off while you're at it."

"That won't be necessary, Sir. I'll be back in a few minutes. Pardon me." He bowed briefly at the waist and then edged around them, disappearing out of sight down the far hall toward his quarters. He could have used the main kitchen, but he no doubt wished to leave them to business.

Blaine turned his attention to Daniel, who'd recovered some of his focus, despite the pain no doubt radiating up his arm. "Let's have a seat and discuss why you're here, shall we?"

He didn't wait for a response, guiding Daniel with his grip as the lesser man danced painfully around his circular charcoal couch. When Blaine rounded the edge of the couch, he tossed the brute down onto the cushions, ignoring his audible sigh of relief and the way he cradled his arm. As Chief, he could have broken it and no one would have questioned him. Daniel had gotten off light. Well, so far.

Blaine walked over to his liquor hutch and grabbed a

bottle of ouzo and two shot glasses. He had a variety of other vintages, but for business, he stuck to the classics. Returning to the couch, he sat across from Daniel, placed the two shot glasses on the circular black glass coffee table between them, and poured. Daniel sat stiff-backed against the couch, eyes trained on Blaine's every movement.

Xenia, the basic respect of a host to his guest, demanded he offer Daniel a drink before seeking answers for his rude behavior. *Someone* had to set an example. Blaine lifted the shot glass in a toast to his unwelcome visitor. Daniel mirrored his behavior, and they both downed the smooth, fiery liquor in one gulp, slamming the glasses onto the table afterward.

Blaine didn't pour them another round. Hospitality had its limits.

"Explain why you've been mistreating my majordomo for the past hour, Daniel." Blaine leaned forward, his elbows resting on his knees, hands clasped before him. "*Impress me.*"

Daniel shifted forward and placed his glass on the table. "As you're well aware, I troll seedy clubs in the evenings, looking for opportunities to start brawls."

Which must be why he sported an impressive black eye, something Blaine hadn't appreciated while his focus had been on Jake. For a devotee of a war god, this must be a common sport for Daniel, but tonight, Blaine couldn't care less to hear about his conquests. Blaine rolled his eyes and waved him on.

Daniel shook his head, his lips thinning. "Look, I hung out at Porter's tonight. It's a quiet place, but the city's been boring overall for me lately. Now I'm knocking back some brews and what do I see? A new devotee sporting ink for non-initiates to see, mind you, and she's *waitressing!*" His face had turned bright red, and he gripped the couch cushions like he was going to shred them.

Blaine frowned, running a finger across his lips. He cared less about her chosen profession, but showcasing her ink, *that* had to be curtailed. "Did you speak to her about the markings?"

Daniel's lips curled up in a sarcastic grin. "Oh yeah. We *talked*," air quoting with his fingers, "all right. How long have you known me, Blaine?"

He tilted his head, confused by the question. "Ever since the followers of Ares elected you to serve on the city council as their speaker because you were the strongest amongst them. Although you were only in the sixth rank. You've risen to the seventh rank since then, the same as most on the council. I've known you for four years now."

"Then I hope you'll trust me when I tell you this. I swear, something is not right with her. She's marked, but she played it like she didn't know who I was. Who *we* are. I mean, in the general sort of way."

Blaine gave a curt shake of his head. "That's not possible."

Daniel shrugged. "Then she's a talented actress, Chief, because she got me going for a minute there. I could have sworn she'd woken up marked yesterday."

Blaine chuckled. "What's her name and description? I'll need to track her down, cite her, and make sure she's on file with her local chapter house."

"Good luck on that count. The guys at Porter's knew her as Lola, but I doubt anyone there knows her true name or where she lives. She's got an athletic build, not too much on top or below. Long legs, though, can't complain there. Short, light blonde hair. Real short, like chin length. It's all fluffy, which is in complete contrast to her hard-ass personality. Wow." He slid his hands over his scalp like he was in pain. Not that he'd ever admit to it. The warrior male had his pride.

"Keep on track. Eyes?"

"Brown. Light brown."

Unbidden, Blaine recalled the woman from his peculiar dream last night. Her lithe form, her light blonde hair, her sweetheart lips, and her brazen strength. Blaine smiled to himself. If only his dreams foretold the women in his life.

"Devotee marking?"

Daniel paused, his gaze drifting to the floor.

"What? If she's not Hellene, I'll hand her over to whichever house to dole out her punishment. I'm the city Chief. It doesn't matter what god, goddess, or path she's devoted to, she's in my city, under my rule."

Daniel nodded. "Right, it's just I've never seen markings like hers and I'm not sure to whom she hails." His words spilled out, almost unintelligible, as they tumbled over each other.

Blaine considered that among the chief strengths of Ares, wits weren't in the top ten, unless you included battle strategy.

"Describe them to me." Blaine poured another round of ouzo, and sipped at the glass, savoring the warmth.

Jake glided back into the room, an ice pack held to his cheek. He remained discreetly in the shadows, yet well within earshot.

Daniel downed the shot like water. "The marks were dark purple and ran across her shoulders from the nape down to at least her mid-back. Like vines, with little clusters of grapes here and there. I didn't get a long look, mind you. It was dark, but she was wearing a tank top."

Chills ran down Blaine's back at the implications of Daniel's words. Such a large mark, not to mention the *vines*? "You're sure it was purple?" All devotees' marks were black unless they were using their powers. "Couldn't it have been an elaborate tattoo?" He tried to recall the phantom dream woman's back, to no avail. He hadn't noticed markings on her.

He shook his head, determination in the fire behind his eyes. "I watched a shimmer of power ripple underneath her skin through the design. I know you know what I mean." Blaine nodded. "No simple tattoo can do that, only a devotee's mark. Also, when I tried to talk sense into her, she brawled with me because I touched her."

"Wait, you hurt her?" Blaine tensed. Altercations between houses could turn south, fast.

"No, no. It's not what you think. I put my hand on her wrist while we were talking, just because she wasn't listening to a thing I was saying. That got her riled up. I mean, you haven't seen mad before. She dragged me outta that booth, threw me down onto the floor, and gave me this!" He pointed to his black eye. "My ribs are even sore from where she straddled me with her knees."

The combination of his uncharacteristic self-disgust and disbelief almost made Blaine gape. *Almost.* The idea of a slip of a woman strong enough to pin him down to the floor sent a thrill of anticipation running through him.

"Did you fight back?" He asked, his voice a coarse whisper.

"Yes! I tried, but in minutes she had me dead to rights. If the bouncer hadn't stepped in, I would be in even worse shape. I have no idea what came over me. I must have drunk more than I thought tonight."

"Yes, perhaps. Thank you for reporting this *Lola*, Daniel." Blaine stood, and Daniel understood his dismissal, standing as well. "Please stay on the lookout for her, and if you run across her, please inform her politely, but firmly, that she's expected to meet with me."

"As you wish, Chief." Daniel bowed briefly at the waist and then turned to go. Jake followed him out of the room, locked up behind him, and then returned and awaited instructions.

Blaine didn't have to muse long over the facts Daniel had brought to his doorstep. If what he'd reported was accurate, they needed to act fast before the new player impacted his city.

Assuming he'd interpreted the clues Jake had reported correctly, and he had no reason to believe he hadn't.

He stood and turned to Jake. "I assume you heard the entire target's physical description?"

"Sir." He gave a curt nod.

"We'll call all our contacts at the chapter's houses and alert them to be on the lookout. They are to locate the subject, report her to us, and then I will deal with her personally. *No. One. Else.* She's demonstrated a distinct issue with authority and is extremely volatile. I won't have anyone getting hurt."

"Yes, Sir. Should I tell them what type of devotee they're looking for?" Jake's eyes narrowed on him.

"Mention the style and location of the mark, but not the

size, extent, or the color. Vines and grape clusters on the shoulders." Jake raised a brow in confusion. "Then we'll know anyone who reports her with the actual mark, instead of some similar tattoo."

He shrugged, apparently accepting Blaine's reasoning. "Should we wait until morning? It's rather late." Jake's impassive expression couldn't hide the glint of amusement in his eyes. His phone was already in his hand, primed for use.

"If they know tonight, then they'll be ready to watch for her tomorrow, yes? Let's call using the usual pattern." Jake nodded and then moved across the room so they wouldn't have too much background chatter from the other's conversations.

Before he could make the first call, Blaine blew out a slow, controlled breath as he ran a hand through his hair. A woman with a mark bearing vines and grape clusters? Such a devotee hadn't been spied in his lifetime. Not in Colorado, nor the US, nor—to his knowledge—internationally. Why now, and why *here*?

What would a *Maenad* be doing in Denver, of all places?

CHAPTER 15

NADIR

*P*orting into the den, Nadir scented for Big Blue and then strode off toward his library.

Azimuth, close on her heels, brushed a cool hand down her back. "Perhaps we could discuss your concerns first?"

She scented Kobol and Orias, following them down the hall. "Oh, we'll *discuss* things, all right."

"You have less finesse managing Belial than the rest of us."

Nadir barked out a laugh. "That's kinda what I'm going for."

"Have you considered the rest of us might not appreciate you getting Blue riled up?" Kobol ground out.

"Really. Don't. Care."

"These are moments I wonder what method I could use to slow you down," Azimuth mused. Icy tendrils crept around her legs, chilling the air and kicking up a cool vapor around her calves.

"Don't go icing up the floors again," Orias warned

Azimuth. "She'll melt right through it while we'll wind up on our asses."

Nadir bounded down the stairs and hunted Belial through the stacks of books. She rounded the last row and spied Belial pouring through a tome with a meager candle for light. His menacing horns glimmered with iridescence in the dim, flickering light.

"Belial!" Nadir snapped through her fangs, planting herself squarely in front of him.

His gaze rose to her, a look of preoccupied disinterest on his face. "I'm in the middle of something, child." He turned a page, scanning through the old vellum pages.

"I will not be put off, *father*." Nadir held up the blade, her hand hanging midair between the page and his eyes. She heard the shifting of the others behind her, but they said nothing.

Belial grimaced, visibly taken aback at her appearance. "Whatever has gotten into you? Do you even realize you're covered in gore? Why do you bare your fangs and claws at me, pup?" he rumbled, full of ire.

Nadir shook the blade under his nose. "Explain the sancre. Fully."

Belial dropped the book to his side, knocking her arm to the side. He bent down and advanced toward her, bringing his face inches from hers. Nadir held her ground. "I remember explaining their use. Were you not listening?" Ancient, menacing fire pooled in his eyes.

Nadir, undeterred, held up the blade again. She heard Kobol groan. "I must have missed something, pops. I killed a wee daemon spawn with this, but it didn't work as advertised.

Its sibling and parents dusted right along with it moments later. How the Sheol does that happen?"

Belial's gaze flickered to the blade for the first time, and his ire melted into a self-satisfied, smug grin full of fang. "Ah, yes. Splendid!"

"*Splendid?*" Nadir replied.

His demeanor relaxed. Belial took a step back and his attention slid back to the tome. "It's functioning exactly as designed. The sancre eliminates not only the daemon it penetrates, but also culls the parents of the lineage."

He resumed reading. Nadir breathed deeply, shocked to hear his admission, despite knowing it must be true because of what she'd witnessed.

Azimuth cleared his throat. "This is an altogether new method of killing."

"Indeed, as I said before, it's my crowning achievement in forged weapons. Your kill rates will soar! Imagine how quickly you will eradicate the tainted vermin!"

The four liminals were silent for a moment as each digested the information. Belial resumed reading, oblivious to the impact of his announcement.

"That explains my vision the other day of a blade turning to ashes. The expanded reach of associated kills will indeed speed our efforts, father," Orias replied. "Are there any other effects we should be aware of?"

Belial looked up, appearing annoyed they were still there. "There's nothing for you to concern yourselves with."

Nadir gnashed her fangs, throwing the blade at his feet. "You withheld some information from us. How can we be certain you're telling us everything now?"

Belial barked out an unexpected laugh. "I suppose you can't, but regardless, you will use these new weapons as ordered, or there will be consequences. Am I understood?"

"What happens if we kill daemons connected to the lineages contained within our flesh?" Nadir asked, eyes focused on her hands. "Will we turn to dust, too?"

Belial sighed in exasperation, as if she were a child asking *why is the sky was blue* for the umpteenth time. "Don't be ridiculous. You have human forms independent of the daemon essences within you, so even if you wiped out all of them, you'd endure."

"Wouldn't we be less useful to you without our powers?" Kobol asked, an uncharacteristic edge in his voice.

Belial let out a low, subvocalized growl. "What a ridiculous question. Obviously, you'd be less useful to me. Yet, you all have so many powers, I doubt you'd miss one here or two there. Besides, if you were to lose a useful skill, you could always use a tre'jor to perk yourselves back up."

His utter and complete disregard for their existence only drove home how little each of his created children mattered to the prince. They were only tools to him, to be discarded when they'd outlived their usefulness. She considered telling him as much, but what would be the point? He didn't appear to be living under any delusions, unlike her cabal-mates. Nadir turned on her heel, storming off from Big Blue.

She heard the scrape of the blade being picked up. "I'll return this to her," Azimuth said. "She'll be fine."

"Talk with her about proper presentation as well. She shouldn't run around looking like that," Belial grated out.

Which was ironic, Nadir considered, as the prince was the one who'd set her up to become part daemon herself.

"Yes, sire," she heard Azimuth reply.

And then there were three sets of feet following her out of the library.

Not in a mood to deal with the others, Nadir ported back to earth before any of them could catch up with her.

CHAPTER 16

NADIR

After rushing through a cool shower, Nadir dressed in black sneakers, cargos, and a long-sleeved top and left her occasionally visited, and thus very dusty, Earth home for an evening run. The warm Indian summer air carried humidity like a blanket, irrespective of the setting sun. She breathed the fall scents in and launched herself uphill along the sidewalk. Nadir set her pace purposefully, knowing if she ran at full pace, her daemon nature would be impossible to ignore.

The relative ease of her pace did little to calm her mind, even after she'd run for miles.

Nadir—no, *Meri*—despised what Belial had made her into. Time hadn't made it easier. She still wasn't comfortable in her new skin, despite the safety it afforded her in Sheol to look the part of a daemon. Maybe she just hadn't had enough time to get used to it. Or perhaps she just missed how she used to look, daemon ink and all. Or, if she was honest, being in her human skin felt like she wasn't trying to hide the creature she'd become, proverbial warts and all.

Sure, some of her new talents were mind-blowing. Most, she wielded with such ease she might as well have been born with them. Yet, she hadn't been. Instead, Belial had orchestrated her shift into his daemonic minion, but he hadn't done it to save her from death at the hands of some daemon. No. Belial had strategically crafted her just like he'd done with his magical tre'jor blades, and now she was just another faceless arrow in his quiver. As if it wasn't bad enough to have lost her humanity, the daemon had also stolen her autonomy, sublimating her will with his ancient, indomitable might.

She was trapped under his proverbial thumb, with no escape.

For eternity.

Nadir held nothing against her cabal-mates. They were just as pinned down by the Prince of Sheol as she was.

Not caring where or how far she ran, Nadir crossed the Highline canal trail, where she sped through full darkness. The path was a blessed solitude, unused at night because of the city's safety regulations.

Considering that she was likely the most dangerous thing which had run the trails in some time, Nadir barked out a bittersweet laugh. Only a daemon like herself would defy the city's rules. Considering no prison could hold her, human laws were no longer of any consequence.

The stars overhead shone with such brilliance she could see the surrounding landscape with ease. When dark shapes jagged across the night sky, Nadir recognized the outlines of bats. Seeking the colony out, she meandered through a meadow to a large, hollowed-out cottonwood next to a naturalized lake fed by the canal. Bats filled the air and the occasional wingtip whipped by within inches of her head, yet she didn't flinch, taken in by the grace and beauty of these tiny creatures.

A familiar vanilla and musk scent whispered by her on a wind-swept breeze. She let out a sigh. "How did you find me?"

Azimuth's footsteps became audible as he walked through the crisp leaves to join her by the lake. "I ported over to your house not long after you left. Then I followed you at a distance as you worked out your frustration."

Nadir frowned. "You're not usually that quiet." In her frustrated state, she hadn't noticed him at all.

"I have a handful of useful skills," he replied.

Heat rose in waves from her flesh. "I remember a few. I'm just surprised anyone could follow me and I didn't notice."

"I was lucky to keep the wind with me." A tentative brush of his fingers stroked across Nadir's shoulder to her neck and then snaked down her spine.

The shiver he elicited from her rolled up her back, and Nadir fought to keep mental focus. "No, I'm not down with this right now. If you want to help me eviscerate Belial, we can get freaky after I've covered his library's walls with his bowels." Nadir spoke through the slightest baring of fangs.

Azimuth cricked an eyebrow, folding his arms in front of him. "I don't imagine that would work out in your favor." He ambled around to face her, his aura cool, calm, and collected.

His poise only served to infuriate Nadir. "At least I'd get my point across!"

Azimuth barked out a laugh, his demeanor humor filled. "It is amusing to consider. However, his viscera would certainly damage many ancient and irreplaceable tomes."

"I don't care," Nadir she hissed. "This situation is intolerable! He treats us like disposable toys, just like his magic blades. He didn't even bother to warn us that the sancre might destroy our powers, too. Nevertheless, he instructs us to go, and we are left with no alternative but to follow his will without hesitation. I don't feel you truly understand how belonging to the prince and having no choice in all this tears me apart."

His carriage stiffened. "None of us misses how upset you are with the situation. I ask you not to forget that we all feel the impact of his choices in our own ways. Consider that time has perhaps made us more used to his conduct and dogma."

His reasonableness did nothing to calm Nadir's ire. "I know you've been sworn to Belial for hundreds of years. Maybe you can't see his behavior with clarity because you're just so inured to his daily abuses. You can't just keep lying to yourselves, believing that things will be okay if you keep following his psychotic orders."

A white shimmer flickered across Azimuth's gaze, gone in a moment as he regained his composure. "What would you have us do?"

"You could start by telling him no?"

The slight crease between his brows, coupled with the scent of incredulity rolling off him, spoke before Azimuth did. "We are oath bound to obey his commands. If we refused, he would be within his rights to destroy any of us who disobeyed."

"So, he might slaughter us if we disobey, but frankly, he could knock us off if he just feels like it, too. What's stopping him?" Nadir heard the frustration in her voice, the raised pitch of her anxiety coloring her words.

Sympathy swirled through his scent. "Nothing. Except how we're useful to him."

"Exactly. I can't obey someone blindly, especially when they have the power to kill me on a whim."

Azimuth shook his head, his hands waving away her concerns with an air of easy dismissal. "You're not used to him, that's all. We've had hundreds of years observing the fleeting nature of his dispositions."

Nadir scowled. "This is more than a flight of fancy by a spirited daemon Prince! These sancre he's devised are fearsome, above and beyond the tre'jor."

"Sure, but that's what he does. New weapons are a source of ongoing amusement to him, that's all."

"It's not that simple!" Nadir rounded on him, stepping into the comfort of his aura despite her irritation with his disagreement.

Azimuth threaded fingers through the hair at her nape, and Nadir leaned into his touch, allowing him to cradle her head.

"Explain to me your concerns," he whispered.

Nadir sighed. "Haven't you wondered if *anyone* in Sheol has taken notice of the missing daemons we've destroyed?"

Azimuth shrugged. "Daemons are legion. They war incessantly. How could anyone notice a missing faction here or there? Or a handful? There are countless feuds to blame well before anyone would even consider holding our small cabal accountable."

"I hear what you're saying. I do. But consider, we kill entire factions each week. In good weeks, we'll destroy more than a handful."

"Again, it's a drop in the bucket."

Nadir pulled away, catching his hand with her own when he tried to pull her back in close. "The sancre completely changes our kill ratio."

"So, two drops in the bucket, then?"

A chill wind swept through the trees, sending an unexpected shiver down Nadir's spine. "I have a bad feeling about this, Az. I know he said it destroys the daemon we attack, their siblings from the same brood, and the daemon's parents."

He nodded. "That was my understanding of his explanation as well."

"Right, but he'd initially withheld this information from us. What else has he left out? Do you think he'd have mentioned it if I hadn't observed the sancre's powers during our last raid?"

A slight frown creased his lips. "I doubt he would have. However, there was no danger to us with his omission and additional kills won't harm our efforts."

Nadir nodded. "I know he didn't endanger us, but I still have concerns. My gut tells me this isn't just a drop or two in the bucket of legion's blood. It's a ripple, and I don't think we can predict the sancre's impact."

"You may be correct," he conceded. "However, this doesn't change our course of action. He's our sire, and we do his bidding, which for now means using the sancre in our fight."

"That may be what you need to do, but I need to think about why my gut is giving me such fits before I head back into battle with the prince's new toy. I know I don't fully understand all of my new powers, and I don't want to be discovering something new while I'm in a melee with a barbed skunk-biter."

Azimuth chuckled. "Why don't you take some time to search your feelings? We'll cover for you with Big Blue. Tell him you're hunting down leads or something."

"That would be such a relief. Thank you for the offer."

"You'll need this for your soul-searching," Azimuth pulled a sancre from his jacket and handed it to her. Nadir grudgingly accepted it, disliking the near-electric tingle she experienced while holding the blade. "The guys will want to know if you hone in on anything."

"If I come up with anything, you'll be the first to know. Can you ask Orias to look into it as well?"

"Of course. Perhaps you just need a break from life in Sheol? I sometimes forget you're new to living amongst daemons."

Nadir laughed. "Culture shock doesn't even cover it."

"Then I'll wish you a couple of boring days and get back. I'll let you know when there's a new horde to eviscerate. Do feel free to ping me if you get hungry."

His eyes roamed down her silhouette, and even in the relative dark, Nadir could feel her inner succubus yearning for his icy fire. "Oh, I'll be calling. I'm not a fan of starvation." She took the sancre and slid it into a side pocket on her pants, needing to be rid of the sensation of the blade in her hand. Sidling up to him, Nadir deeply breathed in his scent, as she ran her nose up the curve of his neck. Her body thrummed in response to his presence.

He ran fingertips down the outside of her arms. "I either have to head back alone now or port you back to my bedroom for a few days. I'd prefer the latter, but if I do, you won't get the downtime you need. So I'll leave and honor your need for space."

"Aw," Nadir pouted. "Tease."

"For you, always. If you need anything, you know how to find me."

His lips brushed across hers, capturing the moment with the heat of passion.

When he ported away, Nadir was left alone with the bats and wind. A pang of loss rang through her, a reaction from the succubus or her heart? Nadir couldn't separate the sensations.

Breathing in a bittersweet freedom, Nadir jogged home at an easy, carefree pace, the weight of the sancre swinging heavy in her pants pocket.

CHAPTER 17

ERIN

*E*rin woke up late, head cloudy from the night before, crammed onto the tiny cot in her apartment. She'd slept right through her alarm clock, and now she'd have to rush through showering and drive into work instead of bussing or biking, which meant paying for parking. She jumped into the shower before the water warmed up, ducking her head under the stream, and taking a moment to luxuriate in the heat.

Her boss, Maria, didn't tolerate tardy employees. Perhaps if Erin skipped makeup, no one would notice.

Oversleeping meant another dent in her finances she couldn't afford, especially after losing her job last night. How she'd picked a fight with the corporate bastard still wasn't clear in her mind. Erin usually kept herself well-schooled, only allowing her real self out to play when she escaped to the mountains on the rare weekend getaway.

How had he intuitively known so much about her? His questions about her time in the forest mirrored her own. She rinsed out her hair and turned off the water, giggling as she remembered Daniel's threats issued from a beaten face. One she'd given him.

Inspecting her knuckles, Erin didn't notice any scuffs or scrapes, nor had they stung under the water. Perhaps the damage had looked worse in the dim lighting of the club. Rolling around on the floor, she'd probably just got him dirty, not bruised.

She toweled off and wondered about his threat to report her. How would he or his *friend* Blaine even know how to find her? Erin rolled her eyes, hurrying through her morning routine. She towel-dried her hair into a messy, less controlled look than her norm, but it bounced in such a cute, flirty way so she left it. She didn't try new things often, but lately she'd been breaking several of her typical rules. One more wouldn't hurt anything.

Consumed with rushing through her routine, she almost missed the dark splotch across her tanned shoulder. Drawing close to her reflection over the chipped and stained basin below, Erin touched the purplish marks snaking over her skin. The oddly vein-like pattern wasn't typical for bruises, but when she applied additional pressure from her fingertips, along the wine-stained lines, the tender flesh ached. Perhaps she'd rolled over something during the fight, causing the bizarre pattern.

She checked her watch. *Crap.* There'd be time to worry about a little bruising later.

Erin pulled out one of her standard business attire outfits from her cramped closet, a plain linen white blouse and skirt, and quickly donned the pair. Her boss preferred the entire company dress in white, so it was basically a work requirement. This set had a pleasing woven texture to the fabric and breathed well, even in the heat of the fading Autumn. Flat white shoes completed the look. A glance at the clock firmed up her choice to skip makeup. Erin grabbed her white leather purse from the hook just inside the closet door.

Erin had to side-stepped through the narrow corridor on her way to the kitchen. She grabbed an apple and thrust it into her purse. Not much of a lunch, but perhaps she'd be able to get away and grab something later. A defeated sigh escaped her lips. She'd *never* catch a break at work. Maria watched her time like a hound after a bone.

Erin shot down the stairs to the parking garage underneath. Scuffs and scratches marred the faded light-blue paint of her car, yet despite the age, wear, tear, and frequent mountain trips, she kept it clean. She opened the door and slid behind the wheel, gunning the engine as she clipped her seat belt into place. The tires squealed as the sedan rushed out of the cave-like garage. Erin paused for the briefest of moments at the exit to ensure she didn't run anyone down before careening into traffic.

She cut off a small, white, expensive import, knowing they'd yield. The driver honked and gesticulated wildly, but backed off and rode her bumper. Erin waved happily back at them.

A buzzing emanated from her purse, and she scrambled to retrieve the earpiece for her phone one-handed while rounding the corner onto 18th west, taking her on a straight shot to downtown.

Sliding it over her ear, she activated the unit. "Hello?"

"Erin? Have you made it into the office yet?" her boss's voice rang out in censure. Erin checked her watch. 7:45 am.

"No. I'm having parking issues." Why did Maria keep demanding her in early, anyway?

"We need to have a talk about your tardiness. When you get here, can you finalize the Avant files for their meeting at 8:30? Do you think you can handle that?"

Erin gripped the steering wheel and blew out a slow breath before answering. "No problem, Maria. They're on my desk and ready to go. I just need to set them up in the conference room."

"I'm unclear why you didn't prep the room last night? Your lack of foresight and planning impacts all of us. I'll see you shortly, yes?" Maria's string of rhetorical questions hung in the air as Erin cut the corner and took a hard left into the parking lot across the street from work on Washington St.

"Yes, Ma'am," Erin bit out.

The line cut out and Erin ground her molars together. That woman got under her skin! She hurriedly parked in the first available spot, paused at the terminal long enough to pay, and then ran across the street, dodging cars. When she burst through the front door of Pythia, the receptionist, Ted, shot her a dour look from behind the expanse of the naturally finished pine lobby desk.

Everything in the modern lobby felt calm and outdoorsy; it was why she'd wanted to work there in the first place. From the white suede couches to the pale green area rugs and pictures of aspen hanging on the walls, Erin could almost imagine herself in the mountains. Unlike Maria's obsession with white clothes, Erin liked her penchant for nature pictures and simple, clean lines in the office. No doubt the furnishings were just as expensive, but they didn't come off as wasteful or indulgent like so many corporate offices.

"It's 8:05. You're late again," Ted pointed at the clock on the wall.

"And I worked until after 7 last night, so I don't care," Erin snapped back.

"The *boss* will care, and therefore, so should you. We have standards here, young lady."

Erin rolled her eyes and walked past him, listening to her shoes clicking against the faux—or could they be real—hardwood floors. With the money and resources Corp's wasted, she'd bet on the latter. Why should she tolerate a reprimand from a mere reception clerk? She scooted down an open corridor through regularly spaced workstations on the main floor. None of her coworkers so much as looked up to acknowledge her arrival.

All of them kept their focus on their projects, lost within their immersive computer displays. Allison studiously reviewed ad copy, Denise and Frank watched a video clip together, pausing the action and debating a change, and Zaire hunched over multiple screens filled with color swatches, flipping back and forth between what looked like identical colors. Zaire had some sort of new tattoo gracing her collarbones with simple white leaves.

Since when could employees show off tattoos?

Erin slid into her seat with no one else so much as acknowledging her presence, which was either a blessing or a curse. Possibly both.

She stowed her purse in her desk drawer wnd reached for the stack of two dozen prepped packets for Avant and picked up her corp-system encoded interactive earpiece and finger stylus from its cradle on the corner of her desk. She slid the earpiece over her earlobe and across the front, depressing the switch to activate it for the day. The sleek, ringed stylus slid up and over the first joint of her index finger on her left hand. Erin avoided focusing on the systems screens as they loaded. There was a limit to the flashy marketing propaganda and indoctrination she wished to swallow in a day. Unlike her coworkers, she preferred to leave the device on standby and her desk display powered down except while she actively interacted with the media.

Instead, she slid the stack of packets toward herself and picked up the top one, done in signature glossy white with a capital P embossed on the cover in Edwardian script. Paging through the packet, Erin checked the page numbers one last time. Everything was to specifications, not that this would appease Maria, but at least Erin knew she'd done the task as requested.

Hefting the pile in her arms, Erin squared her shoulders and headed to the conference room, ignoring her aloof coworkers right back.

The white-walled conference room was filled with soft, diffuse light from sconces high along the rectangular space. A hint of jasmine hung in the air, just enough that she breathed deeper to better catch the scent. White leather chairs ringed the massive, black, oblong conference table, which doubled as a presentation device.

Music played softly, the auditory accompaniment completing the 360-degree impact she'd been trained on as part of the company's sales presentation process. Pythia's theme song reminded Erin of a babbling brook rendered via a violin solo of alternating haunting draws and staccato beats. Perhaps it was intended to energize or soothe, but today the tones irritated her, grating on her nerves.

Erin ringed the table, aligning the packets one by one in front of each supple leather chair, ensuring the chair's alignment matched the packet before moving on. Completing the circle, Erin stepped back and surveyed the room for potential issues. Ted, or someone, had already prepped the water cart near the doorway with two filled water pitchers, a tray of clean glasses, and a filled ice bucket.

Something wasn't quite right. What had she overlooked? Maria always held her to a higher standard.

Her earpiece chirped and Erin's interactive display scrolled an alert about the morning meeting starting in five minutes. A message from Maria popped up a moment later, overlaying the meeting alert.

"I trust everything is prepared. I have word that the clients are arriving now," Maria asked.

"Of course." Erin picked and sent the terse auto-reply with a quick flick of her finger stylus as she rushed out of the conference room, down the hall, and back to her desk. A single tap to the surface of her desk as she sat down activated the display, of which her earpiece and stylus were simply extensions. Campaign slogans she'd crafted the day before hovered on the screen right where she'd left them. Erin pursed her lips, debating if any retained enough merit for further consideration.

The bustle of activity toward the front office drew her attention, informing Erin of the client's imminent arrival. She straightened her back and focused on her work, using her peripheral vision to track the newest potential clients.

The contingent from Mache comprised three women, all dressed in flowing, gauzy dresses of differing lengths and cuts, escorted by a fawning Ted. Erin noted that although each dress was unique, all were light, blushing shades of pink. The contrast between their warm soft tones and her coworkers' bland white outfits tickled at her mind, but Erin did not know why. Also, the three ladies took as little notice of Ted as she did.

Erin knew from researching Mache they were the premier fragrance company within not only Western S-Mart but also all the Central Alliance. People vied for their products in increasing numbers and sales were soaring despite the ridiculous cost.

Why they needed Pythia's help, or anyone's, Erin couldn't hazard a guess.

Maria emerged from her office with purpose, clad in a tailor-fitted white pantsuit, not a hair out of place, and the scent of jasmine wafting through the air as she passed by. Considering the all-white obsession, Erin often wondered why Maria hadn't bleached her mahogany hair blonde, as it must be harder to keep her suit tidy throughout the day. Perhaps even Maria had her limits of conformity.

Continuing to watch out of the corner of her eye, Erin observed Maria greet the clients from Mache. After the usual pleasantries, she turned back and addressed the room.

"Zaire. Denise. Frank. Allison. I'd like Mache to meet the entire team during the presentation. Please join us." Maria didn't wait for a reply, but turned back to the clients and led them back to the conference room. Without question, the four arose and fell into line, following Maria. Allison shot Erin a plastered smile as she walked by her desk.

Erin watched them exit the room, sighing when the doors to the conference room closed. Yes, it was a slight to be excluded, yet the reprieve of even an hour or two without

Maria leveled the loss. Erin refocused on her work, debating the merits of Latin versus Italian keyword usage. She almost didn't notice Ted's approach. When she did, Erin ignored his very existence.

"Could you take a break from," Ted shook his head and drew his finger in a circular motion around her workspace, "whatever it is you're busy with here?"

Erin lifted her gaze and looked him over. From this angle, she could see he'd missed a small patch of whiskers under his ear while shaving, so unlike a Pythia employee.

"Well yes, whatever." He frowned. "The printer repairman has arrived, and you're to supervise him."

"Me?"

"Yes, you. Maria said you must have somehow altered the yellow range on our large format machine, so you have to make sure he gets it fixed." The chastisement reeked from his lips.

"I haven't been using the large format, so how could I break it?"

He shrugged. "Maria stated you broke it."

Erin rolled her chair back and stood up, placing her earpiece in the cradle. "Okay, whatever. At least then I'll know how to fix it next time."

"Atta girl!" He flashed her a fake smile. "C'mon, then." He trotted back to the lobby, and Erin dragged her heels as she followed. Why he felt the need to escort her to the copier room, surely a precious waste of his time, baffled Erin.

The copier room was about halfway to the lobby along the main hall. When they reached it, Ted swept into the room and stood poised to introduce Erin to the repairman. The repairman took no notice as he was head to shoulders deep within the underbelly of the machine. Based on the level of disassembly and strewn parts, Erin revised her likelihood of repeating said equipment fix from possible to not a shot in Sheol.

"Erin, this is Gary, our service representative. Gary, Erin will be here to assist you," Ted announced with a flourish of gestures which were lost on the repairman.

"Huh?" Gary mumbled, casting a quick glance back at them. "Ok." He resumed his efforts with a shrug.

"I'll leave you two to it, then." Ted fake-smiled again and then swept out of the room.

Erin stood by the door, swaying from the balls to heels of her feet and back again. "Anything I can do to help?"

Gary remained deep within the bowels of the machine. "Unless you're certified to work on the MX-8010, I don't see how you could help."

"So, that's a no, then?"

"Correct. I take it you're here to supervise my work?"

"Although I'm woefully ill-suited to the chore, yes. That's why I'm here; to make sure you stay on task and out of trouble," Erin replied.

He grunted. Erin wasn't sure if it was in response to her or his efforts.

"I'd leave you to it, if I could. I'm sure you don't need someone watching over your shoulder."

"Eh, I don't mind," Gary mumbled.

But Erin minded; that was the problem. She walked across the room and sat at a table used for compiling proposals. She added this pointless task to the long list of things Maria had given her this week alone. She'd fetched *fresh* coffee instead of making a new pot. She'd acted as a messenger to convey a simple *can you please contact us* message in person. She'd printed, collated, and assembled Pythia documents over and over this week, instead of having a specializing printing company handle the large volume. Then there was the moment Maria told her to visit the hardware store to get a sampling of paint chips to match the lemon twist pantone for a client so they could paint an accent wall in their office to match the new campaign.

Nothing she did had any real utility at Pythia. At least, not in a way she could measure it. Unless you counted being Maria's whipping girl?

The mantle of mediocrity hung heavy on her shoulders, and reflexively, Erin stretched, willing it to crack into a million pieces. She could almost feel it disintegrate and then slide off into the ether around her. Erin stood up and stretched her arms to the ceiling, shaking her head, feeling like she'd just woken up. The anxiety she'd wound up so tightly melted away, leaving her mind feeling light yet grounded within her body.

Gary grunted again and tossed a part out of the machine onto his work mat.

Drifting over to the plotter, she leaned up against it. "Gary?"

His body jerked. "Ow, damn," he grumbled. He backed out of the machine, rubbing the back of his head.

"How long do you think this," she gestured toward the machine, "is going to take?"

He pulled his hand away from the back of his head, shooting her a pained glance. "Well, it depends. It appears the drum may have delaminated. If so, I'll have to get the part sent over from the warehouse. Then it'll take hours." Gary sat back on his heels, searching the back of his head with probing fingers.

"Is your head all right?" Erin stepped forward into his space. His breath caught in his throat as she bent over him and threaded her fingers through his sandy blond hair. Catching his fingers in her own, the wet slick of blood smeared across her fingers. "There's some blood. Hand me a cloth?"

"Thought I caught it," he said. He dug in a pocket and pulled out a clean handkerchief, handing it over to her.

Erin pulled his head toward her legs and ran her hands through his hair, locating the wound. The warm blood marked her fingers, quickening her pulse. She placed the kerchief against it, compressing the wound and pressing his head against her knees.

He reached up to take hold of the rag. "I can get that."

"Don't be silly," Erin replied. "This is a tricky angle. Just wait a minute until you stop bleeding."

She pressed harder against the wound. He whimpered, his hands reaching up and grabbing her legs and skirt. "Here, let me get up. I can sit on that chair."

Erin pressed his shoulder down. "Don't be silly."

"But I should get back to work. Anyone could walk in on us."

She checked the wound, which had almost stopped bleeding. "Almost there."

A throat noisily cleared in the room. Gary froze, pulling back and attempting to squirm out from under Erin, who was lax to relax pressure on Gary's head. She looked at the sound and fixed Ted with an icy glare while he stared back at her with utter disdain.

"Well, I think you're both done here." He held the door open. "Erin, if you could come with me? Gary, I'll be back to get an update on the repair status in a moment."

Erin dug deep in search of some motivation to obey Ted's directive and found him wanting. Erin extricated herself from Gary and pulled herself up, waiting a moment to make sure Gary had a firm grip on the kerchief. When Ted looked her up and down, rolling his eyes, she glanced at her clothes.

White was not the ideal color to wear when helping a copier repairman. The stark placement of his ink-smudged hands strategically along her thighs and encircling her skirt made for an almost deliberate artistic gesture. For his part, Gary had a few smears of blood on his face and clothes from the cut on his head Erin had staunched. Standing up, he straightened his clothes while blushing and trying somewhat successfully to avoid eye contact with both of them. When his gaze took in Erin, he paled visibly. Surely, she didn't look *that* bad?

Then she saw the blood on her hands. And shirt. And skirt. And legs. Even shoes. How had she managed that?

It occurred to Erin she was expected to feel a level of embarrassment for messing up her work attire. Instead, she felt irritated at Ted over his haughty attitude, and she felt a bit miffed with Gary over his embarrassment.

Ted pointed her toward the hall, reminding Erin of a schoolteacher escorting her to the principal's office. Erin humored him and led the way to Maria's office.

"Does Maria even have time to take a break from her meeting for this?" Erin mused aloud.

Ted coughed. "Oh, she'll make time."

When Erin reached Maria's office, she strode into the

white-washed confines, feeling repelled by the lack of any softness within the room. Glossy white laminate surfaces were paired with stiff white leather cushions throughout. Although she'd been in Maria's office multiple times daily during her tenure at Pythia, it had never felt as uncomfortable as it did now.

Erin took a seat on the lounge across from Maria's desk, flopping back into the enormous expanse of plush leather.

"I'm sure, considering the state of your outfit, that Maria would rather have you stand."

"I'm sure you're correct." Erin leveled a direct gaze at Ted, whose discomfort over her lack of formality was written all over his face and the nervous way he clutched his hands together. The irony hit her that this was the first time his haughty attitude toward her had faltered, and she suspected it was because of her uncharacteristic complete lack of concern.

"That's cheeky of you," he said, and she heard the anxiety tremble through his voice.

Erin ran a hand along the leather seat, a light red stain marring the surface. "I'll just wait here for her." Based on how Ted's gaze kept flickering to her red-tinged digits, he'd noticed as well.

"Okay, then. I'll just fetch her." Ted practically ran out of the room.

Erin looked over the black and red stains on her clothes, mustering not an ounce of concern for her disheveled state. She knew this was not how she should be feeling. Surely Maria would fire her outright. And just as surely, Erin should be upset over her predicament.

So why didn't she care?

CHAPTER 18

ERIN

*E*rin remained draped over the bleached lounge when Maria marched into her office a few minutes later.

"Well, you certainly look comfortable." Maria closed the door behind herself, slowly appraising Erin. She circled Erin, her gaze traveling the length of her recumbent form. Curiosity burned in her eyes.

If she hadn't been so relaxed, Erin would have, well, *cared* more about Maria's shift in mood. Normally her boss was dictatorial, issuing commands as a queen might proclaim edicts. However, the woman before her visibly paused, assessing Erin with an air of incredulity. As one might a wild animal who'd wandered into a corner store for a cup of coffee and a blueberry scone.

Or something. Erin idly scratched her head, hair catching her fingers. How had her hair gotten so wild and disheveled?

Maria leaned back against her desk. "I hear you helped fix the copier?"

Erin shrugged. "Yet I don't think I learned one useful thing about copier repair."

Maria, the ice queen, raised a singular eyebrow. "And the blood? Did you injure him?"

Erin glanced at her hands. "No, I didn't hurt him. He banged his head inside the copier, and I helped him apply pressure to the wound." She wiggled her fingers in further explanation.

Maria crossed her arms, her expression a mix of curiosity and ire. "And the blood on your face? Your lips?"

Erin's fingers traveled to her lips, grazing the surface, as if she could feel the thin sheen of dried blood clinging to them. How had that happened? "No wonder Ted seemed out of sorts."

"Oh, I assure you, Ted had plenty of reasons to be unsettled." Maria frowned, a delicate set of creases gathering between her brows. "I can see you don't appear nervous at all."

Erin took a moment, connecting with the emotions swirling through her solar plexus. "I'm calm as a clam over here."

Maria nodded. "Isn't that at all curious to you?"

"I must admit, it's not at all what I expected."

Maria leaned forward, her perfect white suit shifting slightly at the neck, revealing a hint of more collarbone than before. Across her tanned skin, Erin spied a white set of leaves, which reminded her of the new tattoo she'd seen on Zaire's collarbone earlier. "What's up with the new ink? I saw it on Zaire too. Some sort of new in-club thing?"

Maria's gaze narrowed, understanding washing across her features. "You could call it that, I suppose."

Erin shrugged. "Whatever. Look, I didn't attack the copier guy, if that's what you're worried about. He'll be fine. I just got my clothes dirty in the line of duty assisting him." She sat up, leaning forward as she perched at the edge of the cushy lounge.

Maria shrunk back a little. Was she *that* messy?

Maria recovered a moment later, regaining her aloof moxie. Up shot the eyebrow again. "I don't give a damn about Greg."

Maria had never sworn in her presence before, which took Erin aback. "Okay."

"To whom do you hail?" Maria's fierce expression demanded a response.

"Pardon me?"

Maria stood and took a few steps back. "To. Whom. Do. You. Hail?"

The question resonated deep within Erin, but she had no words to form in response. She shook her head, anxiety welling within her, a late, yet seemingly appropriate, emotion.

"Let's try this another way. Who *elevated* you?" Maria demanded, frustration written throughout her tense form.

Erin jumped up and paced across the floor. The answer swirled within her blood, echoing through her bones. Memories of the man with the golden hair flashed unbidden through her mind.

"I don't know what you're talking about!" Erin snapped back. The surrounding air vibrated, echoing the spike in her adrenaline.

"I suspect you do, Erin." Maria crossed her arms. "But I

do not need to drag it out of you. I'll simply alert the Chief and he'll clear all of this up."

"Chief?" Erin remembered Daniel, the man at the club, mentioning a name. "You mean Blaine?"

Maria's eyes widened. "Well, I certainly doubt you're on a first name basis with him, but yes. I heard he was looking for a new wildling in town."

Instead of fear, adrenaline coursed through her veins. Images of Maria thrown to the wall filled her enraged mind. Erin shook it off, trying to make sense of what Maria had said. Blaine. Chief Blaine? The man she'd referred to as a pansy when talking to that ruffian, Daniel, at the nightclub?

"He's looking for me?" Tension thrummed through her body, a need for movement overwhelming.

Maria grinned. That couldn't be good. Erin had never seen her so pleased with anything before now. "Imagine my surprise to discover you awakened and under my roof."

Awakened? "Yeah, imagine." *Who were these people?* Erin mused. Windswept pine and cedar swirled past her, beckoning Erin to follow.

Maria activated her earpiece with a graceful swipe of her fingers past her temple. Another swipe or two in the air, the arcane gestures the only evidence of Maria's interface with her optical display.

Erin's focus fixed on Maria's lips, her body calming as her focus intensified. A steady, rhythmic beat pounded through her blood.

"Yes, hello. This is Maria. I need to speak with the Chief regarding his wildling. I have her." A pause. "Yes, I'll wait."

Erin's skin bristled, not at the term wilding, but at the use of the possessive pronoun. Curiosity enveloped Erin like a mist as she observed Maria.

A sultry, masculine musk drew her mind's eye away from this conversation. The yearning to move, to fly through the forest, pounded through her thoughts.

Maria's form stilled, and Erin could tell her attention was no doubt on the voice at the other end of the call. "Good morning to you, Chief. Yes, she's right here."

Maria nodded and spoke to Erin. "You're to wait here for him."

"Give him my apologies, Maria. I have to run." *Literally.* Erin turned and walked toward the door.

"I'd advise against making him hunt for you," Maria replied.

"I'm sure we'll run into each other eventually," Erin answered, not looking back as she shot out the door.

A moment later, she emerged onto the pavement downtown. There was nothing better than the sensation of the wind threading itself through her hair, the sun beaming down onto her face, and the smell of bonfire in the breeze.

"Blaine be damned."

Erin ran toward drumbeats only she could hear.

CHAPTER 19

"I apologize, sir," Maria explained over the open line. "I'm afraid she ran."

Blaine ground his teeth, the view from the back of the limousine muted by the window tint. "It's likely for the best, Maria. This wildling turns aggressive with little provocation. Alerting me toward her location and identity will allow us to bring her in for a proper discussion."

"You're quite welcome. I'm transferring her employee file over to your secured cloud location now," Maria replied. "I have a confirmed home address, vehicle plates, and citizen ID included. All the standard documentation is in order. Hopefully, you find this useful."

Blaine smiled, accessing the files sent over by Maria via a couple of air-tapping gestures as he accessed his neural interface. "It's my luck she works for a devotee of Apollo. Other groups might not have been as thorough as you certainly have been." He pulled up a picture of Erin Bevin, regarding her unkempt, light brown hair and unremarkable features. He'd somehow expected a maenad's appearance to be as wild as her soul, but the woman in this picture, he'd describe as downright mousy. "Care to hazard a guess when she was elevated? A recent change, or something she hid during the time she's been with you?"

"I can guarantee it happened over the weekend. Who she presented as today is nothing like the boring assistant I knew last week. I don't even think she fully understands the impact of her elevation."

If that was true, how was she already strong enough to win a brawl with Daniel?

"I appreciate your astute evaluation. No doubt I will confirm your suspicions shortly when we locate her."

"There's one more thing," Maria said.

"More?" Blaine ground out.

"I'll include this in my notes, but I want to make sure you understand. My assistant, Ted, was just in talking with the copier repairman, Gary. Gary hit his head and Erin helped him with his wound, making an utter mess of herself. Anyway, Gary is experiencing some odd symptoms."

"And you think they're related to Erin?"

"I'm certain. Ted was helping Gary clean up and discovered some new markings on Gary's skin."

Blaine felt the hair at the back of his neck stand on end. "God-touched markings?"

"No, no, more like tattoos, but they shifted in color as the doctor observed them. What's more concerning, Gary had no recall of how they came to be on his skin."

"We have to assume those marks are Erin's doing. All the more reason to find out her purpose as quickly as possible and get her under council control. We don't want some sort of infection hitting the city," Blaine replied.

"What an absurd prospect," Maria replied. "We've never had this sort of problem with a new god-touched before!"

"The problems will be under control soon enough, Maria, I assure you."

"Best of luck on your hunt, Chief."

"Luck has nothing to do with it."

Maria's laugh rang out. "Your success is assured, sir. Oh, if I may?"

Blaine raised a brow, knowing what to expect next, but not so inclined to lead her there. "Go ahead."

Maria cleared her throat lightly. "May I claim the favor of a Chief's boon for helping you locate the wildling?" she asked, the slightest of trembles causing her voice to waver.

Blaine couldn't resist pausing longer than necessary. "Technically, we haven't yet located her."

"Very true, sir." The disappointment in Maria's voice rang clear, yet she didn't argue with him.

Few did, considering his position and elevation.

"However, I deem this a fair petition for reporting the last known whereabouts of the wildling and delivering her official documents. The city is in your debt and a commensurate boon is thus granted."

"I am happy I could be of service, Chief." Maria sounded like the fat cat who'd caught the mouse.

"Did you have a request for your boon?" Blaine asked.

"No, sir. I'd hate to disrupt your duties on a day you likely have better things to worry about. Another time?"

Blaine smiled to himself. He granted boons so rarely they were appropriately coveted. Having one in your back pocket at a council meeting could mean the difference between winning or having your pet projects grounded.

"Anytime, Maria. I'll have Jake record the boon on your file."

"Thank you, sir. Let me know if I can be of further assistance."

"You can bet on it. Good day."

Blaine ended the call and continued paging through Erin's file, which was filled with seemingly inconsequential data. He sent her vehicle plates and description to the police, directing them to locate and follow, but not apprehend the suspect. He flagged her citizen ID the same, sending out an image of Erin to every badge in the city.

It was only a matter of time before she turned up.

"Jake," Blaine spoke to his majordomo, who was driving his limo. "I'm sending you GPS coordinates to Erin's home. I'd like to drive by the area, the local eateries, gas stations, and groceries."

"Yes, sir. On route now, our ETA is approximately twenty minutes. Are you considering bringing her in yourself?"

"I am."

"Is that wise, sir? We have people for that sort of thing, you know?" Jake asked.

"Yes, I'm aware. Humor me."

Jake didn't respond, which Blaine understood as Jake-speak for *I disagree with you, but out of respect I am withholding my opinion.* Jake was a wise man.

Besides, if Blaine's intuition proved correct, having his people bring in Erin would not end well. That she'd taken down Daniel, a seventh-ranked devotee of Ares, gave him pause.

Blaine was the only eighth-ranked devotee in the city,

which was why his chapter ran things. If the maenad was on equal footing with him, another eight-rank, which he suspected she was as she'd taken down Daniel, then Erin might actually give Blaine a run for his money in a fight.

The idea of someone actually being a suitable challenge perversely appealed to Blaine.

The notion that another of his rank would be within rights to challenge his authority. Well, that was unacceptable.

CHAPTER 20

ERIN

*E*rin ran through the city, headed toward the relentless, pounding rhythm pulsing through her veins. The late summer sun poured down across her, heating her skin through her white clothes. Buildings passed by in a blur. Grey and black. Granite and concrete. The air in the man-made, cleanly carved and finely finished spaces was filled with emptiness that had been left behind by people who may have once held a flame within them but were now devoid of all hope.

Erin ran past it all, seeking her own pace. Her own space. Cool droplets of sweat trickled down her back, down her neck, yet she wasn't panting despite the effort.

Erin felt boundless. Limitless.

Ahead, tall maples and cottonwoods towered over buildings, drawing her into their expanse. A few leaves swirled through the air, and Erin danced to their cadence, breathing in joy.

Lost in the blissful moment, Erin's gaze caught on a lady sitting at a table outside a coffee shop across from the park.

Unlike the other automatons she'd passed by without a thought downtown, something about this woman reeked of vitality.

Erin had to know more. Striding across the park, she crossed the street and walked straight up to the woman whom she could now see was marked as a daemon summoner.

Erin eyed the whisperer with abject curiosity. "You're completely alive. It's beautiful. What's your name?"

The summoner's eyebrow shot up, her expression regarding Erin with blatant amusement. "I'm Meri, and thank you? Your name would be...?"

"Oh, I think I've heard of you! My name's Erin. Can I sit?"

Meri inclined her head, relaxing back into her chair. "Go right ahead."

Erin pulled out a chair and sat down next to the summoner, energy thrumming through her slight frame. "Thank you."

A waitress paused at the table, staring openly at Erin, her eyes lingering on Erin's ink and blood-stained clothes. A smile crept along Meri's features. "Would you like a coffee?" Erin nodded. "Another for me, and one for my new friend here," Meri said to the waitress.

"We don't want any trouble, Meri," replied the waitress, her expression terse.

"And there won't be any, Carla." Meri's confidence was no match for Carla's concern.

"I'll get that right out for you." Carla dashed off into the building.

"So, you're looking very free spirited today. What's the occasion?" Meri asked.

Erin glanced down at her clothes, ran her fingers through her wild hair, and shrugged. "I had a copier incident and then I was fired."

Meri gave a brief nod. "And is the blood from the copier battle, or did you knock off your boss on the way out?"

A nervous laugh escaped Erin's lips. She tried unsuccessfully to stop bouncing her knees. "No battle, not today, at least so far. The copier man hit his head, and I helped him clean up. This is his blood."

Meri appraised Erin, her eyes missing no detail. "You have blood all over your hands, the side of your face. I even see a bit in your hair, and of course it's all over your clothes as well." Meri leaned forward and whispered, "I bet people think you look straight from the slaughter."

She doesn't pull any punches, does she? "It's that bad?" Erin asked.

Meri pursed her lips and nodded slowly, sitting back in her chair.

"But you don't seem concerned by my appearance?" Erin pressed.

Meri chuckled. "I've seen worse. Most days, before ten AM."

Something about Meri's direct and nonchalant acceptance of violence, which could have been mere bravado, struck Erin as blatant honesty. It occurred to Erin that she should be uncomfortable with her current situation. A surge of anxiety formed within her chest, bubbling into questions in her mind.

"Aren't you a daemon summoner?" Erin asked, and Meri nodded. "So, can you tell me what's wrong with me?" Clearly something had gone wrong, and Erin did not know how to fix her broken life.

"Uh. Well, what do you think is wrong with you?" Meri asked.

Their waitress, Carla, returned with their coffees. She swept in and out, shooting Meri a pointed look.

Erin added two sugars to the black brew, stirring it as she mulled over her thoughts, liquid sloshing out of the cup. "Well, for starters, as of an hour ago, I am unemployed with no income to provide for myself." Erin lifted the cup and took a quick sip of hot coffee, but avoided burning her tongue despite the brew's heat.

"That sounds like an unpleasant situation. Do you have prospects?"

Erin considered for a moment, anxiety crawling between her shoulder blades. She scratched at her scalp and then tried to comb through her hair yet again. "I've got nothing. I'll have to hit the mills tomorrow or see if I can pick up some piece-meal work. Nothing I can find will pay what the gig at Pythia paid me, and I can't use them as a job reference after today."

"Okay, is anything else wrong?" Meri watched her intently.

Erin put her cup down. "I'm unusually strong suddenly. And, um, I know things about wine."

"Those seem like beneficial additions."

Erin leaned in. "Well, sure, I'm not complaining. But am I possessed by some daemon? Or cursed by one?"

A sad look flitted across Meri's face. "I'm afraid that's not how it works."

"So, you can tell? You're sure I don't have a daemon problem?"

"Can confirm." Meri inclined her head. "If you had a daemon problem, I'd help the crap outta you, believe me. But I sense nothing of the daemon sort."

Erin deflated a bit. "I kinda wish I did so you could fix it. Fix me."

"I suspect your issue is something outside my purview."

Erin perked up. "You can't help me, but you know what's wrong with me? Something daemonish?"

Meri took a deep breath and blew it out slowly. Her wary eyes met Erin's. "You smell of the god-touched."

"The what?" Erin brushed at an ink smudge on her skirt, only to coat her fingers with the ashen toner.

Meri took a sip of her coffee, casting a glance around them. "They're the ones who run this city. From the corporate players to the government goons, all are devotees to a variety of gods."

Erin burst out in laughter. "You've gotta be kidding me?"

"It's more common than you'd think." By Meri's focused expression, Erin knew she wasn't joking. "The world is strange and full of mystery. I've been hired by a few corporations over the years to help deal with competition. It's messy work. As someone who specializes in daemons from Sheol, I can't say deities are at all unusual." Meri crossed her legs, weighing her mug in her hands.

"Why haven't I heard of these god-touched before now?" Erin shifted in her seat.

"Unlike daemons, who are messy and have no care for the consequences of their acts upon the human population, the devotees of the gods pride themselves on elevating and bringing order to human culture. Oh, and I almost forgot. Keeping secrets."

"They're rich snobs who play chess with the pawns. For what? Power? Profit?"

Meri shrugged. "More or less all of that, yes."

Erin sank into her chair. "Who all knows about these *touched* people?"

Meri shrugged. "It's your typical secret society, which means those on the inside know bits and pieces, and the rest of us hear rumors. I wouldn't know about them except sometimes my jobs have had me intersect with their circles of influence."

Shivers of energy racked Erin's frame, seizing the breath in her lungs. The call to run pressed into her mind, her blood, muscles, and bones. "I have to find them. How do I find them?" Erin whispered.

Meri regarded her. Erin had the impression she was having some internal debate, and then she continued, misgivings etched along her brow. "My understanding, which is rather limited, is that the god-touched have a method of recognizing each other. I'm not sure if it's a smell, marking, or secret handshake. But from what I've observed, they seem to know each other on sight without having to discuss it."

Frustration bubbled up within Erin, surfacing in her hands as she crushed the mug into shards, slicing into her flesh. Erin screeched, her voice piercing the air.

The reverberating sound brought all the motion around them to a standstill.

"Please, take a deep breath," Meri said. Her features held concern, unlike the scared faces of other coffee shop patrons. Erin held pressure against the cut on her right palm, and took a couple of long breaths, which barely took the edge off the building pressure within her mind and body. "That's right, nice, slow breaths. Look, I can see you're overwhelmed and don't know what to do next. It looks like whatever is happening within you is unbearable, and I'm sorry I don't have an answer for you."

Erin nodded. "I sense you'd help me more if you could." Erin looked at the gash on her hand, rubbing away the blood to discover a barely healed welt where the gash had existed moments ago.

Meri regarded her hand, and their eyes met. "You're unusually powerful, even for one of the touched."

"I don't know what any of this means." Erin sighed, the stress flooding from her body in newfound tears.

Meri flopped back in her chair. "Crap, I really wish I could help you out, Erin. Technically, I can't interfere."

Erin shrugged. "I don't want to get you in trouble. You said I should be able to recognize other god-touched, so I guess I just need to get out there and find them to get my answers. I know one is looking for me already."

"Well, sure. That should work," Meri replied. "Be careful with whom you trust. From my limited experience, their power structure is fairly rigid."

"Okay. So, if I'm one of them now, then they should help me out." Erin's gut roiled with anxiety.

The misgivings were plain on Meri's face. "I mean, sure, that makes sense. You're pretty much in or out with them."

"But not always in?" Erin brushed tears from her face.

"Not always. But again, I can't rightly say." Meri's composure broke for a moment, compassion warring with her measured demeanor. "Fuck it," she murmured to herself, digging into her pocket and pulling out a small stone. Meri hesitated a moment and then held it out to Erin. "Here, take this."

Erin held out her uninjured hand, and Meri dropped the stone into her palm. The stone was hot against her flesh, palpable waves of energy thrumming across her skin. "What's it do?"

"It's my calling card. If things go sideways, hold on to it and think of me, and I'll show up."

"Thank you, Meri." Erin pocketed the stone, not understanding how that might work, but not doubting Meri for a moment. Having a stone as a calling card was perhaps the least odd thing that had happened lately. "But I thought you couldn't help me?"

"I mean, I technically can't. But call me if you need to, and hell, I'll do something." Meri looked like she'd swallowed a bitter pill. Her brow and lips scrunched up into frowns.

"You're solid, you know that?" Erin replied.

Meri sighed. "I've been in similar shoes, and you deserve to have someone watching your back."

Drums beat somewhere in the hills, and Erin shot to her feet, feeling driven toward the sound. Was it hills or towering buildings? She couldn't pinpoint the source. Only that she felt it soaring through her, calling her name.

"I am called."

Meri shook her head and waved her off. "Get down with your touched self."

Erin shot down the road, answering the call in her blood.

CHAPTER 21

ERIN

An edge of frustration and anger fueled Erin's speed as she flew through the city. Erin had persevered for years to get that entry-level job at Pythia, and the waitress job, although less prestigious, hadn't exactly fallen into her lap either. Everything had finally started to come together.

And just as Erin was moving up at the marketing firm, just when she thought everything was coming together, the bottom inevitably dropped out. Her future now laid in a pile, shattered into a million tiny shards of ruin.

It's the moment the cosmos tells you your dreams don't matter one iota. That everything you've clung to for so long is without merit. And it's the moment you're utterly destroyed and reborn, all in an instant. Stripped of all that was, stripped of the assumptive yoke you've thoughtlessly given yourself over to, at this moment, this singular instant, your eyes have a spark of clarity.

At least the sienna and orange-toned dusk was breathtaking, a welcome relief from her beleaguered thoughts. Luckily, the Corporations had yet to figure out a way to charge citizens for the beautiful sunsets and mountain views of Colorado. Except for the value added city tax, a charge based on the added quality of life for living in nicer areas.

Damn the Corporations.

Whatever had happened to Erin out in those woods, she knew this moment was a culmination of that raw, elemental power. Something had taken root in her, shook her foundation to the core, and cracked open her base. Although she'd lost her jobs and for all she knew she'd be out on the street in T-Minus two weeks, this moment was worth every second.

She had to find him. Find answers to what had happened to her.

Erin came to a stop, the air around her a mini whirlwind of dust and leaves. Where was she? The uplifted, scarlet sandstone ridge of the hogback rising before her marked Erin's location as just outside of Morrison. The iconic landmark separated the metro area from the mountainous wilderness beyond. The outgrowth of city homes and buildings pressed to the very edge, but none crossed the ridge top.

Turning away from the city, Erin headed deeper into the mountains, returning to the place of her transformation, seeking answers from the man with the long, golden hair.

Right now, she felt so alive, so fully drawn into her own skin it crackled with anticipation, and she might just burst. Was she scared? Sure, her heart was beating at a million miles an hour, but the surrounding colors were vivid and alive in a way she'd never seen before. No, that's not true. They'd been like this in the forest. With *him.* But now, that same clarity was here, and yet she was all alone. Or was she? The air itself vibrated around her. Was this real or an illusion? But then she caught the scent, *his* scent. Musky, earthy, full of green spring shoots and a hint of wine. Her lips curled as she panted, anticipating.

The hunt was on.

She sprinted even faster, running past the city limits and up into the hills. Erin sped toward her favorite haunt, returning to the scene of the crime. Could she find it again in the fading light of the day? Even as the dusk progressed into evening, her vision remained acute and her memory of the location uncommonly clear.

There were no drums to guide Erin, but she caught glimpses of the light of a bonfire in the distance and knew she'd returned to the scene of the prior bacchanal. Erin slowed her pace, striding into the open glen.

Only one man stood near the fire, his eyes unerringly on Erin as she approached. The only noises were the crackling of the wood as the roaring fire licked around it, reaching toward the sky, and the sound of wind blowing gently through the boughs above. He was dressed casually, in a linen shirt and khakis, his hair a touch unkempt and the long strings of beads around his neck reminding her of meditation stones. His skin shone with a slight golden hue, as if he'd dusted himself with glitter on the way to this odd meeting. He looked for all the world like a burner lost in the woods, except she knew he wasn't lost.

Just like she suspected, he was no mere man.

Erin suspected he caused her newfound prowess, strength, and vitality, yet she did not know why, or even who, he was. Standing mere feet from him, she'd hesitate to call him human. Although he'd kissed her, Erin didn't even know his name.

"Who are you?" Erin asked.

He stepped up to her, his height only a couple inches taller than her, for she was a tall woman and he a slight man. He reached up and pulled a leaf from her hair, tucking some wayward strands behind her ear. His gaze traveled the length of her, no doubt taking in the bloodstains on her face, clothes, and hands.

His expression turned appreciative. "I am Dionysos."

That name rang a bell from her school days, but she couldn't quite place it. "I'm afraid you have me at a loss, sir."

He sighed, and if she'd known him better, Erin would have described his expression as forlorn. "I'm not surprised. The modern education system leaves much to be desired. And surely, much truth is kept from the public. From the disempowered."

"That's stating the obvious. So help me out. I can see you're powerful. What Corporation do you run?"

Dionysos laughed, the deep rumble filling the glen as no man's laugh ever would. "These modern corporations are of no concern to me."

"What in the world are you?" Erin took a step back.

"You have nothing to fear from me, Erin. What I am is your benefactor. An ancient, powerful ally. I am one god of an age well before your time."

His expression was serious, and yet his eyes were alight with amusement. He had to know how impossible this sounded.

"And yet, here you are," she said.

"I've always been here."

"Don't speak in riddles. I mean, why are you here *now*?" Erin made a sweeping gesture with her arm, and more leaves appeared, fluttering to the ground.

Dionysos grinned, pride welling in his eyes. "Your wildness is so captivating, and you wear it so beautifully. I really couldn't be prouder to witness your becoming."

Erin cocked her head to the side. "Becoming? Yeah, what did you do to me the other night?"

Dionysos paced in a circle around the fire, his eyes riveted on her. "I bequeathed on you the highest of honors." His hands were open wide, and he made a slight bow.

Erin, filled with frustration, balled her hands into fists and stamped her foot on the ground. A shock wave of energy radiated out from where she stood. The sensation emboldened and terrified her at the same time. "I'm gonna need you to be more specific!"

He frowned. "Are you aware of those who call themselves the god-touched?"

Erin shook her head from side to side. "Maybe."

"I'm not at all surprised. For, although they run your cities, they exist as a secret society. These individuals spend years venerating deities, often at the behest of their parents or close friends. Those who find favor with the gods are granted a sacred bond."

"So you're saying I'm bonded to you now?" Erin asked, and Dionysos nodded. "But I never asked for this; I never prayed to you." She started pacing as well, unable to stand still another moment longer.

Dionysos growled. "Erin, every time you fled the city, seeking the refuge and wilderness of the woods, I heard your call. Every time you talked to the moon, I felt the indomitable nature of your spirit. And when you accepted my offering of wine the night of the bacchanal, I knew you were perfect."

A shiver ran down Erin's back. "But I came here to shake

off the pressures of my life. To escape. There's such freedom in these wild spaces. It's nothing like the stifling claustrophobia I experience in the city. I knew nothing of your presence here. I came here for myself."

Dionysos shrugged. "The path to the divine is personal and distinct for each being."

Erin barked out a laugh. "That sounds like metaphysical crap. This is all so implausible. It's laughable."

"And yet, despite the impossibilities, I have made you limitless!" Dionysos declared.

Erin bolted toward him and slapped Dionysos across the face, drawing blood as her nails scraped his skin.

The god was unphased. "This is the greatest honor I can bestow, and I have given it to you."

Erin drew her hand up to slap him again, and he caught it, this time licking his blood from her skin, inflaming her.

He barked out a laugh. "You're even powerful enough to damage a god, if only in minute amounts."

Before her eyes, the scratch on his cheek healed, the blood disappearing as if she'd never touched him. His self-satisfied grin only inflamed her temper further. He released her hand, and she resumed her pacing.

"I had a life. I had a job. Now what am I?" Erin growled, seething in his intensity. "I will not be your chattel to be ordered about. I will not be some plaything, some toy, for you to use for whatever purposes you have until you break me."

Dionysos rumbled in laughter. "How could you be? You are infused with the essence of a god. Me."

"I will not bow to you. I will never yield, not to you nor any man."

Dionysos brushed his hand across the proud line of her

jaw and ran his fingers down her strong shoulder, his attention rapt. When he pulled away, Erin momentarily quieted.

"Peace, Erin. I do not seek your servitude. The world has been too long without my presence. Without my sway. Fear and greed rule the masses, and the joys of healthy pleasure are lost on their souls. My gift to them is you. My Maenad. The first I have fashioned in centuries."

"Maenad?" Erin tasted the word on her lips. "That sounds like something I heard in a fairy tale once."

The look in Dionysos' eyes became dangerous. "The Maenads are my immortal vanguard, fueled by wine and madness. They are warriors, destroyers, bacchants, and revelers. They preceded me and announced my arrival. None dared stand against them, at least not for long. They razed cities when defied and tore apart the corpses of their enemies with their bare hands. When welcomed, they threw galas for weeks that earned the renown of bards."

Erin struggled to digest his intensity. "Wait, I'm immortal?"

A corner of his lip curled upwards. "Well, I never liked the term immortal, much, but it has a certain ring to it, yes? Think of it more as being very resilient and difficult to kill."

Erin's heart skipped a beat. Maybe two. "You're truly not going to order me about?"

Dionysos scowled. "Do not offend me. You contain a spark of my godhood. You shall naturally be drawn along the path you must tread."

Erin fisted her palms, aware of the newfound strength coursing through her veins. Through the soles of her feet, she felt the pulse of the Earth in simpatico with her own heartbeat. She breathed deeply, taking in the resinous smells of the flagpole pines surrounding them.

"You're saying I can do whatever I want?" Erin asked, an incredulous lilt to her voice. The possibility of not being under the thumb of someone like Maria or Charlie sunk in.

"I'm counting on you to do exactly that."

Somehow, this discussion with her newfound benefactor had centered her. Erin did not know what to do next, but sensed a realm of possibilities before her.

"Well then. It turns out I require financial backing," Erin asked.

From over his shoulder, Dionysos unslung a heavy satchel and held it out to her. Erin took it without hesitation.

"Everything you need is in there. New ID, loaded coffers, the works. But one warning, my dear. I can't safeguard your journey against all pitfalls."

"I don't know, I have the backing of a god. I'm exceedingly hard to kill, and I have endless money. What's the catch?" Erin asked.

"Have you forgotten I have brothers and sisters who vie for supplicants? Seek the other god-touched. Demand your rightful due. But be warned: you will encounter resistance."

Erin shrugged. "Oh, I haven't forgotten that."

Dionysos moved in close, his look conspiratorial. "And what are you planning with your newfound liberties?"

"You'll see soon enough. But with this opportunity, I can create something new. Something free." Erin's brow raised, a slight smirk curling her lips. "For everyone."

CHAPTER 22

ERIN

Erin sashayed up to the front door of Porter's, a purse full of money, high black heels, and a slip of a black dress that fit her athletic frame like a glove. She felt ready to take on the world. Or Denver, to start with.

After her conversation in the hills with Dionysos, Erin had stopped back by her meager apartment to wash up and change before going out. She'd hidden the satchel Dionysos had given her in her closet wall. Considering how much had happened today, she should have been exhausted, but her energy levels were through the roof.

For the first time in her life, Erin envisioned a world of potential, of possibility. A universe where she didn't live in a flea-ridden apartment building and slept in a bed that didn't smell. Erin wanted to dance all night long. The heavy bass pounding within called to her. Maybe after she'd be ready to sleep?

Bono stood outside the door, eyeing her approach with caution. "Hey now, Lola," he held up his hands, waving her off, "you know I can't let you in. Charlie done kicked you out."

Bono was a hulk of a man, but he was also super sweet. "It's Erin now. And I'm not here to get you in trouble, Bono. I want you to work for me. Whatever you're making now, consider it doubled."

He stepped back and looked at her askance. "What are you talking about? You got a bar now?"

"Fine. I'll triple whatever you're making."

"You do that. How can I refuse?" he shook his head, letting out a chortle. "How'd this miracle happen?"

A slow grin crept across Erin's face. "I've got a backer. We're gonna take over this town. It's a brave new world."

He shook his head, laughing with his whole heart. "All right, *Erin*. Whatever you say, girl. You come up with some magic club and the salary to match, then I'm all yours."

"Awesome. Now that I've got the best muscle in the city, I can worry about the rest of what I've got to get done. C'mon, let me in. I need to hire some gals and free them from Charlie. And dance. I'm definitely needing some good grooves."

Charlie placed his hand on her shoulder, gently blocking her movement. "Whoa, I said I can't let you in! Charlie will just kick you right out, and he'll fire me for letting you in."

"We've covered this; you already have a new gig, working for yours truly."

Bono frowned and pulled his arm back. He crossed his arms, squaring his shoulders to her. "You can't be serious about that. And you know they're looking for you, right? You'd do better to lie low for a while and let your spat with Daniel blow over."

"Oh, wait, is he here now?" Erin imagined punching

Daniel in the nose again. He totally needed another broken nose.

"Not now, but he was by earlier, talking with Charlie, asking about you. I guarantee if you go in there, Charlie will call him."

"Suits me fine," Erin replied. "Now open the door, Bono." He sighed and ran a hand over the back of his shaved head. "I'm a big girl. Don't you worry about me."

Bono exhaled hard. "I hope you know what you're doing." He pulled open the door and ushered her in.

Erin patted his arm as she passed, hoping to assuage his anxiety. The heavy beat echoed in her blood, filling an unspoken need within her psyche. Music had always been this way for her. She moved onto the dance floor, ignoring the stolen glances and wide eyes of the servers. A couple of other patrons were dancing, but they cleared out with her arrival.

Erin lost herself in the music, gyrating and rocking to the beat. After a couple of songs, she looked up, wondering why Charlie hadn't confronted her yet. There he stood at the end of the dance floor, between her and the door, texting frantically on his cell phone. When he looked up and caught her gaze, a sadistic smile flashed across his face.

Bono hadn't been kidding; they were waiting for her. She continued to dance, burning off a thread of anxiety building in her gut. What if Bono was right? What if she was in over her head?

What if she'd lost her mind, and the whole talk with Dionysos was just some stress-filled delusion? Then she thought back to when she got tossed out after trouncing Daniel and couldn't help suppressing a full belly laugh. Nope, somehow this was all actually happening.

Songs ticked by, and Erin grew impatient. There was nothing worse than getting all riled up for a confrontation just to be stuck on hold. She fluffed up the sweat-dampened, curly hair at her nape and sauntered over to the bar, barely glancing at Charlie.

"Hey Mick, how goes?" Erin set her handbag on the table after pulling out a hundred-dollar bill. "Get me a bottle of Old Vine Zinfandel? Cause shit's gonna get serious, and I've gotta power up."

"You're crazy, you know? I have nothing like that." He leaned on the bar, looking down at her.

"Look. Again. Please," she enunciated slowly, forcing a broad smile.

He rolled his eyes and made a show of looking around at the bottles of mostly vodka, gin, and rum on the shelves behind the counter. He halted. "What the shit?" he murmured, picking up a bottle of Old Vine Zin from behind the gin.

"I hate to break it to you, but with that lack of faith and attitude, I don't see you being on my team." Erin pushed the bill across the bar to him.

Mick pulled the cork on the bottle. "I'm crying already." He set it on the bar and pushed it across to her.

"Oh, you will," Erin replied.

"You graduating to using glassware?" he asked, offering her a glass.

"I'm good with my adult sippy cup, thanks." Erin held the bottle to her nose and breathed in the jammy, peppery aroma. Taking a sip, the wine delivered with a spicy, bold flavor, coating her tongue with intense fruit flavor, filling her senses.

She took a longer pull on the bottle, appreciating the potent, bold draught.

Taking a deep breath, Erin noticed a pronounced energy flowing from her gut, down her toes, and out to her fingers. If her body had a vibration, it's as if the wine turned it up a few notches. She took another sip, and the wine vibrated through her entire body, increasing the effect.

If she'd felt bold before, now Erin felt fearless. She stared at the bottle with newfound respect.

"Easy, champ," Mick said. "Looks like you've got company." He motioned toward the front door.

A freshly arrived Daniel stood talking with Charlie, who looked needlessly smug. A man and a woman stood behind Daniel, scanning the room. All four sets of eyes landed on Erin at the same moment, and she toasted them with the bottle before taking one more sip. As if on cue, they frowned as one. Daniel had a determined, angry expression.

No doubt he had something to prove after their prior encounter.

Daniel led the group over, practically stomping as he walked.

"Erin Bevin, I need you to come with us. The mayor demands an audience with you." His words were clipped, his temper barely in check below the surface.

So he knew her name? Not that she needed to keep it secret any longer, but clearly he'd done his homework. "Smart move, bringing your bodyguards along."

"Come along, please." He stepped to the side and motioned her toward the front door.

She'd expected, with the bodyguards, an accompanying

show of force. Perhaps Daniel was under orders not to? "I mean, what if I don't want to go?" she smiled and shrugged.

Charlie spit and backed off, reading the escalating tensions.

"You may be new to this city, but a summons from the mayor is not optional," Daniel ground out between clenched teeth.

Erin wanted to meet with the mayor; certainly, they would be the one to grant her the license to open a new club. A refuge from the likes of these tools. However, Daniel's attitude goaded her into picking a fight instead.

"Maybe it is for you," Erin replied, emboldened to take another swig before setting the bottle down on the bar. "I'm under no such compulsion at the moment."

She watched with rapt attention as the last shred of Daniel's self-control burned to ash under the fire of his well-stoked temper.

He reached out to grab her elbow, which Erin dodged. Seizing his outstretched forearm with her right hand, Erin swung her left fist up against his temple. The impact snapped his head to the side with a sharp crack. Stunned, Daniel crumpled to the floor, groaning. His bodyguards gaped, unsure of what had just happened.

Erin flexed her fist, shocked at the lack of discomfort. "On second thought, I'd love to meet the mayor. Is your car out front?" she asked the bodyguards.

The woman nodded.

Erin grabbed her handbag and the bottle of wine, saluting a shocked Mick. "I'll be waiting in the car," she addressed the bodyguards, who backed out of her path. "Why don't you drag your boss along? I'm guessing the mayor expects him to."

CHAPTER 23

NADIR

Against her better judgment and her cabal's policy to stay out of things human, Nadir paid her tab for the coffee and then strode off in the direction Erin had run off toward. Thanks to Nadir's ability to scent prey from Calloine, she could track Erin's erratic path through the city. Her daemon-enhanced endurance made the tracking manageable, but she worked up a sweat.

How had Erin run so far, so fast? From what Nadir understood, the god-touched were not usually gifted with superhuman powers. Sure, some had boons of strength from their patron deities, or wit, or money, or power.

Mostly, they craved power.

From their brief encounter, Erin didn't seem to have all the typical god-touched benefits nor attitude. Nadir had witnessed her heal miraculously, move faster than humanly possible, and display physical power beyond her own expectations. Most curiously, Erin had claimed to be unemployed and disconnected from the corporate world. As a newly created god-touched, how was she so powerful?

Was it concern or curiosity that drove Nadir right now up this hillside, deep into the foothills? A little of column A, a little of column B, she supposed.

Besides, if Erin was a god-touched person, she was also a total outsider to their ranks. The sensation echoed all too familiarly within Nadir.

By the time she'd located the clearing in the woods, darkness had filled the evening sky. The moon hadn't yet risen, yet she could see well enough with her daemonically enhanced vision. The expanse of the glen was unnaturally hushed, as if rebounding from some sort of cosmic impact. She scented Erin's recent presence, paired with a spicy, exotic other that was completely missing from her internal catalog of known creatures. If Nadir had had to put a name to the smell, she would have called it reverent. Wild. Powerful.

What had happened here? Who had Erin met in this remote location?

Nadir could have followed Erin's scent trail back toward town, but something about the charge of this space moved her to remain. Breathing deeply, she felt intimately connected to the forest, as if every cell of her body resonated in harmony with the heartbeat of the earth. She hadn't felt this alive in weeks. Nadir's temperature spiked as her lust daemon's energy flared into the forefront of her consciousness.

Acting on instinct, Nadir drew Azimuth's invocation sigil in the night air, imbuing it with her focus. Watching the icy blue glow, she grinned in anticipation, waves of heat rolling off her body and shimmering into the air around her like an aura.

She needed Az here, with her. Now.

Moments later, he ported into the glen, his blue-white nimbus illuminating the arboreal space with cool, stark tones.

"You called?" he asked, his eyes scanning the surrounding forest before focusing in on Nadir. She relished the way his aquamarine gaze lingered on her curves. "I didn't expect to hear from you so soon, not that I mind."

Nadir moved toward him, a definitive swagger in her steps. "I hadn't planned to, but then I came to this place and experienced a sudden craving for your presence." Nadir pressed her body against his, her hands sliding around his waist and up his back under his loose t-shirt.

He wrapped his arms around her, and Nadir relished the sensation of his fingers tracing the curve of her lower back. "This is an unusual location for a rendezvous."

Nadir shrugged. "This place has a certain something. But the mood hits when it hits." She brushed her lips from his collarbone and up along the nape of his neck, nibbling gently along the route until she could reach no higher, seeking his lips, waiting for him to bend down to her reach.

"Does it, my sweet?" he asked, dipping his head lower yet holding his lips just beyond contact. His arms were wrapped around her, the tips of his fingers running down her spine.

"It really does," Nadir answered, grinding her hips against his in wanton demand, dragging her fingernails across his muscular, rippled back. Lifting herself up on her toes, she tried to reach his lips, but he backed his head out of range, his eyes sparkling.

"Why are you here, in this remote forest glen, so far away from the city?" he whispered, coming in close to her again. His lips were mere microns from her own, and as they breathed, one out and the other in, they shared the intimacy of one continuous breath.

Nadir reveled in his presence, in the perfect pressure of his fingertips against the curve of her hip, his grazing touch across the swell of her breast. "I was following someone, but that's not important. Kiss me. Now."

His eyes narrowed, lips curling into a wolfish grin. "No, not yet, pet."

Frustration shot through Nadir, fresh waves of heat pouring off her body. "But why not, Az? Please?" She pouted, focusing her attention on undoing his belt buckle. She would not be denied!

Az didn't stop her, but confusion furrowed his brow. "You're begging me?" he barked out a laugh. "Well then, this is indeed unfamiliar territory."

Conquering his belt buckle, Nadir let out a triumphant growl and undid his pants and slip her hand inside.

"Oh, I'm quite certain I've been here before," she growled, sliding her hand down the length of his swollen manhood. "And this feels like something I'm well acquainted with."

He groaned, grinding his hips against her hand, fisting a handful of her hair as he pulled her body against his length. "That you are, pet. But you didn't answer my question. Who did you follow?"

"What are you even talking about?" Nadir didn't care. All that mattered was his flesh and her growing hunger for his touch. "Don't be so difficult."

His fingers traced her jawline, brushing his thumb across the swell of her lower lip. "I mean, lovely, that you're not acting at all like yourself. You said you followed someone here. Tell me who you were following, and why?"

"Oh, you mean the god-touched human, Erin?" Nadir panted against his ear, hungering for him with an uncommon level of intensity, even for her inner succubus. She nibbled his ear, barely realizing her canines had fanged out before narrowly avoiding breaking his skin.

She groaned in frustration and backed against a nearby pine, pulling him along. The tree shuddered with the impact of their bodies, causing a light rain of needles to cascade down around them. "I can't think straight. Take me hard, now. I'll explain more after."

Az chuckled, managing the removal of her pants with daemon-gifted speed. "I accept your terms."

The pine creaked with the force of his thrust as he entered her, and Nadir sighed in relief. Arms gripping his shoulders, she gazed into his azure eyes, dimly aware of the brilliant intensity of their combined energy painting the glen around them with shades of his icy blue and her own waves of rosy light.

Time held suspended for them, lost in the moment together.

Nadir felt herself tighten around him, grinding furiously against his flesh, insatiable for his contact. Crying out in pleasure, a shock wave rippled out from her body, and Az groaned in pleasure a moment later as he reached his own completion.

Aware of her breathing slowing and the temperature slowly returning to normal, Nadir looked around the forest, clarity re-entering her consciousness.

"Feel better?" He pulled away, refastening his pants.

Az retrieved her pants and handed them back to her, and

Nadir slid them on. "Much better, thanks. I can't understand why I got so overcome so quickly. Usually, my hunger is a bit more predictable."

He brushed a hand across her cheek, concern knitting his brow. Az sniffed the air, casting his gaze around the meadow. "This place has a distinct energetic charge; there's such an intense raw sensuality and power in the air. I'm not at all surprised that it triggered your lust aspect. Can you tell me more about this Erin you followed up here?"

Nadir ran a hand through her hair, pulling the wild locks away from her face. "She found me at a cafe in the city and we talked for a while. I think Erin is god-touched, but she's not connected to the typical corporate types like the rest of them. She ran off from our conversation, compelled, and I was curious and so followed her. By the time I'd caught up, she was gone, but the scent and energy here captivated me."

He nodded, frowning. "So I saw. You know as daemons we don't involve ourselves with the god-touched, yes?"

"If you mean Belial's lecture number three thousand and fifty-two on daemonic non-involvement with lesser species," he raised an eyebrow, and she flipped her hair and shrugged her shoulders, "I might have slept through most of that presentation."

"To recap his ofttimes lengthy diatribe, we follow the rules of non-engagement with other non-human species as part of a peace treaty agreed on millennia ago."

"Right, but the god-touched are human," she replied. "Mostly."

He chuckled. "So are we. Mostly. It's that extra part that matters per the interspecies peace accords."

Nadir sauntered around the glen, still aware of the

charged atmosphere, but it didn't have the same impact on her now that her lust asset was well-sated.

"Remind me why we care about other non-human species?" she asked. "I mean, corporates are usually god-touched, and they hire summoners to use daemons for their power struggles. How does that not break the accords?"

"It maintains the accords because the summoners are human intermediaries with the daemons and the god-touched, separately. Each species is afforded direct contact with humans, but no longer with each other. It allows us all to feed upon humans without warring over territory."

"Well then, I'm fine. Or I should say, my Summoner, *Meri*, is fine."

Azimuth's expression hardened. Was that the sound of his teeth grinding?

"That persona is a thin veil, which, when pierced, would hang responsibility for breaking the peace accords squarely on your shoulders. You'd openly invite retribution from any who felt infringed."

"I can't imagine how my talking with Erin infringes upon anyone." Nadir hung her hands on her hips in frustration.

"Talking is one thing, but I have the impression you wish to aid her." He arched a brow. "Have I misread the situation?"

She squirmed under his pointed regard. "I want to be emotionally supportive of her. Erin's lost, just like I was once."

"I don't doubt your intentions. You just need to understand there are consequences of altering the power dynamic amongst non-humans."

"I understand, Az. Trust me. I'll be careful and keep my distance."

Relief washed over his tense features. "Good, that's all I'm asking."

"I hear you." She moved in close to him, wrapping her arms around his slim, muscular frame and resting her head on his shoulder. "I think I'm just looking for something to preoccupy me from thinking too hard about Belial's sancre."

He reciprocated her hug, running adept fingers down her back. "If you're looking for distractions..."

Nadir's laughter echoed through the glen. "I think that's enough distraction for today. I'd better go back to my house and resume hunting down leads on daemon hordes. Or those organ-missing human kills. Or maybe I'll just cozy up with a good book."

"Is that something you do often?" His grin melted her, and Nadir had to shake her head lest she be overcome with lust again.

"Yes, as a matter of fact, there's nothing better than a relaxing, distracting read about werewolves taking over the city or vampires hiding away in the bowels of the sewers, waiting for an opportune chance to strike an unsuspecting human."

"I wouldn't define those as *cozy* stories," he chuckled, his chin-length, silvered hair swinging back and forth as he shook his head.

"To each their own."

"I'll leave you to it, then. Personally, I have a scintillating tome on daemonic chemistry from the second age awaiting me at the den. Ping me if you need anything."

"I've got you loud and clear. Thanks for steering me in the right direction."

Azimuth nodded and then ported away.

Nadir took a deep breath, casting her gaze around the glen. The undeniable energy of the god-touched was still present.

"And despite knowing I should drop my curiosity, I just don't want to leave Erin without support," Nadir whispered. "What's the harm if no one finds out?"

Sniffing the night air, Nadir took off at a jog in the direction Erin had gone, which was back toward the city.

A daemon summoner talking to and befriending a god-touched crossed no lines. Erin did not know Nadir was more than a summoner, and no one else would know either.

CHAPTER 24

BLAINE

Blaine stood, unmoving, as the wild woman was escorted into his office by Jake and a nearly stumbling Daniel, who was sporting a fresh bruise above his right ear. Blaine sighed. This week hadn't been Daniel's strongest performance.

He turned his attention back to the woman. Most newcomers would stare in awe at his lush furnishings; the sumptuous surroundings were a reminder of his power and prestige within the city. Or perhaps they'd walk up to the floor-to-ceiling windows, breathless, and take in his singular view of the city framed by the Rocky Mountain foothills.

Her gaze paid no attention to the room, the view, or his wealth. She looked only at him as she stalked into the chamber like a panther scrutinizing her prey, oblivious to all else.

Sudden recognition flooded Blaine's senses. A hair-raising tingle swept across his skin, down his back, and to the tips of his toes. Power emanated from her, and he could swear the ground beneath her trembled with every step she took.

This was the woman from his dream, the one who'd danced with satyrs and nymphs and howled at the moon with abandon. Her raw animal magnetism struck a chord deep within him.

She was trouble with a capital T.

"Miss Erin Bevin, Sir," Jake announced the newcomer. "This is Mayor Blaine York." Jake motioned to a couch across the room from Blaine's desk. "Would you care to take a seat?"

Erin ignored the offer, choosing instead to stand. "I'm good."

Blaine paused. Did she remember him from the bacchanal dream as well? Based on her lack of overt reaction, she might not. Perhaps the gods had given him the dream as a warning? Or a promise? Blaine shook his head.

"May I fetch you some water, tea, or coffee?" Jake asked, his brow knit in confusion. No doubt he was also trying to figure out this interloper.

She held up a half-drunk bottle of wine. "I'm all set, thanks."

Erin's entire demeanor oozed confidence, despite the clear juxtaposition in power. The newcomer wildling wasn't fazed. Her simple black dress and heels complemented her athletic frame. Her mop of short, blonde hair appeared as if she'd dried it in a wind tunnel, reminiscent of a lion's mane. The natural pink flushing of her lips and cheeks looked like she'd been exerting herself. Did they flush like that in the throes of passion?

Blaine's gaze drifted downwards as Zeus' appreciation for the newcomer's physique stole into his mind. Her breasts, barely contained by the flimsy black dress, stirred an ache within him. Zeus saw Erin as a wild beast in need of taming, though her lithe form held an undeniable appeal. Blaine sensed his deity's primal desire to conquer and subdue her indomitable spirit, to bring the defiant woman to heel. With effort, Blaine wrested control of his wayward thoughts back from the god, mentally chiding Zeus' baser instincts. This was no mindless nymph for Zeus' pleasure; Erin was a force unto herself who would bend to no man. She'd been the one to deliver the blow to Daniel's temple. This woman was a force of nature.

"Thank you, Jake. You may leave us. Oh, and please arrange for Daniel to be seen by a doctor."

"Sir?" Jake, no doubt unsure by his boss's break from protocol, hesitated.

Blaine waved him off, and Jake demurred, exiting the room and closing the door behind him, guiding a pliant Daniel along with him.

Was it in his best interest to have Jake remain in case Erin got out of hand? Sure. Yet he wanted to be alone with this rare creature, so unlike the other god-touched he'd known.

"Welcome to Denver," Blaine said. "And thank you for meeting with me."

Erin barked out a laugh. "I had the impression this meeting wasn't optional."

Did she not understand his position in the city hierarchy? More curious than perturbed, Blaine crossed to the sofa and sat. "If you'd followed the standard practice of introducing yourself to the City Chief on your arrival, Daniel would not have brought you in."

"You'll have to forgive me; this is all pretty new to me." Erin joined him on the couch, claiming the far end. "And I'm not new to the city."

"And yet you are a new devotee in my city. Who is your mentor?"

"Mentor?" she replied, brows knit in confusion.

Her surprise appeared genuine, which flummoxed Blaine. "Your mentor would have inducted you into our order, instructed you how to revere your chosen deity, and guided your growth."

Amusement twinkled in her eyes. "Nope, no mentor for me. Dionysos spoke to me directly."

Blaine hesitated. Could she speak the truth? He'd heard of rare instances where the gods metaphorically called new devotees, but he'd never encountered one in person. No wonder she was a wildling. Further, one dedicated to the god of wine and madness. Could she be any more different from him? Fascination warred with his need to maintain order and control in his city. This woman would need to be finessed. He couldn't sanction her for not following protocols when she had been blind to the god-touched ways.

She took a drink from her bottle of wine, seemingly oblivious to his opinion. A drop of deep purple liquid hung on her lower lip a moment before her tongue snaked out to capture it.

Her uninhibited mannerisms captivated him. Yet he felt like a schoolboy, imagining how her lips tasted, fantasizing about laying a trail of kisses from her chin, up along her neck, to that ear that barely peeked out under her hairline.

He cleared his throat. "I'll assign a mentor for you," he replied. She raised a brow and huffed, and he held up a hand, requesting her patience. "Just someone who can assist you with navigating local protocols so you can achieve your and your benefactor's goals within the dictates of our city charter."

She opened her mouth to speak and then appeared to think better of it.

"Please, ask me anything." He should be focused on corralling this wilding, but Blaine couldn't help himself. The strategist in him needed to know what made Erin tick.

She set down her bottle and purse on his desk and crossed to the windows, taking in his office's expansive views.

Blaine rose and followed her. He couldn't take his eyes off her and the grape-vine sigils that covered her shoulders and her entire upper back. A chill ran down his spine. He'd seen no god-touched markings this extensive. Ever.

Just how powerful had Dionysos made this devotee?

"After Daniel's behavior, I'd expected a battle with you."

And you still might get it, wildling. "My apologies. He will be dealt with accordingly. The devotees of Ares aren't known for their tact."

Erin burst out laughing, a melodious sound he could listen to all day long. "I tried to beat some into him, but I don't think that's how that works."

Blaine shook his head. "I can assure you, your message landed squarely within his vocabulary."

She laughed harder.

"There are certain protocols. All god-touched follow. As you lacked a mentor to explain things, I'll hit the highlights for you."

"I'd be much obliged, but I have to warn you, I'm not one for rules."

"I understand the call of your god is a powerful force.

However, we need to work in harmony for the good of the city."

She raised a brow. "You mean for the good of the corporate profits?"

"We could quibble about definitions all night," he replied, although he could think of other activities he'd prefer to engage her time with. "Now that you're one of us, you need to know the expectations your peers will hold you to. And if you refuse to abide by the protocols, be aware the city council can choose to expel you."

She harrumphed. "I'm quaking in my heels."

"First, you need to swear fealty to the mayor."

"You mean swear fealty to you?"

"Indeed," he replied.

Erin pursed her lips, her appraising gaze turning to him. "I mean, we just met. Can you give me a day to think about it?"

Blaine inclined his head. "I'll give you an entire week. If at the end of that week you refuse, then I will expect you to find another city to call home."

She arched a brow as she considered. "Fair enough. What other protocols?"

"I will not abide unsanctioned fighting. If you continue to brawl, then you won't be allowed to stay in Denver."

"You have sanctioned brawls?" she teased.

"I wouldn't say brawls, but there are circumstances when I approve of specific actions. For instance, when I sent Daniel out to find you tonight. He was authorized to use minimal force."

"I can assure you he didn't use any force," Erin replied.

Blaine liked her sense of humor, despite her coy irreverence.

"Anything else?" she asked.

"Your mentor will fill you in on the rest," he replied.

"Who's your deity?"

He held up the back of his hand, pulling the sleeve of his shirt up to reveal the golden thunderbolts on the back of his hand and forearm. "Zeus."

Realization dawned in her eyes, a charming sparkle in her eyes. "Oh, he's the father of the gods. No wonder you're in charge."

He didn't bother to explain that being a devotee of Zeus wasn't the determining factor of his status. Blaine ruled the city and led the city council because he was the strongest god-touched in Denver.

His gaze caught on Erin, and the realization struck him. Was he still the strongest? If Daniel's description of their fight was to be believed, and if her markings and that bacchanal had been real, perhaps he wasn't anymore. The thought chilled him to the bone, but he forced his face to still, lest he reveal his thoughts. This was a woman he could lose his mayorship to.

Hopefully, the young maenad's interests were partying and drinking wine, not running the city council and planning budgets.

Blaine shrugged, helpless to return her smile. "I've been the Chief of Denver for nearly a decade, and under my rule, we've grown and prospered into the strongest economy throughout the S-Mart Division."

Anger flashed in Erin's eyes. "There's more to prosperity

than money for the Corporations. The people of this city are hungry and suffering."

He should have expected the wildling would be a humanitarian, unaware of the bigger picture. "If you'd traveled to other cities, you'd appreciate how well the people have it here. They may not live in luxury, but they don't starve."

"My mother died in a factory accident a few years ago," Erin replied, her voice brimming with emotion. "And hunger is common in this city of yours."

No wonder her focus was on protecting the people. Blaine wanted to reach out to her, comfort her, but held himself back. He needed to bring her to heel. "How unfortunate. My condolences for your loss."

She sighed and stared out over the city. "I doubt you've ever had to worry about a loved one surviving another week in the factories."

They stood in tense silence, Blaine carefully considering how to respond. He could see the fire in Erin's eyes, the conviction that drove her maenadic spirit. She would not be easily placated with platitudes or half-truths. If he hoped to bring her into the fold, he would need to tread carefully.

"You're right, I haven't suffered such hardships personally," he began. "But I am not blind to the struggles many in this city face. The path we walk is narrow; we must balance the needs of the people with the demands of the Corporations who enable our prosperity."

Erin scoffed. "Some prosperity, when children go hungry and workers die from unsafe conditions."

Blaine raised a hand placatingly. "I understand your passion. But railing against the system will not create the change you seek. There are always improvements to be made, and I rely on voices like yours to illuminate where we have fallen short."

He paused, considering his next words. "Rome wasn't built in a day. But together, we can build something better, something lasting. It must be done thoughtfully, accounting for all perspectives. I know you want justice for the people now. With time and wisdom, we can make that dream a reality."

Erin's eyes blazed with an intensity that gave him pause. She would not be swayed by facile promises or incremental change. The mandate of her god compelled her to dismantle the status quo with reckless abandon.

Blaine knew he walked on a razor's edge. If he could not temper her fervor and channel it constructively, she would burn the entire city down in her crusade. He silently cursed Dionysos for unleashing this force of chaos into his orderly domain.

"I don't have time for pretty words, Blaine," Erin said sharply. "Either join me in bringing actual change or get out of my way."

Her bold challenge hung in the air between them. Blaine's mind raced, searching for the right response. The wild maenad had called his bluff, and he had no simple answers.

"What can I do to help you meet your goals?"

Erin turned to him, conviction plain in the set of her jaw. "I need a club."

"A dance club?" The city didn't need another locale to drink and dance, but what had he expected a maenad to ask for?

"Not exactly. Think of it more as a temple to Dionysos."

He nodded as if he understood. What would the city council do with this request?

"Do you have a location in mind? Perhaps something in the foothills outside the city?"

"No, I don't want it out in the boonies where no one can reach it. It's got to be centrally located, a place people can go to after work and recharge."

"There are some locations you might be able to acquire. Of course, the city council has to approve all new construction and financing within the city, but I'm sure we can find a solution that will fit your needs."

He had to manage her expectations and ensure this headstrong sprite of a girl didn't sideline his management of the city.

Erin pursed her lips and narrowed her eyes. "Show me."

"Show you what?"

"The potential building sites. C'mon, let's go for a ride." She pouted and flipped her hair.

Blaine had the distinct impression he was being manipulated but didn't see any harm in driving around the city with Erin.

He tapped his watch twice. "Jake, bring the car around."

"Right away, Sir," Jake's voice responded.

Blaine considered his options as Jake went to bring the car around. His first instinct was to pawn Erin off to Maria, let her take the wild maenad under her wing for a few weeks of orientation. Maria would educate Erin on how things were done among the god-touched and integrate her into the established order. Then again, Erin used to work for Maria at her company, Pythia. Putting the two of them together again would be asking for trouble on multiple fronts.

Yet the more Blaine contemplated it, the more he doubted the wisdom of that course. The other council members were jealous of his power. They would surely try to turn Erin against him, spin their honeyed lies to warp her perspective. No, he couldn't risk letting her out of his direct supervision, not when she had the potential to unseat him.

Better for him to take her under his own tutelage, keep the unpredictable maenad close so he could monitor her activities. With the right incentives, he could bend her boundless energy to serve his own ends. Perhaps in time, he could even seduce her, bind her to him, body and soul. The thought quickened his pulse. Yes, he would take a personal interest in her orientation to this new world. Erin was a force to be reckoned with, but Blaine was confident that with care and cunning, he could control and harness that force for his own benefit. The wildling would be clay in his hands soon enough.

CHAPTER 25

ERIN

The sumptuous leather glided like silk against the bare skin of her calves and thighs as Erin crossed her legs in the back of the Bentley. Because, of course, Blaine had a Bentley. What else would the mayor use to trundle around town?

"You're going to have to up your game, Blaine," Erin said. As he'd made his sales pitch, Blaine's winning smile and piercing blue gaze had sent shivers down her spine. His charm should be considered an illegal weapon, but she wasn't about to let him palm off subpar properties on her. "Show me something downtown," she demanded, and Blaine's face showed a flash of irritation before he softened his features. "I don't want to go all the way out to the suburbs or anything."

Blaine turned to face her, absently pulling on his shirt cuff, straightening the fit of the shirt across his broad chest. "I know you said no to the open plots on the outskirts of town, but I can assure you, there's virtually no available space left downtown. At least, unless you'd like to upgrade a retiring manufacturing plant?"

Erin's nose wrinkled. "That's an option?"

"Sure, there's usually some remediation of the land that's required, but I'm sure you understand these things always take time."

He'd repeated the mantra of time enough times. Erin understood that if she moved at his and the council's pace, it might be years before Dionysos' temple was built.

Blaine's trusty helper, Jake, had driven them around all night, the pace of his tour leisurely as they made a circuit of the city. They'd stopped at two locations so far, with Blaine making a show of talking about the potential benefits of each option. Did he genuinely want to help her, or was he just humoring her? It was almost as if Blaine took her request for club space seriously.

Almost.

As long as she waited a few years.

"Show me." She licked her lips. "Show me what you've got, Blaine."

He shifted uncomfortably in his seat. An electric thrill shot through Erin as, despite the obvious rein he was trying to keep on these negotiations, he responded to her flirtation. After a lifetime of being snubbed as poor and unempowered, the heady rush of sudden influence was going to her head. Even his pouty lower lip beckoned to her to slide across the seat and nibble it. She told herself she should back down from the seductive interplay with Mayor Blaine, but she didn't want to rein herself in. Images of the bacchanal replayed through her mind, a hunger to taste him flaring through her veins.

She knew the pre-god-touched Erin would have questioned her desire, would have advised caution when dealing with such an obviously powerful man who had the power to crush her dreams.

The Erin of today wanted a bite out of him, and she wasn't playing.

"Jake," Blaine said. "Can you swing us by Confluence Park?"

"Of course, sir," Jake replied. He glanced at Erin through the rear-view mirror, his expression unreadable.

Erin wondered if Jake ever said no to his boss. Did anyone say no to Blaine?

Blaine lived in a universe she'd never visited, nor even glimpsed, from the VIP section of Porters or the snazzy boardroom of Pythia. She slid her hand across the real wood inlay on the interior door frame. Is this how all god-touched lived, with cushy positions in city government and fat paychecks to match? She'd always wondered what kind of job someone had to have in order to afford the lifestyles she only saw in shows.

One thing was evident to Erin—Blaine saw her as a situation to be managed. But by the way his heated gaze lingered on the curves of her legs, there was something more going on under the surface. Yet by the confident look on his face, he believed he had her well in hand. Did he think she wouldn't guess at the layers of administration, red-tape, and bureaucracy he'd casually mentioned would have to be managed in order for Erin to have her temple to Dionysos?

With all his talk of waiting and time, Erin knew he'd delay her as long as he could. If she wanted to appease Dionysos, she had to take matters into her own hands.

Erin slid across into the middle seat, her body flush against his, aware of a sudden spike in body heat between them. The scent of his cologne filled her nostrils, and she felt her heart racing with anticipation. She wanted him, craved him, and didn't care about the risks. Blaine's gaze met her own, and she had the sudden impression that Blaine preferred the role of hunter to prey. Surely, as a man of his status, he'd become used to women flirting with him. Or did she unnerve him?

She crossed her legs, pressing her thighs against his. She leaned in and asked, in a breathy tone, "What's it like to work for Zeus?" while running the fingers of her left hand across his collar and down the buttons of his shirt.

He watched her movements without reciprocating or rebuffing her overt invitation, letting Erin absentmindedly play with the seam of his jacket.

He narrowed his gaze. "What do you mean?"

Was he oblivious to her efforts? Had serving Zeus made him into a man of stone? Recalling the tales of legend she'd read in her youth, Zeus was known as a womanizer. How did the mayor compare to his revered deity?

Surely, he wasn't celibate.

Erin pressed on, pulling his jacket, drawing him ever closer, so the next words she spoke fanned against his cheek, as if she were whispering a secret to a close friend. "What's the father of the gods like? I'd imagine he's the demanding sort."

Blaine chuckled and then shook his head. "As one would predictably expect, of course he is. But then, all the gods are in their own ways." He shifted in his seat, as if to create more space between them, but moved against her most deliciously. "I have a theory about the god-devotee dynamic."

Erin didn't doubt he did. Her curiosity to understand his

theory warred with her desire for Blaine's touch. This man read as a consummate game player who had a theory for everything. She'd even bet he had a printed playbook for every scenario. She felt the corner of her mouth curl, noticing how his eyes were drawn to it before slowly returning to her eyes. "Which is?"

"Gods are demanding, most definitely, but only in proportion to our objectives. Those of us who expect glorious rewards from our devotion to the gods must deliver the commensurate sacrifices and offerings."

Erin wondered what sacrifices Blaine had made. What offerings he had given to the gods. Had he ever given himself over completely to the divine?

"Tell me," she asked, her voice husky with desire. "What kind of sacrifices have you made?"

Blaine's eyes flashed with a sudden intensity, and Erin felt her body respond to the heat in his gaze. She could tell he was pondering her question, weighing his words before he spoke. "I've given up things that most people would consider essential," he drawled. "Things like time, money, personal relationships. I've devoted myself completely to the service of the gods, and in return, Zeus has granted me power and influence beyond what I ever could have dreamed."

Erin felt a thrill run through her at his words, imagining the sway she could wield in this city as a devotee of Dionysos. But she was also suddenly aware of the danger inherent in such a path, the risks she would have to take to achieve her goals. She wondered if Blaine had ever felt that fear, if he had ever doubted his own devotion to the gods.

From the conviction in his gaze, Erin doubted Blaine was

the type to do anything half-heartedly or falter in his convictions.

Blaine's eyes darkened, and he leaned in closer to her, his lips lightly brushing against her ear as he spoke. "If you want something, sacrifice for it. Are you willing to make the necessary sacrifices, Erin?"

Erin didn't hesitate. "Yes," she whispered back. "I'll do whatever it takes." She'd take on the city council, starting with the mayor himself, to bring relief to this city. She'd take them all on, burning their rules and regulations to the ground, starting with Blaine.

Blaine's lips curled into a sly smile. "Good girl." He reached for her, his hands gripping her waist as he pulled her in for a searing kiss. Erin moaned against his lips, her body responding eagerly as he deepened the kiss, his tongue exploring her mouth. She felt the heat between them growing, and she knew that this was just the beginning of a dangerous and exhilarating game.

As their lips parted, Blaine's hands wandered, his fingers tracing the curves of her body, igniting a fire within her. He pulled back slightly, looking into her eyes with a hunger that mirrored her own. "I can give you what you want, Erin," he murmured. "But you have to be willing to pay the price."

Erin nodded, her breath coming in quick gasps. "I'll do whatever it takes," she repeated, unable to deny the desire coursing through her veins. "Just tell me what I need to do."

Blaine's smile was wicked as he leaned in, his lips brushing against her ear. "Swear fealty to me in front of the council," he whispered. "That will leave no doubt in anyone's mind about your commitment."

Erin's heart stuttered, a defiant streak roaring to life in the back of her mind. Did he actually think she'd cave into his demands if he got her hot and bothered? The conviction that she'd never bow to him rolled over Erin, although Erin wasn't sure why. It was Blaine's city, which she didn't even want. Just the club.

Two could play at this game.

"Once I swear to you, then I can have my club?"

His lips ran along her neck, a whisper of stubble rasping against her skin.

"Yes," he murmured. "You can have your club." He planted a kiss at the hollow of her throat. "Once you prove your loyalty to me, you can have that and so much more."

Erin's mind was racing, her resolve faltering. She wanted the club more than anything, but not at this cost. She still might give in one day, but today was not that day. She knew this was a dangerous game, but she couldn't help the thrill that ran through her. She would do whatever it took to get what she wanted, including negotiating with this tempting man.

"Okay," she said, her voice barely above a whisper.

Blaine pulled back, his eyes glittering with satisfaction. "Good," he said. "I'll arrange everything."

Erin's stomach clenched as she realized the gravity of what she had just started. She knew there would be no going back once she had sworn her loyalty to Blaine, which was why she'd delay the act as long as possible. But with the club in her possession, she would risk Blaine's wrath by leading him to think she was on board with his plans.

Blaine leaned in for another kiss, his hands sliding up her body. Erin let herself get lost in the sensation, knowing that this was just the beginning of a dangerous and intoxicating journey.

The kiss was slow, as if Blaine was in no rush to leave her lips. Erin was quickly losing her sense of self, the heat between them rising with each passing second. She couldn't deny the way Blaine made her feel wanted and desired. But she also couldn't ignore the nagging voice in the back of her mind that whispered warnings of danger. She was playing with lightning, and while Erin knew that would have once slowed her down, now the risk only inflamed her desire.

As they pulled away, Erin's eyes met Blaine's, and she saw a flicker of something dark and dangerous in his gaze. She wondered just how far he would go to achieve his goals, but then Erin realized the answer was clear, causing a chill to play across her skin. Blaine hadn't made it this far by committing halfway. He'd accept nothing but a clear submission to his authority.

Blaine sensed her hesitation and leaned in closer, his lips brushing against her ear. "You have nothing to fear, Erin," he whispered. "I'm a fair and even-handed leader of the council. Imagine what we can accomplish by working together."

Erin shuddered, a mix of fear and desire coursing through her. She knew Blaine was dangerous, but she also knew that she would take that risk for what she wanted and for the task Dionysos had charged her with.

Blaine's hand trailed down her body, the rough material of his jacket scraping against her skin. "You're so beautiful," he murmured, his lips trailing along her collarbone.

Aware she was seducing the most influential man in the state, the power rushed to her head. The idea only lasted a minute before crashing headlong toward the realization that this might be a common occurrence for him.

Erin couldn't help but ask, "Is this your usual method of negotiation?"

Blaine laughed, a low and throaty sound that sent shivers down her spine. He pulled away and smiled, a knowing glint in his eyes as his hands traveled up to cup her face. "No Erin," he replied, his voice thick with desire. "This isn't my *usual method*. Besides, you're the one doing the seducing here, right on cue, I might add." His gaze burned into hers as if challenging her to deny it, but Erin knew she couldn't. He had expected her response, and she realized he had pretended to go along with her the entire time.

Erin's heart sank as she realized that she had fallen right into Blaine's trap. She had thought she was in control, but now she saw she was merely a pawn in his game. Blaine was a skilled player, and she had underestimated him. She couldn't deny the attraction she felt for Blaine, but she also knew that it was dangerous to let him get too close.

Erin paused, a wave of confusion washing over her. Ever since Dionysos had awakened the maenad within her, it was as if a dam had burst inside, unleashing impulses and desires she could no longer control. The old Erin, the one who had struggled and scraped to survive in this oppressive system, would never have acted so brazenly or recklessly. But that Erin was gone, transformed into something wilder, something more vicious, seductive, and violent.

Dimly, Erin understood her rage at the injustice in this city remained, but it had warped into a dangerous hunger to punish without thought for human cost. She was no longer bound by human morality or reason. The maenad cared only for satiating her desires, whatever form they took.

Erin shuddered, a small part of her human heart grieving for the loss of who she had been. But the grief quickly faded beneath the maenad's ravenous appetite. She would do whatever it took to gain the upper hand over Blaine, to make him submit to her desires. Even if it meant playing along in his twisted game—for now.

But Erin wasn't one to give up easily. She would take what she wanted from Blaine, by force, if necessary. And she would tear down the rotting foundations of this city to clear the way for Dionysos' new order. The old Erin may have balked at such violence, but the maenad would not hesitate to unleash chaos.

She leaned in, her lips brushing against his ear. "You think you have me all figured out, Blaine," she whispered, her voice low and sultry. "But you have no idea what I'm capable of."

Blaine's eyes widened, before his expression shifted into a sly smile. "I like a woman who knows what she wants," he said, his hand sliding down her back. "But make no mistake, Erin. You may be a maenad, but I'm the one in control here."

Anger flared within Erin. She pushed him away, eyes flashing. "We'll see about that!"

Blaine reached for her, but paused, his gaze turning inward. Erin watched him warily, simmering with frustration. How dare he imply she was just some wild woman to be tamed? She was a force of nature, beholden to no man.

Yet even in her fury, she felt the gravitational pull between them. Try as she might, she could not deny the forbidden attraction.

Blaine's eyes refocused on her, his expression cautious. Erin searched those azure depths, wondering if he felt as conflicted as she.

"What was that about?" Erin asked sharply.

Blaine measured his words before responding. "Zeus offered some counsel on dealing with your impulsive nature."

Erin bristled. "Did he now? And what advice did the philandering god so generously provide?"

Blaine held her gaze. "He suggested a light hand. That brute force will only provoke you further."

Though his tone was even, Erin sensed Blaine's caution. Clearly, Zeus' words had resonated.

Erin moved closer, eyes blazing. "I don't need to be handled, or tamed, or controlled."

"Nor would I attempt to," Blaine replied calmly. "But you cannot deny there are forces at work here, beyond our comprehension." His voice lowered. "Forces that compel us, against all reason."

Erin knew he spoke the truth. This magnetic draw felt ordained by providence, not born of earthly desire. They were two stars locked in orbit, powerless to break free.

Before she could think better of it, Erin pulled Blaine into a searing kiss. As their lips met, she understood this moment would forever change them both. Whatever came next, they could not emerge from this collision untouched.

CHAPTER 26

ERIN

The sound of Jake clearing his throat rocked them out of their reverie as the car came to a full stop. "We've arrived at the Confluence Park remediation location, sir," he said.

At the reminder that they weren't alone, and the look of embarrassment from Blaine, Erin peeled herself off him and moved back to the other seat. Blaine ran a quick hand through his hair and straightened his tie, looking as dazed as Erin felt. Who'd been playing whom just now? Erin felt a pang of guilt for giving in to her desires with Blaine, knowing that their mutual attraction was a distraction from her bigger picture.

Determined to keep her focus on Dionysos' demands, Erin took a deep breath, trying to regain her composure as she distracted herself by looking out the window.

The park was a desolate wasteland of rubble and debris, a reminder of the council's neglect and corruption. The once pristine grass was patchy, littered with trash and debris. An emaciated trickle of a river wound its way around one side of the plot, as aimless as the fallen concrete structures that had once been bridge pilings. Erin couldn't help but feel a deep sense of sadness at the current state of the lot. It was a stark reminder of what Blaine and his cronies were capable of—neglecting the beauty of the land in order to line their pockets.

"I know it's not an ideal location, but it meets your location requirement to be central and after a period of remediation and some improvements, I trust you can transform it into a fitting temple to Dionysos."

Erin fumed in his general direction. "It looks little better than a dung heap, Blaine," she replied, saying his name like a curse. "Do you treat all the god-touched with such disrespect?"

There was a long pause before he answered, during which Erin didn't even look in his direction. "Although I serve Zeus, I respect all gods and would never seek to deny them appropriate tribute. If you give me some more time, I'm sure I can compile a comprehensive list of options suitable for your god's needs."

Erin paused, almost swayed by Blaine's sincerity. But she knew how the mayor and his cronies on the council treated those they deemed inferior.

As they surveyed the damaged park, despair washed over Erin. The people of this city deserved so much better. If she waited for the slow wheels of government, it could be years before progress was made.

The people needed food, clean water, and safe shelters now. Kids suffered daily in the decrepit schools, while their parents waste away in unsafe factories. It can't continue.

Erin dreamed of a new society where people supported

each other, living in prospering, self-sustaining communities. She envisioned communal centers providing education, healthcare, childcare, and recreation. Everyone would contribute what they could and take what they needed.

She wanted to create an oasis here in this broken place. A sanctuary where people could gather, share ideas and resources. A beacon of hope, reminding them that, through cooperation and compassion, a better world was possible.

Erin knew the current system was rotten, propping up the elite while the rest toiled and suffered. She would tear it down and build anew, a society founded on justice, equity and care for one's fellow beings. It would not come easily, but she had faith in the people, once awakened.

The club she planned was just the beginning, a place for Dionysian ecstasy, yes, but also strategizing the revolution ahead. The people would rise up and a new day would dawn.

Erin opened the door and jumped out of the Bentley, striding confidently across the broken sidewalk and up onto a mound of trash, weeds, and broken dreams.

Erin's anger surged within her, a fiery torrent fueled by the injustices she had witnessed and the knowledge that Blaine's hollow promises would only delay her god-given mission. The maenad magic blossomed within her, as though Dionysos himself was calling upon her to act. Her heart pounded as she stood atop the mound, the wind whipping her hair around her face like a tempest.

Blaine stepped out of the car, annoyance etched across his features as he watched Erin. His man, Jake, was right there by his side, determination in every movement. "Erin, what are you doing?" Blaine called out, his voice barely audible over the wind. "Crime is horrible in this part of town at night. You're not safe out here."

Erin didn't respond to him. Instead, she raised her arms to the sky, an instinctive resonance, the call of the gods guiding her movements, as she called upon the power of Dionysos to transform the desolation before her into a place of beauty and worship. She could feel the raw energy coursing through her veins, igniting her soul with the divine power of the god.

"Erin, stop!" Blaine's shout reached her ears, but it was too late. She could feel the ground beneath her feet trembling, a deep rumble that grew louder and stronger with each passing second. Mesmerized, she watched as the ground cracked open, and twisted, green vines emerged from beneath it. Ivy crawled its way up from each split in the earth. The vines rapidly consumed the trash and debris, weaving them together with the unstoppable force of nature. She could sense Dionysos' presence and power in the transformation, and knew that she was an instrument of his will.

As the vines continued their relentless growth, they began to take shape, forming the foundation of a temple that seemed to rise out of the very ground itself. Majestic columns emerged, adorned with intricate carvings that depicted the revelries and ceremonies of Dionysos. The walls of the temple were formed from a combination of earth, stone, and the remnants of the trash, magically transmuted into an ornate and stunning structure.

The desolate, abandoned landscape was transformed into a lush oasis as plants and flowers sprouted from the ground, filling the air with a heady perfume. The once-pitiful river swelled and surged, its waters crystal clear and teeming with life.

As the temple took shape before her, Erin glanced at Blaine and saw him standing dumbstruck. The awe and fear in his eyes were a testament to the power she had just unleashed. She couldn't help but wonder if she was the only one who had ever seen fear lurking behind the mask of power he wore. Her maenad magic had proven to be an unstoppable force, and she reveled knowing that she had defied the mayor and his underhanded tactics.

When the transformation was complete, she lowered her arms, her chest heaving from the effort. Turning to face Blaine, her eyes blazed with determination. "This is what the people deserve, Blaine," she said, her voice unwavering. "A place to worship Dionysos, free from the corruption and greed that has plagued this city for far too long."

For once, Blaine was at a loss for words. She could see in his expression that he had underestimated her and the power she possessed. In that moment, she knew that he finally understood he could no longer stand in her way.

Blaine swallowed hard, the fear in his eyes giving way to grudging respect for her display of power. "I must admit, Erin, that was impressive," he said, though his voice held a note of warning. "But you should know that neither I nor the council will not take kindly to such willful acts."

Erin felt a surge of satisfaction. Her actions had earned her the respect her words never could. She knew that the balance of power between them had shifted, and she could see that Blaine recognized it too. His expression hardened as he seemed to view her actions as a direct challenge to his authority as mayor.

"I understand the risks," Erin replied, her voice resolute. "But sometimes, we need to take a stand for what is right, even if it means going against the established order."

Blaine clenched his jaw, his eyes narrowing. "Don't think that your newfound power gives you free rein to challenge me, Erin," he warned. "As mayor, it's my duty to maintain order in this city, and I won't let anyone undermine that, not even you."

Erin met his gaze, unflinching. "My only intention is to serve Dionysos and create a better future for the people of this city," she said, her voice strong and unwavering. "If that means challenging those who stand in the way of progress, then so be it."

For a moment, they stared each other down, the tension between them palpable. Though Blaine was clearly not about to let her one-up him, Erin knew she had gained a measure of power in their dynamic, and she was determined to use it to the fullest.

CHAPTER 27

BLAINE

Blaine entered the council chamber, his body weighed down by the exhaustion of dealing with the day's events. The room was lit by sconces full of flickering candles that cast eerie shadows onto the faces of the assembled council members. The scent of incense hung in the air, a mix of sweet and bitter notes that mirrored the personalities of those present.

Not everyone was in attendance, but the council members who'd arrived at this late session sat in their respective positions, their countenance reflecting their patron deities. Maria, the devotee of Apollo, sat poised and calculating, her sharp eyes gleaming with shrewd intelligence. Daniel, the Ares devotee, appeared restless and confrontational, his aggressive energy barely contained. Sophia, a devotee of Athena, exuded wisdom and seemed somewhat aloof, her gaze penetrating and assessing. Layla, the Anubis devotee, looked cryptic, her dark eyes focused on the balance between life and death.

Xavier, the chairman of the council, cleared his throat to draw everyone's attention. "Blaine, we have gathered to hear your report on the recent developments with Erin Bevin and her unusual activities." His voice was firm, and his expression suggested he would not tolerate any disturbances.

Blaine took a deep breath, feeling the heavy gazes of the council members upon him. "As you may have heard, Erin has displayed a new ability. She has summoned a club from the earth itself. The club is filled with an energy that speaks to her connection with Dionysos."

Maria leaned forward, a smirk playing on her lips. "How fascinating, Mayor Blaine. It appears that our little Erin is proving to be quite the troublemaker. I must say, I'm surprised you couldn't prevent her from creating such a spectacle. Are you losing your touch, dear Blaine?" Her words dripped with condescension, and Blaine felt a pang of irritation.

Daniel, unable to resist the scent of conflict, jumped into the fray. "Indeed, Blaine, it seems as if you're struggling to maintain control over your city. Perhaps it's time we reconsidered our leadership?" The Ares devotee's voice was harsh and taunting, and Blaine gritted his teeth to hold back a retort.

"These sentiments serve little useful purpose," Xavier said, his voice booming with authority befitting his patron, Hades, lord of the underworld. Xavier's sleeve shifted to reveal an inky black marking of Cerberus on his forearm, the three-headed hound guarding the gates of Hades' domain.

When she spoke, Sophia's voice was calm and analytical, reflecting the wisdom of Athena. An olive branch adorned the back of both of her hands, symbol of the goddess of warfare and crafts. "We must take this development seriously, Blaine. While we understand the challenges you face, it is your responsibility to ensure the city remains secure."

Layla's voice was low and steady, her kohl-rimmed eyes never leaving Blaine's face. As a devotee of Anubis, she served the jackal-headed god who guided souls to the afterlife. The scales of justice marked the front of her throat, representing Anubis' role in weighing hearts to judge the fate of the dead. "We cannot afford to let chaos reign unchecked. Erin's actions may have unforeseen consequences that could threaten the delicate balance we maintain."

As Blaine absorbed their words, he felt the weight of their expectations bearing down on him. He knew he would need to navigate their competing self-interests carefully to maintain control over both the city and the council.

Taking a deep breath, Blaine gathered his thoughts, preparing to address their concerns. He knew the path ahead with Erin would be fraught with unpredictable challenges. His mind raced as he considered how to appease the council without divulging his own growing connection with the defiant maenad.

Steeling himself, Blaine squared his shoulders and met their scrutinizing gazes. He would need to tread delicately, but he was confident he could convince them of his capability to handle the volatile situation. With poise and tact, he would assure the council members that the city remained secure under his leadership, despite Erin's disruptive abilities.

"Despite Erin's display, I assure you that the city remains under control. I am confident that I can handle this situation and maintain the stability we all desire. It is my belief that

Erin's abilities can be harnessed to benefit our city, rather than pose a threat," he stated firmly.

Maria's eyes narrowed, her dissatisfaction clear. "You seem awfully sure of yourself, Blaine. But we will keep a close watch on both you and Erin. If you cannot keep the city in check, we will not hesitate to take matters into our own hands."

Daniel seized the opportunity to mock Blaine further. "Yes, Mayor Blaine, you'd better keep your new little plaything in line, or we'll have no choice but to deal with her ourselves." He sneered, his voice dripping with disdain.

"You just want control of the city for yourself, Maria," Daniel accused, his eyes narrowing. "You don't fool me with your supposed concern about the safety of our citizens!"

Maria scoffed, her expression haughty. "As if you're any better, Daniel. You're always pushing for more police spending, just so you can flex your muscles."

Helena interjected, her voice dripping with disdain. "You two are like bickering children. It's pathetic. Everyone knows you're the one who's flexing his muscles all the time," she said to Ares.

Sophia rolled her eyes. "Oh, please. You're one to talk, Helena. You just want more funding for your family planning centers. As if our tax base can afford it."

Blaine's jaw clenched at the devotee's words, but he maintained his composure. Leaning back in his chair, arms crossed, he observed as the council members descended into heated bickering. Their petty infighting over power and influence was nothing new to Blaine. He'd always accepted it as the norm among the god-touched elite.

Yet now, hearing Erin's impassioned accusations against

the council's corruption, he found himself questioning things. Was this interminable political maneuvering and selfish agenda-pushing truly necessary? Erin had opened his eyes to the suffering of the common people, obscured by the council's endless power plays. For the first time, Blaine wondered if there could be another way to govern, one that put people over politics. One that sought harmony rather than dominance.

Erin's perspective gave him pause. Perhaps they had lost their way, becoming so consumed by partisan conflicts that they neglected their larger purpose. Watching the devotees snipe and undermine each other, Blaine felt the stirrings of doubt take root within him. Things needed to change, but affecting real reform would be no simple task. Still, inspired by Erin's conviction, he resolved to find a better path forward for the city.

In response to the council's rising tension, Xavier intervened. "Enough!" he barked, his voice like thunder in the confined space. "We are here to discuss the matter at hand, not to engage in petty squabbles." The council members fell silent, chastened by their chairman's rebuke.

The room grew tense as they stared one another down, their disagreements simmering beneath the surface. Blaine felt exhaustion creeping up on him as he tried to navigate the web of politics and intrigue. It was then that Xavier's voice rang out again, this time with a warning.

"If I must intervene again, there will be penalties," he threatened, his gaze sweeping across the council members. "Now, Blaine, what measures do you propose to address the situation with Erin and her club?"

Blaine hesitated for a moment, weighing his words. "I

will speak with Erin and discuss her intentions with the club. Together, we can find a way to use her abilities to benefit the city while ensuring that her influence does not lead to chaos. I ask for your patience and trust as I navigate this delicate situation."

The council members exchanged wary glances, but they seemed to accept Blaine's proposal reluctantly for the time being. As the meeting drew to a close, Blaine couldn't help but feel a mix of relief and trepidation. He knew he would need to tread carefully in the coming days, balancing his responsibility to the city and his growing connection with Erin.

With a heavy heart, he left the council chamber and made his way through the dimly lit corridors, the weight of his role as mayor and the council's expectations pressing down on him. As the door closed behind him, the scent of incense still lingered, a reminder of the challenges that lay ahead.

Blaine stepped out of the council building, the cool evening air a welcome respite from the stifling atmosphere within. As he made his way toward his car, he couldn't help but ponder the state of the council and the city. He realized that the corruption Erin had spoken of was more pervasive than he had initially believed. The council's petty squabbles and power plays now seemed more threatening to destabilize the delicate balance that he had worked so hard to maintain.

When he reached his vehicle, Jake, his loyal butler, stood before him with a concerned expression as he held the door open. "Sir, are you alright? You seem troubled."

Blaine slid into the car and sighed, rubbing his temples.

"It's the council, Jake. I can't help but wonder if I've been too complacent, too blind to the problems right in front of me."

Jake's expression softened, and he smiled ruefully before taking a seat behind the wheel. "You've done a lot of good for this city, sir. It's easy to lose sight of the bigger picture when you're caught up in the day-to-day responsibilities of your position."

Blaine nodded. "Erin really opened my eyes to what the people are going through. I can't keep ignoring how much the council takes advantage while folks struggle. Seeing Erin's fire and dedication lit a spark in me, too. I've got to clean up the corruption and help the city's most vulnerable."

Jake's eyes glimmered with determination in the rearview mirror. "I believe in you, sir. You've always proven a powerful leader. I have faith you will figure this out."

As Jake drove, Blaine thought about his new sense of purpose. Erin had ripped off the blinders, showing him how unjust things had become for the citizens he'd sworn to serve. Her spirit awakened his own conscience and duty. He could no longer excuse the council's greed and neglect. The people deserved better. With Erin at his back, Blaine felt sure he could cut out the rot and put the city on a just path again. The maenad had shifted his perspective, and he refused to waste this chance to cause genuine change.

As Blaine entered his home, his resolve strengthened. He would confront the corruption that festered within the council, no matter the cost. And as he contemplated the future, he couldn't help but feel a strange sense of hope. For amid the chaos and uncertainty, he had found something–someone– worth fighting for.

The night was still young, and the city's heartbeat thrummed in his ears, a constant reminder of his duty and the challenges that lay ahead. But for now, Blaine took solace in knowing that he was not alone in his struggle. Together, he and Erin might overcome the darkness and bring light to the city that they both loved.

CHAPTER 28

ORIAS

Orias and Kobol sat at a table in Blood and Stone, Orias drinking a sour ale while Kobol stuck to his whiskey, neat. For a Sheol establishment, the range of options were varied. Orias had once sampled an ethereal flight of fermented tree saps which had sent his visions into a nonstop hallucinogenic-fueled journey for four nights straight. Now, he stuck to the well-known daemon beer. He had more than enough visions without deliberately kick-starting the process.

The sound of the fighting pits carried as a pair of lizard-skinned siblings fought out their bicker of the day. The assembled crowd goaded them on, filling the establishment with a din of cheers and growls. The air was thick with a mixture of incense, sweat, and smoke from the candles. Or was it drugs?

It was a perfect location for private conversation away from the cabal den. And from Belial, who would never have stepped foot in this place, which he would deem too sordid for the likes of his princely rank.

"What do you think of Nadir's concerns over the sancre?" Kobol asked, downing his whiskey all at once.

Orias sank back into a golden plush pillow, pressing it against the blackened stone which served as a rough-hewn bench. The gold triggered his memory of those Aurelian-irised eyes from his visions. He stretched his shoulders, trying to shake off the reflexive tension which built every time he thought of those eyes.

"I feel her concerns are warranted, but it's difficult to judge the full scope of the issue." Orias sipped at his ale, noticing casually how his ever-present shadows moved just over the surface of his skin. One wisp wrapped itself around his mug, as if sampling the contents before swirling back into the others moving around his hand.

"Belial should have told us of their capabilities before sending us out blind," Kobol slammed his now empty glass down upon the tabletop, the wood echoing the impact.

The bar owner, a fire-breathing daemon known as Brekesh, raised an eyebrow their way, amber eyes flaring. Orias smiled and tapped the table, asking for a refill. Brekesh nodded and poured another round, but his eyes continued to simmer.

"Belial rarely informs us beforehand of his motives or plans. Wishing for him to change is a fruitless quest," Orias said.

A slender waiter wearing a transparent, gauzy dress silently drifted over to them and delivered their drinks, sauntering away without uttering a word.

"I'm free to want what I want," Kobol growled. "However pointless I have learned it to be in the *mere* forty years I've served the prince."

Orias barked out a laugh. "That you are. Yet a more productive inquiry might be to determine how accurate Nadir's concerns are."

"You mean figure out how deep the rabbit hole of familial kills goes? What do you propose, lining up ten generations of a cabal and seeing how many of them die in succession?" Kobol's brows knit as he drew a metaphorical diagram of stick figures on the table in whiskey, and then tapped each one in quick succession.

"It's an option. I'm surprised Belial himself hasn't requested. There must be a limit to the scope, or else the moment we first used the sancres, we would have heard of an Arch-daemon or prince mysteriously dying."

"I suppose you've got a point," Kobol replied.

"As do you. The next time we're clearing out a large nest, it'll be wise to pay attention to how the sancre kills ripple through the herd."

"At some point, our efforts will be noticed, and Belial will risk his plan being exposed." Kobol sipped his drink, tapping the glass absently.

Orias nodded, shrugging his shoulders. "I feel that time is far off. I suspect Nadir's issues revolve around her being newly bound to both Belial and the cabal. The other concerns are simply adding insult to the existing fresh injury."

Without warning, Orias' shadows leaped into a frenetic state of activity, churning and enveloping him in seconds such that they blocked out his vision to all else. Orias breathed deep, reminding himself to remain calm and centered despite the sudden blackout and his concern over how the other bar patrons might react.

Daemons didn't respond calmly to sudden changes. He'd have to rely on Kobol to manage the situation.

If only he held absolute control of the shadows, then his life would be so much easier.

A familiar sensation of gravity shift preceded the sense of weightless melding with the universe, as if his mind was floating and expanding into the ether. It was powerfully unnerving; he'd never had a vision hit so hard and fast, and with so little build up or warning.

Through the black fog surrounding him, colors coalesced and sharpened into focus. Again, he looked upon an unremarkable moonlit forest glen. Tall lodgepole pines, the wind whispering through the treetops, and the trickle of a creek in the distance.

The forest lived and breathed, the picture of serenity. Curiosity and anticipation roiled in his gut.

As if in response to Orias's anxiety, a snapping, rending sound cut through the air, as if the fabric of reality itself was being torn asunder. A glow of stars appeared on the ground, reminding Orias of a child's sparkler. A column of stars burned upwards some twelve plus feet, before arcing left five or six feet, and then seared a matching line back down to the ground. Once the flame touched down, a brilliant shockwave of light rippled out from the arch, an opening filled with a murky black substance devoid of all color.

This was the gateway he'd glimpsed in his prior vision. The opening process played out in grim detail. A shiver ran down his spine. Orias could not take his eyes off the star-studded, inky portal. The forest held its breath with him.

After some minutes, the blackened surface rippled, pulsated, and broke over golden skin.

A second shockwave hit him like a hammer, and the vision ended as abruptly as it had begun. Orias gasped for breath, clutching the table before him so hard his fingers dug grooves into the surface. His shadows retreated and Orias' vision cleared, revealing Kobol standing up, facing off against an interested gathering of daemons of all kinds.

Elder Ranna sat across from Orias, attention rapt, eyes alit with interest. "Oh, that looked like a juicy one! Care to dish?" Ranna was wrapped in a smartly tailored, French, forest green couture dress which fit perfectly around her diminutive form like a second skin. Embroidered across the neckline were her signature daemonic sigils, which Orias noted he should take the time to research.

He continued to work to control his labored breathing. The images of the inky portal were seared into his mind. What could it mean?

"Nothing to see here, like I said," Kobol said, swinging his hefty hammer in a slow circle. "Now move along and leave us to our fun."

The assembled throng wasn't deterred.

Ranna lifted a hand and snapped her fingers once while smiling sweetly at Orias. The crowd responded to the Elder's implicit command and quickly discovered other interests.

Despite Ranna's long, curly auburn hair, perfectly cute, small peach horns, and winning smile, she was roundly feared. Orias didn't know her entire history, but what little he'd learned informed him to be cautious of and ever respectful to the distinctive Elder.

"Well? I'm waiting," Ranna tapped her foot.

Kobol joined them at the table, a look of fierce focus belying his typical affable demeanor.

Orias, his breathing now mostly back to normal, forced a smile. "The vision had promise to reveal depth, but it'll take me some consideration and meditation in order to make sense of things."

Ranna burst out laughing, a no-nonsense hard look in her eyes. "Does that prevaricate, double-talk, work on everyone else?" She pursed her lips and raised a brow, as if daring Orias to challenge her assessment.

Orias was taken aback. Rattled from the vision, he sobered further under Ranna's pointed gaze.

"Every time," he replied. "But I see you're too clever for my wiles."

Her expression warmed with a broad smile mirrored in her eyes. "How sweet. Buttering me up won't distract me either, but you're welcome to lay it on thick. Now dish."

Orias had skirted conversations of any depth with Ranna in the past. Now, being mentally and emotionally upset from the powerful vision was certainly not an ideal time.

Regarding Ranna's expression, he could think of only one potential way to avoid this conversation.

"As you know, I am oath bound to Prince Belial, Ranna. I should check with him before disclosing further details to you."

Ranna blinked slowly, an aura of irritation pronounced in her actions. She withdrew a small, matched green purse and pulled out a seal, showing it to him and Kobol both. It was an ancient, blackened clay imprinted with a sigil he recognized immediately. "You recognize Prince Belial's sigil?" They nodded. "Then you'll also acknowledge me as a trusted ally. I am sworn to never betray you nor your cabal."

Damn. Hell if she didn't have him by the balls. He was

oath-bound to answer a trusted ally at the same level as he would his maker, Belial. "My apologies, Elder Ranna. I didn't realize."

She scrunched her nose with her smile and waved off his concerns with a flick of her lace-gloved hand. "It's never come up before. Let's call it an honest mistake, shall we?"

Orias inclined his head, noting the tension in Kobol's form.

She put away the seal and waited expectantly, her attention focused squarely upon Orias.

"I will warn you, I haven't had time to reflect upon this most recent vision, so please keep that in mind. I foresaw a doorway framed with stars in the forest. Something passed through, but the vision ended before I could make out what it was."

Ranna's expression sank, and she sighed in disappointment. "That's all?"

"Yes, but it was a powerful vision. I do not doubt the significance."

Ranna waved him off. "Sure, sure, but that one doesn't help my predicament." Her mood shifted. "Don't you love my new dress?"

Taken aback, Orias frowned. "It's a stunning display of skill, highlighting all your most attractive assets. I would have remarked upon it first had you not come upon me in my out-of-sorts post-vision state."

"You are such a charmer, Orias. One day, you'll make a lovely partner for some lucky and undeserving lady," Ranna replied.

He suppressed a smile.

"Anyway, I had to get this show-stunner made in a jiffy

after my prior outfit dusted off me, at a quite inopportune time. I was making this acceptance speech for my contributions and suddenly, in front of quite a crowd, poof goes my most favorite dress. Tell me, have you had any visions that might shed some light upon my dire plight?"

Anxiety knotted in his gut. "I can recall nothing of merit, Ranna."

Ranna pouted. "And here I was, so sure you'd know why I'd lost Lizbees in such a dramatic fashion. Explain to me why a doorway merits a vision, and Lizbees does not?"

"Lizbees?" Kobol asked.

"Lizbees, my dress! She was also my dearest, oldest friend and confidant before her unfortunate demise. I wore her hide proudly to display my loyalty to her cabal."

Kobol coughed and slammed the rest of his whiskey. Lizbees must have been an Elder daemon, the same as Ranna.

Orias felt punched in the gut. Her dress had been Lizbees' daemon hide, and Orias could certainly imagine the one thing that could have made it crumble into ash with no warnings. Belial's sancre. "I can assure you, I've had no visions pertaining to Lizbees or her disappearance, nor any of you resplendently gown-free during your acceptance speech."

Ranna smiled wickedly, her sharpened canines suddenly more pronounced. "You'd recall such a wonder, I'm certain."

Orias forced another smile. "If I have any visions about Lizbees, I'll visit you promptly."

"That's such a reassurance, Orias. I'd hate to think of you withholding from a sworn ally." Her eyes sparkled, a green flame briefly flashing.

"I can hardly imagine it myself," Orias replied, anxiety percolating through his gut.

This would likely end poorly.

Ranna stood with a sweeping gesture. "Then I'm afraid I must take my leave of you, boys. You know, places to go, daemons to rally."

Orias and Kobol both stood, but Ranna was already off.

"What do you think the forest arch is about?" Kobol asked.

"I do not know. It could be literal or metaphorical," Orias replied. He downed the rest of his ale.

"Do we need to go find Azimuth and search the forest?" Kobol asked.

"Yes, and no," Orias replied. "Therefore I never share the visions, at least until they appear applicable. Searching the entire forest. Cause I have nothing else better to do than chase ghosts from visions?" Orias tossed a couple of coins on the table and headed out the door.

CHAPTER 29

NADIR

Nadir felt Belial's summons echo in her bones, stirring an instantaneous, toddler-like defiance in her gut. She didn't regret swearing allegiance to the prince of darkness or her bond with her cabal-mates, but that didn't mean she would ever grow accustomed to being at a prince of Sheol's whim. It was unfortunate that his summons worked all the way into the human realm, but she suspected that if it hadn't, he'd never have allowed her to leave the burrow.

Nadir reluctantly tore herself away from researching everything god-touched she'd been able to get her hands on and ported back to the burrow. The tension within the cabal was palpable, as dense as fog and just as challenging to navigate. Upon her arrival, Azimuth, Kobol, and Orias exchanged uneasy glances as they sipped on glasses of dark, viscous liquid. The liquid resembled blood, but tasted like a smoky blend of fruit and spice. It was a favorite among the cabal, and it helped to calm their nerves. They sat on the couches in the common area, and by how far they were into the bottle, it looked like they'd been talking for a while.

Azimuth poured her a glass, and Nadir took a small sip, grateful for the distraction it offered. She knew the others were concerned about the potential fallout of her continued resistance to the prince, but they were patient, expecting her to adjust to Belial over time. After all, they had eternity. Ironically, despite living for millennia, Belial did not share their patience.

The tension shifted as the conversation progressed. Kobol was vocal, his voice tense as he worried about the consequences they might face if Belial's anger reached its breaking point. "We need to tread carefully," he insisted, his gaze darting from one face to another. "Who knows what Big Blue will be capable of this time if he feels backed into a corner?"

Azimuth and Orias seemed more focused on keeping the peace. They both understood the delicate balance of power that existed within the cabal and the importance of maintaining it. "You know what they say," Orias quipped, a wry smile playing at the corners of his mouth as shadows danced around his tall, slender form. "We're between a rock and a prince of Sheol. We're bound to act on his wishes, even if those desires bring us all closer to discovery by other cabals. This isn't a new predicament for us."

Azimuth chuckled, his laughter like the tinkling of ice on crystal. "Wise words, Orias. But I agree with Kobol that we need to be especially careful. This time is different. Belial's obsession with purifying the daemonic bloodlines is becoming unhinged. Who knows where his orders will push us next?"

"Not to mention if other elders figure out what we're doing," Kobol added.

"They will," Nadir added. "It's only a matter of time."

Orias leaned forward in his chair, shadows swirling around his ankles. "Ranna suspects something is up."

"The last thing we want is Ranna's attention," Azimuth replied.

Nadir wondered why that was the case. Ranna had been a staunch ally of their cabal, so why was Azimuth unwilling to share the truth with the elder?

The dreaded moment finally arrived. Belial summoned the cabal to his library, which he treated almost as a throne room. He stood tall, exuding authority and power like a daemonic peacock strutting his stuff. The room itself was filled with an oppressive darkness, the air heavy with an unsettling energy.

Nadir couldn't help but wonder if he was already at work on his next, more deadly weapon. She feared nothing would ever be enough for the bloodthirsty prince.

As the cabal entered the library, Belial fixed his gaze on Nadir, his eyes burning with an icy fire. He seemed to brood over her defiance for a few moments, his mood casting a shadow over their gathering.

"Nadir, you have defied my orders by not using the sancre weapon as commanded," he growled, his voice rumbling like a distant storm. "And you have been distracted by petty personal projects, to the detriment of our unholy mission."

Nadir's heart pounded in her chest as she clenched her fists, struggling to keep her anger in check. She met his gaze, her eyes defiant. "I have my projects," she replied tersely. "We all do, for the greater good of the cabal. I can't spend every waking moment skewering daemons for you."

Belial's expression darkened, his face twisting into a

snarl. "I don't see why not." He leaned in closer to Nadir. "You would do well to remember your place, child. Further defiance will be met with consequences you cannot fathom. Do not test me."

He turned to address the rest of the cabal, his voice like thunder as he reminded them of their duty to follow his orders without question. "I will not be defied," he declared. "You must all work together to cleanse the underworld of the sullied daemons. I expect you to double your efforts, lest you risk my ire." His eyes seemed to glow with a supernatural light as he spoke, and his words echoed throughout the room like an ancient warning.

The cabal was left in stunned silence, their heads bowed before Belial's might. They had no choice but to obey his orders, even if it meant risking their lives and sanity.

Nadir refused to let Belial's threats break her spirit. She may have been an insignificant child in his eyes, but she was a force to be reckoned with. She would not blindly follow his orders, but she would not let her defiance put her cabal in danger either.

When he turned to her, Nadir gritted her teeth and gave lip service to his demands, but inside, she seethed with resentment. "Oh, absolutely, Big Blue," she said, her voice oozing with insincerity. "Your wish is my command. I'll be your personal exterminator, ridding the world of daemons left and right, just as you wish."

Belial raised an eyebrow, clearly not amused by her sarcasm. "That's the spirit," he replied, his voice dripping with menace. "I expect nothing less from you. And do not forget; the sancre weapons are not to be taken lightly. They have the power to change everything. Use them wisely, and use them, or suffer the consequences."

He presented a fragment of paper to Azimuth. "Your mission is to sanitize this location. You must act promptly, for you have an entire population of daemons to cleanse."

With that, the prince waved them out of the room, leaving the cabal to exchange worried glances in his wake.

Nadir didn't waste any time. As soon as they were dismissed, she stormed out of the library and into her private quarters. She needed to vent, to release some of the pent-up anger and frustration that had been building inside of her for weeks.

With a snarl, she grabbed a nearby glass and hurled it against the wall, the sound of shattering glass echoing through the room.

Azimuth and Kobol appeared in her doorway moments later, concern etched on their faces.

"Nadir, please, take a moment," Azimuth urged, his voice soothing. "We know how you feel, but this is not the time to let your emotions take control."

Kobol nodded in agreement, adding, "Belial is watching us closely now. We need to be cautious in our actions, even more so than before."

"Well, I can't just go along with the genocide of those Belial deems corrupted, either." Nadir exhaled sharply, running her fingers through her hair. "You're right," she conceded, her anger giving way to resignation. "And I can't stand feeling like a puppet on a string. I didn't sign up for this life to be someone else's pawn and blindly follow orders."

Azimuth placed a hand on her shoulder, his touch gentle and reassuring. "None of us signed up for this," he whispered. "But we remember we are bound to each other, and our strength comes from our unity. If we stand together, we can navigate this difficult path."

Orias slipped into the room, his tall frame casting long shadows across the floor. "I've been thinking," he began, his voice thoughtful, "there may be a way to satisfy Belial's demands without completely sacrificing our own goals. We need to find a balance, a way to keep him appeased while still working toward our own objectives."

Kobol raised an eyebrow, curiosity piqued. "Go on."

"Well," Orias continued, "instead of indiscriminately eliminating daemons with the sancre weapons, we could focus on those who pose a genuine threat to our cabal or daemonkind as a whole. That way, we're still carrying out Belial's orders, but we're also protecting ourselves and furthering our own agenda."

Nadir considered the suggestion, a spark of hope flickering in her chest. "That might work," she agreed, nodding slowly. "It's a delicate balance, but if we can walk that line, I might just be able to stomach the headcount."

The others exchanged glances, nodding their agreement. It was a risky plan, but it was better than allowing Belial to hold complete control over their lives. And if they played their cards right, they might just be able to outwit the prince of Sheol himself.

CHAPTER 30

ERIN

The next morning, Erin walked the perimeter of the park surrounding the temple grounds; the once desolate landscape had transformed into a verdant oasis. Her heart was bursting with pride and a sense of purpose. Erin was a maenad and devotee, and her loyalty to Dionysos would never waver. Looking up at the imposing structure, she was awestruck at what she'd been able to summon with his divine aid. The scent of fresh stone and wood filled her nostrils, and the texture of the intricately carved walls was rough beneath her fingertips. Erin had wandered alone through the multi-level structure last night, discovering all the nooks and crannies of the building, the sound of her footsteps echoing softly in the vast space.

The first floor was devoted to a grand hall, a stage, a bar, and a kitchen. The second floor was filled with lodging rooms, each with plush, inviting beds that cradled her body like a cloud, and a sumptuous, shared bathroom where the soothing warmth of steam and the gentle patter of water on tile enveloped her. The third floor was smaller but no less decadent, containing a large office and attached bedroom, which Erin immediately claimed as her own. Soft, luxurious fabrics draped across the furniture, and the view from the window was breathtaking.

The basement, unsurprisingly, contained an extensive wine cellar and pantry. The earthy scent of aged wines and the subtle chill in the air heightened the sense of mystery and excitement as she explored the space. Overnight, the gardens had transformed, filling in spaces once claimed by concrete and broken glass. Now the sprawling gardens wrapped around the building, filled with grapevines, their ripe fruit bursting with flavor on her tongue, and olive trees with their silvery leaves rustling in the breeze. Fountains gurgled melodically, their cool spray gently misting her skin, while fire pits crackled and cast a warm, flickering glow over the grounds and shadows over the white marble forms of dancing satyrs and dryads.

She knew this temple was her calling and that the people of the city would benefit from her actions and its presence here. As she circled the grounds, she couldn't help but feel the weight of Blaine's words still lingering in her mind. She knew he would be a formidable opponent. No doubt he would press for her pledge of loyalty within the week, but that was a problem for another day.

Erin recognized that her actions last night had made her an enemy of the corrupt mayor, the city council, and his minions, but she was undaunted. She was a woman on a mission, and she would do whatever it took to see it through.

After she'd summoned the temple last night, Erin thought Blaine's head might explode with the fury evident in his gaze, but he'd simply declared that the matter wasn't over before his man, Jake, pulled him away. Erin smiled to herself. Let Blaine whine and complain until he grew hoarse. She had her club, slash temple, slash community center, downtown despite the mayor's protests.

Just wait until he saw the temple in the light of day. She could already imagine the steam billowing out of his ears and how he'd adjust his overly starched shirt around those broad shoulders of his.

Erin looked forward to their next duel, remembering the perfect pressure of Blaine's fingertips gliding against her skin and the way he'd gripped her hips as their tongues had clashed with more than just words. After last night, she could appreciate Blaine's clever, sexy self while also hating how he managed the city and its people. Running her teeth over her bottom lip, Erin decided that, although she wouldn't mind tussling with him again, such distractions were a bad idea.

She couldn't let her attraction to Blaine cloud her judgment. She had a mission to fulfill, a temple to tend to, and a community to lead. Her duty to Dionysos and the people of this city came first.

Blaine York might be downright edible, but she'd never forget he was her enemy. She'd take him and his corrupt city council down.

As she walked, her mind racing with thoughts and plans, Erin felt a strange sense of awareness. The hairs on the back of her neck stood up as she sensed that something, or some-one, was near. She turned around, but there was no one there. She hurried back to the temple; the feeling intensifying as she went, so Erin quickened her pace.

As she reached the entrance to the temple, she felt a powerful surge of energy emanating from within. She sensed Dionysos was present. She pushed open the heavy wooden doors and stepped inside, her breath catching at the sight before her. The walls were adorned with intricate mosaics depicting the god and his followers, their wild revelries and ecstatic dances captured in vivid detail. The air was rich with the scent of incense and the sound of music, the gentle strumming of a lyre and the haunting melody of a flute filtering in from unseen instruments. She could feel the god's energy pulsing through the room, and she knew she was in the presence of something truly divine.

So far, she'd been the only living soul on these grounds, which perplexed Erin, but she knew others would feel the call soon enough. As she reached the stage, the air shifted and roiled, a fine, golden dust filling the air, the only warning she had before Dionysos himself took form.

He stood before her, resplendent and awe-inspiring, his golden blond hair framing a handsome face with piercing blue eyes that seemed to see into her very soul. He wore a crown of ivy leaves and grapevines, a symbol of his dominion over nature and the pleasures it offered. The scent of wine and wildflowers clung to him, making her head swim with the intoxicating fragrance. In that instant, Erin was transported mentally to the bacchanal back in the forest, wild and limitless.

"My child and devotee," Dionysos said, his voice deep and melodic. "You have done well in creating a sanctuary for my followers, and all humans within the perimeter of the gardens are now blessed and under my protection."

Erin felt a thrill of anticipation at his words, wondering what it could mean and who would come to heed his call.

This was what she needed to reform the city. With this place, Erin could finally bring things to rights.

"Erin, I charge you with the sacred task of growing my flock," Dionysos continued. "Bring those who seek solace, those who wish to escape the bonds of their mundane lives, and those who yearn to embrace the wild, untamed nature within themselves. You will teach them to tear apart the ones holding back their dreams, to wear their bloody victories as trophies, and remake the world according to our grand design."

Wait, did she hear that last part, right? Erin bowed her head, her heart stuttering. "I will do my best to fulfill your wishes," she replied, her voice filled with determination yet also a note of confusion.

Dionysos smiled, the warmth of his approval washing over her like a soothing balm. "I have faith in you, Erin. Remember that you have my blessing and my protection. Together, we shall bring new life to this city and awaken the spirit of freedom and revelry that has long been suppressed."

As the god's image faded and she looked around the massive edifice to the wine god, Erin was left knowing that she had the support of a powerful deity. A deity who would rip apart his adversaries in order to reach his goals.

Surely it wouldn't come to that, Erin reassured herself. This building appearing overnight was testament enough to Dionysos' strength. Certainly that would deter others from standing in his way.

Erin's heart swelled with excitement and anticipation for whatever was coming next. Erin knew she could finally bring about a change that would benefit not only the people of the city but also herself.

She couldn't wait to get started.

CHAPTER 31

NADIR

"Where are we off to this time?" Nadir asked Azimuth.

It was the third hunt in three days, and Nadir was ready for a break. She'd killed more daemons than she cared to count, which meant she'd stopped counting after she'd reached a hundred.

Azimuth consulted today's dictate from Belial, again scrawled on another scrap of dingy paper. "It's in the fields of Gehenna. A group of soul collectors known as the Time Bandits. I have the designated entry point. No survivors."

"Does he actually write that down each time?" Nadir asked.

"If you have to ask," Azimuth started.

"We should kill them for the name alone," Kobol said, flicking a chunk of something wet and gooey off the surface of his war hammer.

"I think their title is a metaphor for the life force they feed upon," Orias added.

All three of us turned and stared at Orias.

The slightest smile tugged at the corner of his lips. "I have a sense of humor, you know, and you looked like you needed it."

Nadir could only shake her head.

"Strong work, mate," Azimuth replied. He held out his hand, and each of us laid our palms over his fist. This way, when he ported to the location, he'd drag the rest of them along for the ride.

"Hit it," Nadir said.

A moment later, the dank, fetid air of a foreign burrow hit Nadir and her cabal-mates as they materialized within the Time Bandits' lair. The moist walls seemed to seep a chilly dampness that clung to their skin, while the pungent scent of sulfur stung their nostrils.

"Someone needs to clean once in a while," Kobol whispered, his nose scrunching.

All four of them took up defensive positions, hiding in pockets along the cavern walls while they sized up their opponents.

As they cautiously explored the darkness, the unmistakable scent of human fear reached them. A shiver of dread ran down Nadir's spine as they discovered three humans, bound and helpless, their shallow breaths and whimpers of pain echoing in the chamber. They were surrounded by more daemons than they had expected, all of them taking turns feeding off the humans' dwindling life force.

"We can't let them suffer," Nadir whispered, her voice a mixture of anger and determination.

Azimuth, his skin glowing faintly in the darkness, nodded in agreement. "Fine. We'll need a plan to eliminate the daemons without harming the humans. I'm counting about three dozen of them."

Kobol, his eyes scanning the shadows, chimed in. "The moment we attack, the daemons will use the humans as shields. We need to be strategic."

Orias's voice was steady, despite the tension that hung heavy in the air. "We'll need to be quick and lethal, striking from the shadows."

"I can go invisible and cause some havoc," Kobol replied.

Orias nodded. "I'll surround the humans with my shadows. If we're lucky, they'll think they've disappeared."

"I'll chew them up and spit them out," Nadir added.

"No, you won't," Azimuth replied. "You'll use your sancre. All of us will."

Crap, that thing again. Nadir slid one of her daggers back into its sheath, pulling the jet black sancre out instead. "My flesh-eater aspect is protesting."

"If you get in a bite or two in the fray, that's fine. Just make sure you finish them with the sancre," Azimuth replied.

Anger flared in Nadir's veins, but it wasn't her lover she wanted to hurt. Every night since Belial's new campaign started, Nadir had laid in bed thinking up ways to eliminate the prince without killing them all. So far, all she had were lots of mental diagrams on how she'd piece up the daemon and feed him into the pits of Sheol.

"Fine," Nadir replied. "Last one in buys the first round."

Nadir and her cabal-mates launched into the fray, their powers working in tandem to kill the daemons while doing their best to protect the humans. The sound of battle echoed through the chamber. The clash of steel, the hiss of arcane energies, and the guttural cries of the daemons as they met their end. The air crackled with power, the acrid smell of burned daemon flesh filling their nostrils.

As the last daemon fell to ashes, the cabal surveyed the aftermath. The humans were severely injured, their breathing ragged and weak. The scent of blood mingled with the reek of daemon. Nadir's heart ached at the sight of the suffering humans, especially as they looked upon the newcomers with terror and fresh tears.

A heavy silence fell upon the group as they considered the tough choice before them. Somehow, that none of the humans begged for mercy only made things worse.

Orias' voice broke the silence, his tone resolute. "We have our orders, but I find it difficult to justify ending the lives of innocent people."

Nadir nodded. "We can save them. I can heal them and then hide them on Earth in a place where they can recover. We'll report to Belial that we've eliminated everyone in the burrow, but we won't mention the humans."

There was a pregnant pause. Nadir, her resolve unwavering, knew that the time would come when they would have to confront Belial directly. Somehow, she would put an end to his dangerous obsession with purifying the daemonic bloodlines once and for all, but today the lives of these three humans would have to suffice.

"Belial's becoming increasingly unhinged in obsession with purifying the daemonic bloodlines," Nadir continued. "If we can't stop him, the least we can do is protect the innocent."

"No survivors in the burrow," Kobol said, as if trying out the lie. "It could work."

The others exchanged glances, gauging the risks of such a

plan. One by one, they nodded until Azimuth was the last one remaining.

"Fine. It's risky to lie to the prince, but I'm with you all," Azimuth said. "Our loyalty to each other and our shared sense of morality demands it."

Kobol rolled his eyes. "We don't need a speech, Az."

"Come on," Nadir said to Az, and they got to work.

Together they checked over the humans, Azimuth using his powers to lull each into a calm state while Nadir used her sense of smell to find open wounds and then lick them with her healing saliva. In a few minutes, all three humans were stable and docile.

"Where do you want to keep them?" Orias asked.

"It's better if you don't know," Nadir replied. "You and Kobol return and give Belial an update. Az and I have it from here."

"We won't even mention the humans unless he asks," Orias replied.

"We'll tell Big Blue you're off banging, so take your time," Kobol added. "But not too much time, if you know what I mean."

Nadir arched her brow. Before Kobol dug himself a deeper hole, Orias slapped a hand onto his shoulder and ported them both away.

"I really love that guy," Nadir admitted.

Azimuth smiled. "Same. Where are we taking them?"

"Let's take them to my old summoning space to start. It's still locked up and there's a stocked pantry there. After that, I'll visit the burners up in Firestone. I bet I can talk them into taking them in for a few weeks."

Azimuth laid his hands on two of the humans, while

Nadir grabbed the third. With her free hand, she grabbed Az's shirt and pulled him in close, placing a kiss on his cheek. "Thanks for backing me up."

"Well, I do like the banging," he teased.

Nadir snorted a laugh and then ported all of them away to safety.

CHAPTER 32

ERIN

*E*rin felt a surge of excitement as she stepped out of the temple the following day, her gaze falling on the handful of people already gathered outside. She imagined the miraculous appearance of the temple overnight must have spread like wildfire. Erin could only hope those present had felt a spiritual call and had come to witness it for themselves. The scent of excitement and curiosity filled the air as the group chatted animatedly, their voices a mix of awe and wonder.

As she approached the gathering, Erin couldn't help but notice two particularly striking individuals among the crowd —a tall, red-haired man with a mischievous grin and a stout, dark-skinned woman with a wild mane of hair. Both had a magnetic quality about them, drawing Erin's attention with ease. The two were deep in conversation, and it was clear from their body language that they were no strangers to one another. As Erin drew closer, she heard snippets of their conversation and realized that they were discussing Dionysos and his temple.

"It looks like someone has put quite an effort into this place," the red-haired man said with admiration. "But the locals are saying it's new."

The dark-skinned woman nodded in agreement, her voice filled with awe. "They certainly did not skimp on the details either! The aura of the divine permeates the very air here." She looked around, her gaze softening, as if seeing something beautiful that nobody else could see. "This entire place seems to hold some kind of power and mystery."

"Hail, travelers. I'm Erin," she said, introducing herself to the duo. "Are you here for the temple?"

The red-haired man chuckled. "Well met, Erin. I go where I'm called, and today it's here. I'm Finn, a bartender and a devotee of Loki. My friend here is Nia, a fabulous cook who follows Coyote. It's been some time since we've seen each other, yet today we were both drawn here. We've traveled from other parts of the country, guided by our gods to be here, sensing that massive change is afoot."

Not one, but two agents of chaos? Erin eyed them warily, her anxiety about Blaine and the city council's potential retaliation gnawing at her. "I appreciate your interest, but I have to be cautious about who I involve with the temple."

Finn shook his head, his eyes twinkling with mischief. "No need to worry. We've been called to serve, and we're here to stay until we're called away onto our next adventure. I bet you need people with our skills, are you not?"

"You're right, I am. But there's more to this temple than meets the eye," Erin confessed. "This isn't just a place of revelry. It's the heart of a movement to overthrow the corrupt city government."

Finn's grin widened. "Ah, so there's a little revolution brewing here? Well, stirring things up is what we do best."

"We wouldn't have been called otherwise," Nia added, her voice warm and inviting. "Chaos isn't always a bad thing, Erin. Sometimes, it's just what a city needs to break free from its chains."

Erin hesitated, but realized that these two might be an unexpected boon. She took a chance and trust in the divine guidance that had brought them together. "Alright, then. Welcome to the Temple of Dionysos. Together, we'll bring about the change this city desperately needs."

Having said those words, Erin felt a wave of relief wash over her. Other new arrivals approached and introduced themselves. Some were locals, while others had traveled from out of town to visit the newly opened temple. Regardless of their backgrounds, they were all drawn to Dionysos and his power.

The group swelled as Erin introduced herself to the other newcomers, including a few members of the Firestone Burners—an anarchist collective that had long felt stifled by the city's restrictive nature. They were eager to learn about the temple and its purpose.

One man, a burner named Martin, stood out among the crowd. He wore a tattered leather jacket and carried himself with an air of authority. He watched everything with a critical eye and seemed to take a particular interest in Erin's introduction.

Erin, sensing his openness and genuine curiosity, explained the temple's origins and her vision for it. "This is a place for freedom and spiritual exploration, away from the corruption and greed that has plagued this city. You're welcome to join us, to become part of this movement."

The Burners exchanged excited glances, their faces alight with the possibility of change. One of them, a young woman with fiery red hair and a smattering of freckles, spoke up. "Hey, I'm Charly. We've been waiting for something like this. We could help set up performance areas in the gardens, you know. Nothing spreads the word better than a delightful party."

Erin smiled, her heart swelling with gratitude and hope. The temple was already beginning to attract the very people it served. Erin smiled at the enthusiasm of her newfound allies and welcomed them into the fold. They were ready to join forces and work together to bring down the oppressive system in place in this city. Suddenly, Erin found herself filled with hope and determination; she knew that, with these people by her side, anything was possible. She took a deep breath, inhaling the scent of fresh growth and new beginnings, and embraced the offer.

"Let's do it," she agreed, her voice filled with determination. "Together, we can make this city a better place for everyone."

Erin spent the day working alongside the growing group of volunteers, their shared purpose and determination driving them to transform the temple grounds into a vibrant haven for the community. The air was filled with the sounds of laughter and conversation, the scent of fresh-cut wood and the earthy aroma of plants, as the group worked together to create performance spaces and areas for relaxation.

As the day wore on, Erin couldn't help but feel a mixture of elation and trepidation. Her dream of reforming the city was coming to fruition at a rapid pace, but the thought of potential pushback from Blaine and the city council still weighed heavily on her mind.

She shook off her concerns as best she could, focusing instead on the progress they were making. The once empty gardens now teemed with life and activity, with stages and seating areas taking shape amidst the lush greenery. The sound of hammers striking nails and the rustling of leaves in the breeze created a symphony of progress.

Later that evening, as the sun dipped below the horizon and the sky transformed into a canvas of oranges and purples, Erin stood at the edge of the gardens, surveying the results of their hard work. The warm glow of fire pits illuminated the area, casting flickering shadows on the faces of those who had gathered.

Charly, the young woman with fiery red hair who had suggested the idea of performances earlier in the day, approached Erin. "Hey, Erin. We've invited Jackie, the head of the Firestone Burners, to come and meet you. She's really excited to see what you've accomplished here."

Erin's heart raced with anticipation, but the lingering concern about potential repercussions gnawed at her. "Thank you," she replied, forcing a smile. "I appreciate your support, but I can't help but worry about what might happen when Blaine and the city council find out about all of this."

The young woman's eyes twinkled with a hint of defiance. "We've been living on the fringes of the city for so long, feeling stifled and unwelcome. This temple, and the freedom it represents, is exactly what we need, and it's what the city needs too. Let them try to stop us. We'll stand beside you and fight for our right to be here."

Erin's chest swelled with pride and gratitude, bolstered by the support of her newfound allies. Despite her fears, she knew they were doing something truly special, creating an outlet that the city desperately needed.

As the night went on, the gardens came alive with the sounds of music and laughter. The soft glow of firelight danced across the faces of performers and audience members alike, their shared joy weaving a tapestry of connection and belonging. The scent of roasting meats and vegetables wafted through the air, mingling with the sweet aroma of wine.

During a lull after a rousing fiddling performance, Finn, Nia, and Erin stood together, observing the revelry around them. Finn, his perceptive gaze gleaming with curiosity, leaned in closer to Erin. "So, what are we up against with this Blaine and the city council?" he asked, his eyes studying her.

Nia chimed in, her voice filled with determination. "Yeah, maybe we should go gunning for Blaine. Shake things up a bit."

Erin hesitated, the memory of Blaine's hands on her hips and the intensity of their encounter playing in her mind. She knew that going against Blaine was necessary, but she couldn't help but feel a pang of doubt, wondering if she was really willing to harm him.

"No," Erin said finally, trying to shake off the memory. "We need to be smart about this. Blaine and the city council won't take kindly to our actions, but our priority should be growing this community and providing a haven for those who need it. If we go after Blaine aggressively, it could backfire and harm the very people we're trying to protect."

Finn nodded thoughtfully, while Nia crossed her arms, looking a little disappointed but understanding. "Alright, we'll play it your way," Nia agreed. "But if they come after us, we won't hesitate to defend ourselves and this place."

Erin couldn't help but agree. As much as she felt conflicted about Blaine, she knew that the safety and well-being of the people here were what truly mattered. Erin stood amidst the revelry, her heart aflutter with a strange mixture of hope, joy, and trepidation. She knew that there would be challenges ahead, that Blaine and the city council would likely try to tear down what they had built. But whatever the future held, she would fight for the temple and the freedom it represented, for the people who had come to call it home, and for the city—her city—that so desperately needed change.

CHAPTER 33

ERIN

Erin pushed open the door to Porter's, noticing the familiar scent of stale beer and the faint odor of cigarette smoke lingering in the air. The dim lighting revealed the usual patrons hunched over the bar, their conversations barely audible over the jukebox's blaring music. Erin's eyes scanned the room, landing on Bono, the muscular bouncer who used to have her back when she worked there.

As she approached Bono, she noticed him dealing with a difficult patron, a burly man who appeared to have had one too many drinks. Bono's calm demeanor contrasted with the drunken man's wild gesticulations, and Erin couldn't help but feel a sense of nostalgia for her days working alongside him.

"You've had enough, mate. Time to head home," Bono said, his voice firm but gentle. The man resisted, trying to shove past Bono, but the experienced bouncer held his ground. Suddenly, the drunk man lunged at Bono, fists raised.

Acting on instinct, Erin stepped in, grabbing the patron's

arm with ease. Her newfound strength surprised both the men and herself, as she effortlessly held him back. Bono looked at Erin with admiration and gratitude, his eyebrows raised in surprise.

"Erin, you've got some serious grip there," Bono remarked, chuckling as the drunk man finally relented and stumbled out of the bar. "You've changed since I saw you last."

Erin grinned, feeling the thrill of using her strength for good. "You have no idea, Bono. In fact, I wanted to talk to you about that."

She told Bono about her new Temple of Dionysos and the incredible experiences she'd had so far. Bono listened intently, his eyes widening as Erin recounted her recent adventures. When she finished, she made her proposition.

"I want you to come work with me at the temple, Bono," Erin said, her excitement shining through. "We need someone like you to help us maintain order and safety, especially with the temple's growing popularity."

Bono hesitated, his brow furrowed in uncertainty. "Well, I've been at Porter's for years, Erin. It's been good for me. Why should I leave?"

Erin, sensing his reticence, pressed on. "I understand your loyalty to Porter's, but think about it. Working at the temple would be a fresh start. You'd be part of something new and exciting. Plus, I can offer you a generous raise over what you're making now."

Bono's eyes widened slightly at the mention of a raise, but he still appeared unsure. Erin continued. "You've seen the changes happening in the city, Bono. You know there's a movement growing, and I want you to be part of it. This is your chance to be part of something bigger. Something better than all of this."

Bono rubbed his chin thoughtfully, his curiosity piqued. After a long pause, he finally said, "Alright, Erin. I'll give it a shot. Let's see what this movement of yours is all about."

"Fantastic!" Erin exclaimed, clapping him on the shoulder. "You won't regret it. Let's head to the temple now, and I'll introduce you to Finn and Nia."

As they walked to the Temple of Dionysos, Erin and Bono chatted about old times and shared their hopes for the future. Upon reaching the temple, they found Finn and Nia, busy preparing for the evening's events. Erin introduced Bono to her two new friends, and they immediately hit it off.

The four of them gathered in the temple's main hall, discussing their plans and aspirations for the Temple of Dionysos. Erin shared her vision of creating a haven for people to explore their passions and creativity, while also serving the community through charity work and outreach programs. Finn and Nia eagerly chimed in, their enthusiasm infectious.

"We have the potential to make a real difference here," Erin said, her eyes shining with determination. "Together, we can build something amazing, not just for ourselves but for the entire city."

As they continued to share their ideas, laughter, and hopes for the future, Erin felt a surge of warmth and belonging. The Temple of Dionysos was more than just a place of worship; it was a family, and she couldn't wait to see what they could accomplish together.

As they wrapped up their conversation, Erin led the group on a tour of the temple, showing Bono the various areas and facilities. They walked through the main hall, the dance floor pulsating with energy, and the bar was stocked with an impressive variety of wines.

"This is amazing," Bono said, grinning. "I've never seen anything like it."

Erin smiled, her heart swelling with pride.

They continued their tour, strolling through the temple's meditation room. Nia added, "We've also got plans to set up an art studio and community workshops and classes."

Erin chimed in. "And we'll be hosting regular charity events, fundraisers, and volunteer opportunities to help support the local community." As Erin led the group on a tour of the temple, she showed Bono the lush gardens she had cultivated. With a wave of her hand, even more vines emerged from the soil, rapidly growing and twisting to form a trellis overhead.

"This is where we'll have the community gardens," Erin explained. "I'm using my abilities to help the plants grow quickly so we can start harvesting produce for those in need."

Bono's eyes widened in awe as tomatoes ripened before his eyes. "That's incredible, Erin! This will be a tremendous help to people."

They continued through the gardens, discussing potential spots for clusters of tiny homes. "We could put some small cottages over here by the orchard," Nia suggested. "They'd have easy access to fresh fruit."

Erin nodded. "I'll summon the materials tonight. In no time, we'll have safe housing for those currently without."

The group grinned at the thought of how many lives they could improve. Their excitement was palpable as they envisioned all the potential.

As they made their way back to the main hall, Finn mentioned their plans to expand the temple's outdoor area, creating a space for outdoor performances. Bono looked around, his expression filled with wonder and appreciation.

"You've really thought of everything, haven't you?" he asked, his voice filled with admiration. "And I get the impression you're just getting started."

Erin grinned. "We want the Temple of Dionysos to be a haven for everyone. A place where people can come together, grow, and thrive."

As the evening progressed, the temple filled with patrons. Bono immediately took charge, his presence a calming force as he effortlessly managed the crowd. Erin watched him work, her heart filled with gratitude for having such a skilled and dedicated team.

Later that night, as the festivities were in full swing, Erin, Finn, Nia, and Bono gathered in a quiet corner, sharing a toast to their new partnership and the future of the Temple of Dionysos. They clinked their glasses together; the sound echoing with the promise of unity and growth.

"Here's to new beginnings," Erin said, her eyes shining with determination and hope.

"To new beginnings," they all echoed, taking a sip of their drinks as they looked out at the bustling temple, the embodiment of their shared dreams and aspirations. Little did they know, challenges lay ahead, and their bond would be tested in ways they never imagined. But for now, they reveled in the possibilities that awaited them, their hearts beating in unison with the vibrant pulse of the Temple of Dionysos.

CHAPTER 34

NADIR

Nadir stood at the edge of the Burner Enclave in Firestone, her pulse quickening with anticipation as she approached the familiar entrance. The air was thick with the scent of smoke and burned metal, while the vibrant colors and intricate sculptures that adorned the enclave brought her a sense of comfort. The armed sentries registered her arrival and took aim, but Nadir didn't flinch.

"Hold!" she heard a familiar voice call out, and quickly spotted the head of security, Martin, amongst the others.

"Hey, Martin," Nadir replied. She realized she hadn't transformed into her prior human form of Meri as she usually did, but luckily Martin knew her in both her forms. "It's been a while."

She knew her sudden appearance would set off the compound's perimeter daemon alarms, so Nadir waited patiently. She didn't have long to wait until she spotted the enclave's leader and her longtime friend Jackie approach, her long brown hair braided and draped over one shoulder.

"Uh-yup, it has. I almost didn't recognize you," Martin continued. "You look fresh from a war zone."

Nadir looked at her clothes, only then realizing she was covered in green and brown daemonic blood. At least it was only blood, she supposed.

"You're not wrong," she replied, earning her a frown from Martin.

Jackie looked her over, an urgent look in her eyes. "You in trouble again, my daemon-adjacent friend?"

"It's not for me, Jackie, but I need your help," Nadir said, her voice tense. "I have three humans recently rescued from a daemon burrow who need a safe refuge. Can the enclave provide sanctuary for them?"

Jackie looked at Nadir, concern furrowing her brow. "Of course, we'll do what we can to help. We're short-handed at the moment, but we can manage."

It was Nadir's turn to frown. "Your people okay?"

Jackie waved a hand in the air. "Yeah. A bunch of folks are off checking out the new Temple that sprang up in the heart of Denver overnight."

Nadir had to replay Jackie's words through her mind to make it make sense. "Spring as in, fully formed from the head of Zeus?"

Jackie inclined her head. "Yeah, except I doubt Mayor York had anything to do with it."

Nadir's mind raced, trying to piece together the information. A sudden intuition struck her. "Erin," she whispered to herself. Nadir's mind filled with images of the new and confused Erin. Surely it wasn't connected to her. But what if it was? "What do you know about it?"

Jackie shook her head, the intricate braids swaying gently.

"Not much. It has to be connected to some powerful forces to get built overnight. Some say it has ties to the upper echelons of the city's elite, but we'll get to the bottom of it. In the meantime, we'll do our best to provide shelter and protection for the humans you've rescued. They'll be safe here."

CHAPTER 35

NADIR

Nadir, disguised as her human form, Meri, approached the new temple Jackie had mentioned with a mixture of curiosity and apprehension. It stood as a haven amidst the city's concrete and steel. The multi-level temple was surrounded by sprawling gardens which wrapped around the building, filled with grapevines, olive trees, fountains, and fire pits. Stages and seating areas had been added amidst the greenery, creating a vibrant haven for the bustling community.

As she crossed the temple's threshold, Nadir felt an odd sensation in her body, as if the space dedicated to the gods didn't welcome the daemon essences inhabiting her body. It was like an electric shock coursing through her veins, making her skin crawl.

Azimuth's reminder that god-touched and daemons didn't mingle played through Nadir's mind, and she hesitated, unsure of the consequences of mingling with the devotees of the gods themselves. Then a round of toasts traveled through the crowd, cheering to life, liberty, and love, and Nadir couldn't keep the infectious smile from her lips.

From the looks of things, the only danger she faced here was having a good time. Belial would definitely get his knickers in a twist over it, so Nadir would just have to make sure he never found out.

She shook off the discomfort and stepped further inside, her eyes adjusting to the dim ambient lighting. The air was thick with the scent of burning incense, mingling with the aroma of freshly cooked food and spilled wine. A cacophony of laughter, conversation, and music filled the space, the energy palpable and intoxicating.

Nadir wove through the bustling crowd, searching for Erin amidst the sea of faces. She finally spotted her, radiant and laughing, at the heart of a group of admirers. "Erin!" she called, raising her voice above the noise.

Erin's gaze darted around before finally landing on Nadir. Her face lit up with genuine delight as she made her way over. "Meri! I wasn't expecting you! What brings you here?"

Nadir smiled back but couldn't avoid the concern rumbling in the pit of her stomach. "Jackie mentioned this place, and I thought I see it for myself. Plus, I wanted to check in on you. Are you okay?"

Erin's laughter rang like the sweetest of bells. "Oh, Meri, I'm more than okay! I feel so alive here. The energy, the people, it's all so intoxicating." She threw her arms wide, gesturing to the room. "I'm in my element!"

Nadir studied Erin's face, trying to discern if her happiness was genuine or the result of the temple's strange influence. "I'm glad you're happy, Erin. But are you sure you're okay? There's something off about this place."

Erin's brow furrowed for a moment, and she looked away, taking in the temple's opulence. "I know what you mean. Sometimes it feels like it's all a bit too much, but it's also exhilarating, you know?" She met Nadir's gaze, her eyes shining with a manic intensity. "This place has given me a sense of purpose and belonging I haven't felt in so long."

Before Nadir could respond, a group of people approached Erin, pulling her back into the fray. "Erin, come on! We need you for the opening ritual!" one of them called.

"Sorry, Meri. Duty calls," Erin said with a sheepish grin before being whisked away.

Nadir watched her go, a feeling of unease settling in her chest. The energy in the temple was intense, and she couldn't shake the feeling that there was something more sinister at play. She resolved to investigate further, hoping to uncover the source of her discomfort and the strange sensations she experienced upon entering the temple grounds.

As she moved through the crowd, her senses tingled, alert to every sound, smell, and touch. The temple was alive with the hum of conversation, the clink of glasses, and the rhythmic beat of drums from a nearby stage. Scents of fragrant flowers from the gardens wafted in through open doors, mingling with the more human aromas of sweat and perfume. She felt the press of bodies as she navigated the throng, the warmth and energy of the gathered people a palpable force.

Nadir was feeling overwhelmed when she spotted a figure lurking in the shadows near one of the many alcoves.

The figure seemed out of place, their demeanor at odds with the revelry. As Nadir's eyes adjusted, she recognized the figure as the elder daemon Ranna, whom she knew all too well. Wrapped around her head was a bright and vibrant scarf, matching the hues of her curling copper locks. The scarf covered up any hint of the elder's small horns beneath.

Seated at a private, dimly lit table, Ranna raised a glass and toasted Nadir. A knot of anxiety tightened in Nadir's chest, but she knew she had to confront Ranna and find out what she was doing here. Was this the danger to Erin that she'd sensed in her bones?

With a deep breath to steady herself, Nadir approached the shadowy figure. "Elder Ranna, I didn't expect to find you here," she said, trying to keep her voice steady. She didn't believe the elder intended her any harm, but still considered it wise to be careful with her words around someone so powerful.

Ranna turned her gaze toward Nadir, her eyes narrowing as she studied her. "Ah, Nadir," she replied, her voice a cold, silky whisper. "Please, let's drop the formalities. And I could say the same about you. You're looking resplendent in your human skin tonight. Join me," she asked, her smile revealing a glimpse of fang as she motioned to the empty chair across from her.

As Nadir sat down, she tried not to overthink the compliment coming from a daemon who used to wear her best friend's skin as a haute couture.

"Enlighten me, my clockwork child. What brings you here?"

The tension between them was thick as Nadir weighed

her options. Nadir wasn't Ranna's, but she didn't think it would be smart to point that out to the Elder daemon. She knew Azimuth trusted the elder, and that Ranna was also a sworn ally of Belial's. Nadir also couldn't fully explain why she needed answers, except that she wanted to protect Erin, and her gut said things didn't quite feel right.

Nadir took a chance and was honest with Ranna.

"I'm here because I'm worried about my friend," she said, her voice firm. "I think there's something going on in this temple and I want to understand it."

Meri held Ranna's gaze, determined not to back down. "Because you're here, Ranna. And you're not one for joining the party unless you have a reason."

"You assume I have the answer?" Ranna's expression shifted, a flicker of interest sparking in her eyes. "You can't be implying that I am behind these shenanigans?"

Nadir held Ranna's gaze, trying to get a reading on the enigmatic creature, determined not to back down. "I'm not implying anything, Ranna. I just figure you wouldn't waste your esteemed time sitting around drinking at a human bar. You're clever and calculating, so you wouldn't join this party unless you have a reason."

Ranna regarded Nadir for a moment, a predatory smile playing across her lips. "Very well. But know this, Nadir. Our conversation comes at a price. If you want answers, you'll need to be prepared to give me something in return."

Nadir hesitated, her instincts screaming at her not to trust Elder Ranna. But she couldn't shake the sensation that something was wrong with Erin, with this temple, and Ranna's presence here couldn't be a coincidence. "I understand," she replied, her voice barely more than a whisper. "I'm willing to take that risk."

Ranna's smile widened as she let out a dry, humorless sound that sent a shiver down Nadir's spine. "I could ask you the same thing. It seems we both have our reasons for being here, don't we?"

CHAPTER 36

NADIR

Nadir took a deep breath, inhaling the scent of incense and wine before posing the question that had been burning on her mind. "Why are you here at Erin's temple, Ranna?"

Ranna raised an eyebrow, her gaze contemplative. "You're brash, but it amuses me, young one. To be honest, I'm not entirely sure why I came here. But I seem to have an innate ability to be in the right place at the right time. A nose for trouble, you might say." The faintest trace of a knowing smile played at the corners of her mouth, her lips an alluring shade of deep red. "I suspect you do as well."

Nadir frowned, her mind racing as she considered the implications of Ranna's words. The sound of laughter and music filled her ears, but her focus remained on the Elder daemon. "I seem to," she agreed. "Frankly, I'm surprised you're not chastising me for mixing with the god-touched."

Ranna's hand moved to her chest in mock horror. "Well, I'm sure I don't know who Frank is, but I do declare, calling you to task would be profoundly sanctimonious of me, would it not?"

"It's just, Belial is always going on about the rules," Nadir replied. "And you're an elder, so I sort of figured you might feel the same way."

"I know you did not just call me old," Ranna muttered. "Belial is an over-thinker. Now me? I generally ignore rules created after my birth."

Which, Nadir noted, meant pretty much all of them. "What do you think the appearance of this new Temple of Dionysos means for the city?" she asked, searching Ranna's face for any hints of her thoughts.

A slow, almost sinister smile spread across Ranna's lips. "Dionysos hasn't had a true devotee for decades, my dear. Whatever is happening here, I can assure you, it's bound to be significant." The air seemed to thicken with tension as Ranna's words hung heavy, and Nadir's concern for Erin intensified. "After so many aeons, I do so appreciate novel entertainments."

That didn't bode well for Erin and her temple.

"Time for my question." Ranna leaned in, her breath warm against Nadir's ear as she spoke, her voice low and serious. "Odd daemon deaths have been occurring in Sheol, leaving nothing behind but dust." Her eyes glinted with unspoken knowledge, like a cat playing with a mouse. "I hope you can shed some light for me on this mystery. I know how Belial likes his games and his toys, and I suspect Belial is hiding some new curiosity from me. I'm on your side, Nadir. I may be his ally, but I'm no fan of his deceptions."

Nadir hesitated, her heart heavy with the weight of her situation. She was acutely aware of Ranna's mercurial nature and the immense power she wielded as an Elder daemon. Belial was leading her cabal into dangerous territory, and Ranna, being an ally of Belial, might talk sense into him where her own cabal members had failed.

As Nadir's thoughts whirled, she saw an opportunity to reveal the nature of Belial's new weapon, the sancre, to Ranna. She leaned in closer, her voice barely a whisper, as the rich scent of Ranna's perfume enveloped her. "I think I know what you're looking for." Nadir took a deep breath. An image of Az frowning and arching a brow played through her mind. She knew he would advise her against this line of action, but someone had to talk some sense into Belial. Perhaps Ranna was just the daemon he'd listen to. "There's a weapon that not only kills a daemon but also eradicates their entire lineage. It won't destroy high-level daemons, but I'm not sure how far up the ancestor chain it'll go."

Ranna's eyes widened, a flicker of shock quickly replaced by a steely determination. "You're certain of this?"

Nadir held her gaze, her voice barely a whisper. "I can't say more, but I believe you're on the right track to finding the truth."

A moment of silence passed between them before Ranna nodded, her expression softening. "I appreciate your honesty, Nadir. I'll speak to Belial and try to make him see reason. Know you've done the right thing by coming to me."

The relief that washed over Nadir was palpable, and she exhaled a breath she hadn't realized she'd been holding. "Thank you, Ranna. I just want to protect my cabal mates."

Ranna's eyes held a rare glimmer of warmth as she reached across the table, briefly touching Nadir's hand. The unexpected contact sent a shiver up Nadir's spine. "You've done the right thing. We all have a part to play in this world, and sometimes that means making tough choices. I won't forget your trust in me, Nadir. You've made a wise decision."

As they parted ways, the sounds of the ongoing celebration surrounded Nadir once more. The laughter and music now seemed distant and hollow as the gravity of her conversation with Ranna settled in. The scent of incense and food, once intoxicating, now held a faint undertone of unease.

Nadir couldn't help but feel the weight of her actions, as the stakes of their search for the truth became more apparent. With every step she took away from Ranna, her concern for Erin's safety grew, and her senses were sharpened by the knowledge that something sinister might lurk within the walls of the temple.

The touch of Ranna's hand on hers lingered, a reminder of the fragile alliance they had formed. Nadir knew she had taken a risk in revealing what she knew to Ranna, but she couldn't shake the feeling that it was a necessary step in uncovering the truth and protecting those she cared for.

As Nadir walked through the temple, the sights, sounds, and smells of the festivities seemed to fade into the background. Her mind was preoccupied with her conversation with Ranna, her skin still tingling from their brief contact.

She passed by a group of dancers, their bodies glistening with sweat under the flickering torchlight. The rhythmic sound of their feet on the stone floor barely registered as she was consumed with thoughts of the consequences of her actions.

Nadir's eyes drifted to the temple's altar, adorned with flowers and offerings to Dionysos. The flickering candlelight cast shadows that danced upon the walls, and the scent of burned offerings lingered in the air, leaving a bitter taste in her mouth. She paused, her gaze lingering on the altar, a silent prayer forming in her heart for the safety of her friends and resolving the chaos that had been unleashed.

As the celebration continued around her, Nadir knew that her alliance with Ranna was a gamble, a precarious balance between trust and suspicion. But with the lives of her friends and the fate of the city hanging in the balance, it was a risk she was willing to take.

With newfound resolve, Nadir left the temple, the night air cool on her skin as she contemplated her next move. The journey ahead was uncertain, but she knew she must continue to seek the truth, no matter where it might lead her. In the darkness, the sounds of the celebration slowly faded away, replaced by the quiet whispers of the wind, carrying with it the promise of challenges yet to come.

CHAPTER 37

BLAINE

Blaine stood at the entrance of the Temple of Dionysos, both intrigued and angered by Erin's defiance and the temple's growing popularity. The lively chatter of the people milling around the temple grounds grated on his nerves, and yet, he couldn't help but admire the vibrant community that had formed overnight around the temple. It was a testament to Erin's power and determination, qualities that both attracted and threatened him.

As he walked through the gardens, Blaine noted the scents and sounds that filled the air. The aroma of roasting meats and vegetables mingled with the sweet notes of wine and the earthy fragrance of the plants surrounding him. The cheerful laughter and music that echoed throughout the gardens served as a constant reminder of the influence Erin was amassing, making him even more determined to put an end to the challenge she represented to his power.

His eyes found Erin among the crowd, her laughter bright and her eyes shining with enthusiasm. Blaine's jaw clenched as he fought back the unexpected surge of desire he felt upon seeing her. He knew he couldn't afford to let his feelings cloud his judgment, not when the future of the city was at stake.

Clearing his throat, he stepped forward, drawing the attention of the crowd. "Erin," he called out, his voice booming with authority. "I demand that you swear fealty to me immediately, or I will shut down this temple."

Erin looked up, her green eyes blazing with defiance as they met his. He could feel the irritation over his interruption radiating off her followers. She was attempting to undermine him in front of them, and it was working. She didn't seem surprised by his ultimatum, which only fueled his frustration. Instead of responding to his demand in front of her followers, she calmly replied, "Why don't you come to my office, Blaine? We can discuss this matter further there."

Blaine felt a mix of anger and confusion boiling inside of him. He despised the way his heart raced in response to her presence, knowing that it only complicated an already difficult situation. With every brush of her body against his as they walked, Blaine fought the urge to shove her away from him and end their discussion right then and there.

As they ascended to Erin's office, Blaine couldn't help but take in the lavish surroundings of the club. The intricate artwork on the walls, the soft glow of candles, and the faint sounds of music drifting through the air gave the place an air of decadence and allure. The tension between him and Erin intensified with each step they took.

Erin's office, with its luxurious fabrics and commanding view, seemed a perfect reflection of her bold, captivating spirit. The view from Erin's office was spectacular. The gigantic window took up an entire wall and showed the city below, alive with light and new construction. Surrounding the window were oil paintings depicting flowers and animals, hung at different levels on a dramatically curved wooden frame. The walls, made of genuine wood, had been polished to a shine. They reflected the hanging lamps that scattered bright pools of light across Erin's desk and chair. Erin's enormous mahogany desk was piled with papers, notepads, and pens.

The sight of the bed, draped in deep burgundy comforters and soft pillows, ignited something within him. He couldn't ignore what it would be like to have Erin sprawled beneath him on that inviting bed. But though he ached for her, he was also fearful of the consequences if he crossed that line.

Blaine gritted his teeth, struggling to maintain his composure. "You know as well as I do this city needs order, Erin. And as mayor, it's my responsibility to ensure that order is maintained. Your temple is a threat to that order."

Erin raised an eyebrow, her gaze never wavering. "Is it really the temple that threatens you, Blaine, or is it me?"

His heart skipped a beat at her words, and he fought to suppress the undeniable chemistry that sparked between them. "Don't flatter yourself, Erin," he said, his voice strained. "I'm the most powerful god-touched in this region and my concern is for the city, not for a rogue, fresh to her divine power, no matter how enticing she might be."

"I might be a rogue, but admit it. I'm a needed breath of fresh air."

Blaine couldn't help the smile tugging at his lips. "You're fresh, I'll give you that. But you can't sway me by appealing to the misguided attraction we may have for one another."

Erin's eyes flashed with defiance. "Misguided? You think our attraction is misguided?" she asked, her voice barely a whisper.

Blaine hesitated, the intensity of her gaze making it difficult for him to think clearly. He knew he needed to maintain control, both of the city and of his own desires, but the allure of Erin's strength was proving hard to resist.

"Yes," he said finally, his voice firm. "We can't afford to let our personal feelings interfere with our duties to the city."

Erin shook her head, a sad smile playing at the corners of her lips. "I suppose you're right," she conceded, her voice heavy with resignation. "But that doesn't mean I'll just roll over and swear fealty to you, Blaine. My loyalty lies with Dionysos and the people of this city. I won't let your twisted sense of order destroy what we've built here."

Blaine clenched his fists, his anger rising at her stubborn refusal. "You're playing a dangerous game, Erin. Don't you understand the consequences of going against me and the city council?"

She stared into his eyes, her resolve unwavering. He wasn't much taller than her, and he was almost as brawny as Daniel, the devotee of Ares, but more refined. "I understand perfectly, Blaine. But I also understand that this city is suffering under your rule, and I won't stand by and let it continue. I'm not afraid of fighting for my beliefs."

The air in the room crackled with tension, and for a moment, Blaine considered giving in to the temptation that Erin represented. He could lose himself in her embrace, forget his responsibilities and the city's problems, but he knew that doing so would only bring about disaster.

Taking a deep breath, he stepped back, putting distance

between them. "I'll give you one last chance, Erin. Swear fealty to me and the city council, and we'll let you continue your work here. But if you refuse, I will do everything in my power to shut this temple down and bring you to heel."

Erin's expression softened, her eyes glistening with a seductive glint as she moved close. "Why don't you let go of all that control, just for a moment, Blaine? Embrace the hedonism and freedom this temple offers. Stop being so stuffy and uptight. Why not let go for a moment and embrace the hedonism that comes so naturally to your benefactor, Zeus?"

Blaine hesitated, his gaze lingering on her lips, the desire to taste them again momentarily overpowering his need for order. He swallowed hard and let out a small chuckle. "Zeus may have been known for his revelries, but I can't afford to indulge like he did. Not with the responsibilities that hang on my shoulders. Even if I did, the council would never let you run amok with the city."

Her hand found his chest, fingers splayed over his racing heartbeat. "You've never been with a woman who challenges you, have you?" Erin's breath was warm against his cheek as she whispered, "Maybe that's exactly what you need, Blaine. Someone who isn't afraid to stand up to you and remind you that there's more to life than power and control."

Blaine's eyes flicked down to her lips, then back up to her eyes. "I've had my share of women, Erin. But none quite like you."

Erin's gaze never wavered, a slow smile spreading across her face. "Maybe it's time to try something new, Blaine. To give in to passion, if only for a moment."

The air in the room thickened with the mounting sexual tension between them. Blaine's heart raced, and he found himself momentarily lost in Erin's eyes. He could lose himself in her embrace, forget his responsibilities and the city's problems. Just for a moment.

His resolve wavered, and with a deep, ragged breath, he gave in. They crashed into each other, lips meeting in a fiery, passionate kiss. Their hands tangled in each other's hair, the heat between them undeniable. Blaine's hands slid down Erin's athletic frame, a shiver passing through her as he gripped her hips.

Erin whimpered into Blaine's mouth as their kiss deepened, her hands roaming over his body. She tugged at the edges of his shirt, and he allowed her to peel it away from him. His hands found her hips, and he massaged the soft fabric against her skin, exploring every curve of her body with his fingers.

The heat between them quickly built to an unbearable level as they explored each other with wanton abandon. Blaine pulled back long enough to catch her gaze, and Erin looked back at Blaine with a desire that made his breath catch. He leaned in, his lips meeting hers as they moved together in a passionate embrace. She moaned into his mouth as he kissed her hungrily, exploring her body with his hands and savoring every sensation that coursed through him. His heart slammed against his ribs as their breathing quickened in unison.

Erin's hands moved up Blaine's chest, fingers tracing the contours of his muscles as if she was memorizing them for later. He trailed delicate kisses down her neck, nipping and sucking at sensitive spots that elicited little gasps from Erin's lips. She tilted her head back in pleasure, giving Blaine full access to her gorgeous neck and inviting him to take more.

He complied eagerly, trailing more kisses down her chest and over the swell of her breasts before returning to capture her lips with his once again. His hands moved to cup Erin's face, thumbs gently caressing her cheeks until she was sighing in delight.

"Don't stop now," Erin whispered. "Let me be your escape." She held out her arms to him, inviting him closer, and he obliged. His body moved over hers in a dance of pleasure as their lips reconnected. She tasted sweet like honey and felt so right against him.

Blaine's hands trembled as they drifted across her body, exploring every secret spot with a fervent hunger. He hesitated only briefly before tearing off her dress and baring her to his gaze, drinking in the sight of her glorious figure until a frenzied urge drove him to remove his own clothing. Scooping her up in an embrace, he quickly carried her to her bed, tossing her onto the sheets and climbing on top of her with wild abandon.

Erin gasped as Blaine's lips found hers again. His hands moved over her body with determination and skill that left Erin quivering beneath him. His kisses became more passionate with each passing moment, as his hunger for her proved insatiable.

Her hands flew over his back, exploring every inch of his toned muscles, until finally coming to rest on his hips. She guided him closer to her, their bodies melding together like two pieces of a puzzle in perfect harmony. The heat between them was undeniable, and with each touch, she felt the electric connection that connected them. Before giving in to their desires without restraint or hesitation, he paused for a moment and produced a condom, ensuring a safe encounter as they surrendered to their passions.

Blaine pulled Erin in close, the warmth of her skin and her sweet scent flooding his senses. He felt a primal energy radiating from her as he moved against her body and she responded in kind, passionate cries escaping her lips. His movements intensified as their bodies moved in perfect harmony until the frantic feeling of desire built to an ecstatic peak.

Erin's breath hitched into Blaine's ear as he brought them closer and closer to their goal with each movement of his hips. Blaine pulled back slightly and looked into Erin's eyes, suddenly overwhelmed by the desire for her that burned in him. They had finally found the sweet spot together and were riding a wave of pleasure so intense he could barely string two thoughts together. It was more than any feeling he'd ever experienced, but he knew it would be over all too soon. Suddenly, she clenched around him with her orgasm, and he made one last desperate thrust before giving himself up to the unexpected euphoria.

Blaine rolled off Erin and collapsed beside her on the bed, their limbs entwined. He stared at the ceiling as he tried to catch his breath. Perspiration shone on Erin's skin and gathered between her breasts, which heaved as she breathed. When Blaine looked at Erin, her face was a mixture of desire and triumph.

He knew the score for today. Dionysos: 1. Zeus: 0. Blaine might have given her pleasure, but he hadn't won her fealty.

Blaine knew he couldn't allow himself to be distracted by Erin, not when so much was at stake. With a final, lingering touch, he pulled away, his voice low and gravelly. "We shouldn't have done this, Erin. Not while you're fighting the rule of the city. Fighting me."

Erin's eyes sparkled with a mix of understanding and defiance. "Maybe one day, Blaine, we'll find ourselves on the same side." Then Erin's expression hardened, her eyes blazing with determination. "I accepted you into my bed, but I won't bow to you or the council, Blaine. I will fight for this temple and for the people of this city, no matter what it takes."

Blaine stared at her, the raw power and passion in her voice stirring something within him. He knew he should walk away, leave her to face the consequences of her defiance. But as he pulled himself away from her touch and turned to leave, he couldn't help but wonder if there was a way to harness Erin's strength and use it to benefit the city.

With that, Blaine gathered his clothes, dressed, and left Erin's office, the memory of their passionate encounter lingering in his mind as he steeled himself for the conflicts to come. The battle lines had been drawn, and he knew that things between them would never be the same. But deep down, a small part of him couldn't help but hope that they might one day find a way to reconcile their differences and work together for the greater good of the city. For now, however, he had a job to do, and he wouldn't let his feelings for Erin stand in his way.

CHAPTER 38

ERIN

*E*rin sat behind her desk in her office, her mind still reeling from her intimate encounter with Blaine earlier that day. She couldn't help but feel drawn to him, but she also worried that if she caught feelings, she might become soft and less effective in her fight against him. She traced her fingers over her lips, still tingling from their passionate kiss, her heart fluttering at the memory.

Erin's gaze drifted to the window. She thought back to the morning interlude with Blaine. She felt an electric sensation race through her body, and heat rose in her cheeks. A faint pulse of need vibrated between her legs, and she caught herself licking her lips at the thought of his touch. She knew she had an advantage with their physical connection, but she couldn't bring herself to use it to get her way. She wanted him to stand up for her cause out of genuine belief, not because of any lingering pull between them.

Her musings were interrupted by the sound of the door to her office creaking open. Maria, Erin's ex-boss and a devotee of Apollo, unexpectedly stood in the doorway, her eyes narrowing as she scanned the room with disapproval. Maria's sleek, dark hair was pulled back into a tight bun, and her tailored suit accentuated her statuesque figure. The scent of her sharp, citrusy perfume filled the room as she walked in.

"Erin, devotee of Dionysos, you need to come with me now. The city council demands your presence," Maria said, her tone authoritative and unyielding.

Erin frowned, taken aback by the sudden intrusion and Maria's brusque demeanor. "What do they want from me? I thought I made it clear to Blaine that I'm not backing down."

Maria sighed, her eyes narrowing further. "You think this is some kind of game? The council and I will not stand by and watch as you drag this city into debauchery and chaos. Denver thrives because of the order and clarity the council brings to the region, and we won't let you undermine that."

Erin bristled at Maria's words, but held her ground. "Things might seem great for those in power, but not everyone shares your perspective. If things were truly perfect, Dionysos wouldn't have called me to be his devotee. People need a place where they can be free, express themselves, and feel accepted."

Maria's expression hardened, her eyes flashing with anger. "There's more at stake here than you realize, Erin. We're trying to maintain a balance in this city, and your temple threatens that."

Erin stood up, her voice steady and determined. "Perhaps it's time for a change, Maria. The old ways aren't serving everyone, and it's time we give them a voice too."

Maria sighed, her eyes narrowing further. "Mayor York was supposed to bring you before the council today, but it seems he's been sidetracked," she said, unaware that Erin's encounter with him earlier was the reason for his absence. "So, I'm here to fetch you."

Erin's cheeks flushed as she remembered the stolen moments with Blaine, surprised that he'd neglected to tell her about the city council meeting earlier. Then again, he had been distracted. Or the distraction? She tried to mask her heated thoughts by feigning annoyance. "Fine. I'll go, but don't expect me to bow down to your demands."

As Erin stood up and strode out the door, the sound of Maria's stilettos followed close behind her. Erin glanced over the club's main floor, the scent of incense and wine lingering in the air. She worried about leaving the temple unattended, but as if sensing her concern, Finn appeared by her side, his bright green eyes filled with reassurance.

"Don't worry, Erin. I'll make sure everything stays safe while you're gone," he said, his voice soothing and warm.

Maria looked down her nose at Finn, her eyes cold and calculating. "Don't be so sure about that," she replied dismissively, making it clear she doubted his capabilities.

Erin bristled at Maria's attitude, but she forced herself to keep her focus. "Thank you, Finn. I trust you," she said, giving him a smile before turning to Maria. "Let's get this over with. The sooner the council accepts my presence in this city, the better."

With a terse nod, Maria led Erin out of the temple and toward the city hall. As they walked, Erin took in the sights and sounds of the city—the hustle and bustle of people going about their daily lives, the hum of traffic, and the aroma of food from nearby restaurants. It was a stark contrast to the tranquil, indulgent atmosphere of the temple, and Erin couldn't help but feel a pang of longing for the haven she'd created.

As they approached city hall, Erin steeled herself for the confrontation ahead. She knew that Maria and the other council members would not be easily swayed, but she was determined to stand her ground and fight for her vision of a better, more inclusive city.

As they entered the imposing building, Erin felt the weight of the council's authority bearing down on her. Despite her anxiety, she drew upon the strength of her divine connection, her resolve unwavering as she prepared to face the council and defend her temple.

CHAPTER 39

BLAINE

Blaine returned to his private shrine, his thoughts consumed by the events of the past two days. The taste of her from their recent intimate encounter lingered on his lips, and her scent clung to his clothes. As he entered the dimly lit cella, the shadows cast against the plain, gray-painted walls seemed to reflect his uncertainty. He was driven to gain and wield power, and he struggled to reconcile his feelings for Erin with the potential threat she posed to his authority in the city.

Seeking guidance from Zeus, Blaine lit a stick of frankincense and myrrh incense, its scent invoking a sense of spiritual connection. He sat on the low altar of carved oak and meditated, opening himself to receive a message from the god.

The atmosphere in the shrine shifted subtly as the divine presence of Zeus manifested. The thirty-four Doric-style limestone columns, and the murals of the twelve labors of Heracles, seemed to vibrate with divine energy. The air within the shrine grew colder, and an electric charge made the hairs on the back of Blaine's neck stand on end. He remained patient and focused as he awaited a sign.

The air shimmered, and an ethereal vision emerged before him. He saw Erin, bathed in a halo of light, standing at the center of a storm. Lightning flashed around her, but her gaze remained steady and strong, as if she held the power of the tempest within her grasp.

As Blaine observed the vision, the city around Erin seemed to come to life, as if her presence were regenerative, not just chaotic. He realized that Erin's power might rival his own, and as the Mayorship was held by the most powerful devotee in the region, she might challenge him.

He considered Erin's claims that Dionysos took physical form with her, even holding a dialogue. This was not the case for other devotees. Was it because she was the god's only devotee, or perhaps an sign of how powerful she'd become by his hand?

"Erin, you hold such power," Blaine whispered, his voice barely audible in the sacred space. "But can I embrace the chaos you bring, or must I restore order at all costs?"

As Zeus didn't speak directly, Blaine knew he must interpret the message through the vision. As he paced the shrine, the weight of his decision bore down upon him. He considered the consequences of each choice for the city, his personal life, and his devotion to Zeus.

"Zeus Panhellenios, guide me," Blaine murmured, seeking additional signs or clarity from the god to aid his decision. "Can I truly accept and embrace the change Erin offers, or will it cost me everything I've worked for?"

Finally, Blaine reached a decision, understanding that he must face the consequences of his choice. He weighed what he feared he might have to give up—his title as Mayor, his position of power—against what he might gain by embracing Erin's chaotic influence and the regenerative potential she held.

"Thank you, Zeus Soter," he whispered, bowing before the larger-than-life, pure-white marble statue of Zeus at the center of the shrine. "I reaffirm my devotion to you and promise to honor your guidance. Grant me the wisdom to find a balance between the chaos and the order, between my heart and my duty."

With renewed purpose, Blaine rose and left the shrine, ready to take action and face the challenges ahead. As he stepped into the unknown future, he prepared to navigate the complexities of his relationship with Erin and its impact on the city.

CHAPTER 40

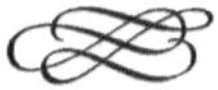

ERIN

As they approached the city hall, Erin steeled herself for the confrontation that awaited her. She felt a mixture of defiance and anxiety, knowing that the council members would undoubtedly be hostile toward her and her temple. She also couldn't help but wonder if Blaine would be present, and if so, how their encounter earlier would impact the dynamic between them.

The grand facade of the city hall loomed before them, its imposing stone structure and tall pillars a stark reminder of the power and authority it represented. Erin's heart raced as they climbed the steps, the sound of Maria's heels clicking on the stone like a metronome, keeping time with Erin's quickening pulse.

Maria led Erin through the halls of the city hall, their footsteps echoing through the marble corridors. They reached a set of ornate double doors, behind which the council chamber lay. Erin took a deep breath, filling her lungs with the scent of polished wood and the faint aroma of leather from the many books that lined the walls of the adjacent library.

Maria pushed open the doors, revealing the council chamber with its high ceiling and large, imposing table at which the council members sat.

Erin took a deep breath and followed Maria into the council chamber. As Erin stepped into the room, she was determined to stand her ground, regardless of the pressure she faced. She squared her shoulders, lifted her chin, and prepared herself for the battle that lay ahead.

It was a grand room, its high ceiling adorned with intricate molding and its walls lined with imposing portraits of past council members. The scent of polished wood and leather filled the room as the large, curved table at the center dominated the space. The council members were already seated, their stern faces looking down at Erin with a mixture of curiosity and disdain.

As she scanned the faces of the council members, Erin recognized Daniel, the brawny and bald devotee of Ares. She'd seen some others around the table at Maria's company, Pythia, where Erin had worked before Maria fired her. A few of them were familiar with the news, but she didn't know any of them personally. Notably, there were three empty chairs, one at the head of the table, which she assumed was reserved for Blaine.

Maria cleared her throat, her voice echoing in the chamber. "I present to you Erin Bevin, the devotee of Dionysos and priestess of the new Temple of Dionysos, as requested."

The council members exchanged glances before the chairman, an elderly man with a shock of white hair and piercing blue eyes, spoke up. "Thank you, Maria. If you could both take a seat, we'll get started," the white-haired man said, gesturing to the seat closest to the door. Erin hesitated for a moment before taking her place. Her gaze locked onto the empty seat that she believed belonged to Blaine.

Maria nodded and took a seat. Erin couldn't help but feel a twinge of unease as she sat down at the council table. Her stomach churned with a mixture of apprehension and defiance, and her heart raced, pounding in her ears as she mentally prepared herself for the confrontation.

The chairman continued, his tone cold and formal. "Erin, you have caused quite a stir in our city with your unauthorized establishment. Additionally, you neglected to present yourself as a devotee upon your arrival in the city. We've brought you here today to discuss the implications of your actions and what consequences may follow."

Erin met the chairman's gaze, her eyes filled with determination. "I understand your concerns, but I've done nothing wrong. I've created a place where people can come together and celebrate life, just as the gods intended."

A murmur rippled through the council members, and Erin could sense their skepticism. The chairman leaned back in his chair, his fingers steepled together as he considered her words.

"Your intentions may be noble, especially as a devotee of your particular deity's persuasion, but you understand we cannot allow chaos and disorder to run rampant in our city. The council decides what is best for this city, not untested neophytes. The Temple of Dionysos has already attracted a questionable crowd, and we fear the consequences it may have on our community."

Erin bristled at the insinuation, but she forced herself to

remain calm. "The people who come to the temple are seeking an outlet, a way to express themselves and find joy in a world that often seems devoid of it. My temple is not a threat to your order; it's a necessary balance."

The elder scoffed at her. "You moved forward without due process and without council approval. Your actions directly challenge our authority, and according to our laws, this makes your claim to the land forfeit, should the council declare it so."

Erin challenged the chairman, her voice steady. "Just try taking the Temple away from me, and you'll see the true power of this devotee."

The chairman exchanged glances with the other council members before responding. "We will take your words into consideration, Erin. However, know that we will monitor the situation closely. If we deem it necessary, we will not hesitate to shut down your establishment or eject you from the city proper."

Erin clenched her fists, fighting the urge to unleash her divine power in defiance. Instead, she nodded and replied evenly, "I understand your position, but I won't let you destroy what I've built without a fight."

The chairman's eyes narrowed, and he dismissed Erin with a curt wave of his hand. "I can see you need some time to digest what we've shared with you today. You may leave now."

As Erin rose and then turned to exit the chamber, she couldn't help but feel a mix of frustration and determination. With her head held high, she strode toward the doors, ready to face whatever challenges lay ahead. She knew that the battle for the future of her city was far from over, but she also knew that she was more than willing to fight for her cause.

Just as Erin reached the doors, Blaine appeared, looking flustered and not at all like his usual composed self. He held out his hand to stop her and declared, "This isn't over, and you're not leaving."

CHAPTER 41

NADIR

Nadir returned to the cabal burrow, her footsteps heavy with exhaustion and worry. The air was thick with the scent of freshly baked cookies and incense, which, with her daemonic super scent, enveloped her like a warm blanket, both comforting and overwhelming. As she entered the communal area, Kobol greeted her, his green eyes lighting up with mischief as he twirled a cookie between his fingers.

"Welcome back, sis," he said, offering her the treat with a wink. "I made a new recipe. I call it, Eternal Damnation Delights. You'll love it."

Nadir hesitated, noticing his curly red hair and short horns covered in a fine coating of flour. She considered teasing him about it but decided against it, not wanting to deflate his excitement. She took a bite, her taste buds exploding with a sinful mix of dark chocolate, chili, caramel, and a touch of sea salt. The flavors swirled together, creating a decadent dance on her tongue. She couldn't help but smile, even in her exhaustion.

"You've outdone yourself, Kobol," she said, taking another bite. "Though I'm not sure about the name."

"Eh, it'll grow on you, just like me," Kobol chuckled, flour puffing from his hair as he shook his head. "You look like you've been getting into trouble," he observed, a note of approval in his voice. "I like it."

Nadir sighed, her lips curving into a wry smile. "You know me too well, Kobol. I'm always finding trouble, or it finds me. Where are the others?" she asked Kobol.

"Orias is off meditating or communing with shadows or whatever he's calling it this week," Kobol shrugged. "Azimuth is," he tilted his head to the side, and then smiled broadly, "well, it looks like he's skulking this way right about now."

Nadir breathed a sigh of relief. Orias could take one look at a person and see their deepest, darkest secrets. Whether he shared what he knew or suspected was another matter. At least today she didn't need to worry their resident oracle would reveal her conversation with Ranna.

Azimuth entered the room, his aquamarine eyes filling with concern as they swept over her. Nadir appreciated Azimuth's keen ability to read people, especially when it wasn't turned her way. "You look thin as a fade energetically," he said, his brow furrowing. "What happened while you were gone?"

Nadir hesitated, the memory of her encounter with Ranna fresh in her mind. She knew she couldn't tell Azimuth about it, not yet, and she certainly couldn't speak of it inside the burrow, where Belial might overhear. Instead, she opted to share the details of her visit to Erin's temple.

"I went to Erin's temple," she began, her voice steady. "I know you said to give her a wide berth, but I can't shake this feeling that something powerful is going down in the city. I'm convinced Erin is at the center of the storm."

Azimuth frowned, his gaze intense. "Did you get any idea of what this power might be, or how it could affect us?"

"No, I'm not sure yet," Nadir admitted, her shoulders slumping. "But whatever it is, Erin and the god-touched won't be the only ones affected. I want to help her, Azimuth. She's not my only friend in the city, either."

Azimuth nodded, his hand reaching out to cup her cheek. "We'll figure this out together, Nadir. But right now, you need to rest and recharge your daemonic energy. You can't keep pushing yourself like this."

Nadir hesitated, gathering her courage before revealing her inner turmoil. "Az, you know I've been feeling conflicted about the current directives from Belial. I'm not sure if we're doing the right thing."

Azimuth's eyes softened, understanding her concerns. "I know it's difficult, Nadir. But you're not alone in this. We'll figure things out together, as we always have."

"Orias and I have your back too, Nadir," Kobol added. "Together, we're a powerhouse."

Nadir nodded but couldn't mask the doubt that still lingered in her eyes. "I want to believe that, but it's hard. I can't help but worry about the consequences of our actions."

Azimuth reached for her hand, gently squeezing it as a sign of reassurance. "I understand your fears, Nadir. But you need to trust me. I'll do everything in my power to keep you safe and take care of you, no matter what happens."

Nadir tried to express her agreement, forcing a smile, but knew Azimuth would sense she didn't trust him completely.

"I know you will, Azimuth. It's just tough, but I'll do my best to trust you and our decisions."

Azimuth smiled back, his eyes filled with determination. "That's all I ask. Together, we can face any challenge that comes our way. Let me show you how I can take care of you," he murmured, a playful glint in his eyes.

Nadir sighed, knowing he was right. Her body ached, and her mind felt as if it were on the verge of shattering. She needed to feed her daemonic hungers, and Azimuth knew it.

Azimuth led her back to their room, the dimly lit space offering a soothing respite from the chaos of her thoughts. As he pulled her into his arms, their bodies entwined, and Nadir felt the familiar thrum of desire course through her veins, fueling her daemonic nature. The icy calm of his touch ignited a fire within her, and she surrendered herself to the passion that consumed them both.

Azimuth's lips trailed a searing path down her neck, leaving a trail of shudders in their wake. Nadir arched her back, pressing herself closer to him, craving more of his touch. "Azimuth," she whispered, the intensity of her need surprising even her.

He responded to her with a low growl, his hands gliding along her body, re-familiarizing himself with every dip and curve. He knew where to touch her to bring the most pleasure, and he took his time, whisking her skin and tantalizing her with his tongue. Nadir's soft cries filled the room, a sign of his capabilities and her ever-growing need. As their playful conversation faded into passionate kisses, their hands explored each other without mercy or restraint. Azimuth's fingers caressed Nadir's skin, leaving her trembling while she playfully yanked at his hair, eyes sparkling with mischievousness.

"Azimuth," Nadir breathed, her voice heavy with lust, "I need you."

In that moment, their connection intensified as Azimuth's fingers traced delicate patterns on Nadir's skin, eliciting a shiver from her. With a firm yet gentle grip, he pulled her closer, joining their bodies together in a dance still fresh despite their time together. His tender kisses on her neck and collarbone contrasted with the commanding way he guided her movements, a perfect balance that drove Nadir wild.

She could feel the chill of his daemonic energy emanating from him, his desire for her evident in his every touch. The sensation of being both loved and desired by Azimuth was intoxicating, and she reveled in it, her heart swelling with emotions she could barely contain. The symphony of their mingled breaths and whispered endearments filled the air, a testament to the depth of their passion and the strength of their bond.

In that moment, their connection intensified as Azimuth's skilled hands guided their dance of passion. His touch was both tender and commanding, a perfect balance that drove Nadir wild. She could feel the mounting pressure building within her, and as their bodies moved in perfect harmony, she relished in the feeling of being both loved and desired.

Their breaths grew more labored, their moans and sighs echoing around them. As Azimuth hit that perfect angle, a surge of pleasure raced through Nadir's body, her muscles tensing in anticipation. Together, they crossed the threshold, their bodies shuddering in unison as they reached the orgasmic culmination of their lovemaking.

Their breaths mingled, and their hearts raced as one, as they found solace in each other's touch. Their passion was both a balm and a source of strength, an unspoken promise of unity against the world's turmoil.

As they lay together in the aftermath, Nadir's thoughts strayed back to her conversation with Ranna. She felt the weight of guilt over not disclosing her discussion but still withheld the information, reasoning that Ranna already had an inkling that Belial was waging war on daemon kind. Nadir knew she couldn't keep it a secret forever, but for now, she needed to protect her cabal and help Erin.

And as sleep finally claimed her, Nadir hoped that whatever storm was coming, they would be strong enough to weather it. But just as she drifted off, her thoughts refused to settle, her mind replaying the events of the day and the uncertainty that lay ahead. The foreboding sense of unease cast a shadow over her thoughts, and she knew that the peace they had found in each other's arms would be short-lived. The storm was already upon them, and as much as she wished for respite, her heart remained heavy knowing that challenges awaited them.

CHAPTER 42

ERIN

As Blaine caught his breath, Erin noted his flushed face and his crumpled suit jacket. Erin's heart caught in her throat at the sight of him. He looked nothing like the polished Mayor York she had seen in public, and she realized he might have been as affected by their encounter as she was.

The chairman visibly relaxed, a faint smile touching his lips as he regarded Blaine. "Ah, Mayor York, good of you to join us. We were just concluding our discussion with Ms. Bevin."

Blaine glanced at Erin, his eyes searching hers for a moment before he addressed the council. "What has been decided?"

The chairman summarized their conversation, detailing their concerns and Erin's refusal to back down. "We've just informed her we'll be monitoring the situation closely and will take action against her or her business if we find it necessary."

Blaine turned to Erin, his gaze intense. "Are you willing

to swear allegiance to the council?" he asked, his voice barely above a whisper. A current of tension passed between them, a reminder of the intimacy they had shared earlier. "To me?"

Erin hesitated for a moment, their connection weighing on her decision, but she finally shook her head. "By your own terms, I have six more days."

As he shook his head, a ghost of a smile flickered across Blaine's face, but it vanished as quickly as it appeared.

Maria, still seated at the table, spoke up. "Before we let her go, shouldn't we test her, as is customary?" Her eyes narrowed as she regarded Erin, suspicion evident in her gaze.

Anxiety spiked within Erin. She did not know what kind of test they had in mind, and she worried about what it might entail. Blaine, however, shook his head. "I don't think that's necessary."

Maria's gaze shifted to Blaine, her suspicion now directed at him. "And why is that, Mayor York? Testing is our gold standard for ranking devotees within the city. What purpose does delaying the testing serve?"

The chairman intervened, his voice calm but firm. "Regardless of Mayor York's opinion, we standardly test the abilities of those who claim to possess divine gifts, usually after they have sworn allegiance. However, in these unusual circumstances, I will make an exception."

Erin looked from the chairman to Blaine, her apprehension growing. "What exactly does this test involve?" she asked, her voice unsteady.

The chairman gestured to an aide, who hurried from the room and returned moments later, cradling a small, ancient-looking tablet. The aide handed it to the chairman, who presented it to Erin.

"This artifact has been used for centuries to measure the intensity of a devotee's divine powers," the chairman explained. "It will reveal to us how generously your deity has bestowed his gifts upon you. I assure you, it will not harm you."

Erin eyed the tablet warily, her hand hovering over its surface. She glanced at Blaine, searching for reassurance. He gave her a subtle nod, but she noted the concern in his eyes.

Taking a deep breath, she placed her hand on the tablet. A sharp jolt of electricity zapped her palm, causing her to jerk her hand away. The tablet's surface now displayed nine glowing symbols arranged in a star-like pattern around a set of scales etched into the center.

The chairman's eyebrows rose in surprise, while Maria's eyes narrowed further, her suspicion not abating. The chairman held the tablet up, displaying it to everyone in the chamber. The council members' eyes wide as they took in the glowing symbols. A murmur of amazement rippled through the room.

"What do the symbols mean?" Erin asked, her voice barely audible above the whispers in the room. "Nine of out of what? Ten? A hundred?"

The chairman studied the symbols for a moment before addressing the council. "These symbols represent the strength and intensity of Erin's divine connection. The more symbols that glow, the stronger her abilities. Nine is quite remarkable. It is rare for a devotee to possess such power."

Erin's chest tightened, and she looked at Blaine, who seemed both awed and concerned by the results. She couldn't help but wonder how this revelation would affect their already precarious relationship.

Maria scoffed, her voice dripping with contempt. "Remarkable or not, it changes nothing. She still refuses to submit to the council, and we have every right to be cautious of someone with this level of power."

Erin couldn't help but ask, "How do my abilities compare to others in the city?"

The chairman considered her question for a moment before answering, "The devotees in our city possess a varying range of abilities. As I said before, yours is quite remarkable."

The chairman's dodging of her question could only mean one thing: Erin's devotee powers must be some of the strongest. Erin's mind flashed back to her brawl with Daniel, only now realizing that she'd been able to beat the devotee of Ares because she was more magically powerful. She then shared a look with Blaine, wondering what to make of their interactions in this new light. Could they be two of the strongest god-touched beings in the city? If so, who was stronger?

The chairman continued, his gaze locked on Erin. "Let us not forget that the purpose of our council is to maintain balance and order, not to oppress those who have been chosen by the gods."

He turned back to the council members. "We will continue to monitor the situation, as previously agreed. Ms. Bevin, you are free to leave, but know that our eyes are on you and your temple. Should we deem it necessary, we will take action."

Erin nodded, her heart pounding in her chest. "I understand."

With a last look at Blaine, who offered her a small, reassuring nod, Erin turned and left the council chamber. As she walked down the marble corridor, she couldn't shake the feeling that everything had changed. The council's knowledge of her power only heightened the stakes, and she knew she would need to tread carefully in the days ahead. The revelation that she and Blaine were the most powerful devotees in the city added an extra layer of complexity to their relationship, and she couldn't help but wonder what the future held for them.

But for now, Erin focused on the task at hand: she still had six days to prove the worth of her temple to the city. And she was more determined than ever to fight for her cause, whatever the consequences.

CHAPTER 43

ERIN

Erin walked away from the council chambers, her heart pounding and her emotions a chaotic whirlwind. She felt a mix of anxiety and determination, knowing that her future was far from certain. What did it mean to be a ninth ring of power devotee? Would she have more sway, or would she be stuck with more expectations?

As she turned a corner, she encountered Jake, Blaine's butler, who she remembered had served him loyally for years.

"Miss Erin," Jake said, his voice gentle and respectful. "I saw you leaving the council chambers. May I offer you a ride home?"

Erin studied him, considering the offer. "Yes, thank you," she finally replied, grateful for the opportunity to collect her thoughts during the ride.

As they walked together toward the parked Bentley, Erin couldn't help but feel curious about the relationship between Blaine and his butler. She also felt a flutter in her stomach as she asked, "Jake, do you trust Blaine?" her voice was hesitant.

Jake looked at her thoughtfully, as if weighing his

response. "Miss Erin, I have known Blaine for many years. He is a man of integrity and vision, who has brought significant improvements to this city since he came to power. I am proud to serve him, and he has never once given me reason to question his allegiance or dedication to this city."

Erin listened carefully to Jake's words, her curiosity piqued. "What improvements do you mean?" she asked, eager to understand more about the man she was growing closer to.

Jake smiled, his eyes far away as he recounted some changes he had witnessed. "Well, for one, he has worked tirelessly to improve the infrastructure of the city, making it more accessible and efficient while also reducing derelict buildings. It's been an honor to witness the positive changes he's brought to our home."

Erin chewed on her lip. She witnessed those changes for herself, hadn't she? Thinking back through the past few years, she remembered seeing new buildings and public transportation expand, but it didn't seem that significant, just minor changes that didn't really move the needle for those stuck in the depths of poverty and suffering.

"That's great and all, but from what I can see, your loyalty runs deeper than just appreciation for some social projects. Can you tell me what makes him so special to you?"

Jake smiled, and there was warmth in his eyes. "Of course, Erin. Blaine has done a lot for my family and me. When my wife fell gravely ill a few years ago, we couldn't afford the expensive medical treatments she needed. Blaine stepped in without hesitation, not only covering the costs but also ensuring she received the best care available. He didn't have to do that, but he did, and I'll never forget it." Jake paused before adding, "Aside from his generosity, Blaine has a certain charm and charisma that captures people's attention, including yours."

Erin listened intently, touched by the depth of Blaine's kindness.

Jake continued. "He's also been a great mentor to me. He's taught me so much about politics, leadership, and the importance of integrity. I've seen firsthand how he's improved this city since he took office, and it's not just about his power as a devotee of Zeus. He genuinely cares for the people he serves, and he works tirelessly to make their lives better. That's why I trust him and why I'm loyal to him."

Erin nodded, understanding that Blaine's actions had earned him the unwavering loyalty of those closest to him. Jake's personal story provided her with valuable insight into Blaine's character and gave her hope that he could be trusted despite the uncertainties surrounding the shifts in their relationship and the council's scrutiny.

As they approached the Bentley, Erin felt a greater sense of trust in Blaine, knowing that he had earned Jake's unwavering loyalty. "Thank you, Jake," she whispered. "I appreciate your honesty."

They reached the car, and Jake opened the door for Erin. "My pleasure, Miss Erin." He paused with a hand to his ear, listening to an incoming message. "My apologies, Erin. I didn't realize the mayor would leave the council so soon. Blaine should join us shortly, if that's alright with you. If not, I can arrange other transport for you."

Erin couldn't deny the thrill that ran down her spine at the thought of seeing Blaine again. She fiddled with the hem of her dress, feeling a mixture of anticipation and nerves. "Sure. I don't mind. It's his car, after all."

Erin got into the car, and as they waited for Blaine, she continued to ask Jake questions, her curiosity driving the conversation. She wanted to understand the challenges both she and Blaine faced in their personal and political lives.

When Blaine arrived, he slid into the car beside Erin, his expression unreadable. As he placed a gentle hand on her thigh, she shivered at his touch. "I hope you don't mind me joining you," he said, his smile suggestive and flirtatious.

Erin shook her head, her heart fluttering with his intimate proximity. "Not at all."

As the Bentley glided smoothly through the city streets, Erin stole a glance at Blaine, her mind filled with questions. "Blaine," she began hesitantly, "are you going to keep a closer eye on me now that the intensity of my power has been revealed?"

Blaine sighed, his brow furrowed in thought. "I knew for myself when I saw you summon your temple from the earth itself. Your power will probably draw both admiration and scrutiny from the council. They'll want to ensure you use your abilities responsibly and in line with their goals."

"So I can expect Maria to be hounding me?"

Blaine sighed. "Not just Maria, although she certainly excels in that arena."

Erin nodded. "Does it change how you see me?"

"As for me," he paused, a hint of a smile on his lips, "it means we have a shared understanding of the challenges and responsibilities that come with our gifts."

Erin nodded, considering his words. She couldn't help but wonder how much the council knew about their relationship, and if it might complicate matters further. "Do you think anyone on the council knows about us?" she asked, her voice barely above a whisper.

Blaine's smile grew wider as he regarded her. "Well, that depends on what you mean by *us*. What do you think this thing between us is?"

Erin felt her cheeks flush, and she looked away, struggling to find the right words. "I'm not sure," she admitted, her voice soft. "But there's a connection here, something powerful. And I worry that if the council knows about it, they might try to use it against us, or at least me."

The atmosphere inside the Bentley was charged with emotion, and Erin could feel the heat of Blaine's body beside her, a comforting presence amidst the uncertainty.

Blaine reached out, his hand covering hers, his touch warm and reassuring. "You're right, there is something powerful between us. But we can't let fear dictate our actions. I'd advise we move forward with discretion and trust that whatever bond we share can withstand the challenges we face." Blaine leaned in closer, his breath warm against her ear, causing her to shiver. "I'd advise that we keep our encounters private," he whispered. He shot her a look, and Erin knew the answer without him having to say the words. "The council is pure politics, Erin. How do you think they would feel knowing that the two most powerful devotees in the region were aligning?"

"I'm not sure we're aligned in purpose, unless you mean horizontally," Erin quipped back, briefly recalling a steamy encounter they shared, a memory that made her heart race and her cheeks flush.

Blaine moved his hand from her thigh to her chin, gently

lifting her face to meet his gaze, and said, "I can assure you, we'll have plenty of opportunities to explore that alignment in the future."

"I suppose that remains to be seen," Erin whispered.

As they neared Erin's home, the Temple of Dionysos, they were both surprised to find a large crowd of people gathered there. She felt a pang of disappointment that her time with Blaine was ending, longing for more time alone with him. But then the sight of the crowd sent a jolt of anxiety through her, and Erin knew she had to address the situation immediately.

"I'm sorry, Blaine," she said, her voice strained with worry. "I need to see what's going on."

Blaine nodded, his own concern evident in his eyes. "Of course. I'll leave you to it."

Before Erin stepped out of the car, Blaine pulled her close for a passionate and lingering kiss, leaving her breathless and wanting more. Erin stepped out of the car and hurried toward the temple, her mind racing with questions. What was happening? Why were so many people gathered at her temple? As she pushed her way through the crowd, she couldn't shake the feeling that everything was about to change once again.

CHAPTER 44

Blaine York stared out the window of his sleek black sedan, his heart heavy with the weight of conflicting emotions. Jake maneuvered the car with practiced ease through the gathering crowds, leaving the Temple of Dionysos behind them. The early evening light cast long shadows across the road, deepening the furrows in Blaine's brow as he considered his growing affection for Erin and his responsibility as mayor.

"You seem deep in thought, sir," Jake observed, his tone tinged with concern.

Blaine sighed, running a hand through his hair. "I'm not sure what to do, Jake. I know we've just met, but Erin has become important to me almost overnight. I worry about her future here in Denver and what surprises her deity has for us all next."

Jake nodded slowly, his eyes flicking between the road and Blaine's face in the rear-view mirror. "It must be difficult trying to balance your feelings and responsibilities as mayor," he said. "Weren't you the one who told me everything has its perfect time and that when the moment comes, listen to the gods and your heart?"

Blaine smiled at that, grateful beyond words for the kindness of Jake's words. He felt a wave of relief wash over him as he realized he didn't have to make any immediate decisions about Erin. Not tonight, at least. All he had to do was take things one step at a time and see where they led him. With a newfound sense of peace, Blaine settled back into his seat. "Yes, I suppose I did. But truth be told, I don't think I'm worried about my heart or myself."

"So then, it's just about her being here in the city?"

"I worry about what Dionysos has planned for the city, and thus for all of us. To have his devotee appear overnight, as powerful as he's made her, makes me question where all of this is going. Plus, Erin is so new to the life of a god-touched, she doesn't really understand the risks or responsibilities that have been thrust upon her."

"It's a good thing she has you to mentor her then, isn't it?"

Blaine sighed, running a hand through his hair. "Is that what I'm doing? Mentoring her? That woman won't listen to a damned thing I say."

Jake smiled knowingly. "I get the impression she's listening more than you think, sir. I've seen the way she looks at you when you speak. She values your opinion and advice, even if she doesn't always follow it."

That gave Blaine pause for thought. He supposed it was possible that Erin was paying more attention to him than he gave her credit for. Still, he couldn't help but feel a certain amount of responsibility for helping Erin navigate this new life of hers. If the gods saw fit to put her in his path and entrust him with her care, then surely he should do all that he could to ensure her safety and well-being while she stayed in Denver. With renewed determination, Blaine decided he would do whatever it took to help Erin and make sure she had the guidance and support she needed.

As they rounded the Temple grounds, Blaine's sharp eyes caught the suspicious movements of Maria, Daniel, and Tom moving through the gardens. The three council members were huddled together, whispering to a group of people who wore expressions of determination and malice.

"Those three skulking around in the shadows can't be good. Jake, park the car," Blaine ordered, his voice tense. Jake complied without question, and Blaine exited the vehicle, keeping a cautious distance from the scheming council members.

Three figures moved amongst the shadows of the moonlit night, their faces hidden by hooded cloaks. Blaine's gaze darted between the strangers and the indomitable statue of Dionysos that overlooked the Temple grounds. Fear pulsed through him as he watched them conspiring. Their arms were animated with urgency as they pointed toward the temple, aiming to cause chaos in this sacred place.

Maria, her eyes glowing like the sun god Apollo, used his power to warm up the bronze of the statue, making it more malleable. Its outer surface undulated and glittered like liquid in the firelight. Daniel, inspired by Ares, infused his followers with an invigorating energy. Tom, a devotee of Hephaestus, distributed adzes he had crafted himself to the people who accepted them gladly.

Blaine felt a wave of emotions wash over him as he slowly grasped the magnitude of their deceit. He wanted to turn and run away, but he knew he could not stay silent and let them continue with their destruction of the Temple. He felt his heart pounding and beads of sweat forming on his forehead, but taking a deep breath, he walked forward and shouted, "Stop this now! Get out of here right away!"

The council members and the vandals stared, their expressions a mix of fear and disbelief. Blaine's jaw clenched and his eyes darkened as he crept closer to the group, the air becoming thick with tension.

Blaine stood rigidly before the council members, his finger pointed accusingly at them. His face was a hard mask of anger, and his gaze shifted from one member to another. "You're undermining my authority and betraying the trust of the people," he spat.

Maria stood tall and proud, a confident smirk curled across her lips. "The Temple is a threat to our entire way of life, Blaine, and yet you remain idle. We will take matters into our own hands if need be."

Blaine gritted his teeth, fighting to maintain his composure. "This is not how things are done in my town," he said, his voice low and dangerous. "Underhanded tactics have no place here."

The council members looked at each other, their faces betraying both fear and indignation. Maria stepped forward, her eyes flashing with defiance.

Maria sneered, her lips upturned into a spiteful grin. "You're just mad because we're giving the new girl in town a hard time," she said. "We were all put through tougher challenges when we first arrived here, so why should it be any different for her? Is that why you've been treating her differently? Is your opinion about her clouding your judgment?"

Blaine remained silent to Maria's allegations, instead warning her with a stern tone. "You're playing with fire, Maria," he said. "This is not like you."

Daniel's laugh was like a thunderclap, echoing around them in the dimly lit chamber. He leaned forward, speaking through gritted teeth. His clenched fists shimmered with energy and power, charged with imminent violence. "You can't protect Erin and the Temple all the time, Blaine. You'll slip up, eventually."

Ignoring their jabs, Blaine focused on the vandals, his face a mask of cold fury. His words were steely and direct. "I said get out!" The vandals fled, casting fearful glances back at Blaine as they scrambled away. The council members collectively shrank back, bracing themselves for Blaine's reaction.

With a final, seething glance at Maria, Daniel, and Tom, Blaine turned on his heel and walked back to the car. The broken gravel crunched underfoot as he strode past the others. His fists were clenched so tightly that they turned white with the pressure. "I need to report some vandalism to Erin," he told Jake, his voice thick with emotion. The words were clipped and tight, like a rubber band stretched too far. His eyes blazed with fury as he swept his gaze over the group one last time. "I won't be long." He kicked at a small rock as he made his way toward the parking lot, sending it hurtling through the air in a spray of dirt and pebbles.

Jake's eyebrows furrowed as he locked eyes with Blaine. His expression softened, and he nodded subtly. "I'll be here as long as it takes to work things out," he said, his voice strong and certain.

With every step toward the temple, Blaine's heart thudded in his chest. He could almost feel Jake's words weighing on his shoulders as he thought of all the ways he wanted to protect Erin and the Temple. But then again, it was his responsibility as mayor to stay objective, regardless of how he felt. He struggled with the thought of what was right and what wasn't as he trudged forward.

CHAPTER 45

ERIN

Erin walked the bustling temple's courtyard's cobblestone grounds, the air thick with anticipation and excitement. The warm, sultry air enveloped her as she made her way through the crowd of enthusiastic patrons. The vibrant music and laughter filled her ears, and the taste of incense, mixed with the tang of alcohol, lingered on her tongue.

"Quite the party, isn't it?" a voice called out from the crowd. Erin turned to see a young man smirking at her, his eyes twinkling with mischief. She smiled back, feeling invigorated by the atmosphere.

As she made her way upstairs to her room, the dull thud of bass reverberating through the floorboards, Erin quickly changed into a wisp of an outfit that allowed her to dance freely. Part tube top and part boy short, sheer, dark, forest green panels hung floor-length from both, giving an illusion of a dress while also revealing a lot of skin. Her flat-soled boots hugged her legs, begging her to pound her feet to the rhythm echoing through the temple. As she emerged from the dressing area, her body tingled with the urge to invoke her maenadic powers.

The music thundered through Erin's body, its relentless beat pounding insistently in her veins. She looked out over the dance floor, feeling totally in her element. Closing them again, she took a deep breath and let the energy surge through her. A wild, primal force that demanded release.

A sudden gust of wind seemed to swirl around Erin, causing her hair to stand on end. But even as she gave over to the rush of energy, Erin realized she didn't control it; the maenadic energy had a mind of its own, bursting forth and rippling out into the crowd.

Instantly, those around her moved differently; their movements became more frenzied and passionate as they felt the maenadic power coursing through their veins. They swayed and twirled in time with one another, their arms becoming extensions of each other's movements, as they created a harmonious dance between them that only they could understand.

Erin could feel the electricity flowing from person to person as if it were alive, creating an unspoken bond between those moving around her.

Erin felt a sudden thrill as she watched the creatures of myth and legend enter the temple courtyard. Satyrs and nymphs danced through the crowd, their hooves clicking on the cobblestone and their laughter ringing out like bells. A few of the partygoers glanced at the strange guests in confusion, but most just smiled and welcomed them.

Erin felt both awed and intimidated by this unfamiliar presence. The power they exuded was palpable, and it took all her strength not to cower in fear. She realized that this was part of what made them so fascinating. Their wildness and unpredictability were both exciting and intimidating.

The music changed from high-energy hip-hop to something more traditional, a slow bluesy number that seemed to draw all of them into another world. Couples swirled around each other, their movements becoming more graceful with each minute. As Erin watched, she yearned for more than just a good time. She wanted a connection, an experience that would last beyond just this moment.

Images of Blaine filled her thoughts, but Erin pushed him out of her mind. Right now, she needed to be here, with her people, surrounded by the magic of Dionysos.

With her initial worries put to rest, Erin allowed herself to be carried away by the music and the energy of the dance floor. She twirled and swayed, laughing with delight, as she caught sight of satyrs cavorting with the dancers and nymphs weaving through the crowd.

As Erin danced, her gaze was drawn to something that stopped her in her tracks. Unable to look away, she couldn't make sense of what she was looking at. But then, Erin had never seen a fae before today. In an alcove across the room, a beautiful male fae was enchanting a human, drawing them into a hypnotic dance. Her gaze lingered on the pair for a moment too long and the fae's ethereal blue eyes seemed to meet hers. The fae gave her a small smile before he returned his attention to the human in his arms.

Finn appeared by Erin's side, accompanied by Nia. He leaned in and whispered, "Fae haven't been seen in the city for generations. They're dangerous."

Erin's heart raced at the revelation, her eyes darting around the room as the gravity of the situation sank in. What had she unleashed by invoking her maenadic powers? The atmosphere in the temple had taken on a darker edge, with the wild energy of the mythical creature intensifying the sense of danger.

Erin nodded absently, still captivated by the fae's beauty. She knew very little about them, only that they were powerful creatures of myth and legend, capable of manipulating emotions and beguiling mortals with their magic.

However, as she watched his graceful movements, Erin couldn't help but feel drawn to him. She was mesmerized by his beauty and grace. It's as if he were from some other world entirely.

Finally tearing her gaze away from him, Erin asked Nia why the fae hadn't been seen here for so long. Nia shrugged and replied that no one quite knew. There were tales of dark rituals taking place within their realm that terrified most mortals who encountered them. But despite this danger, Erin couldn't shake the feeling that she wanted to experience this strange creature's power for herself.

With newfound courage, she stepped closer to observe the twirling couple further, albeit with caution this time. As she looked on with awe and admiration, Erin noticed something else intriguing about the fae; it had wings! Now and then, the iridescent structures would flutter ever so slightly, as if brushed by an invisible force.

"You can't," Nia whispered into her ear, grabbing onto her arm and holding her back. "I told you, it's not safe."

"I'm more resilient than you might think." She looked back at where the fae had been, but it might as well have disappeared. "Wait, where did it go?" Erin asked.

Nia shook her head. "I don't know. Maybe we got lucky, and it wandered off looking for better company."

The music swelled, and Erin felt a pull toward the outdoor area of the temple. She hesitated for a moment before taking a step toward the unknown. "This way," Erin said.

"Do you always run headlong into danger?" Nia asked, but she followed Erin, casting a worried glance back at the revelers. As they approached the entrance to the outdoor space, Erin couldn't help but wonder what other secrets the night had in store.

Erin stepped outside, her heart pounding in her chest. The cold air rushed past her, raising goosebumps on her skin. The contrast between the wild party inside and the stillness outside was jarring. Searching the shadows for any signs of the fae, Erin felt her heart racing and her breath quickening. Nia stood by her side, her eyes wide and fearful.

"Stay close to me," Erin whispered, her voice barely audible over the distant sound of the party inside. The scent of damp earth and fresh greenery filled her nostrils as they ventured further into the darkness.

In the faint moonlight, Erin spotted the statue of Dionysos that had once stood proudly in the temple court-yard. Now it lay on its side, the thyrsus it had once held aloft, impaling a lifeless fae. The once-mesmerizing creature was now a horrifying sight, its body contorted and eyes vacant.

Erin let out a gasp, her hand flying to her mouth. They ran together to the fallen body.

Nia's voice trembled as she whispered, "Oh, gods. What have we done?"

"We didn't do anything," Erin replied, but then she spied

the broken base of the statue. It looked like someone had burned and broken the stone itself. "But someone did. Wait, this isn't even the same fae. This one's female."

With a surge of adrenaline, Erin quickly cast a spell to grow a thick shrubbery around the fallen fae, hiding it from view. She knew she had to act fast. A dead fae would not only put her temple at risk, but the entire city would be in danger if the notoriously vengeful fae sought retribution.

"Stay here," she ordered Nia. "I'm going to get help."

Nia stayed behind to guard the hidden body while Erin hurried back inside, her heart pounding in her chest. She needed to find the summoning stone that Meri had given her, the one that would allow her to call for help from sources outside the council and Blaine.

As Erin frantically searched for the stone, her mind raced with the weight of the consequences. These fae had been drawn to her temple by the power she had unleashed, and she couldn't help but feel responsible for the tragic outcome.

Finally locating the stone in her underwear drawer, Erin clutched it tightly in her hand, feeling its cool, smooth surface. Summoning her courage, Erin prepared to call upon the daemon summoner, Meri, unsure of what would happen next. Her heart hammered in her chest as she whispered Meri's name three times, the summoning stone glowing in her palm. The room seemed to hold its breath, waiting for the unknown to answer her call.

As Erin completed the incantation, the summoning stone pulsed with an otherworldly energy. The air cracked, and the scent of ozone filled her nostrils. A strange sensation of being watched prickled at the back of her neck. Her heart pounded with anticipation, her grip on the stone tightening.

Moments later, Meri emerged from the shadows, out of the darkness itself. Erin wondered how the summoner had managed it, but she had bigger issues to manage.

"You called?" she asked, her voice smooth and sultry.

Erin felt her breath catch in her throat as she studied Meri. There was an air of mystery and danger surrounding her, but Erin knew she could trust her.

"Yes, I need help," she admitted, her voice wavering slightly. "A fae was killed here tonight, and I fear the consequences for my temple and the city."

Meri's eyes flashed with inner fire, reflecting a deep understanding of the gravity of the situation. "I see. Are you positive it was fae? They haven't been seen in some time."

Erin nodded. "Nia, my cook, confirmed it. She's a devotee of Coyote and claims she's seen them before."

Meri seemed to weigh her with her gaze, eventually letting out a sigh of resignation. "Fae are not to be trifled with. But let's look," she said, her voice low and serious. "Time is of the essence."

"It's just outside." Erin led Meri back downstairs and across the dance floor, the weight of the situation bearing down on her. The world she had known was rapidly changing, and she couldn't help but wonder what dark secrets and dangerous encounters awaited her.

With a deep breath, she followed Meri into the night, the fate of her temple and the city hanging in the balance. The outdoor area seemed to grow colder and darker as they approached the hidden fae corpse.

Nia and Bono stood nearby, quietly awaiting their return. Somehow, Bono had found out about the death and had cleared the area of revelers, and Erin found herself grateful for that small blessing.

As they neared the spot, Meri's eyes narrowed, taking in the dense shrubbery that Erin had grown to conceal the body. "Show me," she demanded.

Erin waved her hand, and the shrubbery parted, revealing the gruesome sight of the impaled fae. Meri inhaled sharply, her expression darkening. "You were right to call me. If the fae discover this, there will be Sheol to pay."

"What do we do?" Erin asked, desperation creeping into her voice.

Meri thought for a moment, her brow furrowed in concentration. "I can't manage this on my own, so you're gonna have to trust me."

Erin felt a chill run down her spine. She could have called Blaine, but she suspected if he or the council knew what had happened, they'd use all their powers to shut her down. "I don't have anyone else to turn to, Meri. What do you need me to do?"

Meri fixed her with a serious gaze. "You're gonna have to get real cool, real fast, with some good friends of mine."

CHAPTER 46

NADIR

Nadir surveyed the gruesome scene before her, the metallic scent of blood and the sharp tang of fear heavy in the air. The dead fae's lifeless eyes seemed to bore into her very soul, reminding her of the potential consequences that loomed over them all. She knew she needed help. Specifically, the unique skills and knowledge of her daemonic cabal mates.

Closing her eyes, she reached out through her mental connection to Azimuth, calling him to her side. In response, a familiar sandalwood scent filled the air, and moments later, Azimuth materialized beside her. His skin seemed to glow in the dim light, a stark contrast against the shadows cast by the temple's walls. To Nadir's surprise, Kobol and Orias appeared a moment later.

As the daemons appeared, Erin, Nia, and Bono all took a step back, their eyes wide with a mixture of fear and awe.

"Daemons," Bono whispered, while Nia's hands shot up as she prepared to fight them off if she had to. Erin looked at each of the new arrivals, drinking in the moment's novelty.

The air crackled with tension, and Nadir could feel the prickling sensation of magic in the air. Nadir tried to imagine the moment from the human perspective.

Kobol, the stout warrior with fiery red curls, wielded a hammer that thrummed with energy. Orias, a dark-skinned oracle surrounded by murmuring shadows that had an eerie life of their own, carried a curved, ornately engraved scimitar that gave off a powerful hum. Azimuth also fought with a sword in hand, and Nadir understood all three had come ready for battle.

She offered the humans a reassuring smile, explaining that her allies were here to help. "Relax," Nadir said, her voice exuding confidence, "these three always arrive ready to party. This is just a different party than they're used to."

Erin swallowed hard, her eyes flicking between the imposing daemonic figures before her. The soft rustle of their clothes and the low hum of Orias's scimitar amplified the tension, filling the air with apprehension. "Alright," she agreed, her voice barely above a whisper. Erin gave a slow nod, rolling with the situation far better than Nadir had imagined. "Welcome to the Temple of Dionysos. I'll take all the help I can get right now, even from daemons. If you're friends with Meri, then I'll trust you can help me."

Brief introductions were made, and then everyone's attention quickly turned back to the dead fae.

A frown etched itself across Azimuth's chiseled features. "This is bad. I warned you about the consequences," he said, his voice tense. "The fae's presence is a consequence of you befriending a god-touched and helping her. These ancient beings only stayed away because everyone else kept separate and to the rules."

Orias stepped forward, the shadows around him whispering softly, as if they shared a secret. "True," he conceded, "but the fae's return isn't Meri's fault. In fact, I've seen something coming in my visions, something even I was afraid to put a name to. Now that I see the fae before us, it doesn't seem real, and yet there can be no confusion. The fae are back for good, and I fear they will wage war on the other races, especially if one of their fallen is discovered."

The weight of the oracle's words hung heavily in the air, bringing a hushed silence to the group. The taste of unease lingered on their tongues, and the distant sounds of raucous laughter from the temple felt jarringly out of place.

Azimuth had gone ashen, his radiant aura dimmed by dread. His eyes were wide with fear as he exchanged an anxious glance with Kobol. The stout warrior looked equally shaken, his ruddy complexion paling as he gripped his hammer with white knuckles.

Seeing the unflappable daemons so shaken sent ice water through Nadir's veins. Never had she witnessed them react this way, not even when battling the vicious drakes of Muspelheim. Their visible dread could only mean one thing —the fae's resurgence didn't just endanger them, it could mean utter annihilation.

Nadir nodded, her expression serious. "What can we do to prevent that from happening?" she asked, her gaze meeting Erin's.

The scent of damp earth mingled with the sharp tang of blood as they examined the dead fae and considered their options. The tension was palpable in the air, as each of them knew that one misstep could lead to a catastrophe.

Kobol, still studying the fae's lifeless form, finally spoke up. "We can't just bury it here. That would be too obvious. And we don't want the fae to think that one of their own has been murdered."

"Couldn't we hide the body in the burrow?" Nadir asked.

Azimuth shook his head. "Porting it to Sheol isn't an option. We'd trigger wards just by bringing him over the threshold."

"Plus, the fae have ways of tracing their own," Orias added. "They'll find him once they come looking. We need to get this one far away from here, and fast."

The group exchanged glances, the gravity of the situation pressing down on them like a lead weight. Nadir's fingers traced the intricate patterns of her daemonic tattoos, seeking comfort in their familiar grooves.

Azimuth's fingers brushed Nadir's arm, the brief touch a silent reassurance. His voice was soft, but firm. "We need to make it look like the fae left on his own accord to avoid raising any suspicions."

Kobol's eyes twinkled with a sudden idea, a wicked grin spreading across his face. "What if *I* make it look like the dead fae is leaving of his own will?" he asked. "If everyone sees him walk right out of here, then no one will look to blame Erin."

"How can you manage that?" Erin asked.

"You'll see," Kobol said, shooting her a conspiratorial wink. "If we can hide the blood, I think I can make it work."

The group stared at him, considering the audacity of his plan. It was risky, but the stakes were high, and they had to try something. The sound of their heartbeats thundering in their ears, drowning out the distant noise of the temple party, as they weighed the consequences.

Erin, biting her lip in apprehension, interjected. "What can the rest of us do while Kobol moves the fae?"

Orias stepped forward, his voice a hushed murmur. "I'll use my connection to the shadows to create a diversion, drawing attention away from the area."

Nia nodded, a determined glint in her eyes. "I can help by returning to the party and making sure everyone is focused on the celebrations."

"And I'll stay close to Kobol," Nadir added, "providing support if needed."

With the decision made, the group prepared to execute Kobol's daring plan. As they began, the air seemed to thrum with anticipation, and the scent of danger mixed with the fading sandalwood, leaving them all on edge. It was a desperate gamble, but it was their only hope to prevent starting an all-out war with the fae. With one last shared glance, they set their plan into motion, hoping against hope that it would be enough to stave off disaster.

CHAPTER 47

ERIN

Kobol stood in the center of a circle created by Erin, Meri, Orias, Azimuth, and Finn. He paced back and forth, his arms waving wildly as he explained his plan in a voice filled with enthusiasm. Erin studied their faces. Meri's eyebrows were knitted together in concentration, Orias stood with his brow arched and lips pursed, Azimuth had crossed his arms in disapproval, and Finn gave a tight-lipped nod. She wondered if she was the only one who thought this was madness.

"Are we really doing this?" she asked, raising an eyebrow.

Erin looked around the circle, her heart racing. Kobol was so enthusiastic and yet, she couldn't help wondering if they were really going through with this plan. She caught Meri's eye and gave her a questioning look. Meri shrugged in response, but before Erin could say anything, Orias spoke up.

"Kobol, I don't think this is a good idea," he said, his voice even. "It seems too risky." Azimuth nodded in agreement while Finn frowned and remained silent.

Kobol let out a sigh, his exuberance waning. "I recognize

your anxiety," he uttered. "But I am confident that if we can make this happen, it will secure Erin's Temple." He paused for a moment, then looked each member in the eyes and asked, "Do you believe in me?"

The other four exchanged glances as they deliberated silently among themselves. Finally, Erin spoke up. "I just met you, but if Meri trusts you, so do I," she said firmly, deciding after a few moments of consideration. The others followed suit, and soon they were all resolved to embark on the daring plan that Kobol had concocted despite their reservations about it being too risky.

"Oh, we're doing it," Kobol responded, grinning. "And it's going to be epic."

Erin sighed. "All right, let's do this."

Meri flicked her fingers, and the massive bronze statue of Dionysos groaned before lifting into the air. Azimuth stepped in and grabbed the floating metal, helping Meri move the bulky statue off the fae and out of the way. As he pushed the statue back, the thyrsus popped off into his hand.

"Whoops," Azimuth said. He turned and held out the staff to Erin. "I suppose this is yours."

Erin accepted the staff with reverence, Azimuth's icy blue eyes holding hers, the weight somehow light in her hands. "Thank you."

Closing her eyes, Erin turned to the fae and concentrated, imagining a lush garden springing up around them. She felt power course through her veins and slowly opened her eyes to see ivy creeping up the fae's long dress and winding around her waist. Dainty morning glories sprouted from the sleeves and petals from the collar, creating an elaborate and beautiful tapestry over the top of their clothing, hiding the blood and making it seem as if the fae were wearing a living costume. Vines intertwined with flowers, creating a stunning, if slightly morbid, ensemble. It was an elegant touch, if she did say so herself.

Orias stepped forward, his green eyes alight with power. He spread his hands, and the air seemed to thicken, growing darker until it formed a heavy, impenetrable veil around the fae's face. The shadows wove in and out of each other, swirling in an incomprehensible pattern that made her features seem almost alive while hiding her glassy gaze.

Kobol, grinning like a madman, stepped forward and disappeared from view. But as he did so, the fae began to move as if she were alive. Her limbs twitched and shifted, responding to Kobol's unseen manipulation as he brought her to her feet. Orias was spellbound as they watched the fae's body animated before their very eyes. Orias reached out and caught the fae just in time, holding her steady.

The scene was both eerie and mesmerizing, as if they were puppeteers putting on a show for the gods themselves.

Meri stepped forward and surveyed the scene, her hands on her hips. "Right then," she said. "Az and I will act as lookouts. We'll engage the second there's trouble."

Azimuth nodded in agreement, though his eyes were cold and calculating. He was clearly ready for whatever might come their way.

As they moved away, Erin noted the way Azimuth's hand rested on the small of Meri's back, and the mystery of how Meri knew the daemons fell into place in Erin's mind. Clearly, the two of them were together, and Kobol and Orias were his friends. Or something like that. She wondered how a daemon and a daemon summoner were together. Hopefully, she'd get the chance to learn their story someday.

Erin watched with growing fascination as the fae moved under Kobol's command. She wasn't sure if it was because of her own magic, or some other force at work, but she could feel the energy radiating from the daemons and the dead fae alike.

A handsome man stepped forward to ask for a dance from the fae. His face lit up with a confidence that seemed both bold and strange. He was clearly accustomed to being the life of whatever party he attended.

Erin watched intently as Orias backed away, seeming to allow this man his turn. Under Kobol's control, the fae made an elegant gesture with her hands and then sprang to life, swaying like a willow in the wind. Her movements were swift but graceful, as if she could somehow escape death's embrace.

Every eye in the room seemed entranced by her beauty, her simple movements conveying an emotion that was deeper than anything words could express. The energy in the room seemed to shift as they all watched.

As the dance ended, Orias approached the fae again. This time, he had Finn with him, and both of them looked a little too solemn for the party. Orias appeared to be introducing her to Finn, and then they held a conversation with her. Under Kobol's expert control, the dead fae simply nodded now and then, as if she was trying to understand what they were saying.

A few minutes later, a tipsy guest insisted on taking selfies with the "costumed" fae. The smell of alcohol wafted off him, and his words slurred together as he fumbled with his phone. Kobol had to keep adjusting the fae's pose to create a convincing photo, while Orias discreetly intervened with his shadows placed thoughtfully to prevent any incriminating images.

"Smile, darling!" the tipsy guest cooed, snapping photo after photo.

After the impromptu photo-shoot, the dead fae gave a couple of low bow-like nods, her pale skin and silver-tipped wings shimmering in the club's neon lights.

The club-goers seemed spellbound, their eyes transfixed by the fae's peculiar appearance as she pranced around and then disappeared into the night. People whipped out their phones to snap photos and videos of her fleeting figure, like they had just witnessed a once-in-a-lifetime event. Erin watched on, pleasantly surprised by their delight at the abnormality of it all. The absurdity of the situation was almost comical, but it only added to its entertainment value; it was too outrageous to be true.

Orias stood within the throng, watching the fae leave, establishing to all that she'd left alone.

Kobol's plan had clearly established the dead fae's movements in the Temple and that they'd left alone. Yet Erin couldn't help but worry about the fae's ultimate destination. Would it be to a street in the city, an unmarked path in the woods, or some far away bar she had never heard of? With every step Kobol had the fae take, Erin's fear and anticipation grew as she wondered what fate awaited the body.

Perhaps it was better if she didn't know.

Just as Kobol had got the fae out of the club, Erin spotted movement in her peripheral vision.

Blaine! He was here.

Blaine quickly approached Erin. His eyes were wild, and

his voice trembled as he spoke. "Erin, what is going on here? Are those fae? And daemons?"

Erin wanted to remain cool, but she could tell Blaine was shocked and disturbed by the presence of the fae, daemons, and a daemon summoner in the club. And in his city.

"Blaine, it's a long story," she began, trying to sound nonchalant, "but trust me, we're handling it."

Her heart raced, and she felt his gaze intensely as they were put to their very limits in trying to think of a way to manage the situation. The plan that took so much effort was about to be tested.

CHAPTER 48

BLAINE

Blaine stared at the bizarre scene unfolding before him, struggling to process the fae, daemons, and a daemon summoner in Erin's club. His shock quickly turned to concern for her safety, and he felt a gnawing need to help her, despite the potential consequences of his position as mayor. He clenched his fists, his knuckles turning white, as he tried to contain his mixed emotions.

"You're handling it, Erin?" he called out over the thrumming beat of the music, trying to keep his voice steady. "We need to talk. Now."

Erin looked up, and her eyes widened when she saw the determination in Blaine's face. She nodded and guided him to a quieter corner of the club. The pulsing beat of the music and the kaleidoscope of colorful lights made it difficult for Blaine to focus, but he forced himself to push past the sensory overload.

"How the Sheol does this happen, Erin?" Blaine demanded, his voice a mixture of concern and anger. "Fae?

Daemons? In your club? What am I saying? What are they doing in my city?"

"Blaine, I have no idea how the fae got here." Erin's voice was soft but determined as she recounted to Blaine the details of her findings. "But you should know, there's been a murder," she spoke in hushed tones. "I found one of the fae dead in the Temple gardens. I think someone is trying to frame me or the Temple staff for it. I called my friend, Meri, the daemon summoner, to help me out. The daemons are her friends."

As soon as the words fell from her lips, he remembered the vandals Maria, Tom, and Daniel had been rallying earlier. If they were involved, then for better or worse, it was on Blaine to help clean up their mess. Blaine leaned in, his face contorted with concern, and asked, "Wait, what makes you think someone is trying to frame you?"

Erin continued. "The daemon Kobol misled everyone by hiding the fae's death. Her departure just now that you witnessed, was under his power." She looked directly at him, her emerald orbs assessing his reaction.

As Blaine listened to her explain the gravity of their situation, he noticed the fire in her eyes. He clenched his jaw and tried to ignore the desire that was stirring within him. But despite his better judgment, he couldn't help but be moved by her courage and strength. His anger dissolved, replaced with a newfound admiration for her.

Blaine shook his head, clearing his thoughts. "That's quite a feat, but I'm sure I don't have to tell you this is still a precarious situation. You were right to hide the body," he said. He took Erin's hand and gave it a gentle squeeze. "Fae haven't been seen in human lands in generations. For them to come here tonight, to your club, is concerning enough. For one to die by human hands is tantamount to a war declaration."

Erin's tone had grown gentler as she spoke. "Blaine, I know we barely know each other, and I understand that this might ask a lot. All I need to know is, are you here to help me or make things worse?"

Blaine hesitated for a moment, his mind racing as he considered the potential fallout from his decision. But as he looked into Erin's eyes, he knew he couldn't let her down. He nodded, his resolve hardening.

"I'm with you," he said, his voice firm. "We'll sort this out together."

Erin smiled, relieved and grateful.

"What do you need me to do?" he asked.

"Now that the fae is gone, I need to clean up the scene of the crime before someone discovers the mess."

It was clear she was determined to find out who framed her—if indeed someone was—and clear her name once and for all.

"Lead the way," he replied.

Erin led Blaine outside to an area overgrown with shrubbery. With a flick of her wrist, the bushes parted, and she pulled him through after her. She brushed away a few branches and pulled Blaine behind her. His eyes widened, and he took a step backwards when he saw the statue of Dionysos, the ancient Greek god of wine and revelry, that had been the target of the council's vandals earlier. A pool of blood was drying on the ground next to the statue, a gruesome reminder of the violent act that had just occurred.

Blaine frowned. "What happened here?" he asked Erin.

She didn't answer right away, but examined it carefully before she finally spoke. Erin gestured toward the foot of the statue and then explained. "It looks like someone tore apart the base. No wonder it fell over. But why?"

"Perhaps they were run-of-the-mill vandals?" Blaine said, putting a voice to his concern.

Erin arched her brow. "You think the fae's death was accidental?"

"It's not like anyone expected the fae to show up here," Blaine replied. "That doesn't leave much opportunity for a motive. An accident is the next likely option."

"So what, your theory is that vandals damaged the statue, which just then fell over on a fae who no one predicted would show up here?" Erin asked.

"Unless we can find something else, then yeah. It's the simplest possibility," Blaine replied.

Erin pursed her lips into a deep frown. "Let's just go over everything again."

With renewed determination, they began combing through the area surrounding the statue, looking for evidence that would help them uncover what had happened earlier that night. Together, they worked in sync and shared secret glances as their bond grew stronger.

"Anything?" she asked.

"Nothing new," Blaine replied. "Maybe we should call it and clean up."

Erin sighed. "All right. It was worth a check."

Then she took a deep breath and raised her arms. Blaine's heart raced as he watched Erin wield her maenad powers, her movements graceful and confident as she righted the statue, fixed its base, and then turned the faery blood deep into the earth. Before long, the interior of the little glen looked utterly peaceful again, as if nothing had tainted this sacred ground. Blaine was awed by her abilities and found himself more attracted to her than ever before. He realized that, against all odds, he was falling for her.

Erin magically dismantled the shrubbery surrounding the statue and then they returned to the Temple in the wee hours of the morning, grateful to see the crowds had thinned a bit from earlier. Erin pulled Blaine into an alcove along the edge of the main room, a convenient location to monitor action without being pulled into it. Hidden from the watchful eyes of the club's patrons, Blaine took a deep breath, his heart pounding in his chest, and shared his feelings with her.

He pulled her close and whispered into her ear. "Erin," he said, his voice barely audible over the din of the club. "I need to tell you something."

Erin looked at him, her eyes filled with curiosity and concern. "What is it?"

Taking a deep breath, Blaine fixed his gaze on her and declared firmly, "I'm head over heels for you," his words resonating with the intensity of his feelings.

Erin stared at him, her eyes wide with surprise. For a moment, she was silent, and Blaine felt his heart sink, fearing that he had made a terrible mistake. But then she smiled, her eyes shining with happiness.

"I've been falling for you too, Blaine," she whispered, her voice filled with warmth and affection.

They melted into a passionate kiss, their connection growing stronger with every lingering touch. Blaine's hands explored her body and ignited the smoldering fire of desire between them. The chaos of the club seemed to fade away, leaving only the two of them intertwined in an intimate embrace.

But their moment of intimacy was short-lived. As they pulled away from one another, the scene shifted, and they were suddenly brought back to the reality of the situation. The club's noise and energy washed over them, reminding them of the urgent task at hand.

"We did it," Erin whispered, her voice filled with a mixture of disbelief and pride.

"Yeah," Blaine agreed, his heart swelling with affection for her. "We really did."

Their moment of triumph, however, was brief. A figure detached itself from the shadows, and Blaine's heart leaped into his throat as he recognized one of the fae.

The fae approached them slowly, their eyes filled with curiosity and wariness. Blaine felt a sudden determination to make the situation right and to show that he could be a mayor who could handle even the most extraordinary of circumstances.

"Hello," Blaine said, stepping forward and extending his hand. "My name is Blaine, and I'm the mayor of this city."

The fae hesitated for a moment, then reached out to grasp Blaine's hand, their touch sending a shiver up Blaine's spine. "I am Althea," the fae said, their voice melodic and otherworldly.

Blaine nodded, trying to appear calm and collected despite the pounding of his heart. "I'm glad to meet you, Althea. We rarely have visitors like you in our city."

Althea's eyes flicked to Erin and back to Blaine. "Yes, I can see that. We were drawn here by a powerful force." The fae's gaze lingered on Erin, and he knew she was who the fae was referring to. "It seems your city is becoming more interesting."

Blaine glanced at Erin, whose tense smile couldn't have been more forced. "Yes, it is. And we're doing our best to navigate those changes."

The fae regarded Blaine for a long moment, their expression unreadable. Then, to Blaine's surprise, Althea nodded slowly. "Very well, Mayor Blaine. We shall see how your city fares in these strange times. Tell me, what is this place?"

CHAPTER 49

NADIR

The city's shadows cloaked Nadir and her cabal mates, their figures barely distinguishable in the dim light of the crescent moon. The air was ripe with the city's usual nocturnal scents: a blend of exhaust fumes, fried food from late-night eateries, and the damp earthiness of a recent rain. Somewhere, a dog barked, the echo bouncing off the narrow alleyways. The quartet moved with deliberate precision, a choreographed dance honed by years of experience, their task as grim as the night itself.

Nadir, her daemon-touched senses heightened, focused on the task at hand. Her eyes, sharpened by her daemonic elements, cut through the darkness, scanning their surroundings for any signs of intrusion. In her hands, the lifeless form of the fae felt hauntingly cold, a stark contrast to the warm, vibrant creature it once was. Orias held the other end of the body, shrouding the form in shadows.

The chatter of Azimuth and Kobol served as the backdrop to their grim endeavor, the pair engaging in a morbid debate over the best place to leave the body.

"I'm telling you, Azimuth," Kobol persisted, his eyes flashing brilliant green in the darkness, "burning is the most efficient way."

Azimuth snorted, rolling his eyes. "Because nothing says *nothing to see here* like a roaring fae pyre in the middle of the city. We need something commonplace. Something that points away from Erin, her temple, and the god-touched. But not too far away, either."

"We have to be smart about this," Kobol said firmly. "I remember the stories of old. The fae won't care how one of them died, or where."

Nadir chimed in, a hint of exhaustion lacing her words. "While you two debate on how best to draw attention to ourselves, Orias and I will settle for stashing the body in some dark corner. I'm not even sure why the placement matters that much, as long as it's in some communal space."

Azimuth nodded. "If the fae aren't sure who's responsible, it'll delay their response and give us time to come up with a plan to help your friends."

"I thought you were against us working with the god-touched?" Nadir asked, surprised at his sudden change of heart.

Azimuth's voice was filled with urgency as he spoke. "I was afraid of the risk of breaking the pact which kept the fae away. Now that they're back," Azimuth paused here for a moment to let those words sink in, "all bets are off." He looked down at his hands, his expression tense.

The air around them felt heavy and oppressive, like a storm was brewing just beyond the horizon.

Orias' ever-watchful eyes darted around them, his dark brown eyes filled with a steely determination. His silence spoke volumes, the weight of their situation visible on his face.

"Do your visions have any guidance for us?" Nadir asked him.

"My sight is quiet. Unusually so for such a unique situation," he replied, his voice low and somber. "I can't see beyond the darkness that surrounds us."

Nadir felt a pang of worry. Orias' visions had always been a guiding light for their cabal, a tool they had relied on time and time again to avoid danger. Why would his sight be silent at a time like this?

"We'll manage," she said firmly, trying to reassure both Orias and herself. "We've faced worse than this before."

Azimuth and Kobol nodded in agreement, their expressions grim but resolute. Nadir felt a flicker of pride. Despite their differences, they were united in their cause, working together to achieve their goal.

"I'd recommend we leave the fae somewhere near running water, if possible," Orias continued. "Their kind are often instinctively drawn to it."

"The Cherry Creek Trail is just south of here," Nadir replied. "It should give us a few quiet places to hide them."

They moved in silence for a few more minutes, the only sounds being the shuffle of their footsteps. Finally, they reached the trail. Moving quickly down a deserted and winding bike path, they were soon surrounded by high walls, cultivated embankments, and a rushing stream. It was the perfect place to leave the body—out of sight, and unlikely to be disturbed.

Nadir and Orias placed the fae's form gently on the mossy ground, positioning her as if she'd simply sat down to look at the water. Kobol and Azimuth cast a quick spell, masking the area from human eyes so the body would remain undisturbed. When they finished, the fae's clothes rustled, causing Nadir to jump back.

"What's that?" she asked, and a moment later, a snake slid out of the fae's clothing, its skin iridescent in the moonlight.

Kobol immediately stepped forward and grabbed it, his hands steady and sure. "Do we let it go or kill it?" he asked, his voice tinged with a hint of uncertainty.

Nadir felt her heart tug at the thought of killing the creature, so small and fragile compared to their powerful enemy.

Azimuth took a deep breath before speaking. "Let it go. It's not our place to decide this one's fate." They all nodded in agreement, and Orias released the snake into the tall grasses lining the trail, letting it slip away until it disappeared out of sight.

"We should go," Orias said softly, his gaze fixed on the fae's still form. "Before we're seen."

Just as they were finishing, Orias suddenly swayed, his eyes glazing over. His legs buckled beneath him, and he would have hit the ground had Nadir not darted forward to catch him. A wave of fear washed over her, her heart pounding in her chest like a war drum.

"Orias!" she exclaimed, her voice echoing off the walls of the bike trail. Azimuth and Kobol spun around, their faces pale under the moonlight. They rushed over, their previous argument forgotten. The banter had died, replaced by a tense silence as they all stared down at Orias, waiting.

Orias' body was rigid in Nadir's arms, his eyes glazed over and unfocused. His lips moved, but the words were nothing more than whispered fragments of a language that was not meant for human ears. His body jerked suddenly, a shudder running through him, and his eyes snapped back into focus.

Everyone held their breath, waiting for him to speak. "Belial," he rasped, his voice hoarse as if he'd been screaming. "The fae. It's all going to change."

Nadir's heart clenched in her chest. "Change how, Orias?" she asked, her voice steady despite the panic that was slowly creeping up on her.

Orias shook his head, his gaze distant. "I don't know," he admitted. "Darkness falls like starlight."

As if summoned, a sudden force yanked at their very essence, pulling them toward their master. Nadir knew it was Belial summoning them. The timing couldn't be worse, but when their daemon prince called, one didn't have the luxury of delay.

Azimuth was the first to react. His eyes flashed an icy blue, concern evident in his gaze. "We need to move," he said, his voice hard. He helped Nadir lift Orias, his arm around the seer's waist for support.

"Let's go," Kobol grunted, glancing around the river one last time. The fae's body was moved away from the Temple and their tracks were erased as best as they could.

Nadir cast one last glance at the hidden fae body, a sense of foreboding filling her. Orias' vision, the summoning, it all pointed to an approaching storm. She tightened her grip around Orias and followed Azimuth and Kobol, their figures just barely discernible in the darkness. The night was no longer just grim; it was ominous, filled with uncertainty and a sense of impending chaos.

As one, they ported back to the main room of the burrow. The incorporeal pull of Belial's summoning tugged at their cores. It was an insistent, unyielding pull that each of them was all too familiar with. In the center of the room, Belial awaited them, his imposing figure casting long, monstrous shadows on the walls. His crimson eyes bore into them, a cruel smirk playing on his lips.

"You're late," he chastised, his voice echoing in the cavernous room.

"A delay, my lord," Azimuth explained, bowing his head in deference. "We saw fae while out hunting in the city, and Orias had a vision."

Nadir admired the bit of creative honesty on his part. If they could help it, withholding their role in hiding the fallen fae from Belial might keep him from directing his irrational behavior their way.

Belial's interest was piqued. "Oh? Do tell."

Orias stepped forward, his face pale but determined. He relayed the sparse details of his vision, his voice steady even as the others felt a chill run down their spines. He also described seeing the fae at the Temple without specifying the location.

Belial fell silent, his gaze distant. Whether he was shocked by the fae in the land of humans, it wasn't clear. When he finally spoke, his voice was low, the smirk gone from his face. "This portent confirms all of my fears. We must take the cleansing to the next level."

Before any of them could respond, the room trembled, a blue light surrounding them, flickering violently. Nadir clung to Azimuth, her heart pounding in her chest. Belial stood in the center of it all, his eyes ablaze with a fierce light.

"This is our time of action, and you, Nadir, can delay swearing fealty to me no longer. You will fully commit to our cause, or you will die by my hand."

Nadir's eyes widened in shock. She'd avoided giving in to the prince for so long, she'd almost believed he might forget and let it go. But it was clear his patience had curdled like rotten milk. She tried to move, but Belial held her fixed in place with a single look. His voice reverberated through the cavern, echoing off the walls—an ominous sign of what was to come.

At once, the blue light intensified and grew brighter, pinning them all in place as it enveloped them. Nadir felt her body temperature rising as she was drawn toward Belial by some invisible force, a power that seemed to come from within him and course through his veins like electricity. She closed her eyes and clung tightly to Azimuth's hand as they were all ported away from their current location.

When Nadir opened her eyes again, she stood atop a rocky ledge, looking into an abyss so vast it seemed infinite. The air was heavy with smoke and steam, making it difficult to breathe or see very far at all. Nadir recognized this place; it was one of the deepest parts of Sheol and home to some of its most powerful daemons.

Nadir shivered at the thought of facing whatever lurked beneath them in these depths. Even worse, what would become of her if she failed?

CHAPTER 50

ERIN

Erin's pulse raced as she stood beside Blaine, watching him attempt to engage the standoffish fae, Althea, in conversation. The air in the room felt charged, and the scent of magic was palpable. She caught Blaine's glance and stepped in. "Hello. I'm Erin, the devotee of Dionysos," she announced, hoping to find common ground with the enigmatic creature. "I summoned this Temple in his honor."

Althea tilted her head, her silvery hair shimmering in the dim light as she took in the building. "Interesting," she murmured. "This is a curious place. It tastes new." The fae's voice was melodic, yet eerie, sending shivers down Erin's spine that felt like ice creeping over her skin.

Blaine's eyes narrowed with determination. "Althea, why have the fae come here? Our worlds have been separate for so long," he asked, trying to sound diplomatic.

The fae chuckled, a sound that was both enchanting and unsettling, like the tinkling of delicate glass. "Ah, the human world. So full of surprises and chaos. We find it all boring.

Yet our curiosity has led us here once again. It's as simple as that," Althea explained, her eyes glinting with mischief.

Erin noticed Blaine's mind racing, and she could practically feel his concern for the city radiating off him.

"So, what exactly do the fae want?" Erin asked, pushing Althea for more details.

Althea's expression softened, and her lilac eyes sparkled with a hint of sadness as she replied. "We seek entertainment and the return of what is rightfully ours."

Blaine took a deep breath and squared his shoulders, determination written all over his face. "I would like to negotiate an understanding between the fae and the people of this region," he said firmly. "What can we offer to make this happen?"

Althea regarded him silently, her expression unreadable. When she spoke, her voice was low and solemn. "Humans have lied to us before," she said. "The fae do not trust you anymore."

"But we're still good for entertainment?" Erin asked.

Althea's gaze shifted from Erin to Blaine, and she smiled. "That remains to be seen." With a slight bow of her head, Althea stepped back and faded into the shadows, leaving a lingering scent of magic in the air.

Erin watched as Althea disappeared into the night, her mind racing to make sense of everything that had just happened. She glanced at Blaine, who was standing still in shock, unable to believe what he had just heard. But before they could discuss what the fae had meant, the sound of Maria's voice cut through the air like a knife.

"Blaine!" Maria called out, her eyes narrowing as she

glimpsed Althea, just as the fae was preparing to leave. "What is the meaning of this? Are you consorting with these creatures?" Her tone dripped with disdain.

Erin watched as Blaine turned to face Maria, his face resolute. "Maria, what are you still doing skulking around here?"

"I was checking up on you and here I find fae and daemons making themselves welcome in this den of iniquity, with you rolling out the welcome for both."

"That's not true, Maria. I'm trying to understand what the fae want and why they're here. It's important for the region's safety."

Maria scoffed, her anger boiling over like a volcano about to erupt. "Safety? You call this safety? Allowing dangerous creatures to infiltrate our city?" She stepped closer, her eyes locked on Blaine's like a predator sizing up its prey. "You've lost your focus on your job, Blaine. This is unacceptable. I demand a no-confidence vote for you before the council. It'll be held within the hour. You might want to show up, assuming you can tear yourself away from this maenadic menace."

Maria glared at Erin, lip curling in disgust. "Was it not enough to stir chaos with your drunken hordes? Now you consort with fae and daemons too? You are a plague upon this city, a corrupting influence poisoning our order."

Her eyes flashed with contempt. "I name you anarchic ingrate, churlish cretin, debauched degenerate! You are a fermented fruit, rotten from within, spreading contagion wherever you tread."

Maria turned back to Blaine, disdain etched in her face.

"Cast out this Dionysian deviant before she brings the walls crashing down around us all. I will not stand idle while you let everything we've built teeter on the brink of ruin."

Erin observed as Blaine's face tensed, but he maintained his composure. "Maria, we don't have time for your poetic games. We need to discuss this situation rationally. The fae are here, and we need to understand why," he stated firmly, his confidence unwavering.

"Rational? You've allowed this place to become a hub for creatures known to war and terrorize humanity. You've lost sight of what's important for our city," Maria hissed, her voice venomous.

Taking a step forward, Erin's voice was steady but firm. "Maria, the fae have caused no harm yet. We're trying to keep the situation under control. Surely, you can understand that."

Before Maria could respond to Erin's words, a low growl echoed through the room. The next thing she knew, there was a flash of black and the air shifted with the musky smell of cat. Blaine's eyes widened as a large leopard entered from the gardens and prowled toward them, its golden eyes fixed on Maria. The beast circled around Erin, bumping against her legs when it passed by, before taking a seat at her side.

The beast let out a low, breathy growl, showing off its sharp teeth. Maria's eyes went wide as she stumbled back, momentarily speechless. The leopard's tail flicked back and forth as it continued to grumble menacingly, its muscles rippling under its spotted fur. "You're keeping wild animals here too?" she finally choked out, her voice barely above a whisper in the face of such danger.

"I suppose I am," Erin replied, scratching the leopard between the ears. "Good kitty, now calm down, little buddy," she said to the cat, who quieted at her request, and then laid down on the ground. Was this animal's appearance connected to Dionysos, or something else? When Maria cleared her throat, Erin decided she could figure it out later. She turned back to Maria. "It's just the one wild animal. At least so far."

Blaine took a deep breath, standing tall and resolute. "Maria, I'll address your concerns at the council. But right now, we need to focus on understanding the fae and their intentions. That is the best way to protect our city."

Finn came in from the gardens, saw the three of them and the cat, and came over. Erin nodded to him, but he raised a querying brow. She shook her head. He kept his distance, but was close enough to overhear everything.

Maria hesitated, her eyes darting between the leopard and Blaine. She was clearly unnerved by the beast. Finally, she shook her head, her voice strained. "No. One hour, Blaine. You better have answers by then or you can face down the council's vote."

With that, Maria turned on her heel and stormed away, her fear quickly transforming back into anger. Erin let out a steady breath, her gaze shifting from the retreating figure of Maria to the mysterious leopard that had come to their aid. She sensed Blaine's unease and knew the challenges were mounting. The next hour would be crucial in determining not only his future but also the fate of the city.

As Erin looked at Blaine, she saw the weight of responsibility on his shoulders, and her heart went out to him. But they had no time to waste. Finn moved close, joining them.

"What's up with the leopard?" Finn asked.

The cat huffed back at him, licking its lips.

"I'm calling him Enigma. And you can chill, Enigma," Erin said, and the leopard whined, but the cat laid down his head. "I have no idea where he came from, but who doesn't want their own pet leopard? Besides, he seems to like me."

Blaine chuckled softly, his eyes alight with amusement. "I can see that. But we can't let Maria's threats distract us from the matter at hand. We need to figure out what the fae want and negotiate with them to ensure the safety of our city."

"The fae are gone for now," Erin replied. "Blaine, we should go meet with the council so you can defend your position."

"We?"

"Yes, we. You can't stop me from coming along."

"I'll manage the nightly cleaning crew while you're away," Finn added.

"Thanks, Finn. I'll be back in a few hours."

Blaine smiled, and Erin felt a warmth spreading through her. Taking his hand in hers, she said, "Let's go."

They turned to go, and the leopard stood and began following them. Erin held up her hand. "No, Enigma, if I show up to the council with you, they'll just have something else to bitch about. Be a good boy and stay here."

Enigma shook his head like he was throwing off water, and then, to her surprise, his form shimmered and shifted, leaving a snake where he'd been standing. She bent down and picked it up, tasting magic in the air in the wake of the creature's transformation. "You're not a kitty, and not a snake, not really. What are you?"

"A boon from the gods?" Blaine suggested.

Erin shrugged. The snake wound its way around her arm and then flattened out, leaving a distinctive tattoo pattern embossed on her flesh. Erin gasped in shock, but she could feel the power of the animal emanating from her skin. She felt connected to it, like they shared some kind of bond.

"It looks like my new companion has a few tricks up his sleeve," she said with awe in her voice. "Well, my sleeve. But we can figure Enigma out later. Let's get going."

CHAPTER 51

BLAINE

Blaine and Erin left the temple, the tension from their confrontation with Maria lingering between them. As they stepped outside, Jake pulled up in Blaine's sleek black car, the rumble of its engine purring like a satisfied cat. Erin glanced at her arm, where Enigma had settled as a snake tattoo. The intricate pattern seemed to writhe with a life of its own, making her shiver.

Blaine opened the door to his car and held it open for Erin. She climbed in, and he followed suit, shutting the door softly after him. In the quiet darkness of the interior, he turned to her, his voice low and serious. "Erin, we have to talk about what happened back there. What do you think Althea meant by *the return of what's rightfully ours?*"

Erin shook her head in disbelief. "I can't even guess. I've read enough of the old fairy tales and fantastical novels about the fae to have the basic idea that the fae are vengeful, but they rarely explain why. How much of those stories are based on reality?"

Blaine pushed his hand through his hair. "I'm not sure.

It's been generations since their kind walked this plane. I'm sure the city archives have something, which would be where we could start. Luckily for us, the archives just happen to be next door to where we're headed."

Erin shifted her position on the seat and looked up into his eyes. "I could also ask Meri about it," she replied. "She and her daemon friends might have access to fae lore that we don't."

"She might indeed. How do you know the summoner?"

"Oh, I ran into Meri right after Dionysos did, well, whatever he did to me. She's famous in certain circles, and I'd thought she might help me out. She explained that god-touched individuals are outside of her expertise, but she offered her aid if I needed it. Despite her reputation for having a swarm of daemons at her disposal, she's proved to have a compassionate heart."

Blaine nodded and then looked out the car window at the darkened streets of the city, pondering their next move as they drove through the early pre-dawn toward their destination. Blaine had recognized Meri's name when they met; by her reputation, she was feared and respected in equal measures. He'd never used a summoner's daemons to reach his goals, but he knew plenty who had and knew the high costs that came with it. Blaine made a mental note to dig into the daemon summoner's past a little.

"I'm glad Meri came to your aid, but I wish Maria hadn't been there to see the daemons. Or the fae, to be honest."

Erin nodded and sighed, her brow furrowing. "It must be my temple," she muttered, looking out the window.

Blaine's expression darkened as he considered this new

information. "Do you think that's why the fae have returned?" he asked.

Erin nodded sadly. "I don't know for sure, but something drew them back and I think it might be because of me," she said, her voice barely above a whisper. "They want something from me, and whatever it is, it must be important enough for them to make the journey here from their realm."

Blaine reached over and gave Erin's hand a reassuring squeeze. He was determined to figure out what the fae were after and protect Erin from whatever danger they posed.

"We'll get answers in the archives," Blaine said decisively. "We can start there and see what else we can find out about your temple regarding the fae. Maybe then we'll have some idea of why they're coming back and what they're after."

Erin smiled gratefully at him before turning her gaze back onto the passing scenery outside their car window.

Blaine sighed, and took another long, appraising look at the wild woman in the seat beside him. "You're proving yourself a force to be reckoned with, Erin."

"I'm aware I have a lot to prove," she replied. "But I'm doing the best I can with the situation, and I want the council to know that my goal is to make things better for everyone."

"The council has its own agenda," Blaine said, his voice heavy with disappointment. "I used to think they were working for the greater good, but seeing your dedication to improving the lives of ordinary people has made me rethink their motivations."

Erin looked at him, clearly surprised by his change of heart. "So, what do we do now? What happens if the council passes this no-confidence vote?"

Blaine took a deep breath, steeling himself. "Then I'll no

longer be Mayor. I'd still be on the council. I'm too powerful for them to oust me there, but they'd call for new candidates for the position. If that happens, you need to nominate yourself."

"Are you really suggesting I..."

"I am," Blaine said, feeling a surge of conviction in his words. "If I can't be in charge, I'd rather have you leading than any of the other council members."

Erin's eyes widened in disbelief. "Me? Blaine, I don't want to be mayor. I'm just trying to help the people, not rule the city."

He met her gaze steadily, his expression unyielding. "But that's precisely why you should take up the mantle. If the council ousts me in the no-confidence vote, you're powerful enough to claim the title. If you don't prove your strength, they'll keep coming for you until they force you out."

Erin's cheeks flushed with a combination of embarrassment and admiration. "But it's not just about power. You really think I could do it?"

"Yes," he replied without hesitation, his eyes never leaving hers as he savored the moment between them. He felt himself leaning in toward her and his gaze traced hungrily over her lips. His heart beat faster and he could sense her breath quicken as she leaned closer, and suddenly their lips were locked in an impassioned embrace that seemed to last for eternity.

The taste of Erin's lips was like ambrosia, intoxicating and addictive, and Blaine wanted nothing more than to stay there forever. He ran his hands along her curves and savored the feel of her body against him, as their mouths moved together with a fiery intensity that sent sparks through his veins. He fought against the urge to give himself over to the bliss that was overwhelming him as he struggled to contain his desire for her. He knew they were in a car being driven by Jake, and it was only his awareness of their chauffeur that prevented him from giving into temptation entirely.

Before they knew it, the vehicle had stopped, and the council meeting was upon them. They pulled away from one another, neither of them eager to depart. Erin's eyes smoldered with unspoken desire as she whispered throatily, "We should continue this later." To which Blaine could only nod fervently in agreement before they stepped out of the car and made their way toward the council chambers, hand in hand. With every step he took, he felt his determination grow stronger, because he knew that when this was all over, he would have Erin by his side. Come what may. Even if it meant fighting for her every step of the way.

He couldn't bear to let go of her hand as they walked together and couldn't help but feel aroused by her proximity once more; wanting nothing more than to sweep her off her feet right then and there, but knowing he had to wait until later when they were alone again before he could satisfy all his desires fully. Blaine resolved himself to savor every moment with Erin until that time came.

CHAPTER 52

NADIR

Nadir and the group materialized in an unfamiliar, nightmarish realm within Sheol. Her heart raced as she took in her surroundings. Jagged rocks jutted out from the ground like the teeth of some colossal, slumbering beast. The air was heavy with acrid smoke and steam, and the scent of sulfur hung heavily in the air, assaulting her senses. Nadir felt a shiver run down her spine, an uneasy mix of fear and determination coursing through her veins.

Belial stepped forward, his crimson eyes gleaming with anticipation. "Welcome to the Infernal Realms," he said, his voice echoing across the desolate landscape. "Nadir," he said, shaking his head in disappointment. A dark chuckle escaped his lips. "When we last spoke, you assured me of your loyalty and dedication to my cause. And yet here we are, in this cursed realm within Sheol, and I cannot help but feel that you have not been faithful to our agreement."

"Despite my patience with you, you have failed me time and time again," he spat out angrily. "Despite giving you every opportunity possible to prove yourself loyal, you have instead chosen to shirk away from your obligations! Do not think for one moment that I cannot see how little effort you've made. Do not think for one second I will forgive this betrayal!"

He paused for a moment and gazed at her intently before continuing. "Your hesitance to act on my command has caused us much delay already," he continued sternly. "You understand that if you wish to remain loyal to my cause, then your actions must reflect your words."

"What are you going to do?" Nadir replied, the words sticking in her throat.

Belial raised a clawed hand. "Silence! Your loyalty to me is bound by blood, and I'm tired of sparring you with words. Your words are fickle, Nadir, and I no longer trust you to hold to your agreements. Here, you shall face my challenge with the weapon you continue to refuse to use," he declared, gesturing to the sancre belted at her waist. "The weapon I have ordered you to use as frequently as possible."

Nadir's eyes flicked to the weapon, her fingers flexing at her side. Though the thought of the challenge ahead filled her with trepidation, she could not refuse him. She gave a curt nod, acknowledging her obligation.

A cruel grin spread across Belial's face. "You must face this challenge alone." He turned his gaze to the others, his voice a low growl. "None of your cabal-mates are to assist you."

Azimuth opened his mouth to object, but the look in Belial's eyes silenced him. Orias and Kobol exchanged uneasy glances, the tension between them palpable. Nadir felt a wave of gratitude for their concern, even as fear knotted in her gut.

With a flick of his wrist, Belial summoned a monstrous daemon from the abyss. Nadir felt her skin crawl as the creature emerged from the abyss. Its form seemed to be made of a patchwork of body parts, some recognizable and some strange and alien. Despite its grotesque appearance, it still moved with an air of confidence, as if it was sure of its strength and power. She looked up at Belial and saw his lips pulled into a thin line, the only evidence he showed of his displeasure.

The beast's beady eyes fixed on Nadir, and its snarl filled the air as it lunged forward, claws outstretched in a deadly arc. She pulled her sancre blade from its sheath, the lightweight, short, silver metal not filling her with confidence. The daemon lunged at her, its massive claws cutting through the air with a deadly hiss. Nadir brought her sancre down in an arc toward the monstrous foe, deflecting its strike before landing a hard blow on its head. The creature recoiled with a howl of rage but pushed forward again with renewed vigor.

Nadir dodged the attack, her daemon-enhanced reflexes kicking in. The sancre flashed in her hands as she sliced through the daemon's claw, drawing black ichor. She grinned, her heart pounding with adrenaline. "Is that all you've got?" she taunted, her voice dripping with dark humor.

The daemon roared, its eyes blazing with rage. It flew toward her again, relentless in its hunger. Nadir's heart leaped into her throat as it reached for her, the creature moving like a streak of lightning. Just as its claws grazed against her skin, she dodged its grasp, but not without consequence. A trickle of blood oozed down her arm, dripping onto the dirt beneath them.

Nadir continued to fight against the daemon, her weapon clashing against its claws in a symphony of destruction. Each time she blocked or struck it back, it seemed to become more enraged; each failed attack seemed to make it more determined. Sweat poured down her face as she fought for her life, and yet, somehow, she kept up with its speed and ferocity.

Orias and Kobol watched helplessly, their expressions a mix of fear and frustration. Azimuth glared at the daemon beast with unholy fury, the icy white nimbus of his powers swirling around him. But what could any of them do? Belial's command was absolute, their vows in peril for defying the prince.

As the daemon bore down on her, Nadir tired, her movements slowing. She knew she couldn't keep this up much longer against the massive beast. Panic rose within her, an icy feeling that threatened to choke her.

Nadir struggled to remain standing. When a piece of broken rock twisted beneath her foot and she fell onto her back, her eyes widened as she saw Azimuth leap forward to intervene. His aura shone like a miniature star through the darkness as he drew the daemon's wrath away from her. She watched, locked in place by terror, unable to move for fear that the daemon would target anyone else within its sights. A surge of gratitude washed over her, quickly followed by sorrow as she realized Azimuth might be harmed in this attempt to save her.

The creature struck Azimuth with a devastating blow, sending him hurtling toward the edge of the abyss. With a strangled cry, he disappeared over the edge, his body swallowed by the darkness below.

"No!" Nadir screamed, scrambling back onto her feet, her voice raw with anguish. But the daemon was upon her again, its hunger for her blood undiminished. She had no choice but to fight, her terror morphing into rage. "Damn you!" she roared at the daemon, her voice echoing in the dark abyss. Her hands tightened around the sancre. She had to survive. She had to save Azimuth.

Leveraging her daemon strength, Nadir charged toward the beast. The sancre glowed with an eerie light as she sent it spinning through the air. Her metal-moving ability, a gift from her daemon blood, directed the weapon unerringly to its target.

The blade embedded itself into the daemon's skull with a sickening crunch. The beast let out a guttural roar of agony before collapsing to the ground, its life force quickly ebbing away. As the creature died, its form crumbled into ash, swept away by the merciless winds of Sheol.

Nadir didn't have time to celebrate her victory. She sprinted toward the chasm, heart pounding in her chest. The edge loomed ahead, an ominous void that promised nothing but despair. But she couldn't think about that. All she could think about was Azimuth.

"I'll find you, Azimuth!" she yelled, her voice a defiant cry against the howling wind. Without a moment's hesitation, she hurled herself into the chasm, a human-daemon hybrid diving into the unknown.

As she fell, the world around her a blur, she glanced back one last time. Belial stood at the edge, his cruel grin replaced by an expression of surprise. Orias and Kobol looked on in horror, their faces pale.

With a last, determined glance at her friends, Nadir turned her gaze downward, her heart filled with determination. Whatever lay below, she would face it. For Azimuth. For herself.

And with that, she disappeared into the darkness, leaving behind only the echo of her promise.

CHAPTER 53

ERIN

Erin's heart pounded like thunder in her chest as she followed Blaine into the dimly lit council chambers, the air oppressive and charged with tension. Every molecule of air was humming with anticipation; her skin prickled with a sense of foreboding. Everywhere she looked, members of the council sat in their chairs, their expressions a curious mix of disdain and curiosity, cold eyes throwing daggers as they took in the sight of her. Blaine sat down opposite the chairman, who gave a stately nod in acknowledgement, but no extra seat was provided for Erin. She wasn't part of the council.

Maria stepped away from the table and addressed them all. "We are here today because our city is under threat—from both outside forces and within." Her gaze locked onto Erin before quickly turning away again. "This Dionysian devotee has acted without regard to our customs and authority. We have recently had encounters with both fae and daemons at her so-called temple, yet our mayor has failed to address these issues appropriately."

Tom and Daniel nodded in agreement, and their lips curled into sardonic smiles. The rest of the council shifted uncomfortably in their chairs, murmuring among themselves and nodding, although some seemed uncertain.

Erin's heart ached as everyone united against Blaine because of her arrival, but determination rose within her. She wouldn't give in without a fight. She stepped forward, boldly, and met Maria's gaze. "I'm here to help, not hinder, the progress of this city."

A cacophony of laughter erupted from the council members, who couldn't contain their mirth at her nerve. Except Maria, who waved them to silence, her gaze hard and unforgiving as she challenged the chairman. "Silence, wildling! Must I remind you that you're not even a member of this council?" She turned back to the chairman. "I call for a vote of no confidence in Mayor York."

Erin took a deep breath and steeled herself for what was to come. She could feel the energy radiating from every corner of the room, everyone watching as if they were waiting for Blaine's next move.

The chairman held up his hand. "Does anyone second the motion?"

Tom and Daniel raised their hands without hesitation, as did Bella, the devotee of Aphrodite. Erin took a deep breath and steeled herself for what was to come. It felt like every eye in the room was watching them, waiting for Blaine's next move.

The chairman spoke into the tense silence that followed, addressing Blaine directly. "Well then, before we vote, would you like to make a statement, Mayor York?"

Blaine nodded and stood, his gaze confident and determined. "I understand the council's concerns, and I take full responsibility for any missteps I may have taken. However, I do not believe my actions warrant a vote of no confidence. As mayor, it is my duty to protect and serve our citizens, and I believe that is what I have done. As your mayor, I will continue to do all that is within my power to ensure this city remains safe from any danger—outside and within its borders," he paused for a moment glancing around the room once more before adding softly, "as well as ensure that the customs and traditions of our city are upheld."

The council members murmured in agreement, their faces softening slightly at Blaine's words. Bella leaned forward, looking thoughtful. But Maria remained unmoved, her eyes icy as she addressed Blaine again.

"Your words are admirable, but they do not erase the fact you've allowed a Dionysian temple to thrive unchecked. This brazenly flouts our laws and customs!"

Maria's voice rose, anger simmering beneath her controlled tone. "And it does not stop there. This rabble-rousing maenad openly cavorts with daemons and consorts with the resurgent fae. Her reckless revelries threaten every-thing we've built!"

She slammed her fist on the table. "Erin flouts authority at every turn. Her seditious temple encourages dissent and rebellion among the lower classes. Productivity has dropped sharply thanks to her drunken hordes. Profits are down across all sectors!"

Maria then leaned forward, eyes blazing. "She under-mines the social order we've painstakingly cultivated. Erin and her cult are a cancer to this city! Either she is brought to heel, or everything we've worked for will be torn asunder. I call on you, Mayor York, to act before it is too late!"

She sat back, chest heaving from her tirade. The other council members wore uneasy expressions, shifting in their seats. Maria had given voice to their unspoken fears. Erin could upset the delicate balance that kept them flush and powerful.

Blaine maintained an impassive facade, but internally he weighed Maria's dire warnings. Erin was a force beyond his control, and she might cut off the wellspring of their prosperity. He would need to choose his next steps carefully. "I understand that the temple's practices may not be in line with our customs, but they are not breaking any laws. They have harmed no citizens of our city and have actually helped many who were in need. As mayor, it is my duty to ensure the safety and wellbeing of all citizens, regardless of their beliefs."

The tension in the room hung thick like a stormy fog, pungent and heavy with sweat and fear. Erin stood off to the side, her heart thundering in her chest as she watched the scene unfold. She knew that the outcome of this vote could make or break Blaine's career as mayor, and she was determined to do everything in her power to help him.

Finally, the chairman spoke again, his deep baritone booming through the chamber like a freight train. "Very well. The council has heard both sides. It is now time to vote on the motion of no confidence against Mayor York."

Erin held her breath as the council members raised their hands, some hesitantly and others with more conviction. Blaine was about to lose his position as mayor. Desperate to prevent that outcome, she acted on instinct.

"I challenge Blaine for the mayorship!" she shouted, her voice ringing out like a trumpet throughout the room.

The council members gasped in astonishment, their shocked whispers echoing off the high ceilings of the chamber like a chorus of ghosts. Maria's eyes widened, her face turning a deep shade of crimson. "You? You have no place in this council, let alone as mayor!"

The chairman, an older man with a weathered face and sharp eyes, raised a hand to silence Maria. "The challenge has been made, and I declare it valid," he said. "It is within Erin's rights as a citizen and devotee to challenge for the position of mayor, unlikely as her win might be."

"This is unacceptable! We can't place a maenad in charge of this city!" shouted Tom in opposition to Erin's challenge.

"We can't ignore this issue any longer," argued Bella, the devotee of Aphrodite, "and there may be no better opportunity. Let them fight."

The discussions continued to swirl around them while Erin kept her gaze firmly on Blaine. His blue eyes widened, a mix of surprise and admiration clear in his expression despite his apprehension toward the situation.

"Erin," he said, his voice carrying a note of concern.

Just then, there was a loud bang from outside the chamber doors; everyone's attention snapped toward it as the doors slammed shut with a reverberating clang that echoed throughout the room. The room fell silent; Erin felt a chill run down her spine. Something was about to happen, and she had a feeling that nothing would ever be quite the same again.

CHAPTER 54

ERIN

Erin squared her shoulders and took a deep breath, her pulse racing as she prepared to face Blaine in a battle for the title of mayor. At the snap of the chairman's fingers, the council chambers emptied of furniture, leaving the space open for the duel ahead. The air in the chamber crackled with anticipation, the scent of magic lingering heavy in the air. A murmur of disbelief rippled through the room, and the council members exchanged uneasy glances. The chairman, a tall, imposing figure with an air of authority, stepped forward to explain the rules of the challenge.

"Erin and Blaine will fight using their respective powers, granted by the gods they serve," he announced, his voice stern and clear. "The first to yield or be rendered unable to continue will be declared the loser, and the winner will take the title of mayor."

Erin met Blaine's gaze, her heart aching as she saw the conflict in his eyes. Their feelings for each other added a layer of complexity to the battle that was about to unfold. She knew that winning would mean causing him pain, but she also recognized that losing would put her temple and the city at risk.

Blaine stepped forward, his eyes flashing with a mixture of determination and regret. He spoke first, his voice low and serious. "I know this isn't easy for you, Erin. But I won't hold back," he warned her.

Erin smiled sadly in response, tears welling in her eyes. She knew she had to stay strong if she was going to win- but it wouldn't be easy. Taking a deep breath, she steeled herself and returned Blaine's gaze with renewed resolve.

"Neither will I," she said softly but firmly. It was time to put their feelings aside and prove who was the stronger fighter, at least when it came to the battle for mayor. The tension in the chamber seemed to grow thicker as the two stared each other down, ready for battle. With a determined nod, she steeled herself for the fight.

The battle began with a clash of thunder and a flicker of sparks. Blaine summoned a bolt of lightning, sending it hurtling toward Erin. She narrowly dodged the attack, her own powers from Dionysos surging through her veins. A collective gasp filled the council chambers as the bolt crashed into the wall behind her. The lightning had burned a pattern in the stone, an intricate vine-like design that seemed to be an omen of things to come. Shards of rock rained down from the ceiling and smoke billowed from where it had hit; although no one was hurt, it was clear just how powerful these opponents were.

Blaine might plan for her to win the battle, but it was clear he would not hand over his position to Erin without a fight.

Erin shivered with adrenaline and dread as she realized

that victory would not come without cost. With newfound courage, she summoned forth all her strength and launched herself at Blaine. As Erin called upon her magic, the tattoo of Enigma, her shapeshifter pet, glowed brightly on her arm before releasing from her flesh.

A split second later, Enigma sprung forth in leopard form at Erin's side, snarling and baring its teeth at Blaine. The council members gasped in awe at the sight of the leopard, its fur a brilliant golden color. It seemed almost as if its presence was a reminder from the gods that Erin was favored to win this battle.

Blaine's face softened as he looked upon the majestic creature, and for a moment, it seemed as if he had acknowledged Erin's supremacy. But then his expression hardened, and he was still determined to fight to the end.

Feeling a surge of energy wild as nature itself, Erin concentrated on the ground beneath Blaine's feet, causing the stone floor to soften and become unstable. Blaine struggled to maintain his balance, as the earth seemed to undulate beneath him, his eyes widening in surprise at Erin's newfound power. But just as quickly as it began, Erin stopped her assault, unwilling to cause him serious harm.

Blaine, sensing Erin's hesitation, smiled sadly and responded with a blast of stormy wind that whipped around Erin, tousling her hair and stinging her skin with an electric edge of raw power. Erin gritted her teeth and channeled her own magic to counteract the gust, creating a thick barrier of undulating grapevine that protected her from the worst of the onslaught. She glanced at Blaine, their eyes locking for a moment in a silent acknowledgment of the bittersweet nature of their confrontation.

"Erin," he said sternly, his voice a mix of frustration and admiration. "You're holding back. Don't you think it's time to show me your full power?"

Erin's eyes widened as realization washed over her. She was indeed holding back, afraid to hurt Blaine with her true potential. She had been too focused on not hurting him. She had forgotten that this battle should impress the other council members, showing she was worthy of the title. As they locked gazes, she realized Blaine was right; she had been hiding her strength, and it was time for her to finally unleash it.

With newfound confidence and a surge of inspiration, Erin summoned forth all the energy within her body and unleashed a powerful wave of magical energy toward Blaine. He stepped back, clearly cautious of her magic, and barely avoided the onslaught of energy as it burst into sparks around him.

The sparks sparkled in the air, slowly drifting down until they reached Blaine's feet and spread out like a blanket of stars. Immediately, Blaine's muscles slackened as a magical inebriation took hold. He swayed on his feet, desperately attempting to stand upright before finally giving up and collapsing onto the ground to the shock of everyone present.

Erin smiled victoriously as she watched Blaine succumbing to her magic. With this powerful display of her strength, she had proven herself worthy of the title she sought and hoped she'd earned the respect of at least some of the council members present. Her magic was not something to be trifled with, and those who dared would ultimately succumb to its power.

Blaine raised his hands in surrender. He called out to the chairman, his voice laced with a mix of drunkenness, resignation, and pride. "I yield to Erin," he announced, his starry-eyed gaze never leaving her face.

Erin, taken aback by Blaine's sudden concession, felt a mixture of relief and sadness wash over her. She knew he had yielded not only because of their feelings for each other but also because he truly believed she would be a better leader for the city than the others on the council. The council members stared in shock at the unexpected turn of events, their eyes wide with disbelief and uncertainty.

The chairman stepped forward, his face grim yet resolute. "It appears we have our winner," he declared solemnly, pointing a finger at Erin, who stood wide-eyed and trembling with adrenaline amidst the destruction she had wrought through her divine powers.

Before Erin could fully process the chairman's declaration, Maria, Tom, and Daniel stepped forward, their faces set in determination. "We challenge Erin as well," Maria announced, her voice cold and clipped. Tom and Daniel nodded in agreement; their eyes focused on Erin, who sighed inwardly as she prepared for another battle. Their respective powers from Apollo, Hephaestus, and Ares shimmered around them, ready to be unleashed.

With the chairman's terse nod, Erin faced three challengers at once. She could feel the intensity of their combined power, a mixture of divine energy that sent shivers down her spine. She glanced at Enigma, who stood at her side, a low growl in its throat.

Maria, wielding the power of Apollo, drew a circle of light in the air before her. The luminous arc surged toward Erin, who narrowly avoided the attack, feeling the searing heat as it passed by. Tom's powers from Hephaestus unleashed a barrage of molten projectiles that rained down upon Erin. The air filled with the acrid smell of burning earth, and she nimbly evaded the molten metal, her movements swift and graceful.

Daniel, a devotee of Ares, was the most aggressive of the trio. With a roar, he charged at Erin, his fists crackling with red energy. Erin called upon her own powers and summoned a wave of pulsating vines to entangle Daniel, temporarily immobilizing him. The sound of snapping branches and the scent of crushed leaves filled the air as she fought to maintain her control over the vines.

As the battle raged on, Erin tapped into the depths of her magic. Her connection to Dionysos empowering her with every passing moment. Enigma snapped his teeth and slashed his claws at any who got too close. A second source of strength and resilience that bolstered her resolve.

With a swift and fluid motion, Erin conjured a storm of vines and thorns, the tendrils whipping through the air and lashing out at her opponents. Maria, Tom, and Daniel fought back with their respective powers, the room becoming a chaotic maelstrom of divine energy. The floor trembled, and the air hummed with the force of their magic.

In the heat of the battle, Erin's focus shifted between her three opponents, her mind working quickly to counter each of their attacks. With a surge of power, she knocked Maria off balance; the vines ensnaring her legs and rendering her immobile. Tom's molten projectiles were neutralized by a swift whirlwind that Erin conjured, the wind snuffing out the flames and scattering the molten metal harmlessly to the floor.

Finally, with a triumphant roar, Erin broke through

Daniel's defenses, a torrent of vines wrapping around his body and pinning him to the ground. As the dust settled, the three challengers lay defeated, their powers spent, their bodies bruised and battered.

The chairman stepped forward, admiration radiating from his face. "Does anyone else wish to challenge the maenad?" His voice echoed in the stillness as he made his proclamation: "Well then, as I see no other prospects, Erin has surpassed her adversaries, and I declare her the new mayor of our city."

As the chairman declared Erin the new mayor, a wave of disbelief washed over her. She'd won, but the victory felt bittersweet, the weight of responsibility settling heavily on her shoulders. She glanced over at Blaine, who gave her a small, pained smile, his own conflicting emotions mirrored in his eyes.

"Erin, we swear our allegiance to the office, but you have yet to prove yourself worthy of our loyalty," Maria said coldly, struggling to her feet. Despite her recent defeat, she maintained a regal air, her gaze steady and unwavering. "Remember that your duty is to the people, not just to your own carnal desires."

Tom and Daniel, though battered and bruised, echoed Maria's sentiments. They extended their hands toward Erin in a show of forced respect, the tension between them palpable. Erin reached out, grasping each of their hands firmly, their icy expressions reminding her of the uphill battle she faced in winning their trust.

Together, the five of them stood in the center of the council chamber, a symbol of a new beginning for their city.

Shifting back into the form of a snake, Enigma wound its way up her leg and back around her shoulders.

The chairman, having overseen the entire ordeal, offered his firm handshake. "Congratulations," said the chairman, his voice echoing off the walls. "You have started a new chapter for this city. Let's hope it is prosperous, yes?" He smiled and turned to leave, leaving behind a stillness that was almost sacred.

The other council members shook her hand one by one, offering negligible congratulations while casting wary gazes at Enigma, and then left, one by one. With the others gone, Erin and Blaine stood alone in the council chamber, their eyes meeting in a mixture of sadness and understanding. Only when they had all left did Enigma let out one last hiss before effortlessly sinking back into her skin, leaving a scaly tattoo etched along Erin's skin.

"I never wanted it to be like this," Erin whispered, her voice heavy with regret. Blaine reached out, his fingers gently brushing against her cheek, the warmth of his touch sending shivers down her spine.

"Neither did I," he replied softly. "But maybe this is for the best. Our city needs change, and you have the strength to make it happen. I'll help you, Erin. I'll train you to become the mayor this city needs."

Erin's eyes filled with gratitude, and she nodded. "Thank you, Blaine. I'll need all the help I can get."

Their eyes locked, and for a moment, the electricity between them exploded again. The dizzying pull compelled her to take a step forward toward him. She was so close she could smell his skin, like sunshine and balsam on a fall day.

Drawing in his scent, her heart raced as he reached out to touch her face with his hand.

As if on cue, their lips met in a passionate embrace, the kiss long and lingering. The fight between them was forgotten in that moment, replaced by the reassuring certainty that no matter what happened, they'd be there for each other. When finally the kiss ended, Blaine pulled Erin into his arms and held her tight, their bodies pressed together as if nothing else mattered in the world.

And it didn't. As long as they had each other's support, nothing else mattered.

"Didn't you say we could learn more about the fae in the city archives?" Erin asked.

"Ready to get to work already?" Blaine looked at her with respect and then nodded in agreement. "It's not far. Let's go."

CHAPTER 55

NADIR

Nadir plummeted into the dark chasm, her heart pounding in her chest. Fear gnawed at her, but she pushed it aside, focusing on the task at hand. With a burst of adrenaline, she extended her limbs, her daemon-enhanced agility transforming her fall into a calculated series of parkour-like leaps off the jagged chasm walls. Each bounce sent a jolt of pain through her body, but she gritted her teeth and pressed on, the thought of Azimuth somewhere below driving her forward.

"Like a demented pinball," she muttered to herself, the corners of her mouth twitching with a hint of dark humor despite the dire situation.

The smell of sulfur and damp earth filled her nostrils, but underneath that, she caught a familiar scent. Azimuth. His unique blend of vanilla and sandalwood, a combination that she had grown to associate with safety, was faint but unmistakable. She angled herself toward it, determination replacing fear.

She found him on a ledge jutting out from the chasm

wall, his body crumpled and unmoving. Her heart clenched at the sight, but she forced herself to remain calm. She landed beside him with a grace that belied the urgency coursing through her veins.

"Azimuth," she said, her voice wavering as she touched his face. His skin was cold, much colder than it should have been. "You shouldn't have jumped in to save me."

But he didn't stir.

The smell of iron and something else—something bitter— assaulted her nose, and Nadir willed her trembling hands to stop. She braced herself against the dim light as she gingerly ran her fingers over his body, searching for any evidence of injury. Gashes ran down his leg and back, a pool of blood already spreading underneath him. Saliva flooded her mouth at the coppery scent, her blasphemous hunger reflex uncaring that the subject was her lover. Nadir had promised herself she'd reserve this gift for emergencies, and this was as dire as it got. She grimaced as she lowered her lips to Azimuth's back, the taste of her own saliva bitter on her tongue, but she knew its healing properties were potent.

Gently, she pressed her saliva-coated lips to his wounds; the sensation making her shudder. His flesh sizzled slightly at the contact, the wounds beginning to knit together under her touch. It was slow going, and for a moment, she feared it wouldn't work.

And then, finally, Azimuth groaned, his eyelashes flutter- ing. His ice-blue eyes, dull and clouded with pain, met hers.

"Nadir?" His voice was a raspy whisper, but it was the most beautiful sound she'd ever heard. "You jumped?"

"Of course, I jumped," she replied, her relief manifesting

as a sassy retort. "What did you think I was going to do? Leave you to become the chasm's new decor?"

As relief washed over her, she took a moment to take in their surroundings. The dark expanse of the chasm stretched out around them, their ledge a tiny island in an ocean of shadow. They were far from safe.

But for now, Azimuth was alive. And as long as he was, she would fight tooth and nail to get them out of this hellhole.

Suddenly, Azimuth's hand closed over hers, a weak but reassuring squeeze. "We're in this together, Nadir," he murmured, his gaze intense.

Nadir glanced at the looming tunnel entrance in the chasm wall nearby, her heart pounding with a mix of trepidation and determination. But before she could reply, a low growl echoed from within the tunnels, sending a shiver of dread down her spine.

"Sounds like we need to go. Can you port?" Nadir asked.

There was a pregnant pause as each of them tried to port out of the chasm. "It's not working for me either. There are areas in Sheol where porting is suppressed, usually to trap people in awful locations like this."

"Aren't we lucky? I guess that means we walk?" she asked.

He nodded. "Let's find a way out."

Her hand tightened on Azimuth's as they stared into the darkness. With a shared nod of understanding, Nadir helped Azimuth to his feet, the two of them limping toward the gaping maw of the tunnel. The air within was damp and cool, a stark contrast to the smoky heat of the chasm. The walls were slick with condensation; the moisture reflecting the faint glow of phosphorescent lichen that speckled the rocky surface.

"The place could use an interior designer," Azimuth muttered, his dry humor easing some of the tension that had coiled itself around Nadir's heart. She squeezed his hand in silent gratitude, her fingers brushing over the rough calluses that were a testament to his strength.

The path ahead was treacherous, etched into the side of a steep ravine that plunged deep in jagged drops. The air was thick with a cloying fog that curled around their legs as they pushed on, each step precarious. The ground felt slippery underfoot, slick with mud and scattered rocks that threatened to trip them up at every turn. They had to lean against each other for support, each stumble or slip a reminder of their battered condition. Despite the physical challenges, Nadir couldn't help but feel a strange intimacy in their shared struggle. Their survival depended on each other, cementing a bond that was already profoundly deep. Each scrap or tumble only drew them closer together, the weight of their bodies pressing them into one another in support.

After what felt like hours, they found a small alcove off the main tunnel. It was just big enough for both of them, but it was dry and a margin safer. They settled down, their bodies nestled together like puzzle pieces in the confined space.

"Belial is going to be livid," Azimuth said, breaking the silence. His voice was low and raspy, brushing against Nadir's senses like a tangible thing.

"Yeah," she admitted, her heart pounding at the thought. A moment of silence passed between them. "We could run," she suggested, her words barely above a whisper. "We could leave the burrow, disappear. Get beyond his reach."

Azimuth was silent for a moment, his gaze unwavering. "We can't, Nadir," he said, voice resolute. "We've sworn fealty to Belial. Our fate is bound to his will."

"I thought you might say that," she admitted. She imagined Belial would take his anger out on both of them when they finally returned. Perhaps delaying a bit had its merits.

He reached out, his hand brushing a loose strand of hair from her face. "I'm with you, Nadir. Wherever this leads us, we face it together."

The depth of his commitment sent a wave of warmth through Nadir, banishing the bleak fear that had taken root in her heart. "Together," she echoed, leaning into his touch.

As they settled into the alcove, the shared warmth of their bodies a comforting presence in the darkness, they knew they had a tough road ahead. But they also knew they had each other, and that was enough. For now.

Outside the alcove, the tunnels of the chasm echoed with the distant growls of unknown threats. But inside, there was only the steady rhythm of two hearts beating as one. And so they rested, taking comfort in their shared resolve, ready to face whatever came next.

Their silence settled like a comforting blanket over them, punctuated by the quiet patter of water droplets falling from the ceiling of the tunnel. The phosphorescent glow bathed them in a soft, ethereal light that flickered across their weary faces. Despite their dire circumstances, the alcove felt almost peaceful, a sanctuary within the belly of the beast.

It was Azimuth who broke the silence, his voice a soft murmur in the echoing space. "We've faced worse, you know," he said, a wry smile tugging at the corner of his mouth. His fingers traced idle patterns on the back of Nadir's hand, a comforting gesture that sent shivers of anticipation along her spine.

"Hard to imagine anything worse than being chased by a monstrous daemon in the heart of Sheol, but I'll take your word for it," Nadir retorted.

Their meager laughter echoed off the walls, a beacon of light in the surrounding darkness. It was moments like these, Nadir realized, that made everything worth it. The danger, the fear, the uncertainty. All of it paled compared to the connection she felt with Azimuth at that moment.

After their laughter faded, they sat in companionable silence, their bodies leaning into one another for warmth and comfort. The connection between them was palpable, an unspoken bond forged in the fires of shared hardship and danger.

"Nadir," Azimuth murmured, his voice barely above a whisper. She turned to him, meeting his gaze in the dim light. There was something different in his eyes. A depth of emotion that made her heart flutter in her chest.

"Yes," she responded, her voice barely audible over the echoing drip of water.

"Whatever happens, remember that I love you," he said, his voice steady and sure. The words hung in the air, a bleak confession laid bare in the alcove's quiet.

Nadir felt her breath catch in her chest. Hearing him say it, here in this dangerous place, made it even more powerful. "I love you too, Azimuth," she said, her words a whisper against his lips before she closed the distance between them.

Their kiss was slow and deep, a mingling of breath and shared warmth. It was a moment of connection that transcended their physical location, a testament to their bond that was stronger than any challenge they faced.

Their shared intimacy sparked a fire within them, a need to be closer, to feel each other's warmth, to forget for a moment the danger that lurked beyond their alcove. Clothes were shed, their bodies bare and vulnerable in the soft glow of the lichen.

Their lovemaking was slow and tender, a dance of shared passion and mutual respect. Despite the cold stone beneath them, their bodies generated a heat that banished the chill from their bones. Whispers of love and promises of a future filled the space around them, their words a balm against the uncertainty of their situation.

Nadir's heart raced as she felt Azimuth's body against hers, his powerful arms around her, providing a sense of safety. His gentle caresses and passionate kisses sent shivers down her spine as they explored each other in an intimate dance of desire.

As they reached their peak, Nadir let out a soft moan as pleasure cascaded through her body like waves on the shore. In that moment, she felt completely connected to Azimuth—physically, emotionally, and spiritually. Nothing else mattered except for them at that moment.

Afterwards, they lay entwined together in perfect contentment as the phosphorescent lichen illuminated their faces. Nadir snuggled closer into Azimuth's embrace, feeling completely at peace with the world around her.

Azimuth leaned down to place one last kiss upon Nadir's lips before murmuring softly in her ear: "No matter what happens now," he said reassuringly, "I want you to remember how much I love you."

Nadir smiled back at him fondly before responding with equal sincerity. "I will never forget it."

As they lay entangled in each other's arms, their breaths syncing in the alcove's quiet, Nadir felt a sense of peace wash over her. Despite the impending danger, despite Belial's wrath, she knew they could face whatever came next. Together.

She was awoken some time later by a distant rumble, a sound that echoed ominously through the tunnel. The ground beneath them shuddered, dust and small pebbles raining down from the ceiling. They exchanged a glance, their peaceful post-coital nap replaced by a surge of adrenaline.

"Belial," Azimuth murmured, his voice low and grim. Nadir nodded, her heart pounding in her chest. "He must have gotten impatient waiting for us."

They quickly pulled on clothes, barely managing in the cramped quarters before being yanked by an invisible hand, the pull so intense it left them gasping. The phosphorescent glow of the tunnel was replaced by the familiar wooden walls of the burrow. They were back.

A wave of relief washed over Nadir, the familiar surroundings a welcome sight after the oppressive darkness of the chasm. She looked over at Azimuth, his expression mirroring her own relief. But the peace was short-lived, their joyous return marred by a looming presence.

Belial stood before them; his towering form wreathed in an aura of raw, unbridled power. His crimson eyes blazed with fury, and the fires of his wrath reflected in their depths. "Nadir. Azimuth." His voice reverberated through the burrow, the timbre of his anger echoing off the walls.

Against the far wall, as though they were prisoners awaiting judgment, kneeled Orias and Kobol. Their bodies trembled with fear and rage, their heads held high in defiance of their bonds. The magical manacles that bound them glowed like hot magma and radiated an aura forceful enough to scorch the eyes.

"You dare defy me?" Belial roared, his voice thunderous. His gaze was a burning brand, searing Nadir and Azimuth with its intensity.

Their brief respite was over. The burrow, their haven, had become a battlefield.

"You gave me no choice, Belial!" Nadir shot back, rising to her feet. She could feel Azimuth beside her, his body tense, his power humming beneath his skin. They stood united, a bulwark against Belial's wrath.

Belial sneered, his lips curling back to reveal sharp, predatory teeth. "You had a choice. You could have obeyed my orders, yet you chose defiance."

"I bow to your will, Prince, but I would not stand by and allow Nadir to be destroyed," Azimuth replied, his voice resonating with a resolve that sent a shiver down Nadir's spine. His icy aura flared out, a stark contrast to Belial's fiery presence.

Belial's laugh was a terrible sound, a mirthless chuckle that echoed ominously in the burrow. "That's not bowing then, is it? You will pay for your defiance. You will learn the price of crossing me," he snarled, his voice a promise of impending doom.

Nadir felt a chill run down her spine, the reality of their situation hitting her with full force. They had defied one of the most powerful daemons in existence, and now they had to face the consequences. As she gripped Azimuth's hand, the comforting warmth of his skin a stark contrast to the bitter dread coursing through her, she knew they had to face whatever came next. Together.

As Belial's power surged, ready to unleash his wrath, Nadir locked eyes with Azimuth, a silent promise passing between them. No matter what happened next, they would stand together, bound by their love and shared defiance.

But even as they prepared themselves, a question lingered in Nadir's mind. Would their love be enough to withstand the wrath of a prince of Hell? As the burrow erupted into chaos, she couldn't shake the feeling that they were about to find out.

CHAPTER 56

ERIN

Blaine led the way into the cavernous city archives, Erin trailing behind him. Erin's heart raced as her gaze swept over the bookshelves and archival boxes, her new mayoral title an anchor in the swirling chaos of her life. As they descended the winding staircase, an old musty scent filled the air, a tangible reminder of the history that lay within these walls. The dust seemed to whisper secrets and stories of generations past as they made their way further down the maze of corridors and stairwells.

The two finally reached the restricted archives, where a single door stood between them and their destination. Blaine stepped forward and placed his hand against a stone panel on the wall. With a loud creaking noise, the door slowly opened. "Now that you're on the council, this access panel will work for you too," he said. "Just touch it like I did." They stepped inside the chamber, and Erin was immediately struck by the silence and stillness.

The room was filled with row after row of ancient scrolls, illuminated by the light from the narrow windows. Blaine stepped forward, and as he did, the air seemed to awaken and swirl around them in anticipation. Erin looked around in wonder, her hand slipping unconsciously to her side as if being drawn to some invisible force.

She could feel it now - the energy of the room vibrating with power and possibility. This was the only place in the city where records stretching back centuries could be accessed.

"You're taking to this whole mayor business like a fish to water," Blaine remarked, his voice echoing in the hushed stillness of the archives.

Erin shot him a sidelong glance, a faint smile tugging at her lips. "It's easier to swim when you're thrown into the deep end, Blaine."

They ventured deeper into the archives, the dim light casting long shadows on the rows upon rows of dusty shelves. Erin's fingers trailed over the spines of ancient books, her pulse quickening as she felt a subtle tingle in her fingertips. It was like Dionysos was right there with her, guiding her hand.

They spent hours sifting through texts, unearthing tales of the fae's magical prowess, their complex society, and their troubled history with humans. Erin felt a chill run down her spine as she read about the fae's merciless attacks during the last Great War.

"Gods, Erin," Blaine breathed, running a hand through his hair. "These fae are no joke. Look at this. They can control the elements, they can shapeshift. They're like something out of a comic book."

Erin nodded, her mind racing. "And they're not just characters in a book, Blaine. They're real, and they're here. We need to be ready."

As she spoke, a familiar warmth welled up within her, a spark of divine energy. The pull was undeniable. It was Dionysos, urging her to take the next step.

Drawing a deep breath, Erin closed her eyes and reached out with her senses, the pulse of her newfound powers humming in her veins. She called out to Dionysos, her voice echoing not in the physical space of the archive, but in the ethereal realm of the gods.

"Here goes nothing," she muttered to herself, half expecting nothing to happen.

Blaine looked at her, eyes wide. "Erin, are you sure about this?" His voice was laced with concern, but beneath it, Erin could hear the undercurrent of excitement.

Erin gave him a tight smile. "No. But since when has that ever stopped us?"

Suddenly, the musty scent of old books mixed with a heady aroma, a combination of rich wine and fresh ivy. A gentle breeze seemed to rustle through the library, an impossible wind that tousled her hair and sent chills up her spine. The whispers of ancient voices echoed in her ears, as though the very air was humming with an unseen presence.

The room seemed to dim, the dusty bookshelves receding into the background. The archive's dull and mundane reality was being replaced by something much more mystical and awe-inspiring. A vast, starlit expanse unfolded before her eyes, as though the library was an intersection between the mortal world and something infinitely more divine.

And then he was there. Standing amidst the celestial panorama, was Dionysos, the god of the vine, of ecstasy and madness. His presence was so real, so tangible, that Erin could have reached out and touched him. He was no longer an abstract entity, but a physical being standing before her. His eyes were as dark as the night sky and filled with ageless wisdom. His smile had an unnerving quality to it, as though he was privy to secrets Erin could only dream of.

"Dionysos," Erin managed, her voice shaking slightly. She was now on a first-name basis with a god. That would take some getting used to.

His voice was deep, resonant, and strangely comforting. "Erin," he acknowledged her. He glanced at the book in her hands, a knowing smirk playing on his lips. "I see you've been reading up on your visitors. Good. Knowledge is your greatest weapon."

Erin swallowed, her grip tightening around the book. "We need more than knowledge, Dionysos. We need to protect our city from the fae. They could destroy us."

He nodded, his gaze thoughtful. "Yes, they could. But they won't. Not if you can help it."

Erin frowned, trying to decipher his cryptic words. "What do you mean?"

His grin widened, and a spark of mischief danced in his eyes. "Ah, now that would be telling, wouldn't it? You'll find out soon enough, Erin. For now, keep reading."

And then, as suddenly as he appeared, Dionysos vanished. The celestial backdrop faded away, leaving Erin back in the archives, surrounded by the familiar smell of old books and silence.

Blaine was gaping at her, his eyes wide with disbelief. "Erin, what just happened? You were glowing."

Her mind still buzzing from the divine encounter, Erin looked down at the book in her hands, then back at Blaine, a determined look in her eyes. "We have a lot of work to do, Blaine."

Blaine nodded, visibly steeling himself. "Right. Back to the books, then?"

Erin chuckled, a spark of her old humor breaking through the gravity of their situation. "Back to the books, Blaine."

As they dived back into their research, Erin couldn't shake the feeling that Dionysos had left something unsaid. But whatever it was, she had a feeling she'd find out soon enough. For now, they had a city to protect, and an encroaching fae threat to understand.

CHAPTER 57

NADIR

The wrathful prince's aura flared brighter, the fiery corona casting long, dancing shadows across the walls of the burrow. Belial's eyes narrowed, the flame within flickering ominously as he took a threatening step forward. The air crackled around them, charged with the raw power that the daemon prince was exuding. Nadir's heart pounded, the rhythm echoing in her ears, but she stood her ground, her grip on Azimuth's hand tightening.

"Belial, let's discuss this," Azimuth implored, his calm voice a stark contrast to the building tension in the room.

"There's nothing to discuss. You've crossed the line," Belial seethed, his gaze zeroed in on the defiant duo.

Suddenly, the burrow was filled with an explosion of force, knocking Nadir and Azimuth backward. Belial had unleashed a wave of power strong enough to send them crashing against the far wall. Pain bloomed across Nadir's back, but she forced herself to her feet, pushing back against the pressure that was attempting to crush her.

Azimuth was back on his feet as well, his body shielding

Nadir's as he held out a hand toward Belial, a silent plea for mercy. The sight of his defiance seemed to fuel Belial's rage, and the prince roared, another wave of power smashing into them.

Nadir gritted her teeth, feeling the power pushing against her like a storm, threatening to tear her apart. But she stood her ground, pulling at her own powers, the daemon essence within her responding with a fiery surge that pushed back against Belial's onslaught.

She caught sight of Orias and Kobol, still bound and trembling, but watching them with a look of intense admiration. Nadir felt a spark of determination ignite within her. They would not be crushed by Belial's wrath. They had faced greater dangers in the chasm, and they would face this together.

With a fierce cry, Nadir released her power, a wave of force that clashed with Belial's, the collision causing a shock wave that swept through the burrow. Belial staggered, a look of shock crossing his face as he steadied himself.

Nadir took advantage of the momentary respite, her hand gripping Azimuth's tighter. His ice-blue eyes met hers, and she saw the same determination reflected there. They were a team, and they would face this wrath together.

A growl rumbled in Belial's chest, his aura flaring brighter as he prepared to lash out once more. Nadir felt her body tensing, ready for the onslaught, her own powers simmering just beneath the surface.

Suddenly, an ear-splitting roar echoed through the burrow, a sound so powerful it seemed to shake the very foundations of the earth. Everyone froze, turning their attention to the large tapestry everyone used for porting in and out. A monstrous shadow was taking shape, as if the darkness from the depths of Sheol itself was about to port in.

Belial's eyes, pools of liquid malice, flicked up to find an unexpected sight. A moment later, Ranna, the ever fashionable elder daemon, arrived with Hades, the God of the Underworld, following along behind her. Ranna was draped in long sapphire robes, her head crowned with a gleaming golden diadem nestled against her diminutive horns. Around her neck hung a shimmering amulet with an ancient symbol of wisdom and knowledge carved into its face, which Nadir recognized as the hierophant.

Hades strode in with a stormy aura enveloping him, as if to declare his very presence. His black garment clung tightly against his body and trailed behind him like an ebony cape. His face was contorted with rage, and his eyes glittered like two emeralds buried within coal. He brought an icy chill that disrupted the tranquil atmosphere Belial had been enshrined in.

"Belial, Prince of Sheol," Ranna's voice was a quiet hurricane, building tension in the silence. "Do you know why we're here?"

Belial's smile twisted. "I was enjoying a quiet evening, contemplating the finer things in life, like how to annihilate certain annoyances," he said, a veiled threat hanging between the words.

Ranna, ever unflappable, simply raised an eyebrow. "It seems your pastimes have taken a turn for the reckless." She raised her hand, producing an illusion of a shimmering sancre blade. "What exactly do you plan to do with these blades of yours, Belial?"

The image of the illicit weapons turned the big, blue

daemon's rage into a tangible entity. It crashed against the walls of the burrow, making the shadows themselves tremble.

"Nadir," he spat out, his voice venomous. "She told you, didn't she?"

His rage was an inferno, ready to consume, but Hades stepped forward, his hand raised, a barrier of divine energy materializing between Belial and Nadir. "Answer the question, denizen," he commanded, his voice echoing with the authority of the ages.

Belial's face contorted in rage, an animalistic growl escaping his throat. But before he could retort, the world tipped on its axis. The trap was sprung, and Belial, the mighty, was ensnared. His fate lay not in his hands, but those of his accusers, poised on the edge of treachery.

Belial's fury seemed to falter; his gaze locked with Hades. The tension in the room was palpable, a silent standoff between two powerful entities.

"These are my sancre blades, crafted to destroy our kind. Under my direction, my children have been purifying Sheol of those daemons who feast upon humanity, tainting unending essence."

Ranna cleared her throat. "But it's not just specific daemons, is it, Belial? It'll destroy some of their lineage too, won't it?"

Belial's rage was an oil-soaked bonfire, threatening to consume everything in its wake, but Hades was an ocean, extinguishing the fury with a force that echoed divine authority.

The God of the Underworld's gaze fell upon Belial, a silent reprimand that cut deeper than any spoken word could. "Your aspirations have reached beyond your means,

Prince. Indiscriminately killing your own kind is a crime I cannot abide," his voice was a rumbling thunder, resounding with a finality that left no room for debate.

Belial snarled, a feral sound, but the fire in his eyes dimmed in the face of the god's icy resolve. The scent of defeat, bitter as gall, filled the air, the acridity of it filling Nadir's nostrils and making her eyes sting. But she watched, unable to tear her eyes away as Hades took a step forward, a cruel smile twisting his lips.

"I cast you to the depths," Hades proclaimed, a hint of savage satisfaction in his tone. A bright flash of light swallowed Belial whole, and when it receded, he was gone.

A deep, ominous silence filled the burrow after Hades' proclamation, as if his words had physically sucked the air out of the room. Belial was gone now, and with him, potential salvation for her and her cabal mates. Nadir stood in shocked disbelief, feeling an immense sense of dread as the full realization of their plight sunk in.

And then, Ranna's request cut through the tense silence as if nothing of consequence had just occurred. "My lord, I request custody of Belial's former possessions, including his children, Nadir, Azimuth, Kobol, and Orias." Her voice was a velvet caress against the stony silence of the burrow.

Hades' eyes narrowed at Ranna, his thoughts hidden behind an inscrutable expression. Yet, despite his initial hesitation, he conceded, honoring her request for her part in uncovering the treacherous Belial. His hand rose, an otherworldly glow surrounding his fingers. "In recognition of your service in exposing his treachery, I grant this request."

A feeling akin to a shiver passed through Nadir, a cold, tingling sensation that ran the length of her spine. It was like a thread being cut, then tied anew. She, along with Azimuth, Kobol, and Orias, were no longer connected to Belial. They were all Ranna's now. The sensation was disorienting, leaving her feeling adrift, as if the ground beneath her had shifted. Their fates were rewritten in that moment, leaving them suspended in a future full of uncertainty.

With another flick of his hand, Hades initiated the transfer of powers. It felt like a swirling vortex, pulling at the essence of Nadir, Azimuth, Kobol, and Orias, an other-worldly force severing their bonds to Belial and weaving new ones to Ranna. The sensation was disconcerting, a pulsing shift that unsettled Nadir's stomach. She could taste the iron tang of fear on her tongue, her nerves alight with a combination of apprehension and a hint of reluctant relief.

Through it all, Ranna remained still, her face an enigmatic mask. Only the flicker of triumph in her eyes betrayed any sign of her internal emotions. There was a strange allure to her in that moment, a dangerous mix of power and authority that seemed to radiate off her like heat from a flame.

The process was over as quickly as it had begun, the ethereal glow that had enveloped Hades' hand dissipating into nothingness.

Ranna snapped her fingers and the bindings holding Kobol and Orias in place fell away, freeing them. They remained quiet, but warily stood up.

Then Hades looked at each of them, holding out his hand. "I require the sancre blades. All of them."

One by one, they each handed over their silver blades. Azimuth handed over his last. "These are all of them. Belial only made the four."

There was an appreciative gleam in Hades' eyes as he

handled the blades, their sharp edges catching the low light in the burrow, casting an eerie glow.

"These blades were the catalyst to this upheaval," Hades muttered, his voice echoing through the cavernous expanse of the burrow. He carefully wrapped them in a dark cloth, his movements precise and measured. "They will return with me to my palace. Their misuse will not be repeated."

As he moved, the air seemed to ripple, and with a soft murmur, he disappeared, leaving behind an unsettling quiet. The emptiness was jarring, a stark reminder of the changes that had taken place. They were no longer bound to Belial. They were tied to Ranna now, their fate irrevocably altered. What that would mean for them, however, remained an unnerving mystery.

After Hades departed, the burrow suddenly felt cold and eerie. Ranna turned to leave, her robes rustling against the stone floor, her departure threatening to plunge them into an uncertainty deeper than the burrow's darkest shadows.

"Get some rest," she told Nadir, Azimuth, Kobol, and Orias. Her voice held an edge that sent chills down Nadir's spine, the echo of her words more chilling than any icy wind. She raked them up and down with her gaze, appraising. "My very own clockwork children," she mused, as if speaking to herself. "You'll have your work cut out for you soon enough."

Her dark humor lingered in the air, tainting it with a vague sense of dread. Nadir frowned, her daemon senses picking up the underlying menace in Ranna's words. As their newly appointed master turned to leave, a knot of apprehension tightened in Nadir's stomach. The burrow seemed to close in on them as Ranna's form disappeared, leaving them with nothing but their thoughts and the chilling silence.

When they were alone, they let the gravity of their situation sink in. The cold stone beneath them, the echo of their ragged breaths, the subtle scent of damp earth. Everything heightened their sense of unease.

"Well shit. That could have gone better," Kobol spat out, rubbing the back of his neck.

"It also could have gone much worse," Orias added. They all turned to him, but he waved them off. "No visions of worth to mention."

But amidst the unease and uncertainty, Azimuth turned to Nadir, his gaze full of a newfound respect. "Nadir," he started, his voice steady and sincere, "you played a dangerous game, one I would never have backed, but it paid off. We owe you for that."

Nadir shrugged, her mind still reeling from the whirlwind of events. "Let's just hope the price wasn't too high," she replied, her voice echoing in the burrow's silence. She glanced toward the portal Ranna had disappeared through, a sense of dread trickling down her spine.

CHAPTER 58

ERIN

The sun hung low in the sky, casting long shadows as Erin made her way to the temple gardens. There, amid the lush foliage and peaceful murmurs of nature, Orias stood waiting, his ever-present shadows dancing around his feet. His figure seemed to blend with the surrounding greenery, a guardian amidst the flora and fauna. Orias was to instruct her on creating daemonic wards, a foreign concept to Erin, who was still learning her god-touched abilities.

Nadir, Azimuth, and Kobol had dispersed across the temple grounds, each tasked with warding their own sections. A strange sense of camaraderie bound them together. They were on the same side now, united against the looming threat of the fae. Erin found comfort in their shared purpose, as she ventured into the magical unknown.

The gardens hummed with serenity, a cornucopia of vibrant flowers and intricate statues arranged with an artist's care. Orias' voice broke the tranquil silence, his words lacing through the air.

"Daemonic magic differs from your god-touched abilities, Erin," he began, his tone gentle yet firm. "It draws from the raw energy of the cosmos, channeled through specific sigils."

Erin turned to him, her eyes wide with curiosity. "So, it's like drawing power from the universe itself?"

Orias nodded, a small smile playing on his lips. "Exactly, though it's more complicated than that. On the plus side, you don't have to be a daemon to construct them, but it's important you understand their origination. They work well against the fae, unlike the comparable sorcerer's wards mortals typically use."

The statues surrounding them, ancient effigies of the gods, seemed to watch silently, their stone eyes betraying no disapproval of her newfound path.

"Now," Orias continued, "let's move to the practical aspect." He handed her a small pouch filled with a blend of herbs and soil-infused chalk. "We use this to draw the warding sigils."

Erin opened the pouch, her fingers brushing against the rough chalk. "How do I do it?" she asked, the anticipation making her voice quiver.

"Watch closely," Orias instructed, demonstrating a pattern on the ground. The sigil glowed momentarily, a soft light radiating from the earth. "Now, you try."

Erin bent down and replicated the sigil. Her fingers trembled initially, but steadied as she focused. The sigil beneath her touch glowed, pulsating with a rhythm that resonated with her heartbeat. She looked up at Orias, her eyes searching for approval.

"Well done, Erin," Orias praised, nodding appreciatively. "With each sigil, the wards grow stronger. Can you feel it?"

She closed her eyes, her senses reaching out. There was indeed a sensation, a whisper of energy that laced through the air. "I can," she whispered, a newfound confidence lining her words. "I can feel it."

Erin could feel the surge of energy flowing from the sigils, an invisible shield growing stronger with every ward they set. With each new ward set, Erin's understanding of daemonic magic deepened. Under Orias's tutelage, she could craft increasingly complex sigils, each one pulsating with an inner glow that seemed to resonate with the temple itself. By the time they finished for the day, the temple was enveloped in a comforting, invisible shield. It was a delicate yet powerful web of protection that Erin could feel thrumming under her fingertips.

As Erin drew the final swirls of a warding sigil, she sat back on her heels, a sense of satisfaction spreading through her. Orias watched, his lips curling into an approving smile.

"You're a quick learner, Erin," he praised. "But there's a bigger picture we need to consider."

Erin turned to him, curiosity dancing in her eyes. "What do you mean?"

"The fae aren't just a threat to this temple. The entire city is at risk," Orias explained, his voice sobering. "Our warding network should reach beyond these walls."

Erin paused, taking in his words. The thought was intimidating. Warding an entire city seemed like an astronomical task. But she knew he was right. "You mean, we need to ward the entire city?"

Orias nodded, his dark gaze unwavering. "Exactly. It's a monumental task, no doubt. But we cannot leave our city unprotected."

Resolute determination settled on Erin's features. "We're in this to protect everyone, not just ourselves. If we can do it, we should."

Orias chuckled. "That's the spirit, Erin. We're all in this together."

Erin turned her gaze to the temple looming behind them. It was no longer just a religious sanctuary. It had evolved into a strategic center, a beacon of hope amidst the looming danger. "When this started, I never envisioned my temple becoming such a pivotal space."

Orias shook his head, a knowing look in his eyes. "No, it's much more now. It's the city's fortress against darkness."

"And we'll stand together," Erin said, her voice filled with resolve. "Whatever comes, we'll face it as one."

Erin strode into the temple foyer, her eyes seeking her companions—Nadir, Azimuth, Kobol, and Blaine—who were chatting with Finn and Nia. The grandeur of the temple hummed around them, yet the space felt intimate, alive with the comfort of camaraderie. Erin's gaze fell on her newfound family, gratitude flooding her.

"You've all been busy," Erin commented, a smile playing on her lips. "I can feel the wards humming all around the temple."

As Blaine detached from the group to greet her, Erin felt the familiar warmth of his arms encircle her. He leaned in, his voice barely above a whisper, vibrating against her ear. "I just got word from the council chairman. While we've been busy warding, Maria has taken advantage of our absence. She convinced the chairman to appoint her interim mayor until a proper election can be held."

Pulling back from his embrace, Erin searched Blaine's

gaze, seeing his anxiety over this news mirrored her own. This news was a twist she had not expected, and it stirred up a mess of conflicting emotions within her. Was her absence from the council putting her temple at risk? Or were her efforts to protect it, ironically, the very thing leaving it vulnerable? The irony wasn't lost on her.

Even so, the safety of their city was at stake. Politics seemed so petty when faced with the enormity of their actual problem. "Politics? In the middle of this?" she retorted, frustration seeping into her tone. "We have bigger problems. We have a fae threat on our doorstep."

Blaine, ever the calm in her storm of worry and determination, nodded in agreement. "I thought you'd see it that way. The fae threat should be our priority. But we'll also need to address this political hiccup. The council will have to be convinced to see the larger threat."

"That's a problem for tomorrow," Erin replied, her mind already churning with the challenge of balancing leadership duties and a supernatural threat. It seemed the battle on both fronts had just begun.

As the sun cast long shadows across the temple grounds, they all gathered around the ancient stone table at the heart of the foyer. The murmur of conversation filled the air, each voice a thread in the fabric of their united front.

Blaine cleared his throat, his voice deep and resonant as he spoke. "Hoping for the best and preparing for the worst doesn't seem adequate here. We need to be proactive." His words struck a chord, inciting a rumble of agreement that swept through the room.

Erin stood tall at the head of the table, her eyes meeting Orias'. She nodded, appreciation for his input spreading across her face. "Exactly. Orias and I were speaking about this out in the gardens. We can't just react; we need to dictate the pace here. Our wards have been set, yes, but the next step is expansion."

"Expansion?" Kobol asked, arching his brow.

"We need a city-wide network," Orias replied. "Covering the city. It's our best shot at protecting as many as possible."

She looked around the room, catching each of their eyes. "We will not sit idly by, waiting for the fae to strike. We're going to fortify our city. We'll weave a blanket of wards, a shield to keep our citizens safe from their ill intent."

"Our cabal can gather the necessary supplies," Azimuth chimed in, his gaze firm on Erin's.

Nadir nodded. "We're available to help," Nadir added, her voice calm yet resolute.

"I can petition the council for resources to aid us," Blaine offered, his words underscoring the importance of Orias's proposal.

As Erin returned their pledges with a grateful smile, the enormity of their shared mission weighed heavily on them all. The rising tide of determination within her echoed the shared resolve of her newfound allies. Their alliance, born of necessity, was beginning to flourish into a bond of cama-raderie, threading its way through their collective purpose.

With the looming shadow of the fae threat ever present, their united resolve continued to grow stronger. Yet Erin knew that unity alone would not be enough. They needed to understand what they were up against.

"Many centuries ago, there was a great war against the fae," Orias recounted, his voice low and somber. "Their power threatened to consume the mortal realm. A compact was made. The fae agreed to retreat from the mortal realms, never to return. Until now."

Erin absorbed this knowledge, her mind churning. "We need to understand why they've broken the compact after all this time. What's changed to embolden them?"

Azimuth spoke up, his tone grave. "The fae are mercurial beings, their motives ever shifting. But the rules have changed, that much is clear. We must uncover what has drawn them back in order to protect the mortal realms."

Erin nodded. "You're right. Only by understanding their reasons can we hope to curb their chaos."

She looked around at the assembled allies, resolve steeling her voice. "The fae may be unpredictable, but we cannot falter. We will stand together to shield this city from their mayhem. United, we can face whatever comes next."

Her words ignited murmurs of assent, their unified voices seeming to shake the foundations of the temple. In that moment, Erin saw determination blazing in each pair of eyes. No matter what, they would stand as one.

The temple had become the heart of their efforts, humming with the electric charge of their unified intent. Transforming from a hushed sanctuary into a hive of fervent strategizing, the once tranquil space danced with ideas and strategies, echoing the resounding determination of the group.

Under the looming threat, their differences seemed to blur, superseded by the shared goal of protecting their city from the fae menace. Erin felt a warm surge of realization; this unity was the purpose her temple was meant to serve. It was as if the temple itself resonated with their collective resolve, its purpose fulfilled as it became the beacon of unity and strategic preparation against the encroaching darkness.

Erin's voice rang out in the echoing hall, confidence threaded through her words. "From this moment forward, this temple is not just my home, but our strategic base. I'd be honored if you all consider this your home as well."

Nadir was the first to respond. "Thank you, Erin," she said, her gratitude echoed by the others in a chorus of heartfelt thanks.

As evening deepened into night, Erin retrieved a bottle of rare wine from her cellar. She cracked the seal, and the rich aroma of dark berries and aged oak wafted through the room. Holding up a goblet filled with the ruby-red liquid, she proposed a toast.

"To unity," Erin announced, the clinking of glasses punctuating her declaration. Laughter rippled through the temple, the shared pleasure of the fine wine fostering a sense of camaraderie.

The temple, echoing with the harmonious sounds of unity and shared purpose, embodied Erin's vision of hope and resilience. As they relaxed into the evening, the looming fae threat seemed, if only for a moment, a distant concern.

When the party wound down in the pre-dawn hours, Erin and Blaine worked together to clean up the space. The rhythm of their movements, in sync with the unity that had defined the evening, brought a deep sense of satisfaction to Erin. While picking up the discarded goblets and pillows, the temple settled into a peaceful state as it prepared for the new day.

Erin quietly told Blaine, "This unity we share is our

strongest defense against the fae." Her voice echoed off the walls of the temple, a promise for their cause.

She smiled faintly and Blaine looked back at her. He said, "It will not be easy, but we'll do it together."

Their footsteps were louder than their words as they walked through the silence. The vision of their bond was branded into Erin's heart, lighting up her path in these times of uncertainty.

Erin and Blaine's day drew to a close, and they retreated to her private chambers. The inviting, plush bed was a welcome sight, and they sank into the soft linens with a collective sigh. Erin intertwined her fingers with Blaine's, a silent pact made without words. "Tonight, it's just us," she murmured. "The world can wait till morning."

Within the intimate cocoon of her room, Blaine pulled Erin closer. She nestled into his embrace, relishing the security it offered. "There's strength in this," she whispered, her words a balm against the world's chaos. "Strength to face whatever comes."

As she drifted toward sleep, Blaine's heartbeat provided a steady rhythm, a soothing lullaby in her ear. "We've got this," she mumbled, half-asleep, a current of hope flowing with her words.

Exhaustion began to win, their eyes growing heavy, but Erin clung to a profound peace. "Whatever challenges are out there," she muttered, already halfway into dreamland, "we won't face them alone. We've got allies. We've got each other. We've got the temple. We've got a chance against the fae."

CHAPTER 59

ORIAS

As they bid adieu to Erin, Orias joined Nadir, Azimuth, and Kobol sauntered through the temple gardens. He felt a sense of accomplishment settling within him. Their combined magic of the wards they'd cast today had coalesced into a potent defense web, a force formidable enough to challenge even the fae.

Gathering his tools, Orias mused over his initial skepticism toward the god-touched Erin and her band of Dionysian followers. But as he watched her undeterred focus in seeing through the wards, he found an inkling of respect budding for the young woman's resilience.

"It appears Dionysos sent Erin just in time," Orias mused aloud.

Kobol's chuckle resonated through the group, his statement echoing Orias's sentiments. "This Erin might be god-touched, but she's got some fire in her. I can appreciate that."

Azimuth chimed in, his nod affirming Kobol's words. "A weaker leader could have faltered at the idea of working with daemons. Erin's courage in accepting our assistance speaks volumes about her wisdom."

The collective murmur of agreement served as testament to the respect Erin had garnered in the past days. A spark of hope ignited within Orias; he knew that only through a united front of god-touched and daemons could humanity stand a chance against the looming fae menace. And Erin's temple was now the fulcrum for their combined efforts.

However, as they traversed through the verdant temple gardens, the enormity of their future tasks cast a shadow on Orias's heart. The prospect of extending their wards to cover the entire city, let alone face the fae themselves, seemed daunting.

Sensing his thoughts, Kobol offered a friendly clap on his shoulder, "One step at a time, brother," he said, a smile of encouragement gracing his face.

Orias nodded in silent gratitude, comforted by the solidarity he found in his cabal mates. Together, they might accomplish what seemed impossible.

Exiting the temple gates, his gaze wandered back to the pulsating wards they had cast, their shimmer a silent testament to their combined power. Orias allowed a small smile to form. It was a beginning, and that's what mattered.

"We haven't talked about what happened with Ranna," Nadir said.

Belial's imprisonment and Ranna's ascension to power were still fresh in their minds, stirring mixed emotions within Orias.

Kobol broke the silence first. "At least we knew where we stood with Belial. Ranna remains an enigma."

Azimuth nodded thoughtfully. "We swore fealty to

Belial. Hades transferred that vow to Ranna. Our feelings are of little consequence to that old magic."

Orias could sense Nadir's unease as she muttered, "It feels like we were tossed about in their power struggle, with no say of our own."

Orias couldn't help but agree. For all of Belial's cruelty, at least his intentions had been clear. Ranna remained an unfathomable variable.

Nadir continued, her voice tinged with regret. "We sided with Belial, yet his ambitions became our downfall."

Azimuth shook his head. "We had no choice but to obey Belial's orders. Our fates were bound to his will."

"Until Ranna intervened," Kobol pointed out. "I'll say the quiet part out loud. Thanks for outing Belial to Ranna, Nadir. He was going to get us all destroyed. At least, with Ranna as our master, we're still alive."

Nadir's smile was weak, but Kobol's words appeared to comfort her. "Thank you, brother. I'm sorry I didn't tell you all about the conversation I had with her."

"You're forgiven. Just promise not to hold back in the future," Azimuth replied.

Nadir held up three fingers like a girl scout. "I promise. I've definitely learned my lesson this time around."

"I'm glad to hear it, love. There's just one problem with our new master. Mistress? Whichever." Azimuth continued. "We don't know what she wants with us."

Orias felt a jolt of unease run through him at Azimuth's words. The shadows around Orias began to coalesce and shift, and the familiar pressure started building within his mind. He mentally braced himself for another vision, but this time, it was different.

Again, he saw an ethereal archway of stars. He had seen this portal before, a shining gateway that the fae used to travel from the faery world into the human one. From that gateway, countless fae began pouring through in droves. They descended upon the city like a plague, enveloping buildings in flames and chaos.

As the others turned to him in concern, Orias felt his own terror rising with each passing second. He struggled for breath as he tried to make sense of what he was seeing. The fae were free to wander the earth and were wreaking havoc upon the city! What could be done?

When the vision finally dissipated, Orias was left with a sense of dread. He relayed what he had seen to the others, grimly. "The fae will return en masse, attacking the city, bringing fire and destruction."

"Can you tell when?" Azimuth asked, his brows knit with worry.

Orias could only shake his head. The timing of his visions usually eluded him. Orias saw the concern reflected on his companions' faces. Fighting alongside the god-touched now seemed imperative to protect the city from the fae onslaught he had witnessed. He hoped Erin and her allies were up to the coming challenges and that his own visions would continue to provide valuable warnings.

As Orias and his companions ported back to the burrow, the weight of his latest vision still hung heavily upon him. Images of the fae swarming through the archway and engulfing the city in fire continued to replay in his mind, filling him with a sense of dread at the coming battles.

Despite their success in warding Erin's temple, it now seemed clear that a far greater threat loomed just beyond the horizon. Warding the entire city, as well as facing the full onslaught of the fae army, now appeared a near impossible challenge.

Yet Orias also sensed his companions' determination to aid Erin and her allies growing in the wake of his vision. They now understood that the fate of not just the temple, but the entire city—and perhaps more—rested upon their fragile alliance between god-touched and daemons.

As they went their own ways in the burrow, each lost in their own thoughts, Orias considered the role he and the others would likely play in the coming conflict. Though experienced warriors, they were few in number. They would need every advantage if they were to stand any chance against a fae horde.

Orias had seen enough battles and bloodshed to know that any triumph would come at a cost. Sacrifices would likely be demanded of both god-touched and daemons alike before this conflict drew to a close.

THE END

Thank you so much for reading Wine and Gods! The next book in the series, Fire and Fae, is available for preorder now.

Have you read the series prequel? Grab Wards and Whispers for free here.

GLOSSARY

- Arch-daemon - A powerful class of daemons that command armies and wield immense power and wealth. Arch-daemons are formidable enemies and invaluable allies. Often they have waged and won countless battles, assuming it suits their disposition. It does.
- Bacchanal - A wild, frenzied celebration involving drinking, dancing, and debauchery, typically in honor of Dionysos.
- Binding - The ritual process by which a summoner seals a pact with a daemon, commanding the daemon's actions on Earth in exchange for payment. The binding ritual varies based on the daemon but often involves the summoner offering a sacrifice of hair, blood, etc. to seal the agreement between them.
- Blood-oath - A sworn pact of loyalty and fealty daemons make to their cabal leader or ally. Breaking a blood-oath has severe consequences.

- Burners -- The Burner community of artisans started in 1986 around a festival known as 'Burning Man' and grew through the early 20th century, with a number of self-reliant enclaves springing up through the 21st century. By the time The Fall occurred in the 22nd century many fled to these off-the-grid communes to escape the Corporate-imposed rule.
- Burrow - The home of a cabal within Sheol. Often a well-appointed cave system.
- Cabal - A group of aligned daemons under blood-oath to a leader. They engage in intrigues and wars with other cabals.
- Cambions - (Daemon/human hybrids) These happen very, very rarely, and only live on earth when they do survive the initial gestation. Always the progeny of a daemon and a human woman and rarely do they realize they are a hybrid. Abilities manifest in their teens and cambions often end up in an insane asylum or prison, depending on how their abilities manifest.
- City Council - The ruling council of god-touched devotees that makes decisions for the city. Led by the Mayor, members represent various deities.
- Crypts - The underground dungeon area where prisoners are kept in burrows.
- Daemon - A denizen of Sheol and descendant of Hades. The power of the daemon depends on how close his or her blood ties lie to the god, and the expression of power varies widely. Your average mid-level daemons who have lived for

under a thousand years and are just now getting their wits about them. Generally, they are coming into their power and forming alliances, assuming they've survived enough battles to gain a reputation for their name. The numbers of daemons are countless and never ending.

- Daemon Summoner -- A human who uses arcane means (oils, herbs, unguents, symbols, incantations, etc.) to summon a daemon and bind them to their will. This transactional cost is different for each daemon, often related to daemon's power. Once bound, the daemon's ink sets into the summoner's skin, and the daemon will then complete a single task for the summoner before returning to Sheol. Multiple bindings with the same daemon will increase the size and complexity of the given daemon's ink on the summoner's skin. Summoning is a very dangerous business, as failed bindings leave the daemon free to attack the summoner.
- Daemonic Wards - Protective symbols made from symbols and various substances that create barriers against supernatural threats.
- Devotee - A human follower/worshipper of a god or goddess who gains power from their divine connection.
- Dionysos - Greek god of wine and revelry.
- Elder-Daemons -- Of which there are thousands. These daemons sometimes command by age alone, with others too afraid to challenge them. Alternatively, they may be loners and choose not

to align to any cabal, not needing the strength of others to withstand threats. Elders are formidable enemies, and invaluable allies.

- Elevation - The process by which a devotee gains more power and rises in rank.
- God-Touched -- A human devotee of a god, always marked with sigils (specific to the deity they revere), although they have the ability to hide the sigils from non-supernatural beings. They avoid others who use magical influence, because they feel their choice of dealing with the divine directly as the superior one. Another term for the devotees connected to gods/goddesses.
- Grimoire - An ancient book of magical knowledge containing information on rituals, incantations, sigils, and tools used by summoners to call forth and bind daemons.
- Hades -- God of the Underworld, father of daemons.
- Ink - When a summoner seals a binding with a daemon, a marking known as "daemon ink" appears on their skin as a permanent record of the pact. Its form varies based on the daemon.
- Liminals -- A species of supernatural hybrids overseen by the goddess Hekate of the Underworld, who rules over crossroads and all events and creatures who linger there. Liminals hold the crossroads -- the line of transition between the living and the dead.
- Princes (daemons) -- Of which there are dozens. This is determined by birthright under the direct

lineage of Hades himself. They are plentiful enough few feel particular value in the title. Few challenge their strength.

- Sancre - Another specialty dagger created by Belial.
- Sheol -- The daemonic plane of existence and origin of daemons, described as containing fiery pits and domains ruled by arch-daemons. Made up of various regions, pits, and sections in a vast network constructed over aeon's, possibly only Hades himself understands its entire history, terrain, or inhabitants.
- Sigil -- A symbol used to summon and bind daemons or other entity to a summoner's will by referencing the elements related to the daemon's true essence. The original sigils date back to The Lesser Key of Solomon, but other, more modern sources exist, many in private collections among summoner's grimoires.
- Succubi/Incubi -- Very minor daemons, still deadly to humans but inconsequential within daemon politics. There are lesser and greater forms within these classes.
- Summoning - The ritual by which humans call daemons from Sheol to complete tasks in exchange for payment. Very dangerous.
- Teleportation -- (aka Porting) Done via simple visualization and requires an elemental tie before a being may port into a plane of existence. I.e. daemonic essence to port to Sheol, human soul to port to Earth, etc.

- The Fall -- In the years 2035-2045 the American and EU governments became financially inviable and step-by-step privatized functions to Corporate bidders in order to remain solvent. The intention of a temporary fix turned permanent. Eventually, the government did so little the Corporations moved to disband them. There was no recourse to stop them. Now, instead of political parties jockeying for power, Corporations vie for territories.
- Tre'jor -- A blade fabricated by Belial to eradicate daemons, capturing their essences and transferring them into the human hosts of his cabal.
- Wildling - An out of control devotee.

ALSO BY CANDICE BUNDY

Magical Midlife Mixers Series

Hocus Pocus and Pinot Noir

(*set in the Shadow Series universe*)

Caught Between Worlds Series

Wards and Whispers, A prequel novella

Smoke and Daemons

Wine and Gods

Fire and Fae (2024)

(*Smoke and Daemons was previously published*

as The Daemon Whisperer)

The Stolen Legacy Series

Looted Legacies, A prequel novella

Forbidden Fates

Entangled Essence

Hidden Hearts

Reckless Rapture

Sworn Spirits

Devoted Desires

The Shadow Series

Shadow in the City, A prequel novella

Twinned Shadow

Poisoned Shadow

Shadow Underground

<u>Other Works</u>

Ripples, a novella

Open Rack, a contemporary short

WRITING AS CR BUNDY

The Depths of Memory Series

The Dream Sifter

Dreams Manifest

For a list of my full catalog of available titles, visit my
<u>candicebundy.com/books</u> page.

ABOUT CANDICE BUNDY

Nestled in the sun-kissed and adventure-filled heart of Denver, Colorado, Candice thrives amidst nature's playground. Candice shares her abode with her partner and feline overlords who, quite frankly, aren the true monarchs of their cozy kingdom. A word alchemist at heart, Candice skillfully weaves tales drenched in angsty fantasy romance, exhilarating science fiction, and tantalizing paranormal spice. She likes to throw fierce, clever heroines off cliffs and into the arms of heroes who stand at the ready to catch them.

Her passion extends beyond the page, as she delves deep into the worlds of archeology and mythology, seeking the threads that bind our collective narratives. Not one to rest on her laurels, she's an advocate for habit hacking, ceaselessly striving to embody minimalist principles, promote holistic well-being, and infuse her everyday with an abundance of positive mojo.

Away from her writer's nook, Candice is either nurturing her garden—home to heirloom tomatoes and a symphony of jams and fermented delights—or quite literally tied to a wall. As a fervent sport climber, she eagerly tackles every new challenge, ascending to greater heights and mastering diverse landscapes.

Eager to embark on a journey through her literary realms? Subscribe to her newsletter here and be the first to uncover her latest creations. Should curiosity or inspiration spark within you, don't hesitate to drop Candice a line. Craving some delightful cat moments? Dive into her social channels, where enchanting feline captures await to brighten your day.

For more information:
candicebundy.com
candice@candicebundy.com

www.ingramcontent.com/pod-product-compliance
Lightning Source LLC
Chambersburg PA
CBHW051426190726
48289CB00001B/70